Robert Anson Heinlein was born in Missouri in 1907 and was raised there. He graduated from the U.S. Naval Academy in 1929, but he was forced by illness to retire from the Navy in 1934. Heinlein settled in California and over the next five years held a variety of jobs while doing postgraduate work in mathematics and physics at the University of California. In 1939 he sold his first science fiction story to *Astounding* magazine and soon devoted himself to the genre.

He was a four-time winner of the Hugo Award for his novels *Stranger in a Strange Land* (1961), *Starship Troopers* (1959), *Double Star* (1956), and *The Moon Is a Harsh Mistress* (1966). His Future History series, incorporating both short stories and novels, was first mapped out in 1941. The series charts the social, political, and technological changes shaping human society from the present through several centuries into the future.

Heinlein's books were among the first works of science fiction to reach bestseller status in both hardcover and paperback. He continued to work into his eighties, and his work never ceased to amaze, entertain, and generate controversy. By the time he died in 1988, it was evident that he was one of the formative talents of science fiction: a writer whose unique vision, unflagging energy, and persistence, over the course of five decades, made a great impact on the American mind.

BOOKS BY ROBERT A. HEINLEIN

Stranger in a Strange Land

———

Robert A. Heinlein

ACE
New York

ACE
Published by Berkley
An imprint of Penguin Random House LLC
penguinrandomhouse.com

Copyright © 1961 by Robert A. Heinlein; copyright renewed 1989 by Virginia Heinlein;
copyright assigned 2003 to the Robert A. and Virginia Heinlein Prize Trust
Penguin Random House supports copyright. Copyright fuels creativity, encourages
diverse voices, promotes free speech, and creates a vibrant culture. Thank you for buying
an authorized edition of this book and for complying with copyright laws by not
reproducing, scanning, or distributing any part of it in any form without permission.
You are supporting writers and allowing Penguin Random House to continue to
publish books for every reader.

ACE is a registered trademark and the A colophon is a trademark of
Penguin Random House LLC.

ISBN: 9781984802781

G. P. Putnam's Sons hardcover edition / 1961
Berkley edition / March 1968
Ace mass-market edition / April 1987
Ace premium edition / August 2018

Printed in the United States of America
10

Cover design by Will Staehle
Book design by Tiffany Estreicher

CONTENTS

PART ONE

His Maculate Origin

I

ONCE UPON A time there was a Martian named Valentine Michael Smith.

The first human expedition to Mars was selected on the theory that the greatest danger to man was man himself. At that time, eight Terran years after the founding of the first human colony on Luna, an interplanetary trip made by humans had to be made in free-fall orbits—from Terra to Mars, two hundred fifty-eight Terran days, the same for return, plus four hundred fifty-five days waiting at Mars while the planets crawled back into positions for the return orbit.

Only by refueling at a space station could the *Envoy* make the trip. Once at Mars she might return—if she did not crash, if water could be found to fill her reaction tanks, if a thousand things did not go wrong.

Eight humans, crowded together for almost three Terran years, had better get along much better than humans usually did. An all-male crew was vetoed as unhealthy and unstable. Four married couples was considered optimum, if necessary specialties could be found in such combination.

The University of Edinburgh, prime contractor, subcontracted crew selection to the Institute for Social Studies.

After discarding volunteers useless through age, health, mentality, training, or temperament, the Institute had nine thousand likely candidates. The skills needed were astrogator, medical doctor, cook, machinist, ship's commander, semantician, chemical engineer, electronics engineer, physicist, geologist, biochemist, biologist, atomics engineer, photographer, hydroponicist, rocketry engineer. There were hundreds of combinations of eight volunteers possessing these skills; there turned up three such combinations of married couples—but in all three cases the psychodynamicists who evaluated factors for compatibility threw up their hands in horror. The prime contractor suggested lowering the compatibility figure-of-merit; the Institute offered to return its one dollar fee.

The machines continued to review data changing through deaths, withdrawals, new volunteers. Captain Michael Brant, M.S., Cmdr. D. F. Reserve, pilot and veteran at thirty of the Moon run, had an inside track at the Institute, someone who looked up for him names of single female volunteers who might (with him) complete a crew, then paired his name with these to run problems through the machines to determine whether a combination would be acceptable. This resulted in his jetting to Australia and proposing marriage to Doctor Winifred Coburn, a spinster nine years his senior.

Lights blinked, cards popped out, a crew had been found:

Captain Michael Brant, commanding—pilot, astrogator, relief cook, relief photographer, rocketry engineer;

Dr. Winifred Coburn Brant, forty-one, semantician, practical nurse, stores officer, historian;

Mr. Francis X. Seeney, twenty-eight, executive officer, second pilot, astrogator, astrophysicist, photographer;

Dr. Olga Kovalic Seeney, twenty-nine, cook, biochemist, hydroponicist;

Dr. Ward Smith, forty-five, physician and surgeon, biologist;

Dr. Mary Jane Lyle Smith, twenty-six, atomics engineer, electronics and power technician;

Mr. Sergei Rimsky, thirty-five, electronics engineer, chemical engineer, practical machinist and instrumentation man, cryologist;

Mrs. Eleanora Alvarez Rimsky, thirty-two, geologist and selenologist, hydroponicist.

The crew had all needed skills, some having been acquired by intensive coaching during the weeks before blast-off. More important, they were mutually compatible.

The *Envoy* departed. During the first weeks her reports were picked up by private listeners. As signals became fainter, they were relayed by Earth's radio satellites. The crew seemed healthy and happy. Ringworm was the worst that Dr. Smith had to cope with—the crew adapted to free fall, and anti-nausea drugs were not needed after the first week. If Captain Brant had disciplinary problems, he did not report them.

The *Envoy* achieved a parking orbit inside the orbit of Phobos and spent two weeks in photographic survey. Then Captain Brant radioed: "We will land at 1200 tomorrow GST just south of Lacus Soli."

No further message was received.

II

A QUARTER OF an Earth century passed before Mars was again visited by humans. Six years after the *Envoy* went silent, the drone probe *Zombie*, sponsored by La Société Astronautique Internationale, bridged the void and took up an orbit for the waiting period, then returned. Photographs by the robot vehicle showed a land unattractive by human standards; her instruments confirmed the thinness and unsuitability of Arean atmosphere to human life.

But the *Zombie*'s pictures showed that the "canals" were engineering works and other details were interpreted as ruins of cities. A manned expedition would have been mounted had not World War III intervened.

But war and delay resulted in a stronger expedition than that of the lost *Envoy*. Federation Ship *Champion*, with an all-male crew of eighteen spacemen and carrying twenty-three male pioneers, made the crossing under Lyle Drive in nineteen days. The *Champion* landed south of Lacus Soli, as Captain van Tromp intended to search for the *Envoy*. The second expedition reported daily; three despatches were of special interest. The first was:

"Rocket Ship *Envoy* located. No survivors."

The second was: "Mars is inhabited."

The third: "Correction to despatch 23-105: One survivor of *Envoy* located."

III

CAPTAIN WILLEM VAN Tromp was a man of humanity. He radioed ahead: "My passenger must not be subjected to a public reception. Provide low-gee shuttle, stretcher and ambulance, and armed guard."

He sent his ship's surgeon to make sure that Valentine Michael Smith was installed in a suite in Bethesda Medical Center, transferred into a hydraulic bed, and protected from outside contact. Van Tromp went to an extraordinary session of the Federation High Council.

As Smith was being lifted into bed, the High Minister for Science was saying testily, "Granted, Captain, that your authority as commander of what was nevertheless a scientific expedition gives you the right to order medical service to protect a person temporarily in your charge, I do not see why you now presume to interfere with my department. Why, Smith is a treasure trove of scientific information!"

"I suppose he is, sir."

"Then why—" The science minister turned to the High Minister for Peace and Security. "David? Will you issue instructions to your people? After all, one can't keep Professor Tiergarten and Doctor Okajima, to mention just two, cooling their heels."

The peace minister glanced at Captain van Tromp. The captain shook his head.

"Why?" demanded the science minister. "You admit that he isn't sick."

"Give the captain a chance, Pierre," the peace minister advised. "Well, Captain?"

"Smith isn't sick, sir," Captain van Tromp said, "but he isn't well. He has never before been in a one-gravity field. He weighs two and a half times what he is used to and his muscles aren't up to it. He's not used to Earth-normal pressure. He's not used to *anything* and the strain is too much. Hell's bells, gentlemen, I'm dog-tired myself—and I was born on this planet."

The science minister looked contemptuous. "If acceleration fatigue is worrying you, let me assure you, my dear Captain, that we anticipated that. After all, I've been out myself. I know how it feels. This man Smith must—"

Captain van Tromp decided that it was time to throw a tantrum. He could excuse it by his own very real fatigue, he felt as if he had just landed on Jupiter. So he interrupted. "*Hnh!* 'This man Smith—' This '*man*!' Can't you see that he is *not*?"

"Eh?"

"Smith . . . is . . . not . . . a . . . *man*."

"Huh? Explain yourself, Captain."

"Smith is an intelligent creature with the ancestry of a man, but he is more Martian than man. Until we came along he had never laid eyes on a man. He thinks like a Martian, feels like a Martian. He's been brought up by a race which has *nothing* in common with us—they don't even have *sex*. He's a man by ancestry, a Martian by environment. If you want to drive him crazy and waste that 'treasure trove,' call in your fat-headed professors. Don't give him a chance to get used to this madhouse planet. It's no skin off me; I've done my job!"

The silence was broken by Secretary General Douglas. "And a good job, Captain. If this man, or man-Martian, needs a few days to get adjusted, I'm sure science can wait—so take it easy, Pete. Captain van Tromp is tired."

"One thing won't wait," said the Minister for Public Information.

"Eh, Jock?"

"If we don't show the Man from Mars in the stereo tanks pretty shortly, you'll have riots, Mr. Secretary."

"Hmm—You exaggerate, Jock. Mars stuff in the news, of course. Me decorating the captain and his crew—tomorrow, I think. Captain van Tromp telling his experiences—after a night's rest, Captain."

The minister shook his head.

"No good, Jock?"

"The public expected them to bring back a real live Martian. Since they didn't, we need Smith and need him badly."

"Live Martians?" Secretary General Douglas turned to Captain van Tromp. "You have movies of Martians?"

"Thousands of feet."

"There's your answer, Jock. When the live stuff gets thin, trot on the movies. Now, Captain, about extraterritoriality: you say the Martians were not opposed?"

"Well, no, sir—but they were not for it, either."

"I don't follow you."

Captain van Tromp chewed his lip. "Sir, talking with a Martian is like talking with an echo. You don't get argument but you don't get results."

"Perhaps you should have brought what's-his-name, your semantician. Or is he waiting outside?"

"Mahmoud, sir. Doctor Mahmoud is not well. A—A slight nervous breakdown, sir." Van Tromp reflected that dead drunk was the moral equivalent.

"Space happy?"

"A little, perhaps." These damned groundhogs!

"Well, fetch him around when he's feeling himself. I imagine this young man Smith will be of help, too."

"Perhaps," van Tromp said doubtfully.

THIS YOUNG MAN Smith was busy staying alive. His body, unbearably compressed and weakened by the strange shape of space in this unbelievable place, was at last relieved by the softness of the nest in which these others placed him. He dropped the effort of sustaining it, and turned his third level to his respiration and heart beat.

He saw that he was about to consume himself. His lungs were beating as hard as they did at home, his heart was racing to distribute the influx, all in an attempt to cope with the squeezing of space—and this while smothered by a poisonously rich and dangerously hot atmosphere. He took steps.

When his heart rate was twenty per minute and respiration almost imperceptible, he watched long enough to be sure that he would not discorporate while his attention was elsewhere. When he was satisfied he set a portion of his second level on guard and withdrew the rest of himself. It was necessary to review the configurations of these many new events in order to fit them to himself, then cherish and praise them—lest they swallow him.

Where should he start? When he left home, enfolding these others who were now his nestlings? Or at his arrival in this crushed space? He was suddenly assaulted by lights and sounds of that arrival, feeling it with mind-shaking pain. No, he was not ready to embrace that configuration—back! back! back beyond his first sight of these others who were now his own. Back even before the healing which had followed first grokking that he was not as his nestling brothers . . . back to the nest itself.

None of his thinkings were in Earth symbols. Simple English he had freshly learned to speak, less easily than a Hindu used it to trade with a Turk. Smith used English as one might use a code book, with tedious and imperfect translation. Now his thoughts, abstractions from half a million years of wildly alien culture, traveled so far from human experience as to be untranslatable.

In the adjoining room Dr. Thaddeus was playing cribbage with Tom Meechum, Smith's special nurse. Thaddeus had one eye on his dials and meters. When a flickering light changed from ninety-two pulsations per minute to less than twenty, he hurried into Smith's room with Meechum at his heels.

The patient floated in the flexible skin of the hydraulic bed. He appeared to be dead. Thaddeus snapped, "Get Doctor Nelson!"

Meechum said, "Yessir!" and added, "How about shock gear, Doc?"

"Get Doctor Nelson!"

The nurse rushed out. The intern examined the patient, did not touch him. An older doctor came in, walking with the labored awkwardness of a man long in space and not readjusted to high gravity. "Well, Doctor?"

"Patient's respiration, temperature, and pulse dropped suddenly about two minutes ago, sir."

"What have you done?"

"Nothing, sir. Your instructions—"

"Good." Nelson looked Smith over, studied instruments back of the bed, twins of those in the watch room. "Let me know if there is any change." He started to leave.

Thaddeus looked startled. "But, Doctor—"

Nelson said, "Yes, Doctor? What is your diagnosis?"

"Uh, I don't wish to sound off about your patient, sir."

"I asked for your diagnosis."

"Very well, sir. Shock—atypical, perhaps," he hedged, "but shock, leading to termination."

Nelson nodded. "Reasonable. But this isn't a reasonable case. I've seen this patient in this condition a dozen times. Watch." Nelson lifted the patient's arm, let it go. It stayed where he left it.

"Catalepsy?" asked Thaddeus.

"Call it that if you like. Just keep him from being bothered and call me if there is any change." He replaced Smith's arm.

Nelson left. Thaddeus looked at the patient, shook his head and returned to the watch room. Meechum picked up his cards. "Crib?"

"No."

Meechum added, "Doc, if you ask me, that one is a case for the basket before morning."

"No one asked you. Go have a cigarette with the guards. I want to think."

Meechum shrugged and joined the guards in the corridor; they straightened up, then saw who it was and relaxed. The taller marine said, "What was the excitement?"

"The patient had quintuplets and we were arguing about what to name them. Which one of you monkeys has a butt? And a light?"

The other marine dug out a pack of cigarettes. "How're you fixed for suction?"

"Just middlin'." Meechum stuck the cigarette in his face. "Honest to God, gentlemen, I don't know anything about this patient."

"What's the idea of these orders about 'Absolutely No Women'? Is he a sex maniac?"

"All I know is they brought him in from the *Champion* and said he was to have absolute quiet."

"'The *Champion*!'" the first marine said. "That accounts for it."

"Accounts for what?"

"It stands to reason. He ain't had any, he ain't seen any, he ain't touched any—for months. And he's sick, see? If he was to lay hands on any, they're afraid he'd kill hisself." He blinked. "I'll bet I would."

SMITH HAD BEEN aware of the doctors but had grokked that their intentions were benign; it was not necessary for the major part of him to be jerked back.

At the morning hour when human nurses slap patients' faces with cold, wet cloths Smith returned. He speeded up his heart, increased his respiration, and took note of his surroundings, viewing them with serenity. He looked the room over, noting with praise all details. He was seeing it for the first time, as he had been incapable of enfolding it when he had been brought there. This room was not commonplace to him; there was nothing like it on all Mars, nor did it resemble the wedge-shaped, metal compartments of the *Champion*. Having relived the events linking his nest to this place, he was now prepared to accept it, commend it, and in some degree to cherish it.

He became aware of another living creature. A granddaddy longlegs was making a journey down from the ceiling, spinning as it went. Smith watched with delight and wondered if it were a nestling man.

Doctor Archer Frame, the intern who had relieved Thaddeus, walked in at that moment. "Good morning," he said. "How do you feel?"

Smith examined the question. The first phrase he recognized as a formal sound, requiring no answer. The second was listed in his mind with several translations. If Doctor Nelson used it, it meant one thing; if Captain van Tromp used it, it was a formal sound.

He felt that dismay which so often overtook him in trying to communicate with these creatures. But he forced his body to remain calm and risked an answer. "Feel good."

"Good!" the creature echoed. "Doctor Nelson will be along in a minute. Feel like breakfast?"

All symbols were in Smith's vocabulary but he had trouble believing that he had heard rightly. He knew that he was food, but he did not "feel like" food. Nor had he any warning that he might be selected for such honor. He had not known that the food supply was such that it was necessary to reduce the corporate group. He was filled with mild regret, since there was still so much to grok of new events, but no reluctance.

But he was excused from the effort of translating an answer by the entrance of Dr. Nelson. The ship's doctor inspected Smith and the array of dials, then turned to Smith. "Bowels move?"

Smith understood this; Nelson always asked it. "No."

"We'll take care of that. But first you eat. Orderly, fetch that tray."

Nelson fed him three bites, then required him to hold the spoon and feed himself. It was tiring but gave him a feeling of gay triumph for it was his first unassisted action since reaching this oddly distorted space. He cleaned the bowl and remembered to ask, "Who is this?" so that he could praise his benefactor.

"What is this, you mean," Nelson answered. "It's a synthetic food jelly—and now you know as much as you did before. Finished? All right, climb out of that bed."

"Beg pardon?" It was an attention symbol which was useful when communication failed.

"I said get out of there. Stand up. Walk around. Sure, you're weak as a kitten but you'll never put on muscle floating in that bed." Nelson opened a valve, water drained out. Smith restrained a feeling of insecurity, knowing that Nelson cherished him. Shortly he lay on the floor of the bed with the watertight cover wrinkled around him. Nelson added, "Doctor Frame, take his other elbow."

With Nelson to encourage and both to help, Smith stumbled over the rim of the bed. "Steady. Now stand up," Nelson directed. "Don't be afraid. We'll catch you if necessary."

He made the effort and stood alone—a slender young man with underdeveloped muscles and overdeveloped chest. His hair had been cut in the *Champion* and his whiskers removed and inhibited. His most marked feature was his bland, babyish face—set with eyes which would have seemed at home in a man of ninety.

He stood alone, trembling slightly, then tried to walk. He managed three shuffling steps and broke into a sunny, childlike smile. "Good boy!" Nelson applauded.

He tried another step, began to tremble and suddenly collapsed. They barely managed to break his fall. "Damn!"

Nelson fumed. "He's gone into another one. Here, help me lift him into bed. No—fill it first."

Frame cut off the flow when the skin floated six inches from the top. They lugged him into it, awkwardly because he had frozen into fetal position. "Get a collar pillow under his neck," instructed Nelson, "and call me if you need me. We'll walk him again this afternoon. In three months he'll be swinging through the trees like a monkey. There's nothing really wrong with him."

"Yes, Doctor," Frame answered doubtfully.

"Oh, yes, when he comes out of it, teach him to use the bathroom. Have the nurse help you; I don't want him to fall."

"Yes, sir. Uh, any particular method—I mean, how—"

"Eh? Show him! He won't understand much that you say, but he's bright as a whip."

Smith ate lunch without help. Presently an orderly came in to remove his tray. The man leaned over. "Listen," he said in a low voice, "I've got a fat proposition for you."

"Beg pardon?"

"A deal, a way for you to make money fast and easy."

"'Money?' What is 'money'?"

"Never mind the philosophy; everybody needs money. I'll talk fast because I can't stay long—it's taken a lot of fixing to get me here. I represent Peerless Features. We'll pay sixty thousand for your story and it won't be a bit of trouble to you—we've got the best ghost writers in the business. You just answer questions; they put it together." He whipped out a paper. "Just sign this."

Smith accepted the paper, stared at it, upside down. The man muffled an exclamation. "Lordy! Don't you read English?"

Smith understood this enough to answer. "No."

"Well—Here, I'll read it, then you put your thumb print in the square and I'll witness it. 'I, the undersigned, Valentine Michael Smith, sometimes known as the Man from Mars, do grant and assign to Peerless Features, Limited, all and exclusive rights in my true-fact story to be titled *I Was a Prisoner on Mars* in exchange *for*—"

"Orderly!"

Dr. Frame was in the door; the paper disappeared into the man's clothes. "Coming, sir. I was getting this tray."

"What were you reading?"

"Nothing."

"I saw you. This patient is not to be disturbed." They left; Dr. Frame closed the door behind them. Smith lay motionless for an hour, but try as he might he could not grok it at all.

IV

GILLIAN BOARDMAN WAS a competent nurse and her hobby was men. She went on duty that day as supervisor of the floor where Smith was. When the grapevine said that the patient in suite K-12 had never seen a woman in his life, she did not believe it. She went to pay a call on the strange patient.

She knew of the "No Female Visitors" rule and, while she did not consider herself to be a visitor, she sailed past without attempting to use the guarded door—marines had a stuffy habit of construing orders literally. Instead she went into the adjacent watch room.

Dr. Thaddeus looked up. "Well, if it ain't 'Dimples'! Hi, honey, what brings you here?"

"This is part of my rounds. What about your patient?"

"Don't worry your head, honey chile; he's not your responsibility. See your order book."

"I read it. I want to look at him."

"In one word—no."

"Oh, Tad, don't go regulation."

He gazed at his nails. "If I let you put your foot inside that door, I'd wind up in Antarctica. I wouldn't want Dr. Nelson even to catch you in this watch room."

She stood up. "Is Doctor Nelson likely to pop in?"

"Not unless I send for him. He's sleeping off low-gee fatigue."

"Then what's the idea of being so duty struck?"

"That's all, Nurse."

"Very well, Doctor!" She added, "Stinker."

"Jill!"

"A stuffed shirt, too."

He sighed. "Still okay for Saturday night?"

She shrugged. "I suppose. A girl can't be fussy these days." She went back to her station, picked up the pass key. She was balked but not beaten, as suite K-12 had a door joining it to the room beyond, a room used as a sitting room when the suite was occupied by a high official. The room was not then in use. She let herself into it. The guards paid no attention, unaware that they had been flanked.

She hesitated at the door between the two rooms, feeling the excitement she used to feel when sneaking out of student nurses' quarters. She unlocked it and looked in.

The patient was in bed, he looked at her as the door

opened. Her first impression was that here was a patient too far gone to care. His lack of expression seemed to show the apathy of the desperately ill. Then she saw that his eyes were alive with interest; she wondered if his face was paralyzed?

She assumed her professional manner. "Well, how are we today? Feeling better?"

Smith translated the questions. The inclusion of both of them in the query was confusing; he decided that it might symbolize a wish to cherish and grow close. The second part matched Nelson's speech forms. "Yes," he answered.

"Good!" Aside from his odd lack of expression she saw nothing strange about him—and if women were unknown to him, he was managing to conceal it. "Is there anything I can do?" She noted that there was no glass on the bed-side shelf. "May I get you water?"

Smith spotted at once that this creature was different from the others. He compared what he was seeing with pictures Nelson had shown him on the trip from home to his place—pictures intended to explain a puzzling con-figuration of this people group. This, then, was "woman."

He felt both oddly excited and disappointed. He sup-pressed both in order that he might grok deeply, with such success that Dr. Thaddeus noticed no change in the dials next door.

But when he translated the last query he felt such surge of emotion that he almost let his heartbeat increase. He caught it and chided himself for an undisciplined nestling. Then he checked his translation.

No, he was not mistaken. This woman creature had of-fered him water. It wished to grow closer.

With great effort, scrambling for adequate meanings,

he attempted to answer with due ceremoniousness. "I thank you for water. May you always drink deep."

Nurse Boardman looked startled. "Why, how sweet!" She found a glass, filled it, and handed it to him.

He said, "You drink."

Wonder if he thinks I'm trying to poison him? she asked herself—but there was a compelling quality to his request. She took a sip, whereupon he took one also, after which he seemed content to sink back, as if he had accomplished something important.

Jill told herself that, as an adventure, this was a fizzle. She said, "Well, if you don't need anything, I must get on with my work."

She started for the door. He called out, "No!"

She stopped. "Eh?"

"Don't go away."

"Well . . . I'll have to go, pretty quickly." She came back. "Is there anything you want?"

He looked her up and down. "You are . . . 'woman'?"

The question startled Jill Boardman. Her impulse was to answer flippantly. But Smith's grave face and oddly disturbing eyes checked her. She became aware emotionally that the impossible fact about this patient was true; he did not know what a woman was. She answered carefully, "Yes, I am a woman."

Smith continued to stare. Jill began to be embarrassed. To be looked at by a male she expected, but this was like being examined under a microscope. She stirred. "Well? I look like a woman, don't I?"

"I do not know," Smith answered slowly. "How does woman look? What makes you woman?"

"Well, for pity's sake!" This conversation was further out of hand than any she had had with a male since her twelfth birthday. "You don't expect me to take off my clothes and show you!"

Smith took time to examine these symbols and try to translate them. The first group he could not grok at all. It might be one of those formal sounds these people used . . . yet it had been spoken with force, as if it might be a last communication before withdrawal. Perhaps he had so deeply mistaken right conduct in dealing with a woman creature that it might be ready to discorporate.

He did not want the woman to die at that moment, even though it was its right and possibly its obligation. The abrupt change from rapport of water ritual to a situation in which a newly won water brother might be considering withdrawal or discorporation would have thrown him into panic had he not been consciously suppressing such disturbance. But he decided that if it died now he must die at once also—he could not grok it any other wise, not after giving of water.

The second half contained symbols he had encountered before. He grokked imperfectly the intention but there seemed to be a way to avoid this crisis—by acceding to the suggested wish. Perhaps if the woman took its clothes off neither of them need discorporate. He smiled happily. "Please."

Jill opened her mouth, closed it. She opened it again. "Well, I'll be darned!"

Smith could grok emotional violence and knew that he had offered a wrong reply. He began to compose his mind for discorporation, savoring and cherishing all that he had been and seen, with especial attention to this woman creature. Then he became aware that the woman was bending over him and he knew somehow that it was not about to die. It looked into his face. "Correct me if I am wrong," it said, "but were you asking me to take my clothes off?"

The inversions and abstractions required careful translation but Smith managed it. "Yes," he answered, hoping that it would not stir up a new crisis.

"That's what I thought you said. Brother, you aren't ill."

The word "brother" he considered first—the woman was reminding him that they had been joined in water. He asked the help of his nestlings that he might measure up to whatever this new brother wanted. "I am not ill," he agreed.

"Though I'm darned if I know what is wrong with you. I won't peel down. And I've got to leave." It straightened up and turned toward the side door—then stopped and looked back with a quizzical smile. "You might ask me again, real prettily, under other circumstances. I'm curious to see what I might do."

The woman was gone. Smith relaxed and let the room fade away. He felt sober triumph that he had somehow comported himself so that it was not necessary for them to die . . . but there was much to grok. The woman's last speech had contained symbols new to him and those which were not new had been arranged in fashions not easily understood. But he was happy that the flavor had been suitable for communication between water brothers—although touched with something disturbing and terrifyingly pleasant. He thought about his new brother, the woman creature, and felt odd tingles. The feeling reminded him of the first time he had been allowed to be present at a discorporation and he felt happy without knowing why.

He wished that his brother Doctor Mahmoud were here. There was so much to grok, so little to grok from.

JILL SPENT THE rest of her watch in a daze. The face of the Man from Mars stayed in her mind and she mulled over the crazy things he had said. No, not "crazy"—she had done her stint in psychiatric wards and felt certain that his remarks had not been psychotic. She decided that "innocent" was the term—then decided that the word was not adequate. His expression was innocent, his eyes were not. What sort of creature had a face like that?

She had once worked in a Catholic hospital; she suddenly saw the face of the Man from Mars surrounded by the headdress of a nursing sister, a nun. The idea disturbed her; there was nothing female about Smith's face.

She was changing into street clothes when another nurse stuck her head into the locker room. "Phone, Jill." Jill accepted the call, sound without vision, while she dressed.

"Is this Florence Nightingale?" a baritone voice asked.

"Speaking. That you, Ben?"

"The stalwart upholder of the freedom of the press in person. Little one, are you busy?"

"What do you have in mind?"

"I have in mind buying you a steak, plying you with liquor, and asking you a question."

"The answer is still 'No.'"

"Not *that* question."

"Oh, you know another one? Tell me."

"Later. I want you softened up first."

"Real steak? Not syntho?"

"Guaranteed. Stick a fork in it and it will moo."

"You must be on an expense account, Ben."

"That's irrelevant and ignoble. How about it?"

"You've talked me into it."

"Roof on the medical center. Ten minutes."

She put the suit she had changed into back into her locker and put on a dress kept there for emergencies. It was demure, barely translucent, with bustle and bust pads so subdued that they merely re-created the effect she would have produced wearing nothing. Jill looked at herself with satisfaction and took the bounce tube up to the roof.

She was looking for Ben Caxton when the roof orderly touched her arm. "There's a car paging you, Miss Boardman—that Talbot saloon."

"Thanks, Jack." She saw the taxi spotted for take-off, with its door open. She climbed in, and was about to hand Ben a back-handed compliment when she saw that he was not inside. The taxi was on automatic; its door closed and it took to the air, swung out of the circle and sliced across the Potomac. It stopped on a landing flat over Alexandria and Caxton got in; it took off again. Jill looked him over. "My, aren't we important! Since when do you send a robot to pick up your women?"

He patted her knee and said gently, "Reasons, little one. I can't be seen picking you up—"

"Well!"

"—and you can't afford to be seen with me. So simmer down, it was necessary."

"Hmm . . . which one of us has leprosy?"

"Both of us. Jill, I'm a newspaperman."

"I was beginning to think you were something else."

"And you are a nurse at the hospital where they are holding the Man from Mars."

"Does that make me unfit to meet your mother?"

"Do you need a map, Jill? There are more than a thousand reporters in this area, plus press agents, ax grinders, winchells, lippmanns, and the stampede that arrived when the *Champion* landed. Every one of them has been trying to interview the Man from Mars—and none has succeeded. Do you think it would be smart for us to be seen leaving the hospital together?"

"I don't see that it matters. I'm not the Man from Mars."

He looked her over. "You certainly aren't. But you are going to help me see him—which is why I didn't pick you up."

"Huh? Ben, you've been out in the sun without your hat. They've got a marine guard around him."

"So they have. So we talk it over."

"I don't see what there is to talk about."

"Later. Let's eat."

"Now you sound rational. Would your expense account run to the New Mayflower? You *are* on an expense account, aren't you?"

Caxton frowned. "Jill, I wouldn't risk a restaurant closer than Louisville. It would take this hack two hours to get that far. How about dinner in my apartment?"

"'—Said the Spider to the Fly.' Ben, I'm too tired to wrestle."

"Nobody asked you to. King's X, cross my heart and hope to die."

"I don't like that much better. If I'm safe with you, I must be slipping. Well, all right, King's X."

Caxton punched buttons; the taxi, which had been circling under a "hold" instruction, woke up and headed for the apartment hotel where Ben lived. He punched a phone number and said to Jill, "How much time do you want to get liquored up, sugar foot? I'll tell the kitchen to have the steaks ready."

Jill considered it. "Ben, your mousetrap has a private kitchen."

"Of sorts. I can grill a steak."

"I'll grill the steak. Hand me the phone." She gave orders, stopping to make sure that Ben liked endive.

The taxi dropped them on the roof and they went down to his flat. It was old-fashioned, its one luxury a live grass lawn in the living room. Jill stopped, slipped off her shoes, stepped barefooted into the living room and wiggled her toes among the cool green blades. She sighed. "My, that feels good. My feet have hurt ever since I entered training."

"Sit down."

"No, I want my feet to remember this tomorrow."

"Suit yourself." He went into his pantry and mixed drinks.

Presently she followed and became domestic. Steak was in the package lift; with it were pre-baked potatoes. She tossed the salad, handed it to the refrigerator, set up a combination to grill the steak and heat the potatoes, but did not start the cycle. "Ben, doesn't this stove have remote control?"

He studied the setup, flipped a switch. "Jill, what would you do if you had to cook over an open fire?"

"I'd do darn well. I was a Girl Scout. How about you, smarty?"

They went to the living room; Jill sat at his feet and they applied themselves to martinis. Opposite his chair was a stereovision tank disguised as an aquarium; he switched it on, guppies and tetras gave way to the face of the well-known winchell Augustus Greaves.

"—it can be stated authoritatively," the image was saying, "that the Man from Mars is being kept under drugs to keep him from disclosing these facts. The administration would find it extremely—"

Caxton flipped it off. "Gus old boy," he said pleasantly, "you don't know a durn thing more than I do." He frowned. "Though you might be right about the government keeping him under drugs."

"No, they aren't," Jill said suddenly.

"Eh? How's that, little one?"

"The Man from Mars isn't under hypnotics." Having blurted more than she had meant to, she added, "He's got a doctor on continuous watch, but there aren't any orders for sedation."

"Are you sure? You aren't one of his nurses?"

"No. Uh . . . matter of fact, there's an order to keep women away from him and some tough marines to make sure of it."

Caxton nodded. "So I heard. Fact is, you don't know whether they are drugging him or not."

Jill bit her lip. She would have to tell on herself to back up what she had said. "Ben? You wouldn't give me away?"

"How?"

"Any way at all."

"Hmm . . . that covers a lot, but I'll go along."

"All right. Pour me another." He did so, Jill went on. "I know they don't have the Man from Mars hopped up—because I talked with him."

Caxton whistled. "I knew it. When I got up this morning I said to myself, 'Go see Jill. She's the ace up my sleeve.' Honey lamb, have another drink. Have six. Here, take the pitcher."

"Not so fast!"

"Whatever you like. May I rub your poor tired feet? Lady, you are about to be interviewed. How—"

"No, Ben! You promised. You quote me and I'll lose my job."

"Mmm . . . How about 'from a usually reliable source'?"

"I'd be scared."

"Well? Are you going to let me die of frustration and eat that steak by yourself?"

"Oh, I'll talk. But you can't use it." Ben kept quiet; Jill described how she had out-flanked the guards.

He interrupted. "Say! Could you do that again?"

"Huh? I suppose so, but I won't. It's risky."

"Well, could you slip me in that way? Look, I'll dress like an electrician—coveralls, union badge, tool kit. You slip me the key and—"

"No!"

"Huh? Look, baby girl, be reasonable. This is the greatest human-interest story since Colombo conned Isabella into hocking her jewels. The only thing that worries me is that I may find another electrician—"

"The only thing that worries me is *me*," Jill interrupted. "To you it's a story; to me it's my career. They'd take away my cap, my pin, and ride me out of town on a rail."

"Mmm . . . there's that."

"There sure is that."

"Lady, you are about to be offered a bribe."

"How big? It'll take quite a chunk to keep me in style the rest of my life in Rio."

"Well . . . you can't expect me to outbid Associated Press, or Reuters. How about a hundred?"

"What do you think I am?"

"We settled that, we're dickering over the price. A hundred and fifty?"

"Look up the number of Associated Press, that's a lamb."

"Capitol 10-9000. Jill, will you marry me? That's as high as I can go."

She looked startled. "What did you say?"

"Will you marry me? Then, when they ride you out of town on a rail, I'll be waiting at the city line and take you away from your sordid existence. You'll come back here and cool your toes in my grass—*our* grass—and forget your ignominy. But you've durn well got to sneak me into that room first."

"Ben, you almost sound serious. If I phone for a Fair Witness, will you repeat that?"

Caxton sighed. "Send for a Witness."

She stood up. "Ben," she said softly, "I won't hold you to it." She kissed him. "Don't joke about marriage to a spinster."

"I wasn't joking."

"I wonder. Wipe off the lipstick and I'll tell everything I know, then we'll consider how you can use it without getting me ridden on that rail. Fair enough?"

"Fair enough."

She gave him a detailed account. "I'm sure he wasn't drugged. I'm equally sure that he was rational—although he talked in the oddest fashion and asked the darnedest questions."

"It would be odder still if he hadn't talked oddly."

"Huh?"

"Jill, we don't know much about Mars but we do know that Martians are not human. Suppose you were popped into a tribe so far back in the jungle that they had never seen shoes. Would you know the small talk that comes from a lifetime in a culture? That's a mild analogy; the truth is at least forty million miles stranger."

Jill nodded. "I figured that out. That's why I discounted his odd remarks. I'm not dumb."

"No, you're real bright, for a female."

"Would you like this martini in your hair?"

"I apologize. Women are smarter than men; that is proved by our whole setup. Gimme, I'll fill it."

She accepted peace offerings and went on, "Ben, that order about not letting him see women, it's silly. He's no sex fiend."

"No doubt they don't want to hand him too many shocks at once."

"He wasn't shocked. He was just . . . interested. It wasn't like having a man look at me."

"If you had granted that request for a viewing, you might have had your hands full."

"I don't think so. I suppose they've told him about male and female; he just wanted to see how women are different."

"'Vive la différence!'" Caxton answered enthusiastically.

"Don't be vulgar."

"Me? I was being reverent. I was giving thanks that I was born human and not Martian."

"Be serious."

"I was never more serious."

"Then be quiet. He wouldn't have given me any trouble. You didn't see his face—I did."

"What about his face?"

Jill looked puzzled. "Ben, have you ever seen an angel?"

"You, cherub. Otherwise not."

"Well, neither have I—but that is how he looked. He had old, wise eyes in a completely placid face, a face of unearthly innocence." She shivered.

"'Unearthly' is the word," Ben answered slowly. "I'd like to see him."

"Ben, why are they keeping him shut up? He wouldn't hurt a fly."

Caxton fitted his fingertips together. "Well, they want to protect him. He grew up in Mars gravity; he's probably weak as a cat."

"But muscular weakness isn't dangerous; myasthenia gravis is much worse and we manage all right with that."

"They want to keep him from catching things, too. He's like those experimental animals at Notre Dame; he's never been exposed."

"Sure, sure—no antibodies. But from what I hear around the mess hall, Doctor Nelson—the surgeon in the *Champion*—took care of that on the trip back. Mutual transfusions until he had replaced about half his blood tissue."

"Can I use that, Jill? That's news."

"Just don't quote me. They gave him shots for everything but housemaid's knee, too. But, Ben, to protect him from infection doesn't take armed guards."

"Mmmm . . . Jill, I've picked up a few tidbits you may not know. I can't use them because I've got to protect my sources. But I'll tell you—just don't talk."

"I won't."

"It's a long story. Want a refill?"

"No, let's start the steak. Where's the button?"

"Right here."

"Well, push it."

"Me? You offered to cook dinner."

"Ben Caxton, I will lie here and starve before I will get up to push a button six inches from your finger."

"As you wish." He pressed the button. "But don't forget who cooked dinner. Now about Valentine Michael Smith. There is grave doubt as to his right to the name 'Smith.'"

"Huh?"

"Honey, your pal is the first interplanetary bastard of record."

"The hell you say!"

"Please be ladylike. You remember anything about the *Envoy*? Four married couples. Two couples were Captain and Mrs. Brant, Doctor and Mrs. Smith. Your friend with the face of an angel is the son of Mrs. Smith by Captain Brant."

"How do they know? And who cares? It's pretty snivelin' to dig up scandal after all this time. They're dead— let 'em alone!"

"As to how they know, there probably never were eight people more thoroughly measured and typed. Blood typing, Rh factor, hair and eye color, all those genetic things—you know more about them than I do. It is certain that Mary Jane Lyle Smith was his mother and Michael Brant his father. It gives Smith a fine heredity; his father had an I.Q. of 163, his mother 170, and both were tops in their fields.

"As to who cares," Ben went on, "a lot of people care—and more will, once this shapes up. Ever heard of the Lyle Drive?"

"Of course. That's what the *Champion* used."

"And every space ship, these days. Who invented it?"

"I don't—Wait a minute! You mean *she*—"

"Hand the lady a cigar! Dr. Mary Jane Lyle Smith. She had it worked out before she left even though development remained to be done. So she applied for basic patents and placed it in trust—*not* a non-profit corporation, mind you—then assigned control and interim income to the Science Foundation. So eventually the government got control—but your friend owns it. It's worth millions, maybe hundreds of millions; I couldn't guess."

They brought in dinner. Caxton used ceiling tables to protect his lawn; he lowered one to his chair and another to Japanese height so that Jill could sit on the grass. "Tender?" he asked.

"Ongerful!" she answered.

"Thanks. Remember, I cooked."

"Ben," she said after swallowing, "how about Smith being a—I mean, illegitimate? Can he inherit?"

"He's not illegitimate. Doctor Mary Jane was at Berkeley; California laws deny the concept of bastardy. Same for Captain Brant, as New Zealand has civilized laws. While in the home state of Doctor Ward Smith, Mary Jane's husband, a child born in wedlock is legitimate, come hell or high water. We have here, Jill, a man who is the legitimate child of three parents."

"Huh? Now wait, Ben; he can't be. I'm not a lawyer but—"

"You sure ain't. Such fictions don't bother a lawyer. Smith is legitimate different ways in different jurisdictions—even though a bastard in fact. So he inherits. Besides that, while his mother was wealthy, his fathers were well to do. Brant ploughed most of his scandalous salary as a pilot on the Moon run into Lunar Enterprises. You know how that stuff boomed—they just declared another stock dividend. Brant had one vice, gambling—but the bloke won regularly and invested that, too. Ward Smith had family money. Smith is heir to both."

"Whew!"

"That ain't half, honey. Smith is heir to the entire crew."

"Huh?"

"All eight signed a 'Gentlemen Adventurers' contract, making them mutually heirs to each other—all of them *and* their issue. They did it with care, using as models contracts in the sixteenth and seventeenth centuries that had stood up against every effort to break them. These were highpowered people; among them they had quite a lot. Happened to include considerable Lunar Enterprises stock, too, besides what Brant held. Smith might own a controlling interest, or at least a key bloc."

Jill thought about the childlike creature who had made such a touching ceremony of a drink of water and felt sorry for him. Caxton went on: "I wish I could sneak a look at the *Envoy*'s log. They recovered it—but I doubt if they'll release it."

"Why not, Ben?"

"It's a nasty story. I got that much before my informant sobered up. Dr. Ward Smith delivered his wife by Caesarean section—and she died on the table. What he did next shows that he knew the score; with the same scalpel he cut Captain Brant's throat—then his own. Sorry, hon."

Jill shivered. "I'm a nurse. I'm immune to such things."

"You're a liar and I love you for it. I was on police beat three years, Jill; I never got hardened to it."

"What happened to the others?"

"If we don't break the bureaucrats loose from that log, we'll never know—and I am a starry-eyed newsboy who thinks we should. Secrecy begets tyranny."

"Ben, he might be better off if they gypped him out of his inheritance. He's very . . . uh, unworldly."

"The exact word, I'm sure. Nor does he need money; the Man from Mars will never miss a meal. Any government and a thousand-odd universities and institutions would be delighted to have him as a permanent guest."

"He'd better sign it over and forget it."

"It's not that easy. Jill, you know the famous case of General Atomics versus Larkin, et al.?"

"Uh, you mean the Larkin Decision. I had it in school, same as everybody. What's it got to do with Smith?"

"Think back. The Russians sent the first ship to the Moon, it crashed. The United States and Canada combine to send one; it gets back but leaves nobody on the Moon. So while the United States and the Commonwealth are getting set to send a colonizing one under the sponsorship of the Federation and Russia is mounting the same deal on their own, General Atomics steals a march by boosting one from an island leased from Ecuador—and their men are there, sitting pretty and looking smug when the Federation vessel shows up—followed by the Russian one.

"So General Atomics, a Swiss corporation American controlled, claimed the Moon. The Federation couldn't brush them off and grab it; the Russians wouldn't have held still. So the High Court ruled that a corporate person, a mere legal fiction, could not own a planet; the real owners were the men who maintained occupation—Larkin and associates. So they recognized them as a sovereign nation and took them into the Federation—with melon slicing for those on the inside and concessions to General Atomics and its daughter corporation, Lunar Enterprises. This did not please anybody and the Federation High Court was not all-powerful then—but it was a compromise everybody could swallow. It resulted in rules for colonizing planets, all based on the Larkin Decision and intended to avoid bloodshed. Worked, too—World War Three did *not* result from conflict over space travel and such. So the Larkin Decision is law and applies to Smith."

Jill shook her head. "I don't see the connection."

"Think, Jill. By our laws, Smith is a sovereign nation—and sole owner of the planet Mars."

V

JILL LOOKED ROUND-EYED. "Too many martinis, Ben. I would swear you said that patient owns Mars."

"He does. He occupied it the required period. Smith is the planet Mars—King, President, sole civic body, what you will. If the *Champion* had not left colonists, Smith's claim might have lapsed. But it did and that continues occupation even though Smith came to Earth. But Smith doesn't have to split with them; they are mere immigrants until he grants them citizenship."

"Fantastic!"

"But legal. Honey, you see why people are interested in Smith? And why the administration is keeping him under a rug? What they are doing isn't legal. Smith is also a citizen of the United States and of the Federation; it's illegal to hold a citizen, even a convicted criminal, incommunicado anywhere in the Federation. Also, it has been an unfriendly act all through history to lock up a visiting monarch—which he *is*—and not to let him see people, especially the press, meaning *me*. You still won't sneak me?"

"Huh? You've got me scared silly. Ben, if they had caught me, what would they have done?"

"Mmm . . . nothing rough. Locked you in a padded cell, with a certificate signed by three doctors, and allowed you mail on alternate leap years. I'm wondering what they are going to do to *him*."

"What *can* they do?"

"Well, he might die—from gee-fatigue, say."

"You mean *murder* him?"

"Tut, tut! Don't use nasty words. I don't think they will. In the first place he is a mine of information. In the second place, he is a bridge between us and the only other civilized race we have encountered. How are you on the classics? Ever read H. G. Wells's *The War of the Worlds*?"

"A long time ago, in school."

"Suppose the Martians turn out nasty. They might and we have no way of guessing how big a club they swing. Smith might be the go-between who could make the First

Interplanetary War unnecessary. Even if this is unlikely, the administration can't ignore it. The discovery of life on Mars is something that, politically, they haven't figured out yet."

"Then you think he is safe?"

"For the time being. The Secretary General has to guess right. As you know, his administration is shaky."

"I don't pay attention to politics."

"You should. It's barely less important than your own heart beat."

"I don't pay attention to that, either."

"Don't talk when I'm orating. The patchwork majority headed by Douglas could slip apart overnight—Pakistan would bolt at a nervous cough. There would be a vote of no confidence and Mr. Secretary General Douglas would go back to being a cheap lawyer. The Man from Mars can make or break him. Are you going to sneak me in?"

"I'm going to enter a nunnery. Is there more coffee?"

"I'll see."

They stood up. Jill stretched and said, "Oh, my ancient bones! Never mind coffee, Ben; I've got a hard day tomorrow. Run me home, will you? Or send me home, that's safer."

"Okay, though the evening is young." He went into his bedroom, came out carrying an object the size of a small cigarette lighter. "You won't sneak me in?"

"Gee, Ben, I *want* to, but—"

"Never mind. It is dangerous—and not just to your career." He showed her the object. "Will you put a bug on him?"

"Huh? What is it?"

"The greatest boon to spies since the Mickey Finn. A microminiaturized recorder. The wire is spring driven so it can't be spotted by a snooper circuit. The insides are packed in plastic—you could drop it out of a cab. The power is about as much radioactivity as in a watch dial, but shielded. The wire runs twenty-four hours. Then you slide out a spool and stick in another—the spring is part of the spool."

"Will it explode?" she asked nervously.

"You could bake it in a cake."

"Ben, you've got me scared to go into his room."

"You can go into the room next door, can't you?"

"I suppose so."

"This thing has donkey's ears. Fasten the concave side against a wall—tape will do—and it picks up everything in the room beyond."

"I'm bound to be noticed if I duck in and out of that room. Ben, his room has a wall in common with a room on another corridor. Will that do?"

"Perfect. You'll do it?"

"Umm . . . give it to me. I'll think it over."

Caxton polished it with his handkerchief. "Put on your gloves."

"Why?"

"Possession is good for a vacation behind bars. Use gloves and don't get caught with it."

"You think of the nicest things!"

"Want to back out?"

Jill let out a long breath. "No."

"Good girl!" A light blinked, he glanced up. "That must be your cab. I rang for it when I went to get this."

"Oh. Find my shoes, will you? Don't come to the roof. The less I'm seen with you the better."

"As you wish."

As he straightened up from putting her shoes on, she

took his head in both hands and kissed him. "Dear Ben!
No good can come of this and I hadn't realized you were
a criminal—but you're a good cook as long as I set the
combination . . . I might marry you if I can trap you into
proposing again."

"The offer remains open."

"Do gangsters marry their molls? Or is it 'frails'?" She
left hurriedly.

JILL PLACED THE bug easily. The patient in the room
in the next corridor was bedfast; Jill often stopped to gossip. She stuck it against the wall over a closet shelf while
chattering about how the maids just *never* dusted the
shelves.

Changing spools the next day was easy; the patient was
asleep. She woke while Jill was perched on a chair; Jill di-
verted her with a spicy ward rumor.

Jill sent the exposed wire by mail, as the postal system
seemed safer than a cloak and dagger ruse. But her attempt
to insert a third spool she muffed. She waited for the patient to be asleep but had just mounted the chair when the
patient woke. "Oh! Hello, Miss Boardman."

Jill froze. "Hello, Mrs. Fritschlie," she managed to answer. "Have a nice nap?"

"Fair," the woman answered peevishly. "My back aches."

"I'll rub it."

"Doesn't help. Why are you always fiddling in my closet?
Is something wrong?"

Jill tried to reswallow her stomach. "Mice," she
answered.

"'Mice'? Oh, I'll have to have another room!"

Jill tore the instrument loose and stuffed it into her

STRANGER IN A STRANGE LAND

pocket, jumped down. "Now, now, Mrs. Fritschlie—I was just looking to see if there were mouse holes. There aren't."

"You're *sure*?"

"Quite sure. Now let's rub the back. Easy over."

Jill decided to risk the empty room which was part of K-12, the suite of the Man from Mars. She got the pass key.

Only to find the room unlocked and holding two more marines; the guard had been doubled. One looked around as she opened the door. "Looking for someone?"

"No. Don't sit on the bed, boys," she said crisply. "If you need chairs, we'll send for them." The guard got reluctantly up; she left, trying to conceal her trembling.

The bug was still in her pocket when she went off duty; she decided to return it to Caxton. Once in the air and headed toward Ben's apartment she breathed easier. She phoned him in flight.

"Caxton speaking."

"Jill, Ben. I want to see you."

He answered slowly, "I don't think it's smart."

"Ben, I've got to. I'm on my way."

"Well, okay, if that's how it's got to be."

"Such enthusiasm!"

"Now look, hon, it isn't that I—"

" 'Bye!" She switched off, calmed down and decided not to take it out on Ben—they were playing out of their league. At least she was—she should have left politics alone.

She felt better when she snuggled into his arms. Ben was such a dear—maybe she should marry him. When she tried to speak he put a hand over her mouth, whispered, "Don't talk. I may be wired."

She nodded, got out the recorder, handed it to him. His

eyebrows went up but he made no comment. Instead he handed her a copy of the afternoon *Post*.

"Seen the paper?" he said in a natural voice. "You might glance at it while I wash up."

"Thanks." As she took it he pointed to a column, then left, taking with him the recorder. The column was Ben's own:

THE CROW'S NEST
by Ben Caxton

Everyone knows that jails and hospitals have one thing in common: they can be very hard to get out of. In some ways a prisoner is less cut off than a patient; a prisoner can send for his lawyer, demand a Fair Witness, invoke habeas corpus *and require the jailor to show cause in open court.*

But it takes only a NO VISITORS sign, ordered by one of the medicine men of our peculiar tribe, to consign a hospital patient to oblivion more thoroughly than ever was the Man in the Iron Mask.

To be sure, the patient's next of kin cannot be kept out—but the Man from Mars seems to have no next of kin. The crew of the ill-fated Envoy *had few ties on Earth; if the Man in the Iron Mask—pardon me; I mean the "Man from Mars"—has any relative guarding his interests, a few thousand reporters have been unable to verify it.*

Who speaks for the Man from Mars? Who ordered an armed guard placed around him? What is his dread disease that no one may glimpse him, nor ask

him a question? I address you, Mr. Secretary General;
the explanation about "physical weakness" and "gee-
fatigue" won't wash; if that were the answer, a ninety-
pound nurse would do as well as an armed guard.

Could this disease be financial in nature? Or (let's
say it softly) is it political?

There was more of the same; Jill could see that Ben was
baiting the administration, trying to force them into the
open. She felt that Caxton was taking serious risk in challenging the authorities, but she had no notion of the size
of the danger, nor what form it might take.

She thumbed through the paper. It was loaded with stories on the *Champion*, pictures of Secretary General Douglas pinning medals, interviews with Captain van Tromp
and his brave company, pictures of Martians and Martian
cities. There was little about Smith, merely a bulletin that
he was improving slowly from the effects of his trip.

Ben came out and dropped sheets of onionskin in her
lap. "Here's another newspaper." He left again.

Jill saw that the "newspaper" was a transcription of what
her first wire had picked up. It was marked "First Voice,"
"Second Voice," and so on, but Ben had written in names
wherever he had been able to make attributions. He had
written across the top: "All voices are masculine."

Most items merely showed that Smith had been fed,
washed, massaged and that he had exercised under supervision of a voice identified as "Doctor Nelson" and one
marked "second doctor."

One passage had nothing to do with care of the patient.
Jill reread it:

DOCTOR NELSON: How are you feeling, boy? Strong
  enough to talk?

SMITH: Yes.

DOCTOR NELSON: A man wants to talk to you.

SMITH: (pause) Who? (Caxton had written: All of
  Smith's speeches are preceded by pauses.)

NELSON: This man is our great (untranscribable gut-
  tural word—Martian?). He is our oldest Old One.
  Will you talk with him?

SMITH: (very long pause) I am great happy. The Old
  One will talk and I will listen and grow.

NELSON: No, no! He wants to ask you questions.

SMITH: I cannot teach an Old One.

NELSON: The Old One wishes it. Will you let him ask
  you questions?

SMITH: Yes.

(Background noises)

NELSON: This way, sir. I have Doctor Mahmoud standing by to translate.

Jill read "New Voice." Caxton had scratched this out
and written in: "Secretary General Douglas! ! !"

SECRETARY GENERAL: I won't need him. You say Smith
  understands English.

NELSON: Well, yes and no, Your Excellency. He knows a
  number of words, but, as Mahmoud says, he doesn't
  have any cultural context to hang them on. It can be
  confusing.

SECRETARY GENERAL: Oh, we'll get along, I'm sure.
  When I was a youngster I hitchhiked all through

Brazil, without a word of Portuguese when I started. Now, if you will introduce us—then leave us alone.

NELSON: Sir? I had better stay with my patient.

SECRETARY GENERAL: Really, Doctor? I'm afraid I must insist. Sorry.

NELSON: And I am afraid that *I* must insist. Sorry, sir. Medical ethics—

SECRETARY GENERAL: (interrupting) As a lawyer, I know something of medical jurisprudence—so don't give me that "medical ethics" mumbo-jumbo. Did this patient select you?

NELSON: Not exactly, but—

SECRETARY GENERAL: Has he had opportunity to choose physicians? I doubt it. His status is ward of the state. I am acting as next of kin, *de facto*—and, you will find, *de jure* as well. I wish to interview him alone.

NELSON: (long pause, then very stiffly) If you put it that way, Your Excellency, I withdraw from the case.

SECRETARY GENERAL: Don't take it that way, Doctor. I'm not questioning your treatment. But you wouldn't try to keep a mother from seeing her son alone, now would you? Are you afraid I might hurt him?

NELSON: No, but—

SECRETARY GENERAL: Then what is your objection? Come now, introduce us and let's get on with it. This fussing may be upsetting your patient.

NELSON: Your Excellency, I will introduce you. Then you must select another doctor for your . . . ward.

SECRETARY GENERAL: I'm sorry, Doctor, I really am. I can't take that as final—we'll discuss it later. Now, if you please?

NELSON: Step over here, sir. Son, this is the man who wants to see you. Our great Old One.

SMITH: (untranscribable)

SECRETARY GENERAL: What did he say?

NELSON: A respectful greeting. Mahmoud says it translates: "I am only an egg." More or less that, anyway. It's friendly. Son, talk man-talk.

SMITH: Yes.

NELSON: And you had better use simple words, if I may offer a last advice.

SECRETARY GENERAL: Oh, I will.

NELSON: Good-by, Your Excellency. Good-by, son.

SECRETARY GENERAL: Thanks, Doctor. See you later.

SECRETARY GENERAL: (continued) How do you feel?

SMITH: Feel fine.

SECRETARY GENERAL: Good. Anything you want, just ask for it. We want you to be happy. Now I have something I want you to do for me. Can you write?

SMITH: "Write"? What is "write"?

SECRETARY GENERAL: Well, your thumb print will do. I want to read a paper to you. This paper has a lot of lawyer talk, but stated simply it says that you agree that in leaving Mars you have abandoned—I mean, given up—any claims that you may have there. Understand me? You assign them in trust to the government.

SMITH: (no answer)

SECRETARY GENERAL: Well, let's put it this way. You don't own Mars, do you?

SMITH: (longish pause) I do not understand.

SECRETARY GENERAL: Mmm . . . let's try again. You want to stay here, don't you?

SMITH: I do not know. I was sent by the Old Ones. (Long untranscribable speech, sounds like a bullfrog fighting a cat.)

SECRETARY GENERAL: Damn it, they should have taught him more English by now. See here, son, you don't have to worry. Just let me have your thumb print at the bottom of this page. Let me have your right hand. No, don't twist around that way. *Hold still!* I'm not going to hurt you . . . *Doctor!* Doctor Nelson!

SECOND DOCTOR: Yes, sir?

SECRETARY GENERAL: Get Doctor Nelson.

SECOND DOCTOR: Doctor Nelson? But he left, sir. He said you took him off the case.

SECRETARY GENERAL: Nelson said that? *Damn* him! Well, *do* something. Give him artificial respiration. Give him a shot. Don't just stand there—can't you see the man is dying?

SECOND DOCTOR: I don't believe there is anything to be done, sir. Just let him alone until he comes out of it. That's what Doctor Nelson always did.

SECRETARY GENERAL: Blast Doctor Nelson!

THE SECRETARY GENERAL'S voice did not appear again, nor that of Doctor Nelson. Jill could guess, from gossip she had picked up, that Smith had gone into one of his cataleptiform withdrawals. There were two more entries. One read: No need to whisper. He can't hear you. The other read: Take that tray away. We'll feed him when he comes out of it.

Jill was rereading it when Ben reappeared. He had more onionskin sheets but he did not offer them; instead he said, "Hungry?"

"Starved."

"Let's go shoot a cow."

He said nothing while they went to the roof and took a taxi, still kept quiet during a flight to Alexandria platform, where they switched cabs. Ben picked one with a Baltimore number. Once in the air he set it for Hagerstown, Maryland, then relaxed. "Now we can talk."

"Ben, why the mystery?"

"Sorry, pretty foots. I don't *know* that my apartment is bugged—but if I can do it to them, they can do it to me. Likewise, while it isn't likely that a cab signaled from my flat would have an ear in it, still it might have; the Special Service squads are thorough. But this cab—" He patted its cushions. "They can't gimmick thousands of cabs. One picked at random should be safe."

Jill shivered. "Ben, you don't think they would . . ." She let it trail off.

"Don't I, now! You saw my column. I filed that copy nine hours ago. You think the administration will let me kick it in the stomach without kicking back?"

"But you have always opposed this administration."

"That's okay. This is different; I have accused them of holding a political prisoner. Jill, a government is a living organism. Like every living thing its prime characteristic is the instinct to survive. You hit it, it fights back. This time I've *really* hit it." He added, "But I shouldn't have involved you."

"I'm not afraid. Not since I turned that gadget back to you."

"You're associated with me. If things get rough, that could be enough."

Jill shut up. The notion that she, who had never experienced worse than a spanking as a child and an occasional harsh word as an adult, could be in danger was hard to believe. As a nurse, she had seen the consequences of ruthlessness—but it could not happen to *her*.

Their cab was circling for a landing before she broke the moody silence. "Ben? Suppose this patient dies. What happens?"

"Huh?" He frowned. "That's a good question. If there are no other questions, the class is dismissed."

"Don't be funny."

"Hmm . . . Jill, I've been awake nights trying to answer that. Here are the best answers I have: If Smith dies, his claim to Mars vanishes. Probably the group the *Champion* left on Mars starts a new claim—and almost certainly the administration worked out a deal before they left Earth. The *Champion* is a Federation ship but it is possible that such a deal leaves all strings in the hands of Secretary General Douglas. That could keep him in power a long time. On the other hand, it might mean nothing at all."

"Huh? Why?"

"The Larkin Decision might not apply. Luna was uninhabited, but Mars *is*—by Martians. At the moment, Martians are a legal zero. But the High Court might take a look at the political situation and decide that human occupancy meant nothing on a planet inhabited by non-humans. Then rights on Mars would have to be secured from the Martians."

"But, Ben, that would be the case anyhow. This notion of a single man *owning* a planet . . . it's fantastic!"

"Don't use that word to a lawyer; straining at gnats and swallowing camels is a required course in law schools. Besides, there is precedent. In the fifteenth century the Pope deeded the western hemisphere to Spain and Portugal and nobody cared that the real estate was occupied by Indians with their own laws, customs, and property rights. His grant was effective, too. Look at a map and notice where Spanish is spoken and where Portuguese is spoken."

"Yes, but—Ben, this isn't the fifteenth century."

"It is to a lawyer. Jill, if the High Court rules that the Larkin Decision applies, Smith is in a position to grant concessions which may be worth millions, more likely billions. If he assigns his claim to the administration, then Secretary Douglas controls the plums."

"Ben, why should anybody want that much power?"

"Why does a moth fly toward light? But Smith's financial holdings are almost as important as his position as nominal king-emperor of Mars. The High Court could knock out his squatter's rights but I doubt if anything could shake his ownership of the Lyle Drive and a chunk of Lunar Enterprises. What happens if he dies? A thousand alleged cousins would pop up, of course, but the Science Foundation has fought off such money-hungry vermin for years. It seems possible that, if Smith dies without a will, his fortune reverts to the state."

"Do you mean the Federation or the United States?"

"Another question to which I have no answer. His parents come from two countries of the Federation and he was born outside them all . . . and it will make a crucial difference to some people who votes that stock and licenses those patents. It won't be Smith; he won't know a stock proxy from a traffic ticket. It is likely to be whoever can grab him and hang on. I doubt if Lloyd's would insure his life; he strikes me as a poor risk."

"The poor baby! The poor, poor infant!"

VI

THE RESTAURANT IN Hagerstown had "atmosphere"—tables scattered over a lawn leading down to a lake and more tables in the boughs of three enormous trees. Jill wanted to eat in a tree, but Ben bribed the maiˆtre d'hôtel to set up a table near the water, then ordered a stereo tank placed by it.

Jill was miffed. "Ben, why pay these prices if we can't eat in the trees and have to endure that horrible jitterbox?"

"Patience, little one. Tables in trees have microphones; they have to have them for service. This table is not gimmicked—I hope—as I saw the waiter take it from a stack. As for the tank, not only is it un-American to eat without stereo but the racket will interfere with a directional mike—if Mr. Douglas's investigators are taking an interest."

"Do you really think they're shadowing us, Ben?" Jill shivered. "I'm not cut out for a life of crime."

"Pish and likewise tush! When I was on the General Synthetics scandals I never slept twice in one place and ate nothing but packaged food. You get to like it—stimulates the metabolism."

"My metabolism doesn't need it. All I require is one elderly, wealthy patient."

"Not going to marry me, Jill?"

"After my future husband kicks off, yes. Or maybe I'll be so rich I can keep you as a pet."

"How about starting tonight?"

"*After* he kicks off."

During the dinner the musical show which had been banging their eardrums stopped. An announcer's head filled the tank; he smiled and said, "NWNW, New World Networks and its sponsor, Wise Girl Malthusian Lozenges, is honored to surrender time for a history-making broadcast by the Federation Government. Remember, friends, every wise girl uses Wise Girls. Easy to carry, pleasant to take, guaranteed no-fail, and approved for sale without prescription under Public Law 1312. Why take a chance on old-fashioned, unesthetic, harmful, unsure methods? Why risk losing his love and respect?" The lovely, lupine announcer glanced aside and hurried the commercial: "I give you the Wise Girl, who in turn brings you the Secretary General!"

The 3-D picture cut to a young woman, so sensuous, so mammalian, so seductive, as to make any male unsatisfied with local talent. She stretched and wiggled and said in a bedroom voice, "*I* always use Wise Girl."

The picture dissolved and an orchestra played *Hail to Sovereign Peace*. Ben said, "Do *you* use Wise Girl?"

"None o' your business!" Jill looked ruffled and added, "It's a quack nostrum. Anyhow, what makes you think I need it?"

Caxton did not answer; the tank had filled with the fatherly features of Secretary General Douglas. "Friends," he began, "fellow citizens of the Federation, I have tonight a unique honor and privilege. Since the triumphant return of our trailblazing *Champion*—" He continued to congratulate the citizens of Earth on their successful contact with another planet, another race. He managed to imply that the exploit was the personal accomplishment of every citizen, that any one of them could have led the expedition had he not been busy with serious work—and that he,

Secretary Douglas, had been their humble instrument to work their will. The notions were never stated baldly, the assumption being that the common man was the equal of anyone and better than most—and that good old Joe Douglas embodied the common man. Even his mussed cravat and cowlicked hair had a "just folks" quality.

Ben Caxton wondered who had written it. Jim Sanforth, probably—Jim had the slickest touch of any of Douglas's staff in selecting loaded adjectives to tickle and soothe; he had written commercials before he went into politics and had no compunctions. Yes, that bit about "the hand that rocks the cradle" was Jim's work—Jim was the type who would entice a young girl with candy.

"Turn it off!" Jill demanded.

"Quiet, pretty foots. I must hear this."

". . . and so, friends, I have the honor to bring you our fellow citizen Valentine Michael Smith, the Man from Mars! Mike, we know you are tired and have not been well—but will you say a few words to your friends?"

The stereo scene cut to a semi-close of a man in a wheel chair. Hovering over him was Douglas and on the other side was a nurse, stiff, starched, and photogenic.

Jill gasped. Ben whispered, "Keep quiet!"

The smooth babyface of the man in the chair broke into a shy smile; he looked at the camera and said, "Hello, folks. Excuse me for sitting down. I'm still weak." He seemed to speak with difficulty and once the nurse took his pulse.

In answer to questions from Douglas he paid compliments to Captain van Tromp and his crew, thanked everyone for his rescue, and said that everyone on Mars was terribly excited over contact with Earth and that he hoped to help in welding friendly relations between the two planets. The nurse interrupted but Douglas said gently, "Mike, do you feel strong enough for one more question?"

"Sure, Mr. Douglas—if I can answer it."

"Mike? What do you think of the girls here on Earth?"

"Gee!"

The babyface looked awestruck and ecstatic and turned pink. The scene cut to head and shoulders of the Secretary General. "Mike asked me to tell you," he went on in fatherly tones, "that he will be back to see you as soon as he can. He has to build up his muscles, you know. Possibly next week, if the doctors say he is strong enough." The scene shifted to Wise Girl lozenges and a playlet made clear that a girl who did not use them was not only out of her mind but a syntho in the hay; men would cross the street to avoid her. Ben switched channels, then turned to Jill and said moodily, "Well, I can tear up tomorrow's column. Douglas has him under his thumb."

"Ben!"

"Huh?"

"That's not the Man from Mars!"

"What? Baby, are you *sure*?"

"Oh, it looked like him. But it was not the patient I saw in that guarded room."

Ben pointed out that dozens of persons had seen Smith—guards, interns, male nurses, the captain and crew of the *Champion*, probably others. Quite a few of them must have seen this newscast—the administration would have to assume that some of them would spot a substitution. It did not make sense—too great a risk.

Jill simply stuck out her lower lip and insisted that the

person on stereo was not the patient she had met. Finally she said angrily, "Have it your own way! *Men!*"

"Now, Jill . . ."

"Please take me home."

Ben went for a cab. He did not order one from the restaurant but selected one from the landing flat of a hotel across the way. Jill remained chilly on the flight back. Ben got out the transcripts and reread them. He thought a while, and said, "Jill?"

"Yes, Mr. Caxton?"

"I'll 'mister' you! Look, Jill, I apologize. I was wrong."

"And what leads you to this conclusion?"

He slapped the papers against his palm. "This. Smith could not have shown this behavior yesterday and then given that interview tonight. He would have flipped his controls . . . gone into one of those trance things."

"I am gratified that you have finally seen the obvious."

"Jill, will you kindly kick me, then let up? Do you know what this means?"

"It means they used an actor to fake it. I told you an hour ago."

"Sure. An actor and a good one, carefully typed and coached. But it implies more than that. As I see it, there are two possibilities. The first is that Smith is dead and—"

"Dead!" Jill was suddenly back in that curious water-drinking ceremony and felt the strange, warm, unworldly flavor of Smith's personality, felt it with unbearable sorrow.

"Maybe. In which case this ringer will stay 'alive' as long as they need him. Then the ringer will 'die' and they will ship him out of town, with a hypnotic injunction so strong he would choke up with asthma if he tried to spill it—or maybe even a lobotomy. But if Smith is dead, we can forget it; we'll never prove the truth. So let's assume he's alive."

"Oh, I hope so!"

"What is Hecuba to you, or you to Hecuba?" Caxton misquoted. "If he is alive, it could be that there is nothing sinister about it. After all, public figures do use doubles. Perhaps in two or three weeks our friend Smith will be in shape to stand the strain of public appearance, then they will trot him out. But I doubt it like hell!"

"Why?"

"Use your head. Douglas has already failed one attempt to squeeze out of Smith what he wants. But Douglas can't afford to fail. So I think he will bury Smith deeper than ever . . . and we will never see the true Man from Mars."

"Kill him?" Jill said slowly.

"Why be rough? Lock him in a private nursing home and never let him learn anything."

"Oh, dear! Ben, what are we going to *do*?"

Caxton scowled. "They own the bat and ball and are making the rules. But I am going to walk in with a Fair Witness and a tough lawyer and demand to see Smith. Maybe I can drag it into the open."

"I'll be right behind you!"

"Like mischief you will. As you pointed out, it would ruin you professionally."

"But you need me to identify him."

"Face to face, I can tell a man who was raised by non-humans from an actor pretending to be such. But if anything goes wrong, you are my ace in the hole—a person who knows that they are pulling hanky-panky and has access to the inside of Bethesda Center. Honey, if you don't hear from me, you are on your own."

"Ben, they wouldn't hurt *you*?"

"I'm fighting out of my weight, youngster."

"Ben, I don't like this. Look, if you get in to see him, what are you going to do?"

"I'll ask him if he wants to leave the hospital. If he says yes, I'm going to invite him to come with me. In the presence of a Fair Witness they won't dare stop him."

"Uh . . . then what? He does need medical attention, Ben; he's not able to take care of himself."

Caxton scowled again. "I've been thinking of that. I can't nurse him. We could put him in my flat—"

"—and I could nurse him. We'll do it, Ben!"

"Slow down. Douglas would pull some rabbit out of his hat and Smith would go back to the pokey. And so would both of us, maybe." He wrinkled his brow. "I know one man who might get away with it."

"Who?"

"Ever heard of Jubal Harshaw?"

"Huh? Who hasn't?"

"That's one of his advantages; everybody knows who he is. It makes him hard to shove around. Being both a doctor of medicine and a lawyer he is three times as hard to shove. But most important, he is so rugged and individualist that he would fight the whole Federation with just a pocket knife if it suited him—and *that* makes him eight times as hard. I got acquainted with him during the disaffection trials; he is a friend I can count on. If I can get Smith out of Bethesda, I'll take him to Harshaw's place in the Poconos—and then just let those jerks try to grab him! Between my column and Harshaw's love for a fight we'll give 'em a bad time."

VII

DESPITE A LATE evening Jill relieved as floor nurse ten minutes early. She intended to obey Ben's order to stay out of his attempt to see that Man from Mars but she planned to be close by. Ben might need reinforcements.

There were no guards in the corridor. Trays, medications, and two patients for surgery kept her busy for two hours; she had only time to check the door to suite K-12. It was locked, as was the door to the sitting room. She considered sneaking in through the sitting room, now that the guards were gone, but had to postpone it; she was busy. Nevertheless she kept close check on everyone who came onto her floor.

Ben did not show up and discreet questions asked of her assistant on the switchboard assured her that neither Ben nor anyone had gone into suite K-12 while Jill was elsewhere. It puzzled her; Ben had not set a time but he had intended to storm the citadel early in the day.

Presently she just had to snoop. During a lull she knocked at the door of the watch room, stuck her head in and pretended surprise. "Oh! Good morning, Doctor. I thought Doctor Frame was in here."

The physician at the watch desk smiled as he looked her over. "I haven't seen him, Nurse. I'm Dr. Brush. Can I help?"

At the typical male reaction Jill relaxed. "Nothing special. How is the Man from Mars?"

"Eh?"

She smiled. "It's no secret to the staff, Doctor. Your patient—" She gestured at the inner door.

"Huh?" He looked startled. "Did they have *him* here?"

"Isn't he here now?"

"Not by six decimal places. Mrs. Rose Bankerson—Dr. Garner's patient. We brought her in early this morning."

"Really? What happened to the Man from Mars?"

"I haven't the faintest. Say, did I really just miss seeing Valentine Smith?"

"He was here yesterday."

"Some people have all the luck. Look what I'm stuck with." He switched on the Peeping Tom above his desk; Jill saw in it a water bed; floating in it was a tiny old woman.

"What's her trouble?"

"Mmm . . . Nurse, if she didn't have money to burn, you might call it senile dementia. As it is, she is in for rest and a check-up."

Jill made small talk, then pretended to see a call light. She went to her desk, dug out the night log—yes, there it was: *V. M. Smith, K-12—transfer.* Below that was: *Rose S. Bankerson (Mrs.)—red K-12 (diet kitchen instrd by Dr. Garner—no orders—flr nt respnbl)*

Why had they moved Smith at night? To avoid outsiders, probably. But where had they taken him? Ordinarily she would have called "Reception," but Ben's opinions plus the phony broadcast had made her jumpy; she decided to wait and see what she could pick up on the grapevine.

But first Jill went to the floor's public booth and called Ben. His office told her that Mr. Caxton had left town. She was startled speechless—then pulled herself together and left word for Ben to call.

She called his home. He was not there; she recorded the same message.

BEN CAXTON HAD wasted no time. He retained James Oliver Cavendish. While any Fair Witness would do, the prestige of Cavendish was such that a lawyer was hardly necessary—the old gentleman had testified many times before the High Court and it was said that the wills locked up in his head represented billions. Cavendish had received his training in total recall from the great Dr. Samuel Renshaw and his hypnotic instruction as a fellow of the Rhine Foundation. His fee for a day was more than Ben made in a week, but Ben expected to charge it to the *Post* syndicate—the best was none too good for this job.

Caxton picked up the junior Frisby of Biddle, Frisby, Frisby, Biddle, & Reed, then they called for Witness Cavendish. The spare form of Mr. Cavendish, wrapped in the white cloak of his profession, reminded Ben of the Statue of Liberty—and was almost as conspicuous. Ben had explained to Mark Frisby what he intended to try (and Frisby had pointed out that he had no rights) before they called for Cavendish; once in the Fair Witness's presence they conformed to protocol and did not discuss what he might see and hear.

The cab dropped them on Bethesda Center; they went down to the Director's Office. Ben handed in his card and asked to see the Director.

An imperious female asked if he had an appointment. Ben admitted that he had none.

"Then your chance of seeing Dr. Broemer is very slight. Will you state your business?"

"Tell him," Caxton said loudly, so that bystanders

would hear, "that Caxton of the *Crow's Nest* is here with a lawyer and a Fair Witness to interview Valentine Michael Smith, the Man from Mars."

She was startled but recovered and said frostily, "I shall inform him. Will you be seated, please?"

"Thanks, I'll wait here."

Frisby broke out a cigar, Cavendish waited with the calm patience of one who has seen all manner of good and evil, Caxton jittered. At last the snow queen announced, "Mr. Berquist will see you."

"Berquist? Gil Berquist?"

"I believe his name is Mr. Gilbert Berquist."

Caxton thought about it—Gil Berquist was one of Douglas's platoon of stooges, "executive assistants." "I don't want Berquist; I want the Director."

But Berquist was coming out, hand shoved out, greeter's grin on his face. "Benny Caxton! How are you, chum? Still peddling the same old hoke?" He glanced at the Witness.

"Same old hoke. What are you doing here, Gil?"

"If I ever manage to get out of public service I'm going to get me a column, too—phone in a thousand words of rumor and loaf the rest of the day. I envy you, Ben."

"I said, 'What are you doing here, Gil?' I want to see the Director, then see the Man from Mars. I didn't come here for your high-level brush-off."

"Now, Ben, don't take that attitude. I'm here because Dr. Broemer has been driven frantic by the press—so the Secretary General sent me to take over the load."

"Okay. I want to see Smith."

"Ben, old boy, every reporter, special correspondent, feature writer, commentator, free-lance, and sob sister wants that. Polly Peepers was here twenty minutes ago. *She* wanted to interview him on love life among the Martians." Berquist threw up both hands.

"I want to see Smith. Do I, or don't I?"

"Ben, let's go where we can talk over a drink. You can ask me anything."

"I don't want to ask you anything; I want to see Smith. This is my attorney, Mark Frisby." As was customary, Ben did not introduce the Fair Witness.

"We've met," Berquist acknowledged. "How's your father, Mark? Sinuses giving him fits?"

"About the same."

"This foul climate. Come along, Ben. You, too, Mark."

"Hold it," said Caxton. "I want to see Valentine Michael Smith. I'm representing the *Post* syndicate and indirectly representing two hundred million readers. Do I see him? If not, say so out loud and state your legal authority for refusing."

Berquist sighed. "Mark, will you tell this keyhole historian that he can't burst into a sick man's bedroom? Smith made one appearance last night—against his physician's advice. The man is entitled to peace and quiet and a chance to build up his strength."

"There are rumors," Caxton stated, "that the appearance last night was a fake."

Berquist stopped smiling. "Frisby," he said coldly, "do you want to advise your client concerning slander?"

"Take it easy, Ben."

"I know the law on slander, Gil. But whom am I slandering? The Man from Mars? Or somebody else? Name a name. I repeat," he went on, raising his voice, "that I have heard that the man interviewed on 3-D last night was not the Man from Mars. I want to see him and ask him." ·

The crowded reception hall was very quiet. Berquist glanced at the Fair Witness, then got his expression under control and said smilingly, "Ben, it's possible that you have talked yourself into an interview—as well as a lawsuit. Wait a moment."

He disappeared, came back fairly soon. "I arranged it," he said wearily, "though you don't deserve it, Ben. Come along. Just you—Mark, I'm sorry but we can't have a crowd; Smith is a sick man."

"No," said Caxton.

"Huh?"

"All three, or none of us."

"Ben, don't be silly; you're receiving a very special privilege. Tell you what—Mark can come and wait outside. But you don't need *him*." Berquist nodded toward Cavendish; the Witness seemed not to hear.

"Maybe not. But my column will state tonight that the administration refused to permit a Fair Witness to see the Man from Mars."

Berquist shrugged. "Come along. Ben, I hope that slander suit clobbers you."

They took the elevator out of deference to Cavendish's age, then rode a slide-away past laboratories, therapy rooms, ward after ward. They were stopped by a guard who phoned ahead and were at last ushered into a physio-data display room used for watching critically ill patients. "This is Dr. Tanner," Berquist announced. "Doctor, Mr. Caxton and Mr. Frisby." He did not, of course, introduce Cavendish.

Tanner looked worried. "Gentlemen, I must warn you of one thing. Don't do or say *anything* that might excite my patient. He is in an extremely neurotic condition and falls very easily into a state of pathological withdrawal—a trance, if you choose to call it that."

"Epilepsy?" asked Ben.

"A layman might mistake it for that. It is more like catelepsy."

"Are you a specialist, Doctor? Psychiatry?"

Tanner glanced at Berquist. "Yes," he admitted.

"Where did you do your advanced work?"

Berquist said, "Ben, let's see the patient. You can quiz Dr. Tanner afterwards."

"Okay."

Tanner glanced over his dials, then flipped a switch and stared into a Peeping Tom. He unlocked a door and led them into an adjoining bedroom, putting a finger to his lips.

The room was gloomy. "We keep it semi-darkened because his eyes are not accustomed to our light levels," Tanner explained in a hushed voice. He went to a hydraulic bed in the center of the room. "Mike, I've brought some friends to see you."

Caxton pressed closer. Floating, half concealed by the way his body sank into the plastic skin and covered to his armpits by a sheet, was a young man. He looked at them but said nothing; his smooth, round face was expressionless.

So far as Ben could tell this was the man on stereo the night before. He had a sick feeling that little Jill had tossed him a live grenade—a slander suit that might bankrupt him. "You are Valentine Michael Smith?"

"Yes."

"The Man from Mars?"

"Yes."

"You were on stereo last night?"

The man did not answer. Tanner said, "I don't think he understands. Mike, you remember what you did with Mr. Douglas last night?"

The face looked petulant. "Bright lights. Hurt."

"Yes, the lights hurt your eyes. Mr. Douglas had you say hello to people."

The patient smiled slightly. "Long ride in chair."

"Okay," agreed Caxton. "I catch on. Mike, are they treating you all right?"

"Yes."

"You don't have to stay here. Can you walk?"

Tanner said hastily, "Now see here, Mr. Caxton—" Berquist put a hand on Tanner's arm.

"I can walk . . . a little. Tired."

"I'll see that you have a wheel chair, Mike, if you don't want to stay here, I'll take you anywhere you want to go."

Tanner shook off Berquist's hand and said, "I can't have you interfering with my patient!"

"He's a free man, isn't he?" Caxton persisted. "Or is he a prisoner?"

Berquist answered, "Of course he's free! Keep quiet, Doctor. Let the fool dig his own grave."

"Thanks, Gil. You heard him, Mike. You can go anywhere you like."

The patient glanced fearfully at Tanner. "No! No, no, no!"

"Okay, okay."

Tanner snapped, "Mr. Berquist, this has gone far enough!"

"All right, Doctor. Ben, that's enough."

"Uh . . . one more question." Caxton thought hard, trying to think what he could squeeze out of it. Apparently Jill had been wrong—yet she had *not* been wrong!—or so it seemed last night.

"One more question," Berquist begrudged.

"Thanks. Uh . . . Mike, last night Mr. Douglas asked you some questions." The patient made no comment. "Let's see, he asked you what you thought of the girls here on Earth, didn't he?"

The patient's face broke into a big smile. "Gee!"

"Yes. Mike . . . *when and where did you see these girls?*"

The smile vanished. The patient glanced at Tanner, then stiffened; his eyes rolled up, and he drew himself into fetal position, knees up, head bent, arms across his chest.

Tanner snapped, "Get out of here!" He moved quickly and felt the patient's wrist.

Berquist said savagely, "That tears it! Caxton, will you get out? Or shall I call the guards?"

"Oh, we're getting out," Caxton agreed. All but Tanner left the room and Berquist closed the door.

"Just one point, Gil," Caxton insisted. "You've got him boxed up . . . so just where *did* he see those girls?"

"Eh? Don't be silly. He's seen lots of girls. Nurses . . . laboratory technicians. You know."

"But I don't. I understood he had nothing but male nurses and that female visitors had been rigidly excluded."

"Eh? Don't be preposterous." Berquist looked annoyed, then suddenly grinned. "You saw a nurse with him on stereo last night."

"Oh. So I did." Caxton shut up.

They did not discuss it until the three were in the air.

Then Frisby remarked, "Ben, I don't suppose the Secretary General will sue you. Still, if you have a source for that rumor, we had better perpetuate the evidence."

"Forget it, Mark. He won't sue." Ben glowered at the floor. "How do we know that was the Man from Mars?"

"Eh? Come off it, Ben."

"How do we *know*? We saw a man about the right age in a hospital bed. We have Berquist's word for it—and Berquist got his start in politics issuing denials. We saw a stranger, supposed to be a psychiatrist—and when I tried to find out where he had studied I got euchred out. Mr. Cavendish, did you see anything that convinced you that this bloke was the Man from Mars?"

Cavendish answered, "It is not my function to form opinions. I see, I hear—that is all."

"Sorry."

"Are you through with me in my professional capacity?"

"Huh? Oh, sure. Thanks, Mr. Cavendish."

"Thank *you*, sir. An interesting assignment." The old gentleman took off the cloak that set him apart from ordinary mortals. He relaxed and his features mellowed.

"If I had been able to bring along a crew member of the *Champion*," Caxton persisted, "I could have tied it down."

"I must admit," remarked Cavendish, "that I was surprised at one thing you did not do."

"Huh? What did I miss?"

"Calluses."

"Calluses?"

"Surely. A man's history can be read from his calluses. I once did a monograph on them for *The Witness Quarterly*. This young man from Mars, since he has never worn our sort of shoes and has lived in gravity about one third of ours, should display foot calluses consonant with his former environment."

"Damn! Mr. Cavendish, why didn't you suggest it?"

"Sir?" The old man drew himself up and his nostrils dilated. "I am a Fair Witness, sir. Not a participant."

"Sorry." Caxton frowned. "Let's go back. We'll look at his feet—or I'll bust the place down!"

"You will have to find another Witness . . . in view of my indiscretion in discussing it."

"Uh, yes, there's that." Caxton frowned.

"Calm down, Ben," advised Frisby. "You're in deep enough. Personally, I'm convinced it was the Man from Mars."

Caxton dropped them, then set the cab to hover while he thought. He had been in once—with a lawyer, with a Fair Witness. To demand to see the Man from Mars a second time in one morning was unreasonable and would be refused.

But he had not acquired a syndicated column through being balked. He intended to get in.

How? Well, he knew where the putative "Man from Mars" was kept. Get in as an electrician? Too obvious; he would never get as far as "Dr. Tanner."

Was "Tanner" a doctor? Medical men tended to shy away from hanky-panky contrary to their code. Take that ship's surgeon, Nelson—he had washed his hands of the case simply because—

Wait a minute! Dr. Nelson could tell whether that young fellow was the Man from Mars, without checking calluses or anything. Caxton tried to phone Dr. Nelson, relaying through his office since he did not know where Dr. Nelson was. Nor did Ben's assistant Osbert Kilgallen know, but the *Post* Syndicate's file on Important Persons placed him in the New Mayflower. A few minutes later Caxton was talking with him.

Dr. Nelson had not seen the broadcast. Yes, he had heard about it; no, he had no reason to think it had been faked. Did Dr. Nelson know that an attempt had been made to coerce Smith into surrendering his rights under the Larkin Decision? No, and he would not be interested if it were true; it was preposterous to talk about anyone "owning" Mars; Mars belonged to Martians. So? Let's propose a hypothetical question, Doctor; if someone were trying to—

Dr. Nelson switched off. When Caxton tried to reconnect, a recorded voice stated: "The subscriber has suspended service temporarily. If you care to record—"

Caxton made a foolish statement concerning Dr. Nelson's parentage. What he did next was much more foolish; he phoned the Executive Palace, demanded to speak to the Secretary General.

In his years as a snooper, Caxton had learned that secrets could often be cracked by going to the top and there making himself unbearably unpleasant. He knew that twisting the tiger's tail was dangerous; he understood the psychopathology of great power as thoroughly as Jill Boardman did not—but he relied on his position as a dealer in another sort of power almost universally appeased.

What he forgot was that, in phoning the Palace from a taxicab, he was not doing so publicly.

Caxton spoke with half a dozen underlings and became more aggressive with each one. He was so busy that he did not notice when his cab ceased to hover.

When he did notice, it was too late; the cab refused to obey orders. Caxton realized bitterly that he had let himself be trapped by a means no hoodlum would fall for; his call had been traced, his cab identified, its robot pilot placed under orders of an over-riding police frequency—and the cab was being used to fetch him in, privately and with no fuss.

He tried to call his lawyer.

He was still trying when the taxicab landed inside a courtyard and his signal was cut off by its walls. He tried to leave the cab, found that the door would not open—and was hardly surprised to discover that he was fast losing consciousness—

VIII

JILL TOLD HERSELF that Ben had gone off on another scent and had forgotten to let her know. But she did not believe it. Ben owed his success to meticulous attention to human details. He remembered birthdays and would rather have welched on a poker debt than have omitted a bread-and-butter note. No matter where he had gone, nor how urgently, he could have—*would* have!—taken two minutes in the air to record a message to her.

He *must* have left word! She called his office at her lunch break and spoke with Ben's researcher and office chief, Osbert Kilgallen. He insisted that Ben had left no message for her, nor had any come in since she had called.

"Did he say when he would be back?"

"No. But we always have columns on the hook to fill in when one of these things comes up."

"Well . . . where did he call you from? Or am I being snoopy?"

"Not at all, Miss Boardman. He did not call; it was a statprint, filed from Paoli Flat in Philadelphia."

Jill had to be satisfied with that. She lunched in the nurses' dining room and picked at her food. It wasn't, she told herself, as if anything were wrong . . . or as if she were in love with the lunk . . .

"Hey! Boardman! Snap out of the fog!"

Jill looked up to find Molly Wheelwright, the wing's dietitian, looking at her. "Sorry."

"I said, 'Since when does your floor put charity patients in luxury suites?'"

"We don't."

"Isn't K-12 on your floor?"

"K-12? That's not charity; it's a rich old woman, so wealthy that she can pay to have a doctor watch her breathe."

"Humph! She must have come into money awfully suddenly. She's been in the N.P. ward of the geriatrics sanctuary the past seventeen months."

"Some mistake."

"Not mine—I don't allow mistakes in my kitchen. That tray is tricky—fat-free diet and a long list of sensitivities, plus concealed medication. Believe me, dear, a diet order can be as individual as a fingerprint." Miss Wheelwright stood up. "Gotta run, chicks."

"What was Molly sounding off about?" a nurse asked.

"Nothing. She's mixed up." It occurred to Jill that she might locate the Man from Mars by checking diet kitchens. She put the idea out of her mind; it would take days to visit them all. Bethesda Center had been a naval hospital back when wars were fought on oceans and enormous even then. It had been transferred to Health, Education, & Welfare and expanded; now it belonged to the Federation and was a small city.

But there was something odd about Mrs. Bankerson's case. The hospital accepted all classes of patients, private, charity, and government; Jill's floor usually had government patients and its suites were for Federation Senators or other high officials. It was unusual for a private patient to be on her floor.

Mrs. Bankerson could be overflow, if the part of the Center open to the fee-paying public had no suite available. Yes, probably that was it.

She was too rushed after lunch to think about it, being busy with admissions. Shortly she needed a powered bed. The routine would be to phone for one—but storage was in the basement a quarter of a mile away and Jill wanted it at once. She recalled having seen the powered bed which belonged to K-12 parked in the sitting room of that suite; she remembered telling those marines not to sit on it. Apparently it had been shoved there when the flotation bed had been installed.

Probably it was still there—if so, she could get it at once.

The sitting room door was locked and she found that her pass key would not open it. Making a note to tell maintenance, she went to the watch room of the suite, intending to find out about the bed from the doctor watching Mrs. Bankerson.

The physician was the one she had met before, Dr. Brush. He was not an intern nor a resident, but had been brought in for this patient, so he had said, by Dr. Garner.

Brush looked up as she put her head in. "Miss Boardman! Just the person I need!"

"Why didn't you ring? How's your patient?"

"She's all right," he answered, glancing at the Peeping Tom, "but I am *not.*"

"Trouble?"

"About five minutes' worth. Nurse, could you spare me that much of your time? And keep your mouth shut?"

"I suppose so. Let me use your phone and I'll tell my assistant where I am."

"No!" he said urgently. "Just lock that door after I leave and don't open it until you hear me rap 'Shave and a Hair cut,' that's a good girl."

"All right, sir," Jill said dubiously. "Am I to do anything for your patient?"

"No, no, just sit and watch her in the screen. Don't disturb her."

"Well, if anything happens, where will you be? In the doctors' lounge?"

"I'm going to the men's washroom down the corridor. Now shut up, please—this is *urgent.*"

He left and Jill locked the door. Then she looked at the patient through the viewer and ran her eye over the dials. The woman was asleep and displays showed pulse strong and breathing even and normal; Jill wondered why a "death watch" was necessary?

Then she decided to see if the bed was in the far room. While it was not according to Dr. Brush's instructions, she would not disturb his patient—she knew how to walk through a room without waking a patient!—and she had decided years ago that what doctors did not know rarely hurt them. She opened the door quietly and went in.

A glance assured her that Mrs. Bankerson was in the typical sleep of the senile. Walking noiselessly she went to the sitting room. It was locked but her pass key let her in.

She saw that the powered bed was there. Then she saw that the room was occupied—sitting in a chair with a picture book in his lap was the Man from Mars.

Smith looked up and gave her the beaming smile of a delighted baby.

Jill felt dizzy. Valentine Smith here? He couldn't be; he had been transferred; the log showed it.

Then ugly implications lined themselves up . . . the fake "Man from Mars" on stereo . . . the old woman, ready to die, but in the meantime covering the fact that there was another patient here . . . the door that would not open to her key—and a nightmare of the "meat wagon" wheeling out some night, with a sheet concealing that it carried not one cadaver, but two.

As this rushed through her mind, it carried fear, awareness of peril through having stumbled onto this secret.

Smith got clumsily up from his chair, held out both hands and said, "Water brother!"

"Hello. Uh . . . how are you?"

"I am well. I am happy." He added something in a strange, choking speech, corrected himself and said carefully, "You are here, my brother. You were away. Now you are here. I drink deep of you."

Jill felt herself helplessly split between emotions, one that melted her heart—and icy fear of being caught. Smith did not notice. Instead he said, "See? I walk! I grow strong." He took a few steps, then stopped, triumphant, breathless, and smiling.

She forced herself to smile. "We are making progress,

aren't we? You keep growing stronger, that's the spirit! But I must go—I just stopped to say hello."

His expression changed to distress. "Do not go!"

"Oh, I must!"

He looked woebegone, then added with tragic certainty, "I have hurted you. I did not know."

"Hurt me? Oh, no, not at all! But I must go—and quickly!"

His face was without expression. He stated rather than asked, "Take me with you, my brother."

"What? Oh, I *can't*. And I *must* go, at once. Look, don't tell anyone I was here, please!"

"Not tell that my water brother was here?"

"Yes. Don't tell *anyone*. Uh . . . I'll come back. You be a good boy and wait and don't tell anyone."

Smith digested this, looked serene. "I will wait. I will not tell."

"Good!" Jill wondered how she could keep her promise. She realized now that the "broken" lock had not been broken and her eye went to the corridor door—and saw why she had not been able to get in. A hand bolt had been screwed to the door. As was always the case, bathroom doors and other doors that could be bolted were arranged to open also by pass key, so that patients could not lock themselves in. Here the lock kept Smith in and a bolt of the sort not permitted in hospitals kept out even those with pass keys.

Jill opened the bolt. "You wait. I'll come back."

"I shall waiting."

When she got back to the watch room she heard the *Tock! Tock! Ti-tock, tock! . . . Tock, tock!* signal that Brush had said he would use; she hurried to let him in.

He burst in, saying savagely, "Where were you, Nurse? I knocked three times." He glanced suspiciously at the inner door.

"I saw your patient turn over," she lied quickly. "I was arranging her collar pillow."

"Damn it, I told you simply to sit at my desk!"

Jill knew suddenly that the man was frightened; she counterattacked. "Doctor," she said coldly, "your patient is not my responsibility. But since you entrusted her to me, I did what seemed necessary. Since you questioned it, let's get the wing superintendent."

"Huh? No, no—forget it."

"No, sir. A patient that old can smother in a water bed. Some nurses will take any blame from a doctor—but not me. Let's call the superintendent."

"What? Look, Miss Boardman, I popped off without thinking. I apologize."

"Very well, Doctor," Jill answered stiffly. "Is there anything more?"

"Uh? No, thank you. Thanks for standing by for me. Just . . . well, be sure not to mention it, will you?"

"I won't mention it." You bet your sweet life I won't! But what do I do now? Oh, I wish Ben were in town! She went to her desk and pretended to look over papers. Finally she remembered to phone for the powered bed she had been after. Then she sent her assistant on an errand and tried to think.

Where was Ben? If he were in touch, she would take ten minutes relief, call him, and shift the worry onto his broad shoulders. But Ben, damn him, was off skyoodling and letting her carry the ball.

Or was he? A fret that had been burrowing in her

subconscious finally surfaced. Ben would not have left town without letting her know the outcome of his attempt to see the Man from Mars. As a fellow conspirator it was her right—and Ben *always* played fair.

She could hear in her head something he had said: *"—if anything goes wrong, you are my ace in the hole . . . honey, if you don't hear from me, you are on your own."*

She had not thought about it at the time, as she had not believed that anything could happen to Ben. Now she thought about it. There comes a time in the life of every human when he or she must decide to risk "his life, his fortune, and his sacred honor" on an outcome dubious. Jill Boardman encountered her challenge and accepted it at 3:47 that afternoon.

The Man from Mars sat down when Jill left. He did not pick up the picture book but simply waited in a fashion which may be described as "patient" only because human language does not embrace Martian attitudes. He held still with quiet happiness because his brother had said that he would return. He was prepared to wait, without moving, without doing anything, for several years.

He had no clear idea how long it had been since he had shared water with this brother; not only was this place curiously distorted in time and shape, with sequences of sights and sounds not yet grokked, but also the culture of his nest took a different grasp of time from that which is human. The difference lay not in longer lifetimes as counted in Earth years, but in basic attitude. "It is later than you think" could not be expressed in Martian—nor could "Haste makes waste," though for a different reason: the first notion was inconceivable while the latter was an unexpressed Martian basic, as unnecessary as telling a fish to bathe. But "As it was in the Beginning, is now and ever shall be" was so Martian in mood that it could be translated more easily than "two plus two makes four"—which was not a truism on Mars.

Smith waited.

Brush came in and looked at him; Smith did not move and Brush went away.

When Smith heard a key in the outer door, he recalled that he had heard this sound somewhat before the last visit of his water brother, so he shifted his metabolism in preparation, in case the sequence occurred again. He was astonished when the outer door opened and Jill slipped in, as he had not been aware that it was a door. But he grokked it at once and gave himself over to the joyful fullness which comes only in the presence of one's nestlings, one's water brothers, and (under certain circumstances) in the presence of the Old Ones.

His joy was muted by awareness that his brother did not share it—he seemed more distressed than was possible save in one about to discorporate because of shameful lack or failure. But Smith had learned that these creatures could endure emotions dreadful to contemplate and not die. His Brother Mahmoud underwent a spiritual agony five times daily and not only did not die but had urged the agony on him as a needful thing. His Brother Captain van Tromp suffered terrifying spasms unpredictably, any one of which should have, by Smith's standards, produced immediate discorporation to end the conflict—yet that brother was still corporate so far as he knew.

So he ignored Jill's agitation.

Jill handed him a bundle. "Here, put these on. Hurry!"

Smith accepted the bundle and waited. Jill looked at him and said, "Oh, dear! All right, get your clothes off. I'll help."

She was forced both to undress and dress him. He was wearing a hospital gown, bathrobe, and slippers, not because he wanted to but because he had been told to. He could handle them by now, but not fast enough to suit Jill; she skinned him quickly. She being a nurse and he never having heard of the modesty taboo—nor would he have grasped it—they were not slowed by irrelevancies. He was delighted by false skins Jill drew over his legs. She gave him no time to cherish them, but taped the stockings to his thighs in lieu of garter belt. The nurse's uniform she dressed him in she had borrowed from a larger woman on the excuse that a cousin needed one for a masquerade. Jill hooked a nurse's cape around his neck and reflected that it covered most sex differences—at least she hoped so. Shoes were difficult; they did not fit well and Smith found walking in this gravity field an effort even barefooted.

But she got him covered and pinned a nurse's cap on his head. "Your hair isn't very long," she said anxiously, "but it is as long as some girls wear it and will have to do." Smith did not answer as he had not fully understood the remark. He tried to think his hair longer but realized that it would take time.

"Now," said Jill. "Listen carefully. No matter what happens, don't say a word. Do you understand?"

"Don't talk. I will not talk."

"Just come with me—I'll hold your hand. If you know any prayers, *pray*!"

"Pray?"

"Never mind. Just come along and don't talk." She opened the outer door, glanced outside, and led him into the corridor.

Smith found the many strange configurations upsetting in the extreme; he was assaulted by images he could not bring into focus. He stumbled blindly along, with eyes and senses almost disconnected to protect himself against chaos.

She led him to the end of the corridor and stepped on a slide-away leading crosswise. He stumbled and would have fallen if Jill had not caught him. A chambermaid looked at them and Jill cursed under her breath—then was very careful in helping him off. They took an elevator to the roof, Jill being sure that she could never pilot him up a bounce tube.

There they encountered a crisis, though Smith was not aware. He was undergoing the keen delight of sky; he had not seen sky since Mars. This sky was bright and colorful and joyful—a typical overcast Washington day. Jill was looking for a taxi. The roof was deserted, as she had hoped since nurses going off duty when she did were already headed home and afternoon visitors were gone. But the taxis were gone too. She did not dare risk an air bus.

She was about to call a taxi when one headed in for a landing. She called to the roof attendant. "Jack! Is that cab taken?"

"It's one I called for Dr. Phipps."

"Oh, dear! Jack, see how quick you can get me one, will you? This is my cousin Madge—works over in South Wing—and she has laryngitis and must get out of this wind."

The attendant scratched his head. "Well . . . seeing it's

you, Miss Boardman, you take this and I'll call another for Dr. Phipps."

"Oh, Jack, you're a lamb! Madge, don't talk; I'll thank him. Her voice is gone; I'm going to bake it out with hot rum."

"That ought to do it. Old-fashioned remedies are best, my mother used to say." He reached into the cab and punched the combination for Jill's home from memory, then helped them in. Jill got in the way and covered up Smith's unfamiliarity with this ceremonial. "Thanks, Jack. Thanks loads."

The cab took off and Jill took a deep breath. "You can talk now."

"What should I say?"

"Huh? Whatever you like."

Smith thought this over. The scope of the invitation called for a worthy answer, suitable to brothers. He thought of several, discarded them because he could not translate, settled on one which conveyed even in this strange, flat speech some of the warm growing-closer brothers should enjoy. "Let our eggs share the same nest."

Jill looked startled. "Huh? What did you say?"

Smith felt distressed at the failure to respond in kind and interpreted it as failure on his own part. He realized miserably that, time after time, he brought agitation to these creatures when his purpose was to create oneness. He tried again, rearranging his sparse vocabulary to enfold the thought differently. "My nest is yours and your nest is mine."

This time Jill smiled. "Why, how sweet! My dear, I am not sure I understand you, but that is the nicest offer I have had in a long time." She added, "But right now we are up to our ears in trouble—so let's wait, shall we?"

Smith understood Jill hardly more than Jill understood him, but he caught his water brother's pleased mood and understood the suggestion to wait. Waiting he did without effort; he sat back, satisfied that all was well between himself and his brother, and enjoyed the scenery. It was the first he had seen and on every side there was richness of new things to try to grok. It occurred to him that the apportation used at home did not permit this delightful viewing of what lay between. This almost led him to a comparison of Martian and human methods not favorable to the Old Ones, but his mind shied away from heresy.

Jill kept quiet and tried to think. Suddenly she noticed that the cab was on the final leg toward her apartment house—and realized that home was the last place to go, it being the first place they would look once they figured out who had helped Smith to escape. While she knew nothing of police methods, she supposed that she must have left fingerprints in Smith's room, not to mention that people had seen them walk out. It was even possible (so she had heard) for a technician to read the tape in this cab's pilot and tell what trips it had made and where and when.

She slapped the keys, and cleared the instruction to go to her apartment house. The cab rose out of the lane and hovered. Where could she go? Where could she hide a grown man who was half idiot and could not even dress himself?—and was the most sought-after person on the globe? Oh, if Ben were only here! Ben . . . *where are you?*

She picked up the phone and rather hopelessly punched Ben's number. Her spirits jumped when a man answered—then slumped when she realized that it was not Ben but his major-domo. "Oh. Sorry, Mr. Kilgallen. This is Jill Board-man. I thought I had called Mr. Caxton's home."

"You did. I have his calls relayed to the office when he is away more than twenty-four hours."

"Then he is still away?"

"Yes. May I help you?"

"Uh, no. Mr. Kilgallen, isn't it strange that Ben should drop out of sight? Aren't you worried?"

"Eh? Not at all. His message said that he did not know how long he would be gone."

"Isn't that *odd*?"

"Not in Mr. Caxton's work, Miss Boardman."

"Well . . . *I* think there is something *very* odd about his absence! I think you ought to report it. You ought to spread it over every news service in the country—in the world!"

Even though the cab's phone had no vision circuit Jill felt Osbert Kilgallen draw himself up. "I'm afraid, Miss Boardman, that I must interpret my employer's instructions myself. Uh . . . if you don't mind my saying so, there is always some 'good friend' phoning Mr. Caxton franti-cally whenever he's away."

Some babe trying to get a hammer lock on him, Jill interpreted angrily—and this character thinks I'm the current one. It squelched any thought of asking Kilgallen for help; she switched off.

Where could she go? A solution popped into her mind. If Ben was missing—and the authorities had a hand in it—the last place they would expect to find Valentine Smith would be Ben's apartment . . . unless they connected her with Ben, which seemed unlikely.

They could dig a snack out of Ben's pantry and she could borrow clothes for her idiot child. She set the combination for Ben's apartment house; the cab picked the lane and dropped into it.

Outside Ben's flat Jill put her face to the hush box and said, "Carthago delenda est!"

Nothing happened. Oh *damn*! she said to herself; he's changed the combo. She stood there, knees weak, and kept her face away from Smith. Then she again spoke into the hush box. The same circuit actuated the door or announced callers; she announced herself on the forlorn chance that Ben might have returned. "Ben, this is Jill."

The door slid open.

They went inside and the door closed. Jill thought that Ben had let them in, then realized that she had accidentally hit on his new door combination . . . intended, she guessed, as a compliment—she could have dispensed with the compliment to have avoided that awful panic.

Smith stood quietly at the edge of the thick green lawn and stared. Here was a place so new as not to be grokked at once but he felt immediately pleased. It was less exciting than the moving place they had been in, but more suited for enfolding the self. He looked with interest at the view window at one end but did not recognize it as such, mistaking it for a living picture like those at home . . . his suite at Bethesda had no windows, it being in a new wing; he had never acquired the idea of "window."

He noticed with approval that simulation of depth and movement in the "picture" was perfect—some very great artist must have created it. Up to now he had seen nothing to cause him to think that these people possessed art; his grokking of them was increased by this new experience and he felt warmed.

A movement caught his eye; he turned to find his brother removing false skins and slippers from its legs.

Jill sighed and wiggled her toes in the grass. "Gosh, how my feet hurt!" She glanced up and saw Smith watching with that curiously disturbing baby-faced stare. "Do it yourself. You'll love it."

He blinked. "How do?"

"I keep forgetting. Come here. I'll help." She got his shoes off, untaped the stockings and peeled them off. "There, doesn't that feel good?"

Smith wiggled his toes in the grass, then said timidly, "But these live?"

"Sure, it's alive, it's real grass. Ben paid a lot to have it that way. Why, the special lighting circuits alone cost more than I make in a month. So walk around and let your feet enjoy it."

Smith missed most of this but did understand that grass was living beings and that he was being invited to walk on them. "Walk on living things?" He asked with incredulous horror.

"Huh? Why not? It doesn't hurt this grass; it was specially developed for house rugs."

Smith was forced to remind himself that a water brother could not lead him into wrongful action. He let himself be encouraged to walk around—and found that he did enjoy it and the living creatures did not protest. He set his sensitivity for such as high as possible; his brother was right, this was their proper being—to be walked on. He resolved to enfold and praise it, an effort like that of a human trying to appreciate the merits of cannibalism—a custom which Smith found proper.

Jill let out a sigh. "I must stop playing. I don't know how long we will be safe."

"Safe?"

"We can't stay here. They may be checking on everything that left the Center." She frowned in thought. Her place would not do, this place would not do—and Ben had intended to take him to Jubal Harshaw. But she did not know Harshaw, nor where he lived—somewhere in the Poconos, Ben had said. Well, she would have to find out; she had nowhere else to turn.

"Why are you not happy, my brother?"

Jill snapped out of it and looked at Smith. Why, the poor infant didn't know anything was wrong! She tried to look at it from his point of view. She failed, but did grasp that he had no notion that they were running away from . . . from what? The cops? The hospital authorities? She was not sure what she had done, what laws she had broken; she simply knew that she had pitted herself against the Big People, the Bosses.

How could she tell the Man from Mars what they were up against when she herself did not know? Did they have policemen on Mars? Half the time talking to him was like shouting down a rain barrel.

Heavens, did they even have rain barrels on Mars? Or rain?

"Never mind," she said soberly. "You just do what I tell you to."

"Yes."

It was an unlimited acceptance, an eternal yea. Jill suddenly felt that Smith would jump out the window if she told him to—and she was correct; he would have jumped, enjoyed every second of the twenty-story drop, and accepted without surprise or resentment discorporation on impact. Nor would he have been unaware that such a fall would kill him; fear of death was an idea beyond him. If a water brother selected for him such strange discorporation, he would cherish it and try to grok.

"Well, we can't stand here. I've got to feed us, I've got to get you into different clothes, and we've got to leave. Take those off." She left to check Ben's wardrobe.

She selected a travel suit, a beret, shirt, underclothes, shoes, then returned. Smith was snarled like a kitten in knitting; he had one arm prisoned and his face wrapped in the skirt. He had not removed the cape before trying to take off the dress.

Jill said, "Oh, dear!" and ran to help.

She got him loose from the clothes, then stuffed them down the oubliette . . . she would pay Etta Schere later and she did not want cops finding them—just in case. "You are going to have a bath, my good man, before I dress you in Ben's clean clothes. They've been neglecting you. Come along." Being a nurse, she was inured to bad odors, but (being a nurse) she was fanatic about soap and water . . . and it seemed that no one had bathed this patient recently. While Smith did not stink, he did remind her of a horse on a hot day.

With delight he watched her fill the tub. There was a tub in the bathroom of suite K-12 but Smith had not known its use; bed baths were what he had had and not many of those; his trancelike withdrawals had interfered.

Jill tested the temperature. "All right, climb in."

Smith looked puzzled.

"Hurry!" Jill said sharply. "Get in the water."

The words were in his human vocabulary and Smith did

as ordered, emotion shaking him. This brother wanted him to place *his whole body* in the water of life! No such honor had ever come to him; to the best of his knowledge no one had ever been offered such a privilege. Yet he had begun to understand that these others did have greater acquaintance with the stuff of life . . . a fact not grokked but which he must accept.

He placed one trembling foot in the water, then the other . . . slipped down until water covered him completely.

"Hey!" yelled Jill, and dragged his head above water—was shocked to find that she seemed to be handling a corpse. Good Lord! he couldn't *drown*, not in that time. But it frightened her, she shook him. "Smith! Wake up! Snap out of it."

From far away Smith heard his brother call, and returned. His eyes ceased to be glazed, his heart speeded up, he resumed breathing. "Are you all right?" Jill demanded.

"I am all right. I am very happy . . . my brother."

"You scared me. Look, don't get under the water again. Just sit up, the way you are now."

"Yes, my brother." Smith added something in a croaking meaningless to Jill, cupped a handful of water as if it were precious jewels and raised it to his lips. His mouth touched it, then he offered it to Jill.

"Hey, don't drink your bath water! Now, I don't want it, either."

"Not drink?"

His defenseless hurt was such that Jill did not know what to do. She hesitated, then bent her head and touched her lips to the offering. "Thank you."

"May you never thirst!"

"I hope you are never thirsty, too. But that's enough. If you want a drink, I'll get you one. Don't drink any more of this water."

Smith seemed satisfied and sat quietly. By now Jill knew that he had never had a tub bath and did not know what was expected. No doubt she could coach him . . . but they were losing precious time.

Oh, well! It was not as bad as tending disturbed patients in N.P. wards. Her blouse was wet to the shoulders from dragging Smith off the bottom; she took it off and hung it up. She had been dressed for the street and was wearing a little pediskirt that floated around her knees. She glanced down. Although the pleats were permanized, it was silly to get it wet. She shrugged and zipped it off; it left her in brassière and panties.

Smith was staring with the interested eyes of a baby. Jill found herself blushing, which surprised her. She believed herself to be free of morbid modesty—she recalled suddenly that she had gone on her first bareskin swimming party at fifteen. But this childlike stare bothered her; she decided to put up with wet underwear rather than do the obvious.

She covered discomposure with heartiness. "Let's get busy and scrub the hide." She knelt beside the tub, sprayed soap on him, and started working it into lather.

Presently Smith reached out and touched her right mammary gland. Jill drew back hastily. "Hey! None of that!"

He looked as if she had slapped him. "Not?" he said tragically.

"'Not,'" she agreed firmly, then looked at his face and added softly, "It's all right. Just don't distract me, I'm busy."

Jill cut the bath short, letting water drain and having him stand while she showered him off. Then she dressed while the blast dried him. The warm air startled him and he began to tremble; she told him not to be afraid and had him hold the grab rail.

She helped him out of the tub. "There, you smell better and I bet you feel better."

"Feel fine."

"Good. Let's get clothes on you." She led him into Ben's bedroom. But before she could explain, demonstrate, or assist in getting shorts on him a man's voice scared her almost out of her senses:

"OPEN UP IN THERE!"

Jill dropped the shorts. Did they know anyone was inside? Yes, they must—else they would never have come here. That damned robocab must have given her away!

Should she answer? Or play 'possum?

The shout over the announcing circuit was repeated. She whispered to Smith, *"Stay here!"* then went into the living room. "Who is it?" she called out, striving to keep her voice normal.

"Open in the name of the law!"

"Open in the name of what law? Don't be silly. Tell me who you are before I call the police."

"We *are* the police. Are you Gillian Boardman?"

"Me? I'm Phyllis O'Toole and I'm waiting for Mr. Caxton. I'm going to call the police and report an invasion of privacy."

"Miss Boardman, we have a warrant for your arrest. Open up or it will go hard with you."

"I'm not 'Miss Boardman' and I'm calling the police!"

The voice did not answer. Jill waited, swallowing. Shortly she felt radiant heat against her face. The door's lock began to glow red, then white; something crunched and the door slid open. Two men were there; one stepped in, grinned, and said, "That's the babe! Johnson, look around and find him."

"Okay, Mr. Berquist."

Jill tried to be a road block. The man called Johnson brushed her aside and went toward the bedroom. Jill said shrilly, "Where's your warrant? This is an outrage!"

Berquist said soothingly, "Don't be difficult, sweetheart. Behave yourself and they might go easy on you."

She kicked at his shin. He stepped back nimbly. "Naughty, naughty," he chided. "Johnson! You find him?"

"He's here, Mr. Berquist. Naked as an oyster—three guesses what they were up to."

"Never mind that. Bring him."

Johnson reappeared, shoving Smith ahead, controlling him by twisting one arm. "He didn't want to come."

"He'll come!"

Jill ducked past Berquist, threw herself at Johnson. He slapped her aside. "None of that, you little slut!"

Johnson did not hit Jill as hard as he used to hit his wife before she left him, not nearly as hard as he hit prisoners who were reluctant to talk. Until then Smith had shown no expression and had said nothing; he had simply let himself be forced along. He understood none of it and had tried to do nothing at all.

When he saw his water brother struck by this other, he twisted, got free—and reached toward Johnson—

—and Johnson was gone.

Only blades of grass, straightening up where his big feet had been, showed that he had ever been there. Jill stared at the spot and felt that she might faint.

Berquist closed his mouth, opened it, said hoarsely, "What did you do with him?" He looked at Jill.

"Me? I didn't do *anything*."

"Don't give me that. You got a trap door or something?"

"Where did he *go*?"

Berquist licked his lips. "I don't know." He took a gun from under his coat. "But don't try your tricks on me. You stay here—I'm taking him."

Smith had relapsed into passive waiting. Not understanding what it was about, he had done only the minimum he had to do. But guns he had seen, in the hands of men on Mars, and the expression of Jill's face at having one aimed at her he did not like. He grokked that this was one of the critical cusps in the growth of a being wherein contemplation must bring forth right action in order to permit further growth. He acted.

The Old Ones had taught him well. He stepped toward Berquist; the gun swung to cover him. He reached out— and Berquist was no longer there.

Jill screamed.

Smith's face had been blank. Now it became tragically forlorn as he realized that he must have chosen wrong action at cusp. He looked imploringly at Jill and began to tremble. His eyes rolled up; he slowly collapsed, pulled himself into a ball, and was motionless.

Jill's hysteria chopped off. A patient needed her; she had no time for emotion, no time to wonder how men disappeared. She dropped to her knees and examined Smith.

She could not detect respiration, nor pulse; she pressed an ear to his ribs. She thought that heart action had stopped but, after a long time, she heard a lazy *lub-dub*, followed in four or five seconds by another.

The condition reminded her of schizoid withdrawal, but she had never seen a trance so deep, not even in class demonstrations of hypnoanesthesia. She had heard of such deathlike states among East Indian fakirs but had never really believed the reports.

Ordinarily she would not have tried to rouse a patient in such a state but would have sent for a doctor. These were not ordinary circumstances. Far from shaking her resolve, the last events made her more determined not to let Smith fall back into the hands of the authorities. But ten minutes of trying everything she knew convinced her that she could not rouse him.

In Ben's bedroom she found a battered flight case, too big for hand luggage, too small to be a trunk. She opened it, found it packed with voicewriter, toilet kit, an outfit of clothing, everything a busy reporter might need if called out of town—even a licensed audio link to patch into phone service. Jill reflected that this packed bag showed that Ben's absence was not what Kilgallen thought it was but she wasted no time on it; she emptied the bag and dragged it into the living room.

Smith outweighed her, but muscles acquired handling patients twice her size enabled her to dump him into the big bag. She had to refold him to close it. His muscles resisted force but under gentle steady pressure could be repositioned like putty. She padded the corners with some of Ben's clothes. She tried to punch air holes but the bag was glass laminate. She decided that he could not suffocate with respiration so minimal and metabolic rate as low as it must be.

She could barely lift the packed bag, straining with both hands, and she could not carry it. But it was equipped with "Red Cap" casters. They cut ugly scars in Ben's grass rug before she got it to the parquet of the entrance way.

She did not go to the roof; another cab was the last thing she wanted. She went out by the service door in the basement. There was no one there but a young man checking a kitchen delivery. He moved aside and let her roll the bag out onto the pavement. "Hi, sister. What you got in the keister?"

"A body," she snapped.

He shrugged. "Ask a jerky question, get a jerky answer. I should learn."

PART TWO

His Preposterous Heritage

IX

THE THIRD PLANET from Sol held 230,000 more humans this day than yesterday; among five billion terrestrials such increase was not noticeable. The Kingdom of South Africa, Federation associate, was again cited before the High Court for persecution of its white minority. The lords of fashion, gathered in Rio, decreed that hem lines would go down and navels would be covered. Federation defense stations swung in the sky, promising death to any who disturbed the planet's peace; commercial space stations disturbed the peace with endless clamor of endless trademarked trade goods. Half a million more mobile homes had set down on the shores of Hudson Bay than had migrated by the same date last year; the Chinese rice belt was declared an emergency malnutrition area by the Federation Assembly; Cynthia Duchess, known as the Richest Girl in the World, paid off her sixth husband.

The Reverend Doctor Daniel Digby, Supreme Bishop of the Church of the New Revelation (Fosterite), announced that he had nominated the Angel Azreel to guide Federation Senator Thomas Boone and that he expected Heavenly confirmation later today; news services carried it as straight news, the Fosterites having wrecked newspaper offices in the past. Mr. and Mrs. Harrison Campbell VI had a son and heir by host-mother at Cincinnati Children's Hospital while the happy parents were vacationing in Peru. Dr. Horace Quackenbush, Professor of Leisure Arts at Yale Divinity School, called for a return to faith and cultivation of spiritual values; a betting scandal involved half the professionals of the West Point football squad; three bacterial warfare chemists were suspended at Toronto for emotional instability; they announced that they would carry their cases to the High Court. The High Court reversed the United States Supreme Court in re-primaries involving Federation Assemblymen in the case of *Reinsberg vs. the State of Missouri*.

His Excellency, the Most Honorable Joseph E. Douglas, Secretary General of the World Federation of Free States, picked at his breakfast and wondered why a man could not get a decent cup of coffee. His morning newspaper, prepared by the night shift of his information staff, moved past his eyes at his optimum reading speed in a feedback scanner. The words flowed as long as he looked in that direction. He was looking at it now, but simply to avoid the eyes of his boss across the table. Mrs. Douglas did not read newspapers; she had other ways of finding things out.

"Joseph—"

He looked up, the machine stopped. "Yes, my dear?"

"You have something on your mind."

"Eh? What makes you say that, my dear?"

"Joseph! I've coddled you and darned your socks and kept you out of trouble for thirty-five years—*I* know when something is on your mind."

The hell of it is, he admitted, she does know. He looked

at her and wondered why he had ever let her bully him into a no-termination contract. She had been his secretary, back in "The Good Old Days" when he had been a state legislator. Their first contract had been a ninety-day co-habitation agreement, to economize campaign funds by saving on hotel bills; both had agreed that it was merely a convenience, with "cohabitation" to be construed simply as living under one roof—and she hadn't darned his socks even then!

He tried to remember how it had changed. Mrs. Douglas's biography, *Shadow of Greatness: One Woman's Story* stated that he had proposed during ballot counting in his first election—and such was his romantic need that nothing would do but old-fashioned, death-do-us-part marriage.

Well, there was no use arguing with the official version.

"Joseph! Answer me!"

"Eh? Nothing, my dear. I spent a restless night."

"I know. When they wake you in the night, don't I know it?"

He reflected that her suite was fifty yards across the palace from his. "How do you know it, my dear?"

"Hunh? Woman's intuition. What was the message Bradley brought you?"

"Please, my dear—I've got to finish the news before Council meeting."

"Joseph Edgerton Douglas, don't evade me."

He sighed. "We've lost sight of that beggar Smith."

"Smith? You mean the Man from Mars? What do you mean: '—lost sight of—'? Ridiculous!"

"Be that as it may, my dear, he's gone. Disappeared from his hospital room yesterday."

"Preposterous! How could he?"

"Disguised as a nurse, apparently."

"But—Never mind. He's gone, that's the main thing. What muddle-headed scheme are you using to get him back?"

"Well, we have people searching. Trusted ones. Berquist—"

"*That* garbage head? When you should be using every police officer from the FDS down to truant officers you send *Berquist*!"

"But, my dear, you don't see the situation. We *can't*. Officially he isn't lost. You see there's—well, the *other* chap. The, uh, 'official' Man from Mars."

"*Oh . . .*" She drummed the table. "I told you that substitution scheme would get us in trouble."

"But, my dear, you suggested it."

"I did not. And don't contradict me. Mmm . . . send for Berquist."

"Uh, Berquist is out on his trail. He hasn't reported back yet."

"Uh? Berquist is halfway to Zanzibar by now. He's sold us out. I never did trust that man. I told you when you hired him that—"

"When *I* hired him?"

"Don't interrupt.—that any man who takes money two ways would take it three ways." She frowned. "Joseph, the Eastern Coalition is behind this. You can expect a vote-of-confidence move in the Assembly."

"Eh? I don't see why. Nobody knows it."

"Oh, for Heaven's sake! Everybody will know; the Eastern Coalition will see to that. Keep quiet and let me think."

Douglas shut up. He read that the Los Angeles City-County Council had petitioned the Federation for aid in their smog problem, on the grounds the Ministry of Health had failed to provide something or other—a sop must be thrown to them as Charlie was going to have a tough time being reelected with the Fosterites running their own candidate. Lunar Enterprises was up two points at closing—

"Joseph."

"Yes, my dear?"

"Our 'Man from Mars' is the only one; the one the Eastern Coalition will pop up with is a fake. That is how it must be."

"But, my dear, we can't make it stick."

"What do you mean, we can't? We've *got* to."

"But we *can't*. Scientists would spot the substitution at once. I've had the devil's own time keeping them away from him this long."

"Scientists!"

"But they can, you know."

"I don't know anything of the sort. Scientists indeed! Half guess work and half superstition. They ought to be locked up; they ought to be prohibited by law. Joseph, I've told you repeatedly, the only true science is astrology."

"Well, I don't know, my dear. I'm not running down astrology—"

"You'd better not! After all it's done for *you*."

"—but these science professors are pretty sharp. One was telling me the other day about a star that weighs six thousand times as much as lead. Or was it sixty thousand? Let me see—"

"Bosh! How could they know a thing like that? Keep quiet, Joseph. We admit nothing. Their man is a fake. In the meantime we make full use of our Special Service squads and grab him back, if possible before the Eastern

Coalition makes its disclosure. If strong measures are necessary and this Smith person gets shot resisting arrest or something, well, it's just too bad. He's been a nuisance all along."

"Agnes! Do you know what you are suggesting?"

"I'm not suggesting anything. People get hurt every day. This matter must be cleared up, Joseph, for everybody. The greatest good of the greatest number, as you are always saying."

"I don't want the lad hurt."

"Who said anything about hurting him? You must take firm steps, Joseph; it's your duty. History will justify you. Which is more important?—to keep things on an even keel for five billion people, or to go soft and sentimental about one man who isn't even properly a citizen?"

Douglas didn't answer. Mrs. Douglas stood up. "Well, I can't waste time arguing intangibles; I've got to get Madame Vesant to cast a new horoscope. I didn't give the best years of my life putting you where you are to throw it away through lack of backbone. Wipe the egg off your chin." She left.

The chief executive of the planet stayed for two more cups of coffee before he felt up to going to the Council Chamber. Poor old Agnes! He guessed he had been a disappointment to her . . . and no doubt the change of life wasn't making things easier. Well, at least she was loyal, right to her toes . . . and we all have shortcomings; she was probably as sick of him as he—no point in that!

He straightened up. One damn sure thing!—he wasn't going to let them be rough with that Smith lad. He was a nuisance, granted, but rather appealing in a helpless, half-witted way. Agnes should have seen how easily he was frightened, then she wouldn't talk that way. Smith would appeal to the maternal in her.

But did Agnes have any "maternal" in her? When she set her mouth, it was hard to see it. Oh shucks, all women had maternal instincts; science had proved that. Well, hadn't they?

Anyhow, damn her guts, he wasn't going to let her push him around. She kept reminding him that she had put him into the top spot, but he knew better . . . and the responsibility was his alone. He got up, squared his shoulders, and went to Council.

All day he kept expecting someone to drop the other shoe. But no one did. He was forced to conclude that the fact that Smith was missing was close held in his own staff, unlikely as that seemed. The Secretary General wanted to close his eyes and have the whole horrid mess go away, but events would not let him. Nor would his wife.

Agnes Douglas did not wait for her husband to act in the case of the Man from Mars. Her husband's staff took orders as readily from her as from him—or more readily. She sent for the executive assistant for civil information, as Mr. Douglas's flack was called, then turned to the most urgent need, a fresh horoscope. There was a scrambled private link from her suite to Madame Vesant's studio; the astrologer's plump features came on screen at once. "Agnes? What is it, dear? I have a client."

"Your circuit is hushed?"

"Of course."

"Get rid of the client."

Madame Alexandra Vesant showed no annoyance. "Just a moment." Her features faded out, were replaced by the "Hold" signal. A man entered and stood by Mrs.

Douglas's desk; she saw that it was James Sanforth, the press agent she had sent for.

"Have you heard from Berquist?" she demanded.

"Eh? I wasn't handling that; that's McCrary's pidgin."

She brushed it aside. "You've got to discredit him before he talks."

"You think Berquist sold us out?"

"Don't be naive. You should have checked with me before you used him."

"But I didn't. It was McCrary's job."

"You are supposed to know what is going on. I—" Madame Vesant's face came back on screen. "Wait over there," Mrs. Douglas said to Sanforth. She turned to the screen. "Allie dear, I want fresh horoscopes for Joseph and myself, right away."

"Very well." The astrologer hesitated. "I can be of greater assistance, dear, if you tell me the nature of the emergency."

Mrs. Douglas drummed on the desk. "You don't have to know?"

"Of course not. Anyone possessing the necessary rigorous training, mathematical skill, and knowledge of the stars could calculate a horoscope, knowing nothing but the hour and place of birth of the subject. You could learn it . . . if you weren't so terribly busy. But remember: the stars incline but do not compel. If I am to make a detailed analysis to advise you in a crisis, I must know in what sector to look. Are we most concerned with the influence of Venus? Or possibly with Mars? Or—"

Mrs. Douglas decided. "With Mars," she interrupted. "Allie, I want a third horoscope."

"Very well. Whose?"

"Uh . . . Allie, can I trust you?"

Madame Vesant looked hurt. "Agnes, if you do not trust me, you had best not consult me. Others can give you scientific readings. I am not the only student of the ancient knowledge. Professor von Krausemeyer is well thought of, even though he is inclined to . . ." She let her voice trail off.

"Please, please! I wouldn't think of letting anyone else perform a calculation for me. Now listen. No one can hear from your side?"

"Of course not, dear."

"I want a horoscope for Valentine Michael Smith."

"'Valentine Mich—' The Man from Mars?"

"Yes, yes. Allie, he's been kidnapped. *We've got to find him.*"

Two hours later Madame Alexandra Vesant pushed back from her desk and sighed. She had had her secretary cancel all appointments; sheets covered with diagrams and figures and a dog-eared nautical almanac testified to her efforts. Alexandra Vesant differed from some astrologers in that she did attempt to calculate the "influences" of heavenly bodies, using a paper-backed book titled *The Arcane Science of Judicial Astrology and Key to Solomon's Stone* which had belonged to her late husband, Professor Simon Magus, mentalist, stage hypnotist and illusionist, and student of the Arcanum.

She trusted the book as she had trusted him; there was no one who could cast a horoscope like Simon, when he was sober—half the time he had not needed the book. She knew that she would never have that degree of skill; she always used both almanac and manual. Her calculations were sometimes fuzzy; Becky Vesey (as she had been known) had never really mastered multiplication tables and was inclined to confuse sevens with nines.

Nevertheless her horoscopes were eminently satisfactory; Mrs. Douglas was not her only distinguished client.

She had been a touch panicky when Mrs. Douglas demanded a horoscope for the Man from Mars—she had felt the way she used to feel when some idiot from the audience had retied her blindfold just before the Professor was to ask her questions. But she had discovered 'way back then, as a girl, that she had talent for the right answer; she had suppressed her panic and gone on with the show.

So she had demanded of Agnes the exact hour, date, and place of birth of the Man from Mars, being fairly sure that they were not known.

But precise information had been supplied, after short delay, from the *Envoy*'s log. By then she was not panicky, had simply accepted the data and promised to call back with the horoscopes.

But, after two hours of painful arithmetic, although she had completed findings for Mr. and Mrs. Douglas, she had nothing for Smith. The trouble was simple—and insuperable. Smith had not been born on Earth.

Her astrological bible did not include such an idea; its anonymous author had died before the first rocket to the Moon. She had tried to find a way out of the dilemma, on the assumption that principles were unchanged and that she must correct for displacement. But she grew lost in a maze of unfamiliar relationships; she was not sure the signs of the Zodiac were the same from Mars . . . and what could one do without signs of the Zodiac?

She could as easily have extracted a cube root, that being the hurdle that had caused her to quit school.

She got out a tonic she kept for difficult occasions. She took one dose quickly, poured another, and thought about what Simon would have done. Presently she could hear his steady tones: "Confidence, kiddo! Have confidence and the yokels will have confidence in you. You owe it to them."

She felt much better and started writing the horoscopes for the Douglases. It then turned out to be easy to write one for Smith; she found, as always, that words on paper proved themselves—they were so beautifully *true*! She was finishing as Agnes Douglas called again. "Allie? Haven't you finished?"

"Just completed," Madame Vesant answered briskly. "You realize that young Smith's horoscope presented an unusual and difficult problem in the Science. Born, as he was, on another planet, every aspect had to be recalculated. The influence of the Sun is lessened; that of Diana is almost missing. Jupiter is thrown into a novel, I should say 'unique,' aspect, as I am sure you see. This required computation of—"

"Allie! Never mind that. Do you know the answers?"

"Naturally."

"Oh, thank goodness! I thought you were telling me that it was too much for you."

Madame Vesant showed injured dignity. "My dear, the Science never alters; only configurations alter. The means that predicted the instant and place of the birth of Christ, that told Julius Caesar the moment and method of his death . . . how could it fail? Truth is Truth, unchanging."

"Yes, of course."

"Are you ready?"

"Let me switch on 'recording'—go ahead."

"Very well. Agnes, this is a most critical period in your

life; never have the heavens gathered in such strong con-
figuration. Above all, you must be calm, not hasty, and
think things through. On the whole the portents are in
your favor . . . provided you avoid ill-considered action. Do
not let your mind be distressed by surface appearances—"
She went on giving advice. Becky Vesey always gave good
advice and gave it with conviction because she believed it.
She had learned from Simon that, even when the stars
seemed darkest, there was always a way to soften the blow,
some aspect the client could use toward happiness . . .

The tense face opposite her in the screen calmed and
began nodding agreement as she made her points. "So you
see," she concluded, "the absence of young Smith is a necessity, under the joint influences of three horoscopes. Do
not worry; he will return—or you will hear from him—
very shortly. The important thing is to take no drastic action. Be calm."

"Yes, I see."

"One more point. The aspect of Venus is most favorable
and potentially dominant over that of Mars. Venus sym-
bolizes yourself, of course, but Mars is both your husband
and young Smith—as a result of the unique circumstances
of his birth. This throws a double burden on you and you
must rise to the challenge; you must demonstrate those
qualities calm wisdom and restraint which are peculiarly
those of woman. You must sustain your husband, guide
him through this crisis, and soothe him. You must supply
the earth-mother's calm wells of wisdom. That is your special genius . . . you must use it."

Mrs. Douglas sighed. "Allie, you are simply wonderful!
I don't know how to thank you."

"Thank the Ancient Masters whose humble student I am."

"I can't thank them so I'll thank you. This isn't covered by retainer, Allie. There will be a present."

"No, Agnes. It is a privilege to serve."

"And it is my privilege to appreciate service. Allie, not another word!"

Madame Vesant let herself be coaxed, then switched off, feeling warmly content from having given a reading that she just knew was right. Poor Agnes! It was a privilege to smooth her path, make her burdens a little lighter. It made her feel good to help Agnes.

It made Madame Vesant feel good to be treated as almost-equal by the wife of the Secretary General, although she did not think of it that way, not being snobbish. But young Becky Vesey had been so insignificant that the precinct committeeman could never remember her name even though he noticed her bust. Becky Vesey had not resented it; Becky liked people. She liked Agnes Douglas.

Becky Vesey liked everybody.

She sat a while, enjoying the warm glow and just a nip more tonic, while her shrewd brain shuffled the bits she had picked up. Presently she called her stockbroker and instructed him to sell Lunar Enterprises short.

He snorted. "Allie, that reducing diet is weakening your mind."

"Listen, Ed. When it's down ten points, cover me, even if it is still slipping. Then when it rallies three points, buy again . . . then sell when it gets back to today's closing."

There was long silence. "Allie, you know something. Tell Uncle Ed."

"The stars tell me, Ed."

Ed made a suggestion astronomically impossible. "All right, if you won't, you won't. Mmm . . . I never did have sense enough to stay out of a crooked game. Mind if I ride along?"

"Not at all, Ed. Just don't go heavy enough to let it show. This is a delicate situation, with Saturn balanced between Virgo and Leo."

"As you say, Allie."

Mrs. Douglas got busy at once, happy that Allie had confirmed all her judgments. She gave orders about the campaign to destroy the reputation of the missing Berquist, after sending for his dossier; she summoned Commandant Twitchell of the Special Service Squadrons—he left looking unhappy and made life unbearable for his executive officer. She instructed Sanforth to release another "Man from Mars" stereocast with a rumor "from a source close to the administration" that Smith was about to go, or possibly had gone, to a sanitarium high in the Andes, to provide him with climate as much like Mars as possible. Then she thought about how to nail down Pakistan's votes.

Presently she called her husband and urged him to support Pakistan's claim to a lion's share of the Kashmir thorium. Since he had been wanting to, he was not hard to persuade, although nettled by her assumption that he had been opposing it. With that settled, she left to address the Daughters of the Second Revolution on *Motherhood in the New World*.

X

WHILE MRS. DOUGLAS was speaking freely on a subject she knew little about, Jubal E. Harshaw, LL.B., M.D., Sc.D., bon vivant, gourmet, sybarite, popular author extraordinary, and neo-pessimist philosopher, was sitting by his pool at his home in the Poconos, scratching the grey thatch on his chest, and watching his three secretaries splash in the pool. They were all amazingly beautiful; they were also amazingly good secretaries. In Harshaw's opinion the principle of least action required that utility and beauty be combined.

Anne was blonde, Miriam red-headed, and Dorcas dark; they ranged, respectively, from pleasantly plump to deliciously slender. Their ages spread over fifteen years but it was hard to tell which was the eldest.

Harshaw was working hard. Most of him was watching pretty girls do pretty things with sun and water; one small, shuttered, soundproofed compartment was composing. He claimed that his method of writing was to hook his gonads in parallel with his thalamus and disconnect his cerebrum; his habits lent credibility to the theory.

A microphone on a table was hooked to a voicewriter but he used it only for notes. When he was ready to write he used a stenographer and watched her reactions. He was ready now. "Front!" he shouted.

"Anne is 'front,'" answered Dorcas. "I'll take it. That splash was Anne."

"Dive in and get her." The brunette cut the water; moments later Anne climbed out, put on a robe, and sat down at the table. She said nothing and made no preparations; Anne had total recall.

Harshaw picked up a bucket of ice over which brandy had been poured, took a swig. "Anne, I've got a sick-making one. It's about a little kitten that wanders into a church on Christmas Eve to get warm. Besides being starved and frozen and lost, the kitten has—God knows why—an injured paw. All right; start: 'Snow had been falling since—'"

"What pen name?"

"Mmm . . . use 'Molly Wadsworth'; this one is pretty icky. Title it *The Other Manger*. Start again." He went on talking while watching her. When tears started to leak from her closed eyes he smiled slightly and closed his own. By the time he finished tears were running down his cheeks as well as hers, both bathed in catharsis of schmaltz.

"Thirty," he announced. "Blow your nose. Send it off and for God's sake don't let me see it."

"Jubal, aren't you ever ashamed?"

"No."

"Someday I'm going to kick you right in your fat stomach for one of these."

"I know. Get your fanny indoors and take care of it before I change my mind."

"Yes, Boss."

She kissed his bald spot as she passed behind his chair. Harshaw yelled, "Front!" and Miriam started toward him. A loudspeaker mounted on the house came to life:

"Boss!"

Harshaw uttered one word and Miriam clucked. He added, "Yes, Larry?"

The speaker answered, "There's a dame down here at the gate—and she's got a *corpse* with her."

Harshaw considered this. "Is she pretty?"

"Uh . . . yes."

"Then why are you sucking your thumb? Let her in." Harshaw sat back. "Start," he said. "City montage dissolving into medium two-shot interior. A cop is seated in a straight chair, no cap, collar open, face covered with sweat. We see the back of the other figure, depthed between us and cop. Figure raises a hand, bringing it back and almost out of the tank. He slaps the cop with a heavy, meaty sound, dubbed." Harshaw glanced up and said, "Pick up from there." A car was rolling up the hill toward the house.

Jill was driving; a young man was beside her. As the car stopped the man jumped out, as if happy to divorce himself from it. "There she is, Jubal."

"So I see. Good morning, little girl. Larry, where is this corpse?"

"Back seat, Boss. Under a blanket."

"But it's *not* a corpse," Jill protested. "It's . . . Ben said that you . . . I mean—" She put her head down and sobbed.

"There, my dear," Harshaw said gently. "Few corpses are worth tears. Dorcas—Miriam—take care of her. Give her a drink and wash her face."

He went to the back seat, lifted the blanket. Jill shrugged off Miriam's arm and said shrilly, "You've got to listen! He's not dead. At least I hope not. He's . . . oh dear!" She started to cry again. "I'm so dirty . . . and so scared!"

"Seems to be a corpse," Harshaw mused. "Body temperature down to air temperature, I judge. Rigor not typical. How long has he been dead?"

"But he's not! Can't we get him out of there? I had an *awful* time getting him in."

"Surely. Larry, help me—and quit looking green; if you puke, you'll clean it up." They got Valentine Michael Smith out and laid him on the grass; his body remained stiff, huddled together. Dorcas fetched Dr. Harshaw's stethoscope, set it on the ground, switched it on and stepped up the gain.

Harshaw stuck the headpiece in his ears, started sounding for heart beat. "I'm afraid you're mistaken," he said gently to Jill. "This one is beyond my help. Who was he?"

Jill sighed. Her face was drained of expression and she answered in a flat voice, "He was the Man from Mars. I tried so hard."

"I'm sure you did—*the Man from Mars?*"

"Yes. Ben . . . Ben Caxton said you were the one to come to."

"Ben Caxton, eh? I appreciate the confid—*hush*!" Harshaw gestured for silence. He looked puzzled, then surprise burst over his face. "Heart action! I'll be a babbling baboon. Dorcas—upstairs, the clinic—third drawer in the locked part of the cooler; the code is 'sweet dreams.' Bring the drawer and a one cc. hypo."

"Right away!"

"Doctor, no stimulants!"

Harshaw turned to Jill. "Eh?"

"I'm sorry, sir. I'm just a nurse . . . but this case is different. I *know*."

"Mmm . . . he's my patient now, nurse. But about forty years ago I found out I wasn't God, and ten years later I discovered I wasn't even Aesculapius. What do you want to try?"

"I want to try to wake him. If you do anything to him, he goes deeper into it."

"Hmm . . . go ahead. Just don't use an ax. Then we'll try my methods."

"Yes, sir." Jill knelt, started trying to straighten Smith's limbs. Harshaw's eyebrows went up when he saw her succeed. Jill took Smith's head in her lap. "Please wake up," she said softly. "This is your *water brother*."

Slowly the chest lifted. Smith let out a long sigh and his eyes opened. He looked up at Jill and smiled his baby smile. He looked around, the smile left him.

"It's all right," Jill said quickly. "These are friends."

"Friends?"

"All of them are your friends. Don't worry—and don't go away again. Everything is all right."

He lay quiet with eyes open, staring at everything. He seemed as content as a cat in a lap.

Twenty-five minutes later both patients were in bed. Jill had told Harshaw, before the pill he gave her took hold, enough to let him know that he had a bear by the tail. He looked at the utility car Jill had arrived in. Lettered across it was: READING RENTALS—Permapowered Ground Equipment—"Deal with the Dutchman!"

"Larry, is the fence hot?"

"No."

"Switch it on. Then polish every fingerprint off that heap. When it gets dark, drive over to the other side of Reading—better go almost to Lancaster—and leave it in a ditch. Then go to Philadelphia, catch the Scranton shuttle, come home from there."

"Sure thing, Jubal. Say—is he *really* the Man from Mars?"

"Better hope not. If he is and they catch you before you dump that wagon and connect you with him, they'll quiz you with a blow torch. I think he is."

"I scan it. Should I rob a bank on the way back?"

"Probably the safest thing you can do."

"Okay, Boss." Larry hesitated. "Mind if I stay over night in Philly?"

"Suit yourself. But what in God's name can a man do at night in Philadelphia?" Harshaw turned away. "Front!"

Jill slept until dinner, awoke refreshed and alert. She sniffed the air from the grille overhead and surmised that the doctor had offset the hypnotic with a stimulant. While she slept someone had removed her dirty torn clothes and had left a dinner dress and sandals. The dress was a fair fit; Jill concluded that it must belong to the one called Miriam. She bathed and painted and combed and went down to the living room feeling like a new woman.

Dorcas was curled in a chair, doing needle point; she nodded as if Jill were part of the family, turned back to her fancy work. Harshaw was stirring a mixture in a frosty pitcher. "Drink?" he said.

"Uh, yes, thank you."

He poured large cocktail glasses to their brims, handed her one. "What is it?" she asked.

"My own recipe. One third vodka, one third muriatic acid, one third battery water—two pinches of salt and add pickled beetle."

"Better have a highball," Dorcas advised.

"Mind your business," Harshaw said. "Hydrochloric acid aids digestion; the beetle adds vitamins and protein."

He raised his glass and said solemnly, "Here's to our noble selves! There are damned few of us left." He emptied it.

Jill took a sip, then a bigger one. Whatever the ingredients it seemed to be what she needed; well-being spread from her center toward her extremities. She drank about half, let Harshaw add a dividend. "Look in on our patient?" he asked.

"No, sir. I didn't know where he was."

"I checked a few minutes ago. Sleeping like a baby—I think I'll rename him Lazarus. Would he like to come down to dinner?"

Jill looked thoughtful. "Doctor, I don't know."

"Well, if he wakes I'll know it. He can join us, or have a tray. This is Freedom Hall, my dear. Everyone does as he pleases . . . then if he does something I don't like, I kick him the hell out. Which reminds me: I don't like to be called 'Doctor.'"

"Sir?"

"Oh, I'm not offended. But when they began handing out doctorates for comparative folk dancing and advanced flyfishing, I became too stinkin' proud to use the title. I won't touch watered whiskey and take no pride in watered-down degrees. Call me Jubal."

"Oh. But the degree in medicine hasn't been watered down."

"Time they called it something else, so as not to confuse it with playground supervisors. Little girl, what is your interest in this patient?"

"Eh? I told you, Doct—Jubal."

"You told me what happened; you didn't tell me why. Jill, I saw the way you spoke to him. Are you in love with him?"

Jill gasped. "Why, that's preposterous!"

"Not at all. You're a girl; he's a boy—that's a nice setup."

"But—No, Jubal, it's not that. I . . . well, he was a prisoner and I thought—or Ben thought—that he was in danger. We wanted to see him get his rights."

"Mmm . . . my dear, I'm suspicious of a disinterested interest. You look as if you had normal glandular balance, so it's my guess that it is either Ben, or this poor boy from Mars. You had better examine your motives, then judge which way you are going. In the meantime, what do you want *me* to do?"

The scope of the question made it hard to answer. From the time Jill crossed her Rubicon she had thought of nothing but escape. She had no plans. "I don't know."

"I thought not. On the assumption that you might wish to protect your license, I took the liberty of having a message sent from Montreal to your Chief of Nursing. You asked for leave because of illness in your family. Okay?"

Jill felt sudden relief. She had buried all worry about her own welfare; nevertheless down inside was a heavy lump caused by what she had done to her professional standing. "Oh, Jubal, thank you!" She added, "I'm not delinquent in watch standing yet; today was my day off."

"Good. What do you want to do?"

"I haven't had time to think. Uh, I should get in touch with my bank and get some money—" She paused, trying to recall her balance. It was never large and sometimes she forgot to—

Jubal cut in. "If you do, you will have cops pouring out of your ears. Hadn't you better stay here until things level off?"

"Uh, Jubal, I wouldn't want to impose on you."

"You already have. Don't worry, child; there are always freeloaders around here. Nobody imposes on me against my will, so relax. Now our patient: you said you wanted him to get his 'rights.' You expected my help?"

"Well . . . Ben said—Ben seemed to think you would help."

"Ben does not speak for me. I am not interested in this lad's so-called rights. His claim to Mars is lawyers' hogwash; as a lawyer myself I need not respect it. As for the wealth that is supposed to be his, the situation results from other people's passions and our odd tribal customs; he has earned none of it. He would be lucky if they bilked him of it—but I would not scan a newspaper to find out. If Ben expected me to fight for Smith's 'rights' you have come to the wrong house."

"Oh." Jill felt forlorn. "I had better arrange to move him."

"Oh, no! Not unless you wish."

"But you said—"

"I said I was not interested in legal fictions. But a guest under my roof is another matter. He can stay, if he likes. I just wanted to make clear that I had no intention of meddling with politics to suit romantic notions you or Ben Caxton may have. My dear, I used to think I was serving humanity . . . and I pleasured in the thought. Then I discovered that humanity does not want to be served; on the contrary it resents any attempt to serve it. So now I do what pleases Jubal Harshaw." He turned away. "Time for dinner, isn't it, Dorcas? Is anyone doing anything?"

"Miriam." She put down her needle point and stood up.

"I've never figured out how these girls divide up the work."

"Boss, how would you know?—you never do any." Dorcas patted him on the stomach. "But you never miss any meals."

A gong sounded, they went in to eat. If Miriam had cooked dinner, she had done so with modern shortcuts; she was seated at the foot of the table and looked cool and beautiful. In addition to the secretaries there was a man slightly older than Larry called "Duke" who treated Jill as if she always lived there. Service was by non-android machines, keyed from Miriam's end of the table. The food was excellent and, so far as Jill could tell, none was syntho.

But it did not suit Harshaw. He complained that his knife was dull, the meat was tough; he accused Miriam of serving leftovers. No one seemed to hear him but Jill was becoming embarrassed on Miriam's account when Anne put down her fork. "He mentioned his mother's cooking," she stated.

"He is beginning to think he is boss again," agreed Dorcas.

"How long has it been?"

"About ten days."

"Too long." Anne gathered Dorcas and Miriam by eye; they stood up. Duke went on eating.

Harshaw said hastily, "Girls, not at meals! Wait until—" They moved toward him; a machine scurried out of the way. Anne took his feet, each of the others an arm; French doors slid aside; they carried him out, squawking.

The squawks ended in a splash.

The women returned, not noticeably mussed. Miriam sat down and turned to Jill. "More salad, Jill?"

Harshaw returned in pajamas and robe instead of evening jacket. A machine had covered his plate as he was dragged away; it now uncovered it, he went on eating. "As I was saying," he remarked, "a woman who can't cook is a waste of skin. If I don't start having service I'm going to swap you all for a dog and shoot the dog. What's dessert, Miriam?"

"Strawberry shortcake."

"That's more like it. You are all reprieved till Wednesday."

After dinner Jill went into the living room intending to view a news stereocast, being anxious to find out if she played a part in it. She could find no receiver, nor anything which could conceal a tank. Thinking about it, she could not recall having seen one. Nor any newspapers, although there were plenty of books and magazines.

No one joined her. She began to wonder what time it was. She had left her watch upstairs, so she looked around for a clock. She failed to find one, then searched her memory and could not remember seeing clock or calendar in any room she had been in. She decided that she might as well go to bed. One wall was filled with books; she found a spool of Kipling's *Just So Stories* and took it happily upstairs.

The bed in her room was as modern as next week, with automassage, coffee dispenser, weather control, reading machine, etc.—but the alarm circuit was missing. Jill decided that she would probably not oversleep, crawled into bed, slid the spool into the reading machine, lay back and scanned the words streaming across the ceiling. Presently the control slipped from relaxed fingers, lights went out, she slept.

Jubal Harshaw did not get to sleep as easily; he was

vexed with himself. His interest had cooled and reaction set in. Half a century earlier he had sworn a mighty oath never again to pick up a stray cat—and now, so help him, by the multiple paps of Venus Genetrix he had picked up two at once . . . no, three, if he counted Caxton.

That he had broken his oath more times than there were years intervening did not trouble him; he was not hobbled by consistency. Nor did two more pensioners under his roof bother him; pinching pennies was not in him. In most of a century of gusty living he had been broke many times, had often been wealthier than he now was; he regarded both as shifts in the weather and never counted his change.

But the foofooraw that was bound to ensue when the busies caught up with these children disgruntled him. He considered it certain that catch up they would; that naive Gillian infant would leave a trail like a club-footed cow!

Whereupon people would barge into his sanctuary, asking questions, making demands . . . and he would have to make decisions and take action. He was convinced that all action was futile, the prospect irritated him.

He did not expect reasonable conduct from human beings; most people were candidates for protective restraint. He simply wished they would leave him alone!—all but the few he chose for playmates. He was convinced that, left to himself, he would have long since achieved nirvana . . . dived into his belly button and disappeared from view, like those Hindu jokers. Why couldn't they leave a man *alone*?

Around midnight he put out his twenty-seventh cigarette and sat up; lights came on. "Front!" he shouted at a microphone.

Dorcas came in, dressed in robe and slippers. She yawned and said, "Yes, Boss?"

"Dorcas, the last twenty or thirty years I've been a worth-less, no-good parasite."

She yawned again. "Everybody knows that."

"Never mind the flattery. There comes a time in every man's life when he has to stop being sensible—a time to stand up and be counted—strike a blow for liberty—smite the wicked."

"Ummm . . ."

"So quit yawning, the time has come."

She glanced down. "Maybe I had better get dressed."

"Yes. Get the other girls up, too; we're going to be busy. Throw a bucket of water over Duke and tell him to dust off the babble machine and hook it up in the study. I want the news."

Dorcas looked startled. "You want *stereovision*?"

"You heard me. Tell Duke, if it's out of order, to pick a direction and start walking. Now git; we've got a busy night."

"All right," Dorcas agreed doubtfully, "but I ought to take your temperature first."

"Peace, woman!"

Duke had Harshaw's receiver hooked up in time to let Jubal see a rebroadcast of the second phony interview with the "Man from Mars." The commentary included a rumor about moving Smith to the Andes. Jubal put two and two together, after which he was calling people until morning. At dawn Dorcas brought him breakfast, six eggs beaten into brandy. He slurped them while reflecting that one advantage of a long life was that eventually a man knew almost everybody of importance—and could call on them in a pinch.

Harshaw had prepared a bomb but did not intend to

trigger it until the powers-that-be forced him. He realized that the government could haul Smith back into captivity on grounds that he was incompetent. His snap opinion was that Smith was legally insane and medically psychopathic by normal standards, the victim of a double-barreled situational psychosis of unique and monumental extent, first from being raised by non-humans and second from being pitched into another alien society.

But he regarded both the legal notion of sanity and the medical notion of psychosis as irrelevant. This human animal had made a profound and apparently successful adjustment to a non-human society—but as a malleable infant. Could he, as an adult with formed habits and canalized thinking, make another adjustment just as radical and much more difficult for an adult? Dr. Harshaw intended to find out; it was the first time in decades he had taken real interest in the practice of medicine.

Besides that, he was tickled at the notion of balking the powers-that-be. He had more than his share of that streak of anarchy which was the birthright of every American; pitting himself against the planetary government filled him with sharper zest than he had felt in a generation.

XI

AROUND A MINOR G-type star toward one edge of a medium-sized galaxy planets swung as they had for billions of years, under a modified inverse square law that shaped space. Four were big enough, as planets go, to be noticeable; the rest were pebbles, concealed in the fiery skirts of the primary or lost in black reaches of space. All, as is always the case, were infected with that oddity of distorted entropy called life; on the third and fourth planets surface temperatures cycled around the freezing point of hydrogen monoxide; in consequence they had developed life forms similar enough to permit a degree of social contact.

On the fourth pebble the ancient Martians were not disturbed by contact with Earth. Nymphs bounced joyously around the surface, learning to live and eight out of nine dying in the process. Adult Martians, enormously different in body and mind from nymphs, huddled in faerie, graceful cities and were as quiet as nymphs were boisterous—yet were even busier and led a rich life of the mind.

Adults were not free of work in the human sense; they had a planet to supervise; plants must be told when and where to grow, nymphs who had passed 'prenticeships by surviving must be gathered in, cherished, fertilized; the resultant eggs must be cherished and contemplated to encourage them to ripen properly, fulfilled nymphs must be persuaded to give up childish things and metamorphose into adults. All these must be done—but they were no more the "life" of Mars than is walking the dog twice a day the "life" of a man who bosses a planet-wide corporation between those walks—even though to a being from Arcturus III those walks might seem to be the tycoon's most significant activity—as a slave to the dog.

Martians and humans were both self-aware life forms but they had gone in vastly different directions. All human behavior, all human motivations, all man's hopes and fears, were colored and controlled by mankind's tragic and oddly beautiful pattern of reproduction. The same was true of Mars, but in mirror corollary. Mars had the efficient bipolar pattern so common in that galaxy, but Martians had it in form so different from Terran form that it would be "sex" only to a biologist and emphatically not have been "sex" to a human psychiatrist. Martian nymphs were female, all adults were male.

But in each in function only, not in psychology. The man-woman polarity which controlled human lives could not exist on Mars. There was no possibility of "marriage." Adults were huge, reminding the first humans to see them of ice boats under sail; they were physically passive, mentally active. Nymphs were fat, furry spheres, full of bounce and mindless energy. There was no parallel between human and Martian psychological foundations. Human bipolarity was both binding force and driving energy for all human behavior, from sonnets to nuclear equations. If any being thinks that human psychologists exaggerated this, let it search Terran patent offices, libraries, and art galleries for creations of eunuchs.

Mars, geared unlike Earth, paid little attention to the *Envoy* and the *Champion*. The events were too recent to be significant—if Martians had used newspapers, one edition a Terran century would have been ample. Contact with other races was nothing new to Martians; it had happened before, would happen again. When a new other race was thoroughly grokked, then (in a Terran millennium or so) would be time for action, if needed.

On Mars the currently important event was a different sort. The discorporate Old Ones had decided almost absent-mindedly to send the nestling human to grok what he could of the third planet, then turned attention back to

serious matters. Shortly before, around the time of the Terran Caesar Augustus, a Martian artist had been composing
a work of art. It could have been called a poem, a musical
opus, or a philosophical treatise; it was a series of emotions
arranged in tragic, logical necessity. Since it could be experienced by a human only in the sense in which a man blind
from birth might have a sunset explained to him, it does
not matter which category it be assigned. The important
point was that the artist had accidentally discorporated before he finished his masterpiece.

Unexpected discorporation was rare on Mars; Martian
taste in such matters called for life to be a rounded whole,
with physical death at the appropriate selected instant. This
artist, however, had become so preoccupied that he forgot
to come in out of the cold; when his absence was noticed
his body was hardly fit to eat. He had not noticed his discorporation and had gone on composing his sequence.

Martian art was divided into two categories: that sort
created by living adults, which was vigorous, often radical,
and primitive; and that of the Old Ones, which was usually
conservative, extremely complex, and was expected to
show much higher standards of technique; the two sorts
were judged separately.

By what standards should this opus be judged? It
bridged from corporate to discorporate; its final form had
been set throughout by an Old One—yet the artist, with
the detachment of all artists everywhere, had not noticed
the change in his status and had continued to work as if
corporate. Was it a new sort of art? Could more such pieces
be produced by surprise discorporation of artists while
they were working? The Old Ones had been discussing the
exciting possibilities in ruminative rapport for centuries

and all corporate Martians were eagerly awaiting their verdict.

The question was of greater interest because it was religious art (in the Terran sense) and strongly emotional: it described contact between the Martian Race and the people of the fifth planet, an event that had happened long ago but which was alive and important to Martians in the sense in which one death by crucifixion remained alive and important to humans after two Terran millennia. The Martian Race had encountered the people of the fifth planet, grokked them completely, and had taken action; asteroid ruins were all that remained, save that the Martians continued to cherish and praise the people they had destroyed. This new work of art was one of many attempts to grok the whole beautiful experience in all its complexity in one opus. But before it could be judged it was necessary to grok how to judge it.

It was a pretty problem.

On the third planet Valentine Michael Smith was not concerned with this burning issue; he had never heard of it. His Martian keeper and his keeper's water brothers had not mocked him with things he could not grasp. Smith knew of the destruction of the fifth planet just as any human school boy learns of Troy and Plymouth Rock, but he had not been exposed to art that he could not grok. His education had been unique, enormously greater than that of his nestlings, enormously less than that of an adult; his keeper and his keeper's advisers among the Old Ones had taken passing interest in seeing how much and of what sort this alien nestling could learn. The results had taught them more about the human race than that race had yet learned about itself, for Smith had grokked readily things that no other human being had ever learned.

At present Smith was enjoying himself. He had won a new water brother in Jubal, he had acquired many new friends, he was enjoying delightful new experiences in such kaleidoscopic quantity that he had no time to grok them; he could only file them away to be relived at leisure.

His brother Jubal told him that he would grok this strange and beautiful place more quickly if he would learn to read, so he took a day off to do so, with Jill pointing to words and pronouncing. It meant staying out of the swimming pool that day, which was a great sacrifice, as swimming (once he got it through his head that it was *permitted*) was not merely a delight but almost unbearable religious ecstasy. If Jill and Jubal had not told him to, he would never have come out of the pool at all.

Since he was not permitted to swim at night he read all night long. He was zipping through the Encyclopedia Britannica and sampling Jubal's medicine and law libraries as dessert. His brother Jubal saw him leafing through one of the books, stopped and questioned him about what he had read. Smith answered carefully, as it reminded him of tests the Old Ones had given him. His brother seemed upset at his answers and Smith found it necessary to go into meditation—he was sure that he had answered with the words in the book even though he did not grok them all.

But he preferred the pool to the books, especially when Jill and Miriam and Larry and the rest were all splashing each other. He did not learn at once to swim, but discovered that he could do something they could not. He went to the bottom and lay there, immersed in bliss—whereupon they hauled him out with such excitement that he was almost forced to withdraw, had it not been clear that they were concerned for his welfare.

Later he demonstrated this for Jubal, remaining on the bottom a delicious time, and tried to teach it to his brother Jill—but she became disturbed and he desisted. It was his first realization that there were things he could do that these new friends could not. He thought about it a long time, trying to grok its fullness.

SMITH WAS HAPPY; Harshaw was not. He continued his usual loafing, varied by casual observation of his laboratory animal. He arranged no schedule for Smith, no program of study, no regular physical examinations, but allowed Smith to run wild, like a puppy on a ranch. What supervision Smith received came from Gillian—more than enough, in Jubal's grumpy opinion; he took a dim view of males' being reared by females.

However, Gillian did little more than coach Smith in social behavior. He ate at the table now, dressed himself (Jubal thought he did; he made a note to ask Jill if she still had to assist him); he conformed to the household's informal customs and coped with new experiences on a "monkey-see-monkey-do" basis. Smith started his first meal at the table using only a spoon and Jill cut up his meat. By the end of the meal he was attempting to eat as others ate. At the next meal his manners were a precise imitation of Jill's, including superfluous mannerisms.

Even the discovery that Smith had taught himself to read with the speed of electronic scanning and appeared to have total recall of all that he read did not tempt Jubal Harshaw to make a "project" of Smith, with controls, measurements, and curves of progress. Harshaw had the arrogant humility of a man who has learned so much that he is aware of his own ignorance; he saw no point in "measurements" when he did not know what he was measuring.

But, while Harshaw enjoyed watching this unique animal develop into a mimicry copy of a human being, his pleasure afforded him no happiness.

Like Secretary General Douglas, Harshaw was waiting for the shoe to drop.

Having found himself coerced into action by expectation of action against him it annoyed Harshaw that nothing happened. Damn it, were Federation cops so stupid that they couldn't track an unsophisticated girl dragging an unconscious man across the countryside? Or had they been on her heels?—and now were keeping a stake-out on his place? The thought was infuriating; the notion that the government might be spying on his home, his castle, was as repulsive as having his mail opened.

They might be doing that, too! Government! Three-fourths parasitic and the rest stupid fumbling—oh, Harshaw conceded that man, a social animal, could not avoid government, any more than an individual could escape bondage to his bowels. But simply because an evil was inescapable was no reason to term it "good." He wished that government would wander off and get lost!

It was possible, even probable, that the administration knew where the Man from Mars was and chose to leave it that way.

If so, how long would it go on? And how long could he keep his "bomb" armed and ready?

And where the devil was that young idiot Ben Caxton?

* * *

JILL BOARDMAN FORCED him out of his spiritual thumb-twiddling. "Jubal?"

"Eh? Oh, it's you, bright eyes. Sorry, I was preoccupied. Sit down. Have a drink?"

"Uh, no, thank you. Jubal, I'm worried."

"Normal. That was a pretty swan dive. Let's see another like it."

Jill bit her lip and looked about twelve years old. "Jubal! Please listen! I'm terribly worried."

He sighed. "In that case, dry yourself off. The breeze is chilly."

"I'm warm enough. Uh, Jubal? Would it be all right if I left Mike here?"

Harshaw blinked. "Certainly. The girls will look out for him, he's no trouble. You're leaving?"

She didn't meet his eye. "Yes."

"Mmm . . . you're welcome here. But you're welcome to leave, if you wish."

"Huh? But, Jubal—I don't *want* to!"

"Then don't."

"But I *must*!"

"Play that back. I didn't scan it."

"Don't you *see*, Jubal? I like it here—you've been wonderful to us! But I can't stay. Not with Ben missing. I've *got* to look for him."

Harshaw said one earthy word, then added, "How do you plan to look for him?"

She frowned. "I don't know. But I can't lie around, loafing and swimming—with Ben missing."

"Gillian, Ben is a big boy. You're not his mother—nor

his wife. You haven't any call to go looking for him. Have you?"

Jill twisted one toe in the grass. "No," she admitted. "I haven't any claim on Ben. I just know . . . that if *I* were missing . . . Ben would look—until he found me. So *I've* got to look for *him*!"

Jubal breathed malediction against all gods involved in the follies of the human race, then said, "All right, let's get some logic into it. Do you plan to hire detectives?"

She looked unhappy. "I suppose that's the way to do it. Uh, I've never hired a detective. Are they expensive?"

"Quite."

Jill gulped. "Would they let me pay, uh, in monthly installments?"

"Cash at the stairs is their policy. Quit looking grim, child; I brought that up to dispose of it. I've already hired the best in the business to try to find Ben—there is no need to hock your future to hire second best."

"You didn't tell me!"

"No need to."

"But—Jubal, what did they find out?"

"Nothing," he admitted, "so there was no need to put you in the dumps by telling you." Jubal scowled. "I had thought you were unnecessarily nervy about Ben—I figured the same as his assistant, that fellow Kilgallen, that Ben had gone yiping off on some trail and would check in when he had the story." He sighed. "Now I don't think so. That knothead Kilgallen—he does have a message on file telling him that Ben would be away; my man saw it and sneaked a photograph and checked. The message was sent."

Jill looked puzzled. "Why didn't Ben send me one, too? It isn't like him—Ben's very thoughtful."

Jubal repressed a groan. "Use your head, Gillian. Just because a package says 'Cigarettes' does not prove it contains cigarettes. You got here Friday; the code groups on that statprint show it was filed from Philadelphia—Paoli Station Landing Flat—at ten thirty the morning before— 10:30 A.M. Thursday. It was transmitted and received at once; Ben's office has its own statprinter. All right, *you* tell *me* why Ben sent a printed message to his own office— during working hours—instead of telephoning?"

"Why, I don't think he would. At least I wouldn't. The telephone is the normal—"

"You aren't Ben. I can think of a dozen reasons for a man in Ben's business. To avoid garbles. To insure a record in the files of I.T.&T. for legal purposes. To send a delayed message. Lot of reasons. Kilgallen saw nothing odd—and the fact that Ben goes to the expense of a statprinter in his office shows that Ben uses it.

"However," Jubal went on, "that message placed Ben at Paoli Flat at ten thirty-four on Thursday. Jill, it was not sent from there."

"But—"

"One moment. Messages are either handed in or telephoned. If handed over the counter, the customer can have facsimile transmission of handwriting and signature . . . but if filed by phone, it has to be typed before it can be photographed."

"Yes, of course."

"Doesn't that suggest anything, Jill?"

"Uh . . . Jubal, I'm so worried I can't think."

"Quit breast-beating; it wouldn't have suggested

anything to me, either. But the pro working for me is a sneaky character; he went to Paoli with a statprint faked from the photograph taken under Kilgallen's nose—and with credentials that made it appear that he was 'Osbert Kilgallen,' the addressee. Then, with his fatherly manner and sincere face, he conned a young lady into telling things which she should have divulged only under court order— very sad. Ordinarily she wouldn't remember one message out of hundreds—they go in her ears, out her fingertips, and are gone, save for filed microprints. But this lady is one of Ben's fans; she reads his columns every night—a hideous vice." Jubal blinked. *"Front!"*

Anne appeared, dripping. "Remind me," Jubal told her, "to write an article on the compulsive reading of news. The theme will be that most neuroses can be traced to the unhealthy habit of wallowing in the troubles of five billion strangers. Title is 'Gossip Unlimited'—no, make that 'Gossip Gone Wild.'"

"Boss, you're getting morbid."

"Not me. Everybody else. See that I write it next week. Now vanish; I'm busy." He turned to Gillian. "She noticed Ben's name—thrilled because she was speaking to one of her heroes . . . but was irked because Ben hadn't paid for vision as well as voice. Oh, she remembers . . . and she remembers that the service was paid for by cash from a public booth—in Washington."

"'In Washington'?" repeated Jill. "Why would Ben call from—"

"Of course!" Jubal agreed pettishly. "If he's at a booth in Washington, he can have voice and vision with his assistant, cheaper, easier, and quicker than he could phone a message to be sent *back* to Washington from a hundred miles away. It doesn't make sense. Or it makes just one kind. Hanky-panky. Ben is as used to hanky-panky as a bride is to kisses. He didn't get to be the best winchell in the business through playing his cards face up."

"Ben is not a winchell! He's a lippmann!"

"Sorry, I'm colorblind in that range. He might have believed that his phone was tapped but his statprinter was not. Or suspected that both were tapped—and used this round-about relay to convince whoever was tapping him that he was away and would not be back soon." Jubal frowned. "In that case we would do him no favor by finding him. We might endanger his life.".

"Jubal! No!"

"Jubal, yes," he answered wearily. "That boy skates close to the edge; that's how he made his reputation. Jill, Ben has never tackled a more dangerous assignment. If he disappeared voluntarily—do you want to call attention to the fact? Kilgallen has him covered, Ben's column appears every day. I've made it my business to know."

"Canned columns!"

"Of course. Or perhaps Kilgallen is writing them. In any case, Ben Caxton is still officially on his soap box. Perhaps he planned it, my dear—because he was in such danger that he did not dare get in touch even with you. Well?"

Gillian covered her face. "Jubal . . . I don't know what to do!"

"Snap out of it," he said gruffly. "The worst that can happen to him is death . . . and that we all are in for—in days, or weeks, or years. Talk to Mike. He regards 'discorporation' as less to be feared than a scolding. Why, if I told Mike we were going to roast him for dinner, he would thank me for the honor with his voice choked with gratitude."

"I know," Jill agreed in a small voice, "but I don't have his philosophical attitude."

"Nor I," Harshaw agreed cheerfully, "but I'm beginning to grasp it—and it is a consoling one to a man my age. A capacity for enjoying the inevitable—why, I've been cultivating that all my life . . . but this infant, barely old enough to vote and too unsophisticated to stand clear of the horse cars, has me convinced that I've just reached kindergarten. Jill, you asked if Mike was welcome. Child, I want to keep that boy until I've found out what he knows and I don't! This 'discorporation' thing . . . it's not the Freudian 'death-wish'—none of that 'Even the weariest river' stuff—it's more like Stevenson's 'Glad did I live and gladly die and I lay me down with a will!' I suspect that Stevenson was whistling in the dark or enjoying the euphoria of consumption, but Mike has me halfway sold that he knows what he is talking about."

"I don't know," Jill answered dully. "I'm just worried about Ben."

"So am I," agreed Jubal. "Jill, I don't think Ben is hiding."

"But you said—"

"Sorry. My snoops didn't limit themselves to Ben's office and Paoli Flat. On Thursday morning Ben called at Bethesda Medical Center with a lawyer and a Fair Witness—James Oliver Cavendish, in case you follow such things."

"I don't, I'm afraid."

"No matter. The fact that Ben retained Cavendish shows how serious he was; you don't hunt rabbits with elephant guns. They were taken to see the 'Man from Mars'—"

Gillian gasped, then said, "That's impossible!"

"Jill, you're disputing a Fair Witness . . . and not just any Fair Witness. If Cavendish says it, it's gospel."

"I don't care if he's the Twelve Apostles! He wasn't on my floor last Thursday morning!"

"You didn't listen. I didn't say that they were taken to see Mike—I said they were taken to the 'Man from Mars.' The phony one, obviously—that fellow they stereovised."

"Oh. Of course. And Ben caught them!"

Jubal looked pained. "Little girl, Ben did not catch them. Even Cavendish did not—at least he won't say so. You know how Fair Witnesses behave."

"Well . . . no, I don't. I've never met one."

"So? *Anne*!"

Anne was on the springboard; she turned her head. Jubal called out, "That house on the hilltop—can you see what color they've painted it?"

Anne looked, then answered, "It's white on this side."

Jubal went on to Jill, "You see? It doesn't occur to Anne to infer that the other side is white, too. All the King's horses couldn't force her to commit herself . . . unless she went there and looked—and even then she wouldn't assume that it stayed white after she left."

"*Anne* is a Fair Witness?"

"Graduate, unlimited license, admitted to testify before the High Court. Sometime ask her why she gave up public practice. But don't plan anything else that day—the wench will recite the whole truth and nothing but the truth, which takes time. Back to Mr. Cavendish—Ben retained him for open witnessing, full disclosure, without enjoining privacy. So when Cavendish was questioned, he answered, in boring detail. The interesting part is what he does *not* say. He never states that the man they saw was *not* the Man from Mars . . . but not one word indicates that Cavendish accepted the exhibit as being the Man from Mars. If you knew Cavendish, this would be conclusive. If Cavendish had seen Mike, he would have reported with such exactness that you and I would *know* that he had seen Mike. For example, Cavendish reports the shape of this exhibit's ears . . . and it does not match Mike's ears. Q.E.D.; they were shown a phony. Cavendish knows it, though he is professionally restrained from giving opinions."

"I told you. They never came near my floor."

"But it tells us more. This occurred hours before you pulled your jail break; Cavendish sets their arrival in the presence of the phony at nine fourteen Thursday morning. So the government had Mike under their thumb at that moment; they could have exhibited Mike. Yet they risked offering a phony to the most noted Fair Witness in the country. Why?"

Jill answered, "You're asking me? I don't know. Ben told me that he intended to ask Mike if he wanted to leave the hospital—and help him if he said, 'Yes.'"

"Which Ben did try, with the phony."

"So? But, Jubal, they couldn't have known that Ben intended to . . . and, anyhow, Mike wouldn't have left with Ben."

"Later he left with you."

"Yes—but I was his 'water brother,' just as you are now. He has this crazy idea that he can trust anyone with whom he has shared a drink of water. With a 'water brother' he is docile . . . with anybody else he is stubborn as a mule. Ben couldn't have budged him." She added, "At least that is the way he was last week—he's changing awfully fast."

"So he is. Too fast, maybe. I've never seen muscle tissue develop so rapidly. Never mind, back to Ben—Cavendish reports that Ben dropped him and the lawyer, a chap named Frisby, at nine thirty-one, and Ben kept the cab. An hour later he—or somebody who said he was Ben—phoned that message to Paoli Flat."

"You don't think it was Ben?"

"I do not. Cavendish reported the number of the cab and my scouts tried to get a look at its daily trip tape. If Ben used his credit card, his charge number should be on the tape—but even if he fed coins into the meter the tape should show where the cab had been."

"Well?"

Harshaw shrugged. "The records show that cab in for repairs and never in use Thursday morning. So either a Fair Witness misremembered a cab's number or somebody tampered with the record." He added, "Maybe a jury would decide that even a Fair Witness could misread a number, especially if he had not been asked to remember it—but *I* don't believe it—not when the Witness is James Oliver Cavendish. He would either be certain—or his report would never mention it."

Harshaw scowled. "Jill, you're forcing me to rub my nose in it—and I don't like it! Granted that Ben could have sent that message, it is most unlikely that he could tamper with the record of that cab . . . and still less believable that he had reason to. Ben went somewhere—and somebody who could get at the records of a public carrier went to a lot of trouble to conceal where he went . . . and sent a phony message to keep anyone from realizing that he had disappeared."

"'Disappeared!' Kidnapped, you mean!"

"Softly, Jill. 'Kidnapped' is a dirty word."

"It's the only word! Jubal, how can you sit there when you ought to be shouting it from the—"

"Stop it, Jill! Instead of kidnapped, Ben might be dead."

Gillian slumped. "Yes," she agreed dully.

"But we'll assume he is not, until we see his bones. Jill, what's the greatest danger about kidnapping? It is a hue-and-cry—because a frightened kidnapper almost always kills his victim."

Gillian looked woeful. Harshaw went on gently, "I'm forced to say that it is likely that Ben is dead. He has been gone too long. But we've agreed to assume that he is alive. Now you intend to look for him. Gillian, how will you do this? Without increasing the risk that Ben will be killed by the unknown parties who kidnapped him?"

"Uh—But we know who they are!"

"Do we?"

"Of course! The same people who kept Mike a prisoner—the government!"

Harshaw shook his head. "That's an assumption. Ben has made many enemies with his column and not all of them are in government. However—" Harshaw frowned. "Your assumption is all we have to go on. But it's too sweeping. 'The government' is several million people. We must ask ourselves: Whose toes were stepped on? What individuals?"

"Why, Jubal, I told you, just as Ben told me. The Secretary General himself."

"No," Harshaw denied. "No matter who did what, if it is rough or illegal, it won't be the Secretary General, even if he benefits. Nobody could prove that he even knew it. It is likely he would *not* know—not about rough stuff. Jill, we need to find out which lieutenant in the Secretary General's staff of stooges handled this operation. That isn't as hopeless as it sounds—I think. When Ben was taken to see that phony, one of Douglas's assistants was with him—tried to talk him out of it, then went with him. It now appears that this same top-level stooge also dropped out of sight last Thursday. I don't think it's coincidence, since he appears to have been in charge of the phony 'Man from Mars.' If we find him, we may find Ben. Gilbert Berquist is his name and I have reason—"

"Berquist?"

"That's the name. I have reason to—Jill, what's the trouble? Don't faint or I'll dunk you in the pool!"

"Jubal. This 'Berquist.' Is there more than one Berquist?"

"Eh? He does seem to be a bit of a bastard; there might be only one. I mean the one on the Executive staff. Do you know him?"

"I don't know. But if it is the same one . . . I don't think there's any use looking for him."

"Mmm . . . talk, girl."

"Jubal . . . I'm terribly sorry—but I didn't tell you everything."

"People rarely do. All right, out with it."

Stumbling and stammering, Gillian told about the men who had disappeared. "And that's all," she concluded sadly. "I screamed and scared Mike . . . and he went into that trance—and then I had a *terrible* time getting here. I told you about that."

"Mmm . . . yes. I wish you had told me this, too."

She turned red. "I didn't think anybody would believe me. And I was scared. Jubal, can they do anything to us?"

"Eh?" Jubal seemed surprised.

"Send us to jail, or something?"

"Oh. My dear, it is not a crime to be present at a miracle.

Nor to work one. But this has more aspects than a cat has hair. Let me think."

Jubal held still about ten minutes. Then he opened his eyes and said, "I don't see your problem child. He's probably on the bottom of the pool—"

"He is."

"—so dive in and get him. Bring him to my study. I want to see if he can repeat this . . . and we don't want an audience. No, we need one; tell Anne to put on her Witness robe—I want her in her official capacity. I want Duke, too."

"Yes, Boss."

"You're not privileged to call me 'Boss'; you're not tax deductible."

"Yes, Jubal."

"Mmm . . . I wish we had somebody who never would be missed. Can Mike do this stunt with inanimate objects?"

"I don't know."

"We'll find out. Haul him out and wake him up." Jubal blinked. "What a way to dispose of—no, I mustn't be tempted. See you upstairs, girl."

XII

A FEW MINUTES later Jill reported to Jubal's study. Anne was there in the white robe of her guild; she glanced up, said nothing. Jill found a chair and kept quiet, as Jubal was dictating to Dorcas; he did not look up and went on:

"—under the sprawled body, soaking a corner of the rug and seeping out in a dark red pool on the hearth, where it was attracting the attention of two unemployed flies. Miss Simpson clutched at her mouth. 'Dear me!' she said in a distressed voice, 'Daddy's favorite rug! . . . and Daddy, too, I do believe.' End of chapter, Dorcas, and of first installment. Mail it off. Git."

Dorcas left, taking her shorthand machine and smiling to Jill. Jubal said, "Where's Mike?"

"Dressing," answered Gillian. "He'll be along soon."

"'Dressing'?" Jubal repeated peevishly. "I didn't say the party was formal."

"But he has to dress."

"Why? It makes no never-mind whether you kids wear skin or overcoats. Chase him in."

"Please, Jubal. He's got to learn."

"Humph! You're forcing on him your own narrow-minded, middle-class, Bible Belt morality."

"I am not! I'm simply teaching him necessary customs."

"Customs, morals—is there a difference? Woman, here, by the grace of God and an inside straight, we have a personality untouched by the psychotic taboos of our tribe—and *you* want to turn him into a copy of every fourth-rate conformist in this frightened land! Why not go whole hog? Get him a briefcase."

"I'm not doing anything of the sort! I'm just trying to keep him out of trouble. It's for his own good."

Jubal snorted. "That's the excuse they gave the tomcat before his operation."

"Oh!" Jill appeared to count to ten. She said bleakly, "This is your house, Doctor Harshaw, and we are in your debt. I will fetch Michael at once." She stood up.

"Hold it, Jill."

"Sir?"

"Sit down—and quit trying to be as nasty as I am; you don't have my years of practice. Now let's get something straight: you are not in my debt. Impossible—because I never do anything I don't want to. Nor does anyone, but in my case I know it. So please don't invent a debt that does not exist, or next you will be trying to feel gratitude—and that is the treacherous first step toward complete moral degradation. You grok that?"

Jill bit her lip, then grinned. "I'm not sure what 'grok' means."

"Nor I. I intend to go on taking lessons from Mike until I do. But I was speaking seriously. 'Gratitude' is a euphemism for resentment. Resentment from most people I do not mind—but from pretty little girls it is distasteful."

"Why, Jubal, I don't resent you—that's silly."

"I hope you don't . . . but you will if you don't root out of your mind this delusion that you are indebted to me. The Japanese have five ways to say 'thank you'—and every one translates as resentment, in various degrees. Would that English had the same built-in honesty! Instead, English can define sentiments that the human nervous system is incapable of experiencing. 'Gratitude,' for example."

"Jubal, you're a cynical old man. I do feel grateful to you and I shall go on feeling grateful."

"And you are a sentimental young girl. That makes us a complementary pair. Let's go to Atlantic City for a weekend of illicit debauchery, just us two."

"Why, Jubal!"

"You see how deep your gratitude goes?"

"Oh. I'm ready. When do we leave?"

"Hummph! We should have left forty years ago. The second point is that you are right; Mike must learn human customs. He must take off his shoes in a mosque, wear his hat in a synagogue, and cover his nakedness when taboo requires, or our shamans will burn him for deviationism. But, child, by the myriad aspects of Ahriman, don't brainwash him. Make sure he is cynical about it."

"Uh, I'm not sure I can. Mike doesn't seem to have any cynicism in him."

"So? Well, I'll lend a hand. Shouldn't he be dressed by now?"

"I'll go see."

"In a moment. Jill, I explained why I am not anxious to accuse anyone of kidnapping Ben. If Ben is unlawfully detained (to put it at its sweetest), we have not crowded anyone into getting rid of evidence by getting rid of Ben. If he is alive, he stands a chance of staying alive. But I took other steps the first night you were here. You know your Bible?"

"Uh, not very well."

"It merits study, it contains practical advice for most emergencies. '—every one that doeth evil hateth the light—' John something or other, Jesus to Nicodemus. I have been expecting an attempt to get Mike away from us, for it didn't seem likely that you had covered your tracks. But this is a lonely place and we haven't any heavy artillery. There is one weapon that might balk them. Light. The glaring spotlight of publicity. So I arranged for any ruckus here to have publicity. Not just a little that might be hushed up—but great gobs, world wide and all at once. Details do not matter—where cameras are mounted and what linkages have been rigged—but if a fight breaks out here, it will be seen by three networks and hold-for-release messages will be delivered to a spread of V.I.P.s—all of whom would like to catch our Honorable Secretary General with his pants down."

Harshaw frowned. "But I can't maintain it indefinitely. When I set it up, my worry was to move fast enough— I expected trouble at once. Now I think we are going to have to force action, while I can still keep a spotlight on us."

"What sort of action, Jubal?"

"I've been fretting about it the past three days. You gave me a glimmering of an approach with that story of what happened in Ben's apartment."

"I'm sorry I didn't tell you sooner, Jubal. I didn't think anybody would believe me— and it makes me feel good that you do."

"I didn't say I believed you."

"What? But you—"

"I think you told the truth, Jill. But a dream is a true experience of a sort and so is a hypnotic delusion. But what happens in this room during the next hour will be seen by a Fair Witness and by cameras which are—" He pressed a button. "—rolling now. I don't think Anne can be hypnotized when she's on duty and I'll lay odds that cameras can't be. We will find out what kind of truth we're dealing with— after which we can consider how to force the powers-that-be to drop the other shoe . . . and maybe figure a way to help Ben, too. Go get Mike."

MIKE'S DELAY WAS not mysterious. He had tied his left shoe-string to his right—had stood up, tripped himself, fallen flat, and jerked the knots almost hopelessly tight. He spent the rest of the time analyzing his predicament and slowly getting the snarl untied and the strings correctly tied. He was not aware that he had taken long but was troubled that he had failed to repeat correctly something which Jill had taught him. He confessed his failure even though he had it repaired when she came to fetch him.

She soothed him, combed his hair, herded him in. Harshaw looked up. "Hi, son. Sit down."

"Hi, Jubal," Valentine Michael Smith answered gravely, sat down—waited.

Harshaw said, "Well, boy, what have you learned today?"

Smith smiled happily, then answered—as always with a pause. "I have today learned to do a one-and-a-half gainer. That is a jumping, a dive, for entering our water by—"

"I know, I saw you. Keep your toes pointed, knees straight, and feet together."

Smith looked unhappy. "I rightly did not it do?"

"You did it very rightly, for a first time. Watch Dorcas."

Smith considered this. "The water groks Dorcas. It cherishes him."

"'Her.' Dorcas is 'her,' not 'him.'"

"'Her,'" Smith corrected. "Then my speaking was false? I have read in Webster's New International Dictionary of the English Language, Third Edition, published in Springfield, Massachusetts, that the masculine gender includes the feminine gender in speaking. In Hagworth's Law of Contracts, Fifth Edition, Chicago, Illinois, 1978, on page 1012, it says—"

"Hold it," Harshaw said hastily. "Masculine forms do include the feminine, when you are speaking in general—but not when talking about a particular person. Dorcas is always 'she' or 'her'—never 'he' or 'him.'"

"I will remember."

"You had better—or you may provoke Dorcas into proving just how female she is." Harshaw blinked thoughtfully. "Jill, is the lad sleeping with you? Or one of you?"

She hesitated, then answered flatly, "So far as I know, Mike doesn't sleep."

"You evaded my question."

"Then you can assume that I intended to. However, he is not sleeping with *me*."

"Mmm . . . damn it, my interest is scientific. Mike, what else have you learned?"

"I have learned two ways to tie my shoes. One way is only good for lying down. The other way is good for walking. And I have learned conjugations. I am, thou art, he is, we are, you are, they are, I was, thou wast—"

"Okay, that's enough. What else?"

Mike smiled delightedly. "To yesterday I am learning to drive the tractor, brightly, brightly, and with beauty."

"Eh?" Jubal turned to Jill. "When was this?"

"Yesterday while you were napping, Jubal. It's all right—Duke was careful not to let him get hurt."

"Umm . . . well, obviously he didn't. Mike, have you been reading?"

"Yes, Jubal."

"What?"

"I have read," Mike recited, "three more volumes of the Encyclopedia, Maryb to Mushe, Mushr to Ozon, P to Planti. You have told me not to read too much of the Encyclopedia at one reading, so I then stopped. I then read the *Tragedy of Romeo and Juliet* by Master William Shakespeare of London. I then read the *Memoirs of Jacques Casanova de Seingalt* as translated into English by Arthur Machen. I then read *The Art of Cross-Examination* by

Francis Wellman. I then tried to grok what I had read until Jill told me that I must come to breakfast."

"And did you grok it?"

Smith looked troubled. "Jubal, I do not know."

"Something bothering you?"

"I do not grok all fullness of what I read. In the history written by Master William Shakespeare I found myself full of happiness at the death of Romeo. Then I read on and learned that he had discorporated too soon—or so I thought I grokked. Why?"

"He was a blithering young idiot."

"Beg pardon?"

"I don't know, Mike."

Smith considered this. Then he muttered in Martian and added, "I am only an egg."

"Eh? You say that when you want to ask a favor, Mike. What is it?"

Smith hesitated. Then he blurted, "Jubal my brother, would please you ask Romeo why he discorporated? I cannot ask him; I am only an egg. But you can—and then you could teach me the grokking of it."

Jubal saw that Mike believed that Romeo had been a living person and managed to grasp that Mike expected him to conjure up Romeo's ghost and demand explanations for his conduct in the flesh. But to explain that the Capulets and Montagues had never had corporated existence was another matter. The concept of fiction was beyond Mike's experience; there was nothing on which it could rest. Jubal's attempts to explain were so upsetting to Mike that Jill was afraid that he was about to roll up into a ball.

Mike saw how perilously close he was to that necessity

and had learned that he must not resort to this refuge in the presence of friends, because (with the exception of his brother Doctor Nelson) it caused them emotional disturbance. So he made a mighty effort, slowed his heart, calmed his emotions, and smiled. "I will waiting till a grokking comes of itself."

"Good," agreed Jubal. "Hereafter, before you read anything, ask me or Jill, or somebody, whether or not it is fiction. I don't want you mixed up."

"I will ask, Jubal." Mike decided that, when he did grok this strange idea, he must report the fullness to the Old Ones . . . and found himself wondering if the Old Ones knew about "fiction." The incredible idea that there might be something as strange to the Old Ones as it was to himself was so much more revolutionary than the weird concept of fiction that he put it aside to cool, saved it for meditation.

"—but I didn't," his brother Jubal was saying, "call you in to discuss literary forms. Mike, remember the day that Jill took you away from the hospital?"

"'Hospital'?" Mike repeated.

"I'm not sure, Jubal," Jill interrupted, "that Mike knew it was a hospital. Let me try."

"Go ahead."

"Mike, you remember where you were, where you lived alone in a room, before I dressed you and took you away."

"Yes, Jill."

"Then we went to another place and I undressed you and gave you a bath."

Smith smiled in recollection. "Yes. It was great happiness."

"Then I dried you off—and two men came."

Smith's smile wiped away. He began to tremble and huddle into himself.

Jill said, "Mike! Stop it! Don't you dare go away!"

Mike took control of his being. "Yes, Jill."

"Listen, Mike. I want you to think about that time—but you mustn't get upset. There were two men. One of them pulled you out into the living room."

"The room with the joyful grasses," he agreed.

"That's right. He pulled you into the room with the grass floor and I tried to stop him. He hit me. Then he was gone. You remember?"

"You are not angry?"

"What? No, no, not at all. One man disappeared, then the other pointed a gun at me—and then he was gone. I was frightened—but I was not angry."

"You are not angry with me now?"

"Mike, dear—I have *never* been angry with you. Jubal and I want to know what happened. Those two men were there; you did something . . . and they were gone. What was it you did? Can you tell us?"

"I will tell. The man—the big man—hit you . . . and I frightened, too. So I—" He croaked in Martian, looked puzzled. "I do not know words."

Jubal said, "Mike, can you explain it a little at a time?"

"I will try, Jubal. Something is in front of me. It is a wrong thing and must not be. So I reach out—" He looked perplexed. "It is an easy thing. Tying shoe laces is much more hard. But the words not are. I am very sorry." He considered it. "Perhaps the words are in Plants to Raym, or Rayn to Sarr, or Sars to Sorc. I will read them tonight and tell you at breakfast."

"Maybe," Jubal admitted. "Just a minute, Mike." He

went to a corner and returned with a case which had contained brandy. "Can you make this go away?"

"This is a wrong thing?"

"Well, assume that it is."

"But—Jubal, I must *know* that it is a wrong thing. This is a box. I do not grok it exists wrongly."

"Mmm—Suppose I picked this up and threw it at Jill?"

Smith said with gentle sadness, "Jubal, you would not do that to Jill."

"Uh . . . damn it, I guess not. Jill, will you throw the box at me? Hard—a scalp wound at least, if Mike can't protect me."

"Jubal, I don't like the idea."

"Oh, come on! In the interest of science . . . and Ben Caxton."

"But—" Jill jumped up, grabbed the box, threw it at Jubal's head. Jubal intended to stand fast—but reflex won; he ducked.

"Missed me," he said. "Confound it, I wasn't watching. I meant to keep my eyes on it." He looked at Smith. "Mike, is that the—What's the matter, boy?"

The Man from Mars was trembling and looking unhappy. Jill put her arms around him. "There, there, it's all right, dear! You did it beautifully. It never touched Jubal. It simply vanished."

"I guess it did," Jubal admitted, looking around and chewing his thumb. "Anne, were you watching?"

"Yes."

"What did you see?"

"The box did not simply vanish. The process lasted some fraction of a second. From where I am sitting it appeared to shrink, as if it were disappearing into the distance. But it did not go outside the room; I could see it up to the instant it disappeared."

"Where did it go?"

"That is all I can report."

"Mmm . . . we'll run films later—but I'm convinced. Mike—"

"Yes, Jubal?"

"Where is that box?"

"The box is—" Smith paused. "Again I have not words. I am sorry."

"I'm confused. Son, can you reach in and haul it out?"

"Beg pardon?"

"You made it go away; now make it come back."

"How can I? The box is *not*."

Jubal looked thoughtful. "If this method becomes popular, it'll change the rules for corpus delicti. 'I've got a little list . . . they never will be missed.' Mike, how close do you have to be?"

"Beg pardon?"

"If you had been in the hallway and I had been back by the window—oh, thirty feet—could you have stopped it from hitting me?"

Smith appeared mildly surprised. "Yes."

"Hmm . . . come to the window. Suppose Jill and I were on the far side of the pool and you were here. Could you have stopped the box?"

"Yes, Jubal."

"Well . . . suppose Jill and I were down at the gate, a quarter of a mile away. Is that too far?"

Smith hesitated. "Jubal, it is not distance. It is not seeing. It is knowing."

"Hmm . . . let's see if I grok it. It doesn't matter how far. You don't even have to see it. If you know that a bad thing is happening, you can stop it. Right?"

Smith looked troubled. "Almost is right. But I am not long out of the nest. For knowing I must see. An Old One does not need eyes to know. He knows. He groks. He acts. I am sorry."

"I don't know why you're sorry," Jubal said gruffly. "The High Minister for Peace would have declared you Top Secret ten minutes ago."

"Beg pardon?"

"Never mind." Jubal returned to his desk, picked up a heavy ash tray. "Jill, don't aim at my face. Okay, Mike, stand in the hallway."

"Jubal . . . my brother . . . *please* not!"

"What's the trouble? I want one more demonstration— and this time I won't take my eyes off it."

"Jubal   "

"Yes, Jill?"

"I grok what is bothering Mike."

"Well, tell me."

"We did an experiment where I was about to hurt you with that box. But we are his water brothers—so it upset Mike that I even tried. I think there is something very unMartian about such a situation."

Harshaw frowned. "Maybe it should be investigated by the Committee on unMartian Activities."

"I'm not joking, Jubal."

"Nor I. All right, Jill, I'll re-rig it." Harshaw handed the ash tray to Mike. "Feel how heavy it is, son. See those sharp corners."

Smith examined it gingerly. Harshaw went on, "I'm going to throw it up—and let it hit me in the head as it comes down."

Mike stared. "My brother . . . you will now discorporate?"

"Eh? No, no! But it will hurt me—unless you stop it. Here we go!" Harshaw tossed it straight up within inches of the high ceiling.

The ash tray topped its trajectory, stopped.

Harshaw looked at it, feeling stuck in one frame of a motion picture. He croaked, "Anne. What do you see?"

She answered in a flat voice, "That ash tray is five inches from the ceiling. I do not see anything holding it up." She added, "Jubal, I *think* that's what I'm seeing . . . but if the cameras don't show the same thing, I'm going to tear up my license."

"Um. Jill?"

"It floats . . ."

Jubal went to his desk and sat down without taking his eyes off the ash tray. "Mike," he said, "why didn't it disappear?"

"But, Jubal," Mike said apologetically, "you said to stop it; you did not say to make it go away. When I made the box go away, you wanted it to be again. Have I done wrongly?"

"Oh. No, you have done exactly right. I keep forgetting that you take things literally." Harshaw recalled insults common in his early years—and reminded himself *never* to use such to Mike—if he told the boy to drop dead or get lost, Harshaw felt certain that the literal meaning would ensue.

"I am glad," Smith answered soberly. "I am sorry I

could not make the box be again. I am sorry twice that I wasted food. Then a necessity was. Or so I grokked."

"Eh? What food?"

Jill said hastily, "He's talking about those men, Jubal. Berquist and the man with him."

"Oh, yes." Harshaw reflected that he retained unMartian notions of food. "Mike, don't worry about wasting that 'food.' I doubt if a meat inspector would have passed them. In fact," he added, recalling the Federation convention about "long pig," "they would have been condemned as unfit to eat. Besides, it was a necessity. You grokked the fullness and acted rightly."

"I am much comforted," Mike answered with relief in his voice. "Only an Old One can always be sure of right action at a cusp . . . and I have much learning to learn and growing to grow before I may join the Old Ones. Jubal? May I move it? I am tiring."

"You want to make it go away? Go ahead."

"But I cannot."

"Eh? Why not?"

"Your head is no longer under it. I do not grok wrongness in its being, where it is."

"Oh. All right. Move it." Harshaw continued to watch, expecting it to float to the spot now over his head and thus regain a wrongness. Instead the ash tray slanted downward until it was close above his desk, hovered, then came in to a landing.

"Thank you, Jubal," said Smith.

"Eh? Thank *you*, son!" Jubal picked up the ash tray. It was as commonplace as ever. "Yes, thank *you*. For the most amazing experience I've had since the hired girl took me up into the attic." He looked up. "Anne, you trained at Rhine."

"Yes."

"Have you seen levitation before?"

She hesitated. "I've seen what was called telekinesis with dice—but I'm no mathematician and cannot testify that it was telekinesis."

"Hell's bells, you wouldn't testify that the sun had risen if the day was cloudy."

"How could I? Somebody might be supplying artificial light above the cloud layer. One of my classmates could apparently levitate objects about the mass of a paper clip—but he had to be three drinks drunk. I was not able to examine it closely enough to testify . . . because I had been drinking, too."

"You've never seen anything like this?"

"No."

"Mmm . . . I'm through with you professionally. If you want to stay, hang up your robe and drag up a chair."

"Thanks, I will. But, in view of your lecture about mosques and synagogues, I'll change in my room."

"Suit yourself. Wake up Duke and tell him I want the cameras serviced."

"Yes, Boss. Don't let anything happen until I get back." Anne headed for the door.

"No promises. Mike, sit at my desk. Now, can you pick up that ash tray? Show me."

"Yes, Jubal." Smith reached out and took it in his hand.

"No, no!"

"I did wrongly?"

"No, it was my mistake. I want to know if you can lift it *without* touching it?"

"Yes, Jubal."

"Well? Are you tired?"

"No, Jubal."

"Then what's the matter? Does it have to have a 'wrongness'?"

"No, Jubal."

"Jubal," Jill interrupted, "you haven't *told* him to—you just asked if he could."

"Oh." Jubal looked sheepish. "Mike, will you please, without touching it, lift that ash tray a foot above the desk?"

"Yes, Jubal." The ash tray raised, floated above the desk. "Will you measure, Jubal?" Mike said anxiously. "If I did wrongly, I will move it."

"That's fine! Can you hold it? If you get tired, tell me."

"I will tell."

"Can you lift something else, too? Say this pencil? If you can, do it."

"Yes, Jubal." The pencil ranged itself by the ash tray.

By request, Mike added other articles to the floating objects. Anne returned, pulled up a chair, and silently watched. Duke came in carrying a step ladder, glanced, looked a second time, said nothing, and set up the ladder. At last Mike said uncertainly, "I am not sure, Jubal. I—" He seemed to search for a word. "I am idiot in these things."

"Don't wear yourself out."

"I can think one more. I hope." A paper weight stirred, lifted—and the dozen-odd floating objects all fell down. Mike seemed about to weep. "Jubal, I am utmostly sorry."

Harshaw patted his shoulder. "You should be proud. Son, what you just did is—" Jubal searched for a comparison within Mike's experience. "What you did is harder than tying shoe-strings, more wonderful than doing a one-and-a-half gainer perfectly. You did it, uh, 'brightly, brightly, and with beauty.' You grok?"

Mike looked surprised. "I should not feel shame?"

"You should feel proud."

"Yes, Jubal," he answered contentedly. "I feel proud."

"Good. Mike, I cannot lift even one ash tray without touching it."

Smith looked startled. "You cannot?"

"No. Can you teach me?"

"Yes, Jubal. You—" Smith stopped, looked embarrassed. "I again have not words. I will read and read and read, until I find words. Then I will teach my brother."

"Don't set your heart on it."

"Beg pardon?"

"Mike, don't be disappointed if you do not find the words. They may not be in the English language."

Smith considered this. "Then I will teach my brother the language of my nest."

"You may have arrived fifty years late."

"I have acted wrongly?"

"Not at all. You might start by teaching Jill your language."

"It hurts my throat," objected Jill.

"Try gargling aspirin." Jubal looked at her. "That's a feeble excuse, Nurse. You're hired as research assistant for Martian linguistics . . . which includes extra duties as may be necessary. Anne, put her on the payroll—and be sure it gets in the tax records."

"She's been doing her share in the kitchen. Shall I date it back?"

Jubal shrugged. "Don't bother me with details."

"But, Jubal," Jill protested, "I don't think I *can* learn Martian!"

"You can *try*."

"But—"

"What was that about 'gratitude?' Do you take the job?"

Jill bit her lip. "I'll take it. Yes . . . Boss."

Smith timidly touched her hand. "Jill . . . I will teach."

Jill patted his. "Thanks, Mike." She looked at Harshaw. "I'm going to learn it just to spite you!"

He grinned at her. "That motive I grok—you'll learn it. Mike, what else can you do that we can't?"

Smith looked puzzled. "I do not know."

"How could he," protested Jill, "when he doesn't know what we can and can't do?"

"Mmm . . . yes. Anne, change that title to 'assistant for Martian linguistics, culture, and techniques.' Jill, in learning their language you are bound to stumble onto things that are different, really different—and when you do, tell me. And, Mike, if you notice anything which you can do but we don't, tell me."

"I will tell, Jubal. What things will be these?"

"I don't know. Things like you just did . . . and being able to stay on the bottom of the pool longer than we can. Hmm . . . Duke!"

"Boss, I've got both hands full of film."

"You can talk, can't you? I noticed the pool is murky."

"I'm going to add precipitant tonight and vacuum it in the morning."

"How's the count?"

"It's okay, the water is safe enough to serve at the table. It just looks messy."

"Let it be. I'll let you know when I want it cleaned."

"Hell, Boss, nobody likes to swim in dishwater."

"Anybody too fussy can stay dry. Quit jawing, Duke. Films ready?"

"Five minutes."

"Good. Mike, do you know what a gun is?"

"A gun," Smith answered carefully, "is a piece of ord-nance for throwing projectiles by force of some explosive, as gunpowder, consisting of a tube or barrel closed at one end, where the—"

"Okay, okay. Do you grok it?"

"I am not sure."

"Have you ever seen a gun?"

"I do not know."

"Why, certainly you have," Jill interrupted. "Mike, think back to that time we talked about, in the room with the grass floor—but don't get upset! One man hit me."

"Yes."

"The other pointed something at me."

"He pointed a bad thing at you."

"That was a gun."

"I had thought that the word for that bad thing might be 'gun.' Webster's New International Dictionary of the English Language, Third Edition, published in—"

"That's fine, son," Harshaw said hastily. "Now listen. If someone points a gun at Jill, what will you do?"

Smith paused longer than usual. "You will not be angry if I waste food?"

"No. Under those circumstances no one would be an-gry at you. But I want to know something else. Could you make the gun go away, without making the man go away?"

Smith considered it. "Save the food?"

"Uh, that isn't what I mean. Could you cause the gun to go away without hurting the man?"

"Jubal, he would not hurt. I would make the gun go away, the man I would just stop. He would feel no pain.

He would simply discorporate. The food would not damage."

Harshaw sighed. "Yes, I'm sure that's the way it would be. But could you cause to go away just the gun? Not 'stop' the man, not kill him, just let him go on living?"

Smith considered it. "That would be easier than doing both at once. But, Jubal, if I left him corporate, he might still hurt Jill. Or so I grok it."

Harshaw stopped to remind himself that this baby innocent was neither babyish nor innocent—was in fact sophisticated in a culture which he was beginning to realize was far in advance of human culture in mysterious ways . . . and that these naive remarks came from a superman—or what would do for a "superman." He answered Smith, choosing words carefully as he had in mind a dangerous experiment.

"Mike . . . if you reach a—'cusp'—where you must do something to protect Jill, you do it."

"Yes, Jubal. I will."

"Don't worry about wasting food. Don't worry about anything else. Protect Jill."

"Always I will protect Jill."

"Good. But suppose a man pointed a gun—or simply had it in his hand. Suppose you did not want to kill him . . . but needed to make the gun go away. Could you do it?"

Mike paused briefly. "I think I grok it. A gun is a wrong thing. But it might be needful for the man to remain corporate." He thought. "I can do it."

"Good. Mike, I am going to show you a gun. A gun is a wrong thing."

"A gun is a wrong thing. I will make it go away."

"Don't make it go away as soon as you see it."

"Not?"

"Not. I will lift the gun and start to point it at you. Before I can get it pointed at you, make it go away. But don't stop me, don't hurt me, don't kill me, don't do *anything* to *me*. Don't waste me as food, either."

"Oh, I never would," Mike said earnestly. "When you discorporate, my brother Jubal, I hope to be allowed to eat of you myself, praising and cherishing you with every bite . . . until I grok you in fullness."

Harshaw controlled a reflex and answered gravely, "Thank you, Mike."

"It is I who must thank you, my brother—and if it should be that I am selected before you, I hope that you will find me worthy of grokking. Sharing me with Jill. You would share me with Jill? Please?"

Harshaw glanced at Jill, saw that she kept her face serene—reflected that she probably was a rock-steady scrubbed nurse. "I will share you with Jill," he said solemnly. "But, Mike, none of us will be food any time soon. I am going to show you this gun—and you wait until I say . . . and then be very careful, because I have many things to do before I am ready to discorporate."

"I will be careful, my brother."

"All right." Harshaw opened a drawer. "Look in here, Mike. See the gun? I'm going to pick it up. But don't do anything until I tell you." Harshaw reached for the gun, an elderly police special, took it out. "Get ready, Mike. *Now!*" Harshaw did his best to aim the weapon at Smith.

His hand was empty.

Jubal found that he was shaking, so he stopped. "Perfect!" he said. "You got it before I had it aimed."

"I am happy."

"So am I. Duke, did that get in the camera?"

"Yup."

"Good." Harshaw sighed. "That's all, kids. Run along."

Anne said, "Boss? You'll tell me what the films show?"

"Want to stay and see them?"

"Oh, no! I couldn't, not the parts I Witnessed. But I want to know—later—whether or not they show that I've slipped my clutches."

"Okay."

XIII

WHEN THEY HAD gone, Harshaw started to give orders to Duke—then said grumpily, "What are you looking sour about?"

"Boss, when do we get rid of that ghoul?"

"'Ghoul'? Why, you provincial lout!"

"Okay, so I'm from Kansas. Never was any cannibalism in Kansas. I'm eating in the kitchen until he leaves."

Harshaw said icily, "So? Anne can have your check ready in five minutes. It ought not to take more than ten to pack your comic books and your other shirt."

Duke had been setting up a projector. He stopped. "Oh, I didn't mean I was quitting."

"It means that to me, son."

"But—what the hell? I've eaten in the kitchen lots of times."

"Other circumstances. Nobody under my roof refuses to eat at my table because he won't eat with others who eat there. I am an almost extinct breed, an old-fashioned gentleman—which means I can be a cast-iron son of bitch when it suits me. It suits me right now . . . which is to say that no ignorant, superstitious, prejudiced bumpkin is permitted to tell me who is fit to eat at *my* table. I dine with publicans and sinners, that is my business. I do not break bread with Pharisees."

Duke said slowly, "I ought to pop you one—and I would, if you were my age."

"Don't let that stop you. I may be tougher than you think. If not, the commotion will fetch the others. Do you think you can handle the Man from Mars?"

"*Him?* I could break him in two with one hand!"

"Probably . . . if you could lay a hand on him."

"Huh?"

"You saw me try to point a pistol at him. Duke—*where's that pistol?* Find that pistol. Then tell me whether you still think you can break Mike in two. But find the pistol first."

Duke went ahead setting up the projector. "Some sleight-of-hand. The films will show it."

Harshaw said, "Duke. Stop fiddling with that. Sit down. I'll take care of it after you've left."

"Huh? Jubal, I don't want you touching this projector. You always get it out of whack."

"Sit down, I said."

"But—"

"Duke, I'll bust the damned thing if it suits me. I do not accept service from a man after he has resigned."

"Hell, I didn't resign! You got nasty and fired me—for no reason."

"Sit down, Duke," Harshaw said quietly, "and let me try to save your life—or get off this place as fast as you can. Don't stop to pack. You might not live that long."

"What the hell do you mean?"

"Exactly what I say. Duke, it's irrelevant whether you resigned or were fired; you ended your employment when you announced that you would not eat at my table. Nevertheless I would find it distasteful for you to be killed on my premises. So sit down and I will do my best to avoid it."

Duke looked startled and sat down. Harshaw went on, "Are you Mike's water brother?"

"Huh? Of course not. Oh, I've heard such chatter—it's nonsense, if you ask me."

"It is not nonsense and nobody asked you; you aren't competent to have an opinion." Harshaw frowned. "Duke, I don't want to fire you; you keep the gadgetry working and save me from annoyance by mechanical buffoonery. But I must get you safely off the place—and then find out who else is not a water brother to Mike . . . and see that they become such—or send them away, too." Jubal chewed his lip. "Maybe it would be enough to exact a promise from Mike not to hurt anyone without my permission. Mmmm . . . no, too much horse play around here—and Mike is prone to misinterpret things. Say if you—or Larry, since you won't be here . . . picked up Jill and tossed her into the pool, Larry might wind up where that pistol went before I could explain to Mike that Jill was not in danger. Larry is entitled to live his life without having it cut short through my carelessness. Duke, I believe in everyone's working out his own damnation but that is no excuse to give a dynamite cap to a baby."

Duke said slowly, "Boss, you've come unzipped. Mike wouldn't hurt anybody—shucks, this cannibalism talk makes me want to throw up but don't get me wrong; he's a savage, he doesn't know any better. But he's gentle as a lamb—he would never hurt anybody."

"You think so?"

"I'm certain."

"So. You've got guns in your room. I say he's dangerous. It's open season on Martians; pick a gun, go down to the pool and kill him. Don't worry about the law; I guarantee you'll never be indicted. Go ahead, do it!"

"Jubal . . . you don't mean that."

"No. Not really. Because you *can't*. If you tried, your gun would go where my pistol went—and if you hurried him you'd go with it. Duke, you don't know what you are fiddling with. Mike is *not* 'gentle as a lamb' and he is *not* a savage. I suspect we are savages. Ever raise snakes?"

"Uh . . . no."

"I did, when I was a kid. One winter down in Florida I caught what I thought was a scarlet snake. Know what they look like?"

"I don't like snakes."

"Prejudice again. Most snakes are harmless, useful, and fun to raise. The scarlet snake is a beauty—red, black, and yellow—docile and makes a fine pet. I think this little fellow was fond of me. I knew how to handle snakes, how not to alarm them and not give them a chance to bite—even the bite of a non-poisonous snake is a nuisance. This baby was my prize. I used to take him out and show him to people, holding him back of his head and letting him wrap himself around my wrist.

"I got a chance to show my collection to the herpetologist of the Tampa zoo—I showed him my prize first. He almost had hysterics. My pet was not a scarlet snake—it was a young coral snake. The most deadly snake in North America. Duke, do you see my point?"

"That raising snakes is dangerous? I could have told you."

"Oh, for Pete's sake! I had rattlesnakes and water moccasins, too. A poisonous snake is *not* dangerous, no more than a loaded gun is dangerous—in each case, you must handle it properly. The thing that made that snake dangerous was that I hadn't known what it could do. If, in my ignorance, I had handled it carelessly, it would have killed me as casually and innocently as a kitten scratches. That's what I'm trying to tell you about Mike. He seems like an ordinary young male human, rather underdeveloped, clumsy, abysmally ignorant but bright and docile and eager to learn. But, like my snake, Mike is more than he appears to be. If Mike does not trust you, he can be much more deadly than that coral snake. Especially if he thinks you are harming one of his water brothers, such as Jill—or me."

Harshaw shook his head. "Duke, if you had given way to your impulse to take a poke at me and if Mike had been standing in that doorway, you would have been dead before you knew it, much too quickly for me to stop him. Mike would then have been apologetic over having 'wasted food'—namely your beefy carcass. But he wouldn't feel guilty about killing you; that would be a necessity you forced on him . . . and not important, even to you. You see, Mike believes that your soul is immortal."

"Huh? Well, hell, so do I. But—"

"Do you?" Jubal said bleakly. "I wonder."

"Why, certainly I do! Oh, I don't go to church much, but I was brought up right. I've got faith."

"Good. Though I've never understood how God could expect his creatures to pick the one true religion by faith— it strikes me as a sloppy way to run a universe. However, since you believe in immortality, we need not trouble over the probability that your prejudices will cause your demise. Do you want to be cremated or buried?"

"Oh, for cripe's sake, Jubal, quit trying to get my goat."

"Not at all. I can't guarantee your safety since you persist in thinking that a coral snake is a harmless scarlet snake— any blunder may be your last. But I promise I won't let Mike eat you."

Duke's chin dropped. Then he answered, explosively, profanely, incoherently. Harshaw listened, then said testily, "All right, pipe down. Make any arrangements with Mike you like." Harshaw bent over the projector. "I want to see these pictures. Damn!" he added. "The pesky thing savaged me."

"You tried to force it. Here—" Duke completed the adjustment Harshaw had muffed, then inserted a spool. Neither reopened the question of whether Duke was, or was not, working for Jubal. The projector was a tabletop tank, with adapter to receive solid-sight-sound 4 mm. film. Shortly they were watching events leading up to the disappearance of the empty brandy case.

Jubal saw the box hurtle toward his head, saw it wink out in mid-air. "Anne will be pleased to know that the cameras back her up. Duke, let's repeat that in slow motion."

"Okay." Duke spooled back, then announced, "This is ten-to-one."

The scene was the same but slowed-down sound was useless; Duke switched it off. The box floated from Jill's hands toward Jubal's head, then ceased to be. But under slow-motion it could be seen shrinking, smaller and smaller until it was no longer there.

"Duke, can you slow it still more?"

"Just a sec. Something has fouled the stereo."

"What?"

"Darned if I know. It looked all right on the fast run. But when I slowed it, the depth effect was reversed. That box went away from us, mighty fast—but it always looked closer than the wall. Swapped parallax, of course. But I never took that cartridge off the spindle."

"Oh. Hold it, Duke. Run the film from the other camera."

"Unh . . . I see. That'll give us a ninety-degree cross and we'll see properly even if I did jimmy this film." Duke changed cartridges. "Zip through the first part. Then undercranked on the last part?"

"Go ahead."

The scene was unchanged save for angle. When the image of Jill grabbed the box, Duke slowed action and again they watched the box go away.

Duke cursed. "Something fouled the second camera, too."

"So?"

"It was shooting from the side so the box should have gone out of frame to one side. Instead it went straight away from us again. You saw it."

"Yes," agreed Jubal. "'Straight away from us.'"

"But it *can't*—not from both angles."

"What do you mean, 'it can't'? It *did*." Harshaw added, "If we had used doppler-radar in place of cameras, I wonder what it would have shown?"

"How should I know? I'm going to take these cameras apart."

"Don't bother."

"But—"

"Duke, the cameras are okay. What is ninety degrees from everything else?"

"I'm no good at riddles."

"It's not a riddle. I could refer you to Mr. A. Square from Flatland, but I'll answer it. What is perpendicular to everything else? Answer: two bodies, one pistol, and an empty case."

"What the deuce do you mean, Boss?"

"I never spoke more plainly in my life. Try believing the evidence instead of insisting that the cameras must be at fault because what they saw was not what you expected. Let's see the other films."

They added nothing to what Harshaw already knew. The ash tray when near the ceiling had been out of camera, but its leisurely descent had been recorded. The pistol's image in the tank was small but, so far as could be seen, the pistol had shrunk away into the distance without moving. Since Harshaw had been gripping it tightly when it had left his hand, he was satisfied—if "satisfied" was the word.

"Duke, I want duplicate prints of all those."

Duke hesitated. "I'm still working here?"

"What? Oh, damn it! You can't eat in the kitchen, that's flat. Duke, try to forget your prejudices and listen."

"I'll listen."

"When Mike asked for the privilege of eating my stringy old carcass, he was doing me the greatest honor he knows of—by the only rules he knows. What he 'learned at his mother's knee,' so to speak. He was paying me his highest compliment—and asking a boon. Never mind what they think in Kansas; Mike uses values taught him on Mars."

"I'll take Kansas."

"Well," admitted Jubal, "so will I. But it is not free choice for me, nor you—nor Mike. It is almost impossible to shake off one's earliest training. Duke, can you get it through your skull that if *you* had been brought up by Martians, you would have the same attitude toward eating and being eaten that Mike has?"

Duke shook his head. "I won't buy it, Jubal. Sure, about most things it's just Mike's hard luck that he wasn't brought up civilized. But this is different, this is an instinct."

"'Instinct,' *Dreck*!"

"But it is. I didn't get 'training at my mother's knee' not to be a cannibal. Hell, I've always known it was a sin—a nasty one. Why, the thought turns my stomach. It's a basic instinct."

Jubal groaned. "Duke, how could you learn so much about machinery and never learn anything about how you yourself tick? Your mother didn't have to say, 'Mustn't eat your playmates, dear; that's not nice,' because you soaked it up from our culture—and so did I. Jokes about cannibals and missionaries, cartoons, fairy tales, horror stories, endless things. Shucks, son, it couldn't be instinct; cannibalism is historically a most widespread custom in every branch of the human race. Your ancestors, my ancestors, everybody."

"*Your* ancestors, maybe."

"Um. Duke, didn't you tell me you had some Indian blood?"

"Huh? Yeah, an eighth. What of it?"

"Then, while both of us have cannibals in our family trees, chances are that yours are many generations closer because—"

"Why, you bald-headed old—"

"Simmer down! Ritual cannibalism was common among aboriginal American cultures—look it up. Besides that, as North Americans, we stand a better than even chance of having a touch of Congo without knowing it . . . and there you are again. But even if we were Simon-pure North European stock (a silly notion, casual bastardy is far in excess of that ever admitted)—but if we were, such ancestry would merely tell us *which* cannibals we are descended from . . . because *every* branch of the human race has cannibalism. Duke, it's silly to talk about a practice being 'against instinct' when hundreds of millions have followed it."

"But—All right, I should know better than to argue with you, Jubal; you twist things. But suppose we did come from savages who didn't know any better—What of it? We're civilized now. Or at least *I* am."

Jubal grinned. "Implying that I am not. Son, aside from my own conditioned reflex against munching a roast haunch of—well, you, for example—aside from that trained-in prejudice, I regard our taboo against cannibalism as an excellent idea . . . because we are *not* civilized."

"Huh?"

"If we didn't have a taboo so strong that you believed it was instinct, I can think of a long list of people I wouldn't trust with my back turned, not with the price of beef what it is today. Eh?"

Duke grudged a grin. "I wouldn't take a chance on my ex-mother-in-law."

"Or how about our charming neighbor on the south,

who is so casual about other people's livestock during hunting season? Want to bet that you and I wouldn't wind up in his freezer? But Mike I trust—because Mike is civilized."

"Huh?"

"Mike is utterly civilized, Martian style. Duke, I've talked enough with Mike to know that Martian practice isn't dog-eat-dog . . . or Martian-eat-Martian. They eat their dead, instead of burying them, or burning them, or exposing them to vultures; but the custom is formalized and deeply religious. A Martian is never butchered against his will. In fact, murder doesn't seem to be a Martian concept. A Martian dies when he decides to, having discussed it with friends and received consent of his ancestors' ghosts to join them. Having decided to die, he does so, as easily as you close your eyes—no violence, no illness, not even an overdose of sleeping pills. One second he is alive and well, the next second he's a ghost. Then his friends eat what he no longer has any use for, 'grokking' him, as Mike would say, and praising his virtues as they spread the mustard. The ghost attends the feast; it is a bar mitzvah or confirmation service by which the ghost attains the status of 'Old One'—an elder statesman, as I understand it."

Duke made a face. "God, what superstitious junk!"

"To Mike it's a solemn—but joyful—religious ceremony."

Duke snorted. "Jubal, you don't believe that stuff about ghosts. It's just cannibalism combined with rank superstition."

"Well, I wouldn't go that far. I find these 'Old Ones' hard to swallow—but Mike speaks of them the way we talk about last Wednesday. As for the rest—Duke, what church were you brought up in?" Duke told him; Jubal went on:

"I thought so; in Kansas most people belong to yours or to one enough like it that you have to look at the sign to tell the difference. Tell me—how did you feel when you took part in the symbolic cannibalism that plays so paramount a part in your church's rituals?"

Duke stared. "What the devil do you mean?"

Jubal blinked solemnly back. "Were you a member? Or simply went to Sunday School?"

"Huh? Why, certainly I was a member, I still am—though I don't go much."

"I thought perhaps you weren't entitled to receive it. Well, you know what I'm talking about if you stop to think." Jubal stood up. "I shan't argue differences between one form of ritual cannibalism and another. Duke, I can't spend more time trying to shake you loose from prejudice. Are you leaving? If you are, I had better escort you off the place. Or do you want to stay? Stay and eat with the rest of us cannibals?"

Duke frowned. "Reckon I'll stay."

"I wash my hands of it. You saw those movies; if you're bright enough to pound sand, you've figured out that this man-Martian can be dangerous."

Duke nodded. "I'm not as stupid as you think, Jubal. But I won't let Mike run me off the place." He added, "You say he's dangerous. But I'm not going to stir him up. Shucks, Jubal, I *like* the little dope, most ways."

"Mmm . . . damn it, you still underestimate him, Duke. See here, if you feel friendly toward him, the best thing you can do is to offer him a glass of water. Understand me? Become his 'water brother.'"

"Uh . . . I'll think about it."

"But, Duke, don't fake it. If Mike accepts your offer, he'll be dead serious. He'll trust you utterly—so don't do it unless you are willing to trust him and stand by him, no matter how rough things get. Either all out—or don't do it."

"I understood that. That's why I said, 'I'll think about it.'"

"Okay. Don't take too long making up your mind . . . I expect things to get very rough soon."

XIV

IN LAPUTA, ACCORDING to Lemuel Gulliver, no person of importance listened or spoke without help of a "climenole"—or "flapper" in English translation, as such servant's duty was to flap the mouth and ears of his master with a bladder whenever, *in the opinion of the servant*, it was desirable for his master to speak or listen. Without the consent of his flapper it was impossible to converse with any Laputian of the master class.

The flapper system was unknown on Mars. Martian Old Ones would have as little use for flappers as a snake has for shoes. Martians still corporate could have used flappers but did not; the concept ran contrary to their way of living.

A Martian needing a few minutes or years of contemplation simply took it; if a friend wished to speak with him, the friend would wait. With eternity to draw on there could be no reason for hurrying—"hurry" was not a concept in Martian. Speed, velocity, simultaneity, acceleration, and other abstractions of the pattern of eternity were part of Martian mathematics, but not of Martian emotion.

Contrariwise, the unceasing rush of human existence came not from mathematical necessities of time but from the frantic urgency implicit in human sexual bipolarity.

On the planet Terra the flapper system developed slowly. Time was when any Terran sovereign held public court so that the lowliest might come before him without intermediary. Traces of this persisted long after kings became scarce—an Englishman could "Cry Harold!" (although none did) and the smarter city bosses still left their doors open to any gandy dancer or bindlestiff far into the twentieth century. A remnant of the principle was embalmed in Amendments I & IX of the United States Constitution, although superseded by the Articles of World Federation.

By the time the *Champion* returned from Mars the principle of access to the sovereign was dead in fact, regardless of the nominal form of government, and the importance of a personage could be told by the layers of flappers cutting him off from the mob. They were known as executive assistants, private secretaries, secretaries to private secretaries, press secretaries, receptionists, appointment clerks, et cetera—but all were "flappers" as each held arbitrary veto over communication from the outside.

These webs of officials resulted in unofficials who flapped the Great Man without permission from official flappers, using social occasions, or back-door access, or unlisted telephone numbers. These unofficials were called: "golfing companion," "kitchen cabinet," "lobbyist," "elder statesman," "five-percenter," and so forth. The unofficials grew webs, too, until they were almost as hard to reach as the Great Man, and secondary unofficials sprang up to circumvent the flappers of primary unofficials. With a personage of foremost importance the maze of unofficials was as complex as the official phalanxes surrounding a person merely very important.

DR. JUBAL HARSHAW, professional clown, amateur subversive, and parasite by choice, had an almost Martian attitude toward "hurry." Being aware that he had but a short time to live and having neither Martian nor Kansan faith in immortality, he purposed to live each golden moment as eternity—without fear, without hope, with sybaritic gusto. To this end he required something larger than Diogenes' tub but smaller than Kubla's pleasure dome; his was a simple place, a few acres kept private with electrified fence, a house of fourteen rooms or so, with running secretaries and other modern conveniences. To support his austere nest and rabble staff he put forth minimum effort for maximum return because it was easier to be rich than poor—Harshaw wished to live in lazy luxury, doing what amused Harshaw.

He felt aggrieved when circumstances forced on him a necessity for hurry and would never admit that he was enjoying himself.

This morning he needed to speak to the planet's chief executive. He knew that the flapper system made such contact all but impossible. Harshaw disdained to surround himself with flappers suitable to his own rank—he answered his telephone himself if he happened to be at hand because each call offered odds that he could be rude to some stranger for daring to invade his privacy without cause—"cause" by Harshaw's definition. He knew that he would not find such conditions at the Executive Palace;

Mr. Secretary General would not answer his own phone. But Harshaw had years of practice in outwitting human customs; he tackled the matter cheerfully, after breakfast.

His name carried him slowly through several layers of flappers. He was sufficiently a narrow-gauge V.I.P. that he was never switched off. He was referred from secretary to secretary and wound up speaking to an urbane young man who seemed willing to listen endlessly no matter what Harshaw said—but would not connect him with the Honorable Mr. Douglas.

Harshaw knew that he would get action if he claimed to have the Man from Mars with him, but he did not think that the result would suit him. He calculated that mention of Smith would kill any chance of reaching Douglas while producing reaction from subordinates—which he did not want. With Caxton's life at stake Harshaw could not risk failure through a subordinate's lack of authority or excess of ambition.

But this soft brush-off tried his patience. Finally he snarled, "Young man, if you have no authority, let me speak to someone who has! Put me through to Mr. Berquist."

The stooge suddenly lost his smile and Jubal thought gleefully that he had at last pinked him. So he pushed on. "Well? Don't just sit there! Get Gil on your inside line and tell him you've kept Jubal Harshaw waiting."

The face said woodenly, "We have no Mr. Berquist here."

"I don't care where he is. Get him! If you don't know Gil Berquist, ask your boss. Mr. Gilbert Berquist, personal assistant to Mr. Douglas. If you work around the Palace you've seen Mr. Berquist—thirty-five, six feet and a hundred and eighty pounds, sandy hair thin on top, smiles a lot and has perfect teeth. If you don't dare disturb him, dump it in your boss's lap. Quit biting your nails and move!"

The young man said, "Please hold on. I will inquire."

"I certainly will. Get me Gil." The image was replaced by an abstract pattern; a voice said, "Please wait while your call is completed. This delay is not charged to your account. Please relax while—" Soothing music came up; Jubal sat back and looked around. Anne was reading, out of the telephone's vision angle. On his other side the Man from Mars was also out of pickup and was watching stereovision and listening via ear plugs.

Jubal reflected that he must have that obscene babble box returned to the basement. "What you got, son?" he asked, reached over and turned on the speaker.

Mike answered, "I don't know, Jubal."

The sound confirmed what Jubal had feared: Smith was listening to a Fosterite service; the Shepherd was reading church notices: " junior Spirit-in-Action team will give a demonstration, so come early and see the fur fly! Our team coach, Brother Hornsby, has asked me to tell you boys to fetch only your helmets, gloves, and sticks—we aren't going after sinners this time. However, the Little Cherubim will be on hand with their first-aid kits in case of excessive zeal." The Shepherd paused and smiled broadly, "And now wonderful news, My Children! A message from Angel Ramzai for Brother Arthur Renwick and his good wife Dorothy. Your prayer has been approved and you will go to Heaven at dawn Thursday morning! Stand up, Art! Stand up, Dottie! Take a bow!"

Camera made reverse cut, showing the congregation and centering on Brother and Sister Renwick. To wild applause and shouts of *"Hallelujah!"* Brother Renwick was responding with a boxer's handshake, while his wife blushed and smiled and dabbed at her eyes beside him.

Camera cut back as the Shepherd held up his hand for silence. He went on briskly, "The Bon Voyage party starts at midnight and doors will be locked at that time—so get here early and let's make this the happiest revelry our flock has ever seen; we're all proud of Art and Dottie. Funeral services will be held thirty minutes after dawn, with breakfast immediately following for those who have to get to work early." The Shepherd suddenly looked stern and camera zoomed in until his head filled the tank. "After our last Bon Voyage, the sexton found an empty pint bottle in one of the Happiness rooms—of a brand distilled by sinners. That's past and done; the brother who slipped confessed and paid penance sevenfold, even refusing the usual cash discount—I'm sure he won't backslide. But stop and think, My Children—Is it worth risking eternal happiness to save a few pennies on an article of worldly merchandise? Always look for that happy, holy seal-of-approval with Bishop Digby's smiling face on it. Don't let a sinner palm off on you something 'just as good.' Our sponsors support us; they deserve your support. Brother Art, I'm sorry to have to bring up such a subject—"

"That's okay, Shepherd! Pour it on!"

"—at a time of such great happiness. But we must never forget that—" Jubal switched off the speaker circuit.

"Mike, that's not anything you need."

"Not?"

"Uh—" Shucks, the boy was going to have to learn about such things. "All right, go ahead. But talk to me later."

"Yes, Jubal."

Harshaw was about to add advice to offset Mike's

tendency to take literally anything he heard. But the telephone's "hold" music went down and out, and the screen filled with an image—a man in his forties whom Jubal labeled as "cop."

Jubal said aggressively, "You aren't Gil Berquist."

"What is your interest in Gilbert Berquist?"

Jubal answered with pained patience, "I wish to speak to him. See here, my good man, are you a public employee?"

The man hesitated. "Yes. You must—"

"I 'must' nothing! I am a citizen and my taxes help pay your wages. All morning I have been trying to make a simple phone call—and I have been passed from one butterfly-brained bovine to another, every one of them feeding out of the public trough. And now *you*. Give me your name, job title, and pay number. Then I'll speak to Mr. Berquist."

"You didn't answer my question."

"Come, come! I don't have to; I am a private citizen. You are *not*—and the question I asked any citizen may demand of any public servant. O'Kelly versus State of California 1972. I demand that you identify yourself—name, job, number."

The man answered tonelessly, "You are Doctor Jubal Harshaw. You are calling from—"

"So that's what took so long? That was stupid. My address can be obtained from any library, post office, or telephone information. As to who I am, everyone knows. Everyone who can read. Can you read?"

"Dr. Harshaw, I am a police officer and I require your cooperation. What is your reason—"

"Pooh, sir! I am a lawyer. A citizen is required to cooperate with police under certain conditions only. For example, during hot pursuit—in which case the police officer may still be required to show credentials. Is this 'hot pursuit,' sir? Are you about to dive through this blasted instrument? Second, a citizen may be required to cooperate within reasonable and lawful limits in the course of police investigation—"

"This is an investigation."

"Of what, sir? Before you may require my cooperation, you must identify yourself, satisfy me as to your bonafides, state your purpose, and—if I so require—cite the code and show that 'reasonable necessity' exists. You have done none of these. I wish to speak to Mr. Berquist."

The man's jaw muscles were jumping but he answered, "I am Captain Heinrich of the Federation S.S. Bureau. The fact that you reached me by calling the Executive Palace should be proof that I am who I say I am. However—" He took out a wallet, flipped it open, and held it to his pickup. Harshaw glanced at the I.D.

"Very well, Captain," he growled. "Will you now explain why you are keeping me from speaking with Mr. Berquist?"

"Mr. Berquist is not available."

"Then why didn't you say so? Transfer my call to someone of Berquist's rank. I mean one of the people who work directly with the Secretary General, as Gil does. I don't propose to be fobbed off on some junior assistant flunky with no authority to blow his own nose! If Gil isn't there, then for God's sake get me someone of equal rank!"

"You have been trying to telephone the Secretary General."

"Precisely."

"Very well, you may explain what business you have with the Secretary General."

"And I may not. Are you a confidential assistant to the Secretary General? Are you privy to his secrets?"

"That's beside the point."

"That's exactly the point. As a police officer, you know better. I shall explain, to some person known to me to be cleared for sensitive material and in Mr. Douglas's confidence, just enough to make sure that the Secretary General speaks to me. Are you sure Mr. Berquist can't be reached?"

"Quite sure."

"Then it will have to be someone else—of his rank."

"If it's that secret, you shouldn't be calling over a phone."

"My good Captain! Since you had this call traced, you know that my phone is equipped to receive a maximum-security return call."

The S.S. officer ignored this. Instead he answered, "Doctor, I'll be blunt. Until you explain your business, you aren't going to get anywhere. If you call again, your call will be routed to this office. Call a hundred times—or a month from now. Same thing. Until you cooperate."

Jubal smiled happily. "It won't be necessary now, as you have let slip—unwittingly, or was it intentional?—the one datum needed before we act. If we must. I can hold them off the rest of the day . . . but the code word is no longer 'Berquist.'"

"What the devil do you mean?"

"My dear Captain, please! Not over an unscrambled circuit—But you know, or should know, that I am a senior philosophunculist on active duty."

"Repeat?"

"Haven't you studied amphigory? Gad, what they teach in schools these days! Back to your pinochle game; I don't need you." Jubal switched off, set the phone for ten minutes' refusal, said, "Come along, kids," and returned to his loafing spot near the pool. He cautioned Anne to keep her Witness robe at hand, told Mike to stay in earshot, and gave Miriam instructions concerning the telephone. Then he relaxed.

He was not displeased. He had not expected to reach the Secretary General at once. His reconnaissance had uncovered one weak spot in the wall surrounding the Secretary and he expected that his bout with Captain Heinrich would bring a return call from a higher level.

If not, the exchange of compliments with the S.S. cop had been rewarding in itself and had left him in a warm glow. Harshaw held that certain feet were made for stepping on, in order to improve the breed, promote the general welfare, and minimize the ancient insolence of office; he had seen at once that Heinrich had such feet.

But he wondered how long he could wait? In addition to the pending collapse of his "bomb" and the fact that he had promised Jill to take steps on behalf of Caxton, something new was crowding him: Duke was gone.

Gone for the day, gone for good (or for bad), Jubal did not know. Duke had been at dinner, had not shown up for breakfast. Neither was noteworthy in Harshaw's household and no one else seemed to miss Duke.

Jubal looked across the pool, watched Mike attempt to perform a dive exactly as Dorcas had just performed it, and admitted to himself that he had not asked about Duke this morning, on purpose. The truth was that he did not want to ask the Bear what had happened to Algy. The Bear might answer.

Well, there was only one way to cope with weakness. "Mike! Come here."

"Yes, Jubal." The Man from Mars got out of the pool and trotted over like an eager puppy. Harshaw looked him over, decided that he must weigh twenty pounds more than he had on arrival . . . all of it muscle. "Mike, do you know where Duke is?"

"No, Jubal."

Well, that settled it; the boy didn't know how to lie— wait, hold it! Jubal remembered Mike's computer-like habit of answering only the question asked . . . and Mike had not appeared to know where that pesky box was, once it was gone. "Mike, when did you see him last?"

"I saw Duke go upstairs when Jill and I came downstairs, this morning when time to cook breakfast." Mike added proudly, "I helped cooking."

"That was the last time you saw Duke?"

"I am not see Duke since, Jubal. I proudly burned toast."

"I'll bet you did. You'll make some woman a fine husband, if you aren't careful."

"Oh, I burned it most carefully."

"Jubal—"

"Huh? Yes, Anne?"

"Duke grabbed an early breakfast and lit out for town. I thought you knew."

"Well," Jubal temporized, "I thought he intended to leave after lunch." Jubal suddenly felt a load lifted. Not that Duke meant anything to him—of course not! For years he had avoided letting any human being be important to him—but it would have troubled him. A little, anyhow.

What statute was violated in turning a man ninety degrees from everything else?

Not murder, as long as the lad used it only in self-defense, or in the proper defense of another, such as Jill. Pennsylvania laws against witchcraft might apply . . . but it would be interesting to see how an indictment would be worded.

A civil action might lie—Could harboring the Man from Mars be construed as "maintaining an attractive nuisance"? It was likely that new rules of law must evolve. Mike had already kicked the bottom out of medicine and physics, even though the practitioners of such were aware of the chaos. Harshaw recalled the tragedy that relativity had been for many scientists. Unable to digest it, they had taken refuge in anger at Einstein. Their refuge had been a dead end; all that inflexible old guard could do was die and let younger minds take over.

His grandfather had told him of the same thing in medicine when germ theory came along; physicians had gone to their graves calling Pasteur a liar, a fool, or worse—without examining evidence which their "common sense" told them was impossible.

Well, he could see that Mike was going to cause more hoorah than Pasteur and Einstein combined. Which reminded him—"Larry! Where's Larry?"

"Here, Boss," the loudspeaker behind him announced. "Down in the shop."

"Got the panic button?"

"Sure. You said to sleep with it. I do."

"Bounce up here and give it to Anne. Anne, keep it with your robe."

She nodded. Larry answered, "Right away, Boss. Count down coming up?"

"Just do it." Jubal found that the Man from Mars was still in front of him, quiet as a sculptured figure. Sculpture? Uh—Jubal searched his memory. Michelangelo's

"David"! Yes, even the puppyish hands and feet, the serenely sensual face, the tousled, too-long hair. "That was all, Mike."

"Yes, Jubal."

But Mike waited. Jubal said, "Something on your mind, son?"

"About what I was seeing in that goddam-noisy-box. You said, 'But talk to me later.'"

"Oh." Harshaw recalled the Fosterite broadcast and winced. "Yes, but don't call that thing a 'goddam noisy box.' It is a stereovision receiver."

Mike looked puzzled. "It is not a goddam-noisy-box? I heard you not rightly?"

"It is indeed a goddam noisy box. But *you* must call it a stereovision receiver."

"I will call it a 'stereovision-receiver.' Why, Jubal? I do not grok."

Harshaw sighed; he had climbed these stairs too many times. Any conversation with Smith turned up human behavior which could not be justified logically, and attempts to do so were endlessly time consuming. "I do not grok it myself, Mike," he admitted, "but Jill wants you to say it that way."

"I will do it, Jubal. Jill wants it."

"Now tell me what you saw and heard—and what you grok of it."

Mike recalled every word and action in the babble tank, including all commercials. Since he had almost finished the encyclopedia, he had read articles on "Religion," "Christianity," "Islam," "Judaism," "Confucianism," "Buddhism," and related subjects. He had grokked none of this.

Jubal learned that: (a) Mike did not know that the

Fosterite service was religious; (b) Mike remembered what he had read about religions but had filed such for future meditation, not having understood them; (c) Mike had a most confused notion of what "religion" meant, although he could quote nine dictionary definitions; (d) the Martian language contained no word which Mike could equate with *any* of these definitions; (e) the customs which Jubal had described to Duke as Martian "religious ceremonies" were not; to Mike such matters were as matter-of-fact as grocery markets were to Jubal; (f) it was not possible to separate in the Martian tongue the human concepts: "religion," "philosophy," and "science"—and, since Mike thought in Martian, it was not possible for him to tell them apart. All such matters were "learnings" from the "Old Ones." Doubt he had ever heard of, nor of research (no Martian word for either); the answers to any questions were available from the Old Ones, who were omniscient and infallible, whether on tomorrow's weather or cosmic teleology. Mike had seen a weather forecast and had assumed that this was a message from human "Old Ones" for those still corporate. He held a similar assumption concerning the authors of the Encyclopedia Britannica.

But last, and worst to Jubal, Mike had grokked the Fosterite service as announcing impending discorporation of two humans to join the human "Old Ones"—and Mike was tremendously excited. Had he grokked it rightly? Mike knew that his English was imperfect; he made mistakes through ignorance, being "only an egg." But had he grokked *this* correctly? He had been waiting to meet the human "Old Ones," he had many questions to ask. Was this an opportunity? Or did he require more learnings before he was ready?

Jubal was saved by the bell; Dorcas arrived with sandwiches and coffee. Jubal ate silently, which suited Smith as
his rearing had taught him that eating was a time of meditation. Jubal stretched his meal while he pondered—and
cursed himself for letting Mike watch stereo. Oh, the boy
had to come up against religions—couldn't be helped if he
was going to spend his life on this dizzy planet. But, damn
it, it would have been better to wait until Mike was used
to the cockeyed pattern of human behavior . . . and not
Fosterites as his first experience!

A devout agnostic, Jubal rated all religions, from the
animism of Kalahari Bushmen to the most intellectualized
faith, as equal. But emotionally he disliked some more
than others and the Church of the New Revelation set his
teeth on edge. The Fosterites' flat-footed claim to gnosis
through a direct line to Heaven, their arrogant intoler-
ance, their football-rally and sales-convention services—
these depressed him. If people must go to church, why the
devil couldn't they be dignified, like Catholics, Christian
Scientists, or Quakers?

If God existed (concerning which Jubal maintained
neutrality) and if He wanted to be worshipped (a proposition which Jubal found improbable but nevertheless possible in the light of his own ignorance), then it seemed
wildly unlikely that a God potent to shape galaxies would
be swayed by the whoop-te-do nonsense the Fosterites offered as "worship."

But with bleak honesty Jubal admitted that the Fosterites might own the Truth, the exact Truth, nothing but the
Truth. The Universe was a silly place at best . . . but the
least likely explanation for it was the no-explanation of random chance, the conceit that abstract somethings "just

happened" to be atoms that "just happened" to get together in ways which "just happened" to look like consistent laws and some configurations "just happened" to possess self-awareness and that two "just happened" to be the Man from Mars and a bald-headed old coot with Jubal inside.

No, he could not swallow the "just-happened" theory, popular as it was with men who called themselves scientists. Random chance was not a sufficient explanation of the Universe—random chance was not sufficient to explain random chance; the pot could not hold itself.

What then? "Least hypothesis" deserved no preference; Occam's Razor could not slice the prime problem, the Nature of the Mind of God (might as well call it that, you old scoundrel; it's an Anglo-Saxon monosyllable not banned by four letters—and as good a tag for what you don't understand as any).

Was there any basis for preferring any sufficient hypothesis over another? When you did not understand a thing: No! Jubal admitted that a long life had left him not understanding the basic problems of the Universe.

The Fosterites might be right.

But, he reminded himself savagely, two things remained: his taste and his pride. If the Fosterites held a monopoly on Truth, if Heaven were open only to Fosterites, then he, Jubal Harshaw, gentleman, preferred that eternity of painfilled damnation promised to "sinners" who refused the New Revelation. He could not see the naked Face of God . . . but his eyesight was good enough to pick out his social equals—and those Fosterites did not measure up!

But he could see how Mike had been misled; the Fosterite "going to Heaven" at a selected time did sound like the voluntary "discorporation" which, Jubal did not doubt, was the practice on Mars. Jubal suspected that a better term for the Fosterite practice was "murder"—but such had never been proved and rarely hinted. Foster had been the first to "go to Heaven" on schedule, dying at a prophesied instant; since then, it had been a Fosterite mark of special grace . . . it had been years since any coroner had had the temerity to pry into such deaths.

Not that Jubal cared—a good Fosterite was a dead Fosterite.

But it was going to be hard to explain.

No use stalling, another cup of coffee wouldn't make it easier—"Mike, who made the world?"

"Beg pardon?"

"Look around you. All this. Mars, too. The stars. Everything. You and me and everybody. Did the Old Ones tell you who made it?"

Mike looked puzzled. "No, Jubal."

"Well, have you wondered? Where did the Sun come from? Who put the stars in the sky? Who started it? All, everything, the whole world, the Universe . . . so that you and I are here talking." Jubal paused, surprised at himself. He had intended to take the usual agnostic approach . . . and found himself compulsively following his legal training, being an honest advocate in spite of himself, attempting to support a religious belief he did not hold but which was believed by most human beings. He found that, willy-nilly, he was attorney for the orthodoxies of his own race against—he wasn't sure what. An unhuman viewpoint. "How do your Old Ones answer such questions?"

"Jubal, I do not grok . . . that these are '*questions*.' I am sorry."

"Eh? I don't grok your answer."

Mike hesitated. "I will try. But words are . . . are *not* . . . rightly. Not 'putting.' Not 'mading.' A *nowing*, World is. World was. World shall be. *Now*."

"'As it was in the beginning, so it is now and ever shall be, World without end—'"

Mike smiled happily. "You grok it!"

"I don't grok it," Jubal answered gruffly, "I am quoting something, uh, an 'Old One' said." He decided to try another approach; God the Creator was not the aspect of Deity to use as an opening—Mike did not grasp the idea of Creation. Well, Jubal wasn't sure that he did, either—long ago he had made a pact with himself to postulate a created Universe on even-numbered days, a tail-swallowing eternal-and-uncreated Universe on odd-numbered days—since each hypothesis, while paradoxical, avoided the paradoxes of the other—with a day off each leap year for sheer solipsist debauchery. Having tabled an unanswerable question he had given no thought to it for more than a generation.

Jubal decided to explain religion in its broadest sense and tackle the notion of Deity and Its aspects later.

Mike agreed that learnings came in various sizes, from little learnings that a nestling could grok on up to great learnings which only an Old One could grok in fullness. But Jubal's attempt to draw a line between small learnings and great so that "great learnings" would have the meanings of "religious questions" was not successful; some religious questions did not seem to Mike to be questions (such as "Creation") and others seemed to him to be "little" questions, with answers obvious to nestlings—such as life after death.

Jubal dropped it and passed on to the multiplicity of human religions. He explained that humans had hundreds of ways by which "great learnings" were taught, each with its own answers and each claiming to be the truth.

"What is 'truth'?" Mike asked.

("What is Truth?" asked a Roman judge, and washed his hands. Jubal wished that he could do likewise.) "An answer is truth when you speak rightly, Mike. How many hands do I have?"

"Two hands. I see two hands," Mike amended.

Anne glanced up from reading. "In six weeks I could make a Witness of him."

"Quiet, Anne. Things are tough enough. Mike, you spoke rightly; I have two hands. Your answer is truth. Suppose you said that I had seven hands?"

Mike looked troubled. "I do not grok that I could say that."

"No, I don't think you could. You would not speak rightly if you did; your answer would not be truth. But, Mike listen carefully—each religion claims to be truth, claims to speak rightly. Yet their answers are as different as two hands and seven hands. Fosterites say one thing, Buddhists say another, Muslims still another—many answers, all different."

Mike seemed to be making great effort. "All speak rightly? Jubal, I do not grok."

"Nor I."

The Man from Mars looked troubled, then suddenly smiled. "I will ask the Fosterites to ask your Old Ones and then we will know, my brother. How will I do this?"

A few minutes later Jubal found, to his disgust, that he had promised Mike an interview with some Fosterite bigmouth. Nor had he been able to dent Mike's assumption that Fosterites were in touch with human "Old Ones." Mike's difficulty was that he didn't know what a lie was—definitions of "lie" and "falsehood" had been filed in his mind with no trace of grokking. One could "speak wrongly" only by accident. So he had taken the Fosterite service at its face value.

Jubal tried to explain that *all* human religions claimed to be in touch with "Old Ones" one way or another; nevertheless their answers were all different.

Mike looked patiently troubled. "Jubal my brother, I try . . . but I do not grok how this can be right speaking. With my people, Old Ones speak always rightly. Your people—"

"Hold it, Mike."

"Beg pardon?"

"When you said, 'my people' you were talking about Martians. Mike, you are not a Martian; you are a man."

"What is 'Man'?"

Jubal groaned. Mike could, he was sure, quote the dictionary definitions. Yet the lad never asked a question to be annoying; he asked always for information—and expected Jubal to be able to tell him. "I am a man, you are a man, Larry is a man."

"But Anne is not a man?"

"Uh . . . Anne is a man, a female man. A woman."

("Thanks, Jubal."—"Shut up, Anne.")

"A baby is a man? I have seen pictures—and in the goddamnoi—in stereovision. A baby is not shaped like Anne . . . and Anne is not shaped like you . . . and you are not shaped like I. But a baby is a nestling man?"

"Uh . . . yes, a baby is a man."

"Jubal . . . I think I grok that my people—'Martians'—are man. Not shape. Shape is not man. Man is grokking. I speak rightly?"

Jubal decided to resign from the Philosophical Society and take up tatting! What was "grokking"? He had been using the word for a week—and he didn't grok it. But what was "Man"? A featherless biped? God's image? Or a fortuitous result of "survival of the fittest" in a circular definition? The heir of death and taxes? The Martians seemed to have defeated death, and they seemed not to have money, property, nor government in any human sense—so how could they have taxes?

Yet the boy was right; shape was irrelevant in defining "Man," as unimportant as the bottle containing the wine. You could even take a man out of his bottle, like that poor fellow whose life those Russians had "saved" by placing his brain in a vitreous envelope and wiring him like a telephone exchange. Gad, what a horrible joke! He wondered if the poor devil appreciated the humor.

But *how*, from the viewpoint of a Martian, did Man differ from other animals? Would a race that could levitate (and God knows what else) be impressed by engineering? If so, would the Aswan Dam, or a thousand miles of coral reef, win first prize? Man's self-awareness? Sheer conceit, there was no way to prove that sperm whales or sequoias were not philosophers and poets exceeding any human merit.

There was one field in which man was unsurpassed; he showed unlimited ingenuity in devising bigger and more efficient ways to kill off, enslave, harass, and in all ways make an unbearable nuisance of himself to himself. Man was his own grimmest joke on himself. The very bedrock of humor was—

"Man is the animal who laughs," Jubal answered.

Mike considered this. "Then I am not a man."

"Huh?"

"I do not laugh. I have heard laughing and it frighted me. Then I grokked that it did not hurt. I have tried to learn—" Mike threw his head back and gave out a raucous cackle.

Jubal covered his ears. *"Stop!"*

"You heard," Mike agreed sadly. "I cannot rightly do it. So I am not man."

"Wait a minute, son. You simply haven't learned yet . . . and you'll never learn by trying. But you will, I promise you. If you live among us long enough, one day you will see how funny we are—and you will laugh."

"I will?"

"You will. Don't worry, just let it come. Why, son, even a Martian would laugh once he grokked us."

"I will wait," Smith agreed placidly.

"And while you are waiting, don't doubt that you are man. You are. Man born of woman and born to trouble . . . and some day you will grok its fullness and laugh—because man is the animal that laughs at himself. About your Martian friends, I do not know. But I grok that they may be 'man.'"

"Yes, Jubal."

Harshaw thought that the interview was over and felt relieved. He had not been so embarrassed since a day long gone when his father had explained the birds and the bees and the flowers—*much* too late.

But the Man from Mars was not yet done. "Jubal my brother, you were ask me, 'Who made the World?' and I did not have words why I did not grok it rightly to be a question. I have been thinking words."

"So?"

"You told me, 'God made the World.'"

"No, no!" Harshaw said. "I told you that, while religions said many things, most of them said, 'God made the World.' I told you that I did not grok the fullness, but that 'God' was the word that was used."

"Yes, Jubal," Mike agreed. "Word is 'God.'" He added, "You grok."

"I must admit I don't grok."

"You grok," Smith repeated firmly. "I am explain. I did not have the word. You grok. Anne groks. I grok. The grasses under my feet grok in happy beauty. But I needed the word. The word is God."

"Go ahead."

Mike pointed triumphantly at Jubal. *"Thou art God!"*

Jubal slapped a hand to his face. "Oh, Jesus H.—*What have I done?* Look, Mike, take it easy! You didn't understand me. I'm sorry. I'm very sorry! Just forget what I've said and we'll start over another day. But—"

"Thou are God," Mike repeated serenely. "That which groks. Anne is God. I am God. The happy grasses are God. Jill groks in beauty always. Jill is God. All shaping and making and creating together—" He croaked something in Martian and smiled.

"All right, Mike. But let it wait. Anne! Have you been getting this?"

"You bet I have, Boss!"

"Make a tape. I'll have to work on it. I *can't* let it stand. I must—" Jubal glanced up, said, "Oh, my God! General Quarters, everybody! *Anne!* Set the panic button on 'dead man'—and for God's sake keep your thumb on it; they may not be coming here." He glanced up again, at two air cars approaching from the south. "I'm afraid they are. Mike! Hide in the pool! Remember what I told you—down in the deepest part, stay there, hold still—don't come up until I send Jill."

"Yes, Jubal."

"Right now! *Move!*"

"Yes, Jubal." Mike ran the few steps, cut water and disappeared. He kept his knees straight, toes pointed, feet together.

"*Jill!*" Jubal called out. "Dive in and climb out. You too, Larry. If anybody saw that, I want 'em confused as to how many are using the pool. Dorcas! Climb out fast, child, and dive again. Anne—No, you've got the panic button."

"I can take my cloak and go to the edge of the pool. Boss, do you want delay on this 'dead-man' setting?"

"Uh, thirty seconds. If they land, put on your Witness cloak and get your thumb back on the button. Then wait—and if I call you to me, let the balloon go up. I don't dare shout 'Wolf!' unless—" He shielded his eyes. "One of them is going to land . . . and it's got that Paddy-wagon look. Oh, damn, I thought they would parley."

The first car hovered, dropped for a landing in the garden around the pool; the second started circling at low altitude. The cars were squad carriers in size, and showed a small insignia: the stylized globe of the Federation.

Anne put down the radio relay link, got quickly into professional garb, picked up the link and put her thumb on the button. The door of the first car opened as it touched and Jubal charged towards it with the belligerence of a Pekingese. As a man stepped out, Jubal roared, "Get that God damned heap off my rose bushes!"

The man said, "Jubal Harshaw?"

"Tell that oaf to raise that bucket and move it *back*! Off the garden and onto the grass! Anne!"

"Coming, Boss."

"Jubal Harshaw, I have a warrant for—"

"I don't care if you've got a warrant for the King of England; move that junk off my flowers! Then, so help me, I'll sue you for—" Jubal glanced at the man, appeared to see him for the first time. "Oh, so it's *you*," he said with bitter contempt. "Were you born stupid, Heinrich, or did you have to study? When did that uniformed jackass learn to fly?"

"Please examine this warrant," Captain Heinrich said with careful patience. "Then—"

"Get your go-cart out of my flower beds or I'll make a civil-rights case that will cost you your pension!"

Heinrich hesitated. *"Now!"* Jubal screamed. "And tell those yokels getting out to pick up their feet! That idiot with the buck teeth is standing on a prize Elizabeth M. Hewitt!"

Heinrich turned his head. "You men—careful of those flowers. Paskin, you're standing on one. *Rogers!* Raise the car and move back clear of the garden." He turned to Harshaw. "Does that satisfy you?"

"Once he moves it—but you'll still pay damages. Let's see your credentials . . . and show them to the Fair Witness and state loud and clear your name, rank, organization, and pay number."

"You know who I am. I have a warrant to—"

"I have a warrant to part your hair with a shotgun unless you do things legally and in order! *I* don't know who you are. You look like a stuffed shirt I saw over the telephone—but I don't identify you. *You* must identify yourself, in specified fashion. World Code paragraph 1602, part II, before you may serve a warrant. And that goes for those other apes, too, and that pithecan parasite piloting for you."

"They are police officers, acting under my orders."

"*I* don't know that they are. They might have hired those ill-fitting clown suits at a costumer's. The letter of the law, sir! You've come barging into my castle. You *say* you are a police officer—and you allege that you have a warrant for this intrusion. But *I* say you are trespassers until you prove otherwise . . . which invokes my sovereign right to use force to eject you—which I shall start to do in about three seconds."

"I wouldn't advise it."

"Why are *you* to advise? If I am hurt in attempting to enforce this my right, your action becomes constructive assault—with deadly weapons, if the things those mules are toting are guns, as they appear to be. Civil and criminal, both—why, my man, I'll have your hide for a door mat!" Jubal drew back a skinny arm and clenched a fist. "*Off* my property!"

"Hold it, Doctor. We'll do it your way." Heinrich had turned red, but he kept his voice under tight control. He offered his identification, which Jubal glanced at, then handed back for Heinrich to show to Anne. He then stated his full name, said that he was a captain of police, Federation Special Service Bureau, and recited his pay number. One by one, the other troopers and the driver went through the rigmarole at Heinrich's frozen-faced orders.

When they were done, Jubal said sweetly, "And now, Captain, how may I help you?"

"I have a warrant for Gilbert Berquist, which warrant names this property, its buildings and grounds."

"Show it to me, then show it to the Witness."

"I will do so. I have another warrant, similar to the first, for Gillian Boardman."

"Who?"

"Gillian Boardman. The charge is kidnapping."

"My goodness!"

"And another for Hector C. Johnson . . . and one for Valentine Michael Smith . . . and one for *you*, Jubal Harshaw."

"Me? Taxes again?"

"No. Accessory to this and that . . . and material witness on other things . . . and I'd take you in on my own for obstructing justice if the warrant didn't make it unnecessary."

"Oh, come, Captain! I've been most cooperative since you identified yourself and started behaving in a legal manner. And I shall continue to be. Of course, I shall still sue you—and your immediate superior and the government— for your illegal acts *before* that time . . . and I am not waiving any rights or recourses with respect to anything any of you may do hereafter. Mmm . . . quite a list of victims. I see why you brought an extra wagon. But—dear me!— something odd here. This, uh, Mrs. Barkmann?—I see that she is charged with kidnapping this Smith fellow . . . but in this other warrant *he* seems to be charged with fleeing custody. I'm confused."

"It's both. He escaped—and she kidnapped him."

"Isn't that difficult to manage? Both, I mean? And on what charge was he being held? The warrant does not seem to state?"

"How the devil do I know? He escaped, that's all. He's a fugitive."

"Gracious me! I think I shall have to offer my services as counsel to each of them. Interesting case. If a mistake has been made—or mistakes—it could lead to other matters."

Heinrich grinned coldly. "You won't find it easy. You'll be in the pokey, too."

"Oh, not for long, I trust." Jubal raised his voice and turned his head toward the house. "I think, if Judge Holland were listening, habeas corpus proceedings—for all of us—might be rather prompt. And, if the Associated Press happened to have a courier car nearby, there would be no time lost in knowing *where* to serve such writs."

"Always the shyster, eh, Harshaw?"

"Slander, my dear sir. I take notice."

"A fat lot of good it will do you. We're alone."

"Are we?"

XV

VALENTINE MICHAEL SMITH swam through murky water to the deepest part, under the diving board, and settled on the bottom. He did not know why his water brother had told him to hide; he did not know he was hiding. Jubal had told him to do this and remain until Jill came for him; that was sufficient.

He curled up, let air out of his lungs, swallowed his tongue, rolled his eyes up, slowed his heart, and became effectively "dead" save that he was not discorporate. He elected to stretch his time sense until seconds flowed past like hours, as he had much to meditate.

He had failed again to achieve the perfect understanding, the mutually merging rapport—the grokking—that should exist between water brothers. He knew the failure was his, caused by his using wrongly the oddly variable human language, because Jubal had become upset.

He knew that his human brothers could suffer intense emotion without damage, nevertheless Smith was wistfully sorry to have caused upset in Jubal. It had seemed that he had at last grokked a most difficult human word. He should have known better because, early in his learnings under his brother Mahmoud, he had discovered that long human words rarely changed their meanings but short words were slippery, changing without pattern. Or so he seemed to grok. Short human words were like trying to lift water with a knife.

This had been a very short word.

Smith still felt that he grokked rightly the human word "God"—confusion had come from his failure in selecting other words. The concept was so simple, so basic, so necessary, that a nestling could explain it—in Martian. The problem was to find human words that would let him speak rightly, make sure that he patterned them to match in fullness how it would be said in his own people's language.

He puzzled over the fact that there should be any difficulty in saying it, even in English, since it was a thing everyone knew . . . else they could not grok alive. Possibly he should ask the human Old Ones how to say it, rather than struggle with shifting meanings. If so, he must wait until Jubal arranged it, for he was only an egg.

He felt brief regret that he was not privileged to attend discorporation of brother Art and brother Dottie.

Then he settled down to review Webster's New International Dictionary of the English Language, Third Edition, published in Springfield, Massachusetts.

FROM A LONG way off Smith was roused by uneasy awareness that his water brothers were in trouble. He paused between "sherbacha" and "sherbet" to ponder this. Should he leave the water of life and join them to grok and share their trouble? At home there could have been no question; trouble is shared, in joyful closeness.

But Jubal had told him to wait.

He reviewed Jubal's words, trying them against other human words, making sure that he grokked. No, he had grokked rightly; he must wait until Jill came.

Nevertheless he was so uneasy that he could not go back to his word hunt. At last an idea came that was filled with such gay daring that he would have trembled had his body been ready.

Jubal had told him to place his body under water and leave it there until Jill came . . . but had Jubal said that *he himself* must wait with the body?

Smith took a long time to consider this, knowing that slippery English words could lead him into mistakes. He concluded that Jubal had not ordered him to stay with his body . . . and that left a way out of the wrongness of not sharing his brothers' trouble.

So Smith decided to take a walk.

He was dazed at his own audacity, for, while he had done it before, he had never "soloed." Always an Old One had been with him, watching over him, making sure that his body was safe, keeping him from becoming disoriented, staying with him until he returned to his body.

There was no Old One to help him now. But Smith was confident that he could do it alone in a fashion that would fill his teacher with pride. So he checked every part of his body, made certain that it would not damage while he was gone, then got cautiously out of it, leaving behind that trifle of himself needed as caretaker.

He rose up and stood on the edge of the pool, remembering to behave as if his body were with him as a guard against disorienting—against losing track of pool, body, everything, and wandering off into unknown places where he could not find his way back.

Smith looked around.

A car was just landing in the garden and beings under it were complaining of injuries and indignities. Was this the trouble he could feel? Grasses were for walking on, flowers and bushes were not—this was a wrongness.

No, there was more wrongness. A man was stepping out of the car, one foot about to touch the ground, and Jubal was running toward him. Smith could see the anger that Jubal was hurling toward the man, a blast so furious that, had one Martian hurled it toward another, both would discorporate.

Smith noted it as something to ponder and, if it was a cusp of necessity, decided what he must do to help his brother. Then he looked over the others.

Dorcas was climbing out of the pool; she was troubled but not too much so; Smith could feel her confidence in Jubal. Larry was at the edge and had just gotten out; drops of water falling from him were in the air. Larry was excited and pleased; his confidence in Jubal was absolute. Miriam was near him; her mood was midway between those of Dorcas and Larry. Anne was standing nearby, dressed in the long white garment she had had with her all day. Smith could not fully grok her mood; he felt in her the cold unyielding discipline of an Old One. It startled him, as Anne was always soft and gentle and warmly friendly.

He saw that she was watching Jubal closely and was ready to help him. And so was Larry! . . . and Dorcas! . . . and Miriam! With a burst of empathy Smith learned that all these friends were water brothers of Jubal—and therefore of him. This release from blindness shook him so that he almost lost anchorage. Calming himself, he stopped to praise and cherish them all, one by one and together.

Jill had one arm over the edge of the pool and Smith knew that she had been down under, checking on his safety. He had been aware of her when she had done it . . . but now he knew that she had not alone been worried about his safety; Jill felt other and greater trouble, trouble that was not relieved by knowing that her charge was safe under the water of life. This troubled him much and he considered going to her, making her know that he was with her and sharing her trouble.

He would have done so had it not been for a faint feeling of guilt: he was not certain that Jubal wanted him to walk around while his body was in the pool. He compromised by telling himself that he would share their trouble—and let them know that he was present if it became needful.

Smith then looked over the man who was stepping out of the air car, felt his emotions and recoiled from them, forced himself to examine him carefully, inside and out.

In a shaped pocket strapped around his waist the man was carrying a gun.

Smith was almost certain it was a gun. He examined it in detail, comparing it with guns he had seen, checking it against the definition in Webster's New International Dictionary of the English Language, Third Edition, published in Springfield, Massachusetts.

Yes, it was a gun—not alone in shape but also in wrongness that surrounded and penetrated it. Smith looked down the barrel, saw how it must function, and wrongness stared back at him.

Should he turn it and let it go elsewhere, taking its wrongness with it? Do it before the man was fully out of the car? Smith felt that he should . . . and yet Jubal had once told him not to do this to a gun until Jubal told him that it was time.

He knew now that this was indeed a cusp of necessity . . . but he resolved to balance on the point of cusp until he grokked all—since it was possible that Jubal, knowing that a cusp was approaching, had sent him under water to keep him from acting wrongly.

He would wait . . . but he would watch this gun. Not being limited to eyes, being able to see all around if needful, he continued to watch gun and man while he went inside the car.

More wrongness than he would have believed possible! Other men were in there, all but one crowding toward the door. Their minds smelled like a pack of Khaugha who had scented an unwary nymph . . . and each one held in his hands a something having wrongness.

As he had told Jubal, Smith knew that shape was never

a prime determinant; it was necessary to go beyond shape to essence in order to grok. His own people passed through five major shapes: egg, nymph, nestling, adult—and Old One which had no shape. Yet the essence of an Old One was patterned in the egg.

These somethings seemed like guns. But Smith did not assume that they were; he examined one most carefully. It was larger than any gun he had ever seen, its shape was different, its details were quite different.

It was a gun.

He examined each of the others just as carefully. They were guns.

The one man still seated had strapped to him a small gun.

The car had built into it two enormous guns—plus other things which Smith could not grok but in which he felt wrongness.

He considered twisting car, contents, and all—letting it topple away. But, in addition to his lifelong inhibition against wasting food, he knew that he did not grok what was happening. Better to move slowly, watch carefully, and help and share at cusp by following Jubal's lead . . . and if right action was to remain passive, then go back to his body when cusp had passed and discuss it with Jubal later.

He went outside the car and watched and listened and waited.

The first man to get out talked with Jubal concerning things which Smith could only file without grokking; they were beyond his experience. The other men got out and spread out; Smith spread his attention to watch them all. The car raised, moved backwards, stopped again, which relieved the beings it had sat on; Smith grokked with them, trying to soothe their hurtings.

The first man handed papers to Jubal; they were passed to Anne. Smith read them with her. He recognized their word shapings as being concerned with human rituals of healing and balance, but since he had encountered these rituals only in Jubal's law library, he did not try to grok the papers, especially as Jubal seemed untroubled by them—the wrongness was elsewhere. He was delighted to recognize his own human name on two papers; he always got an odd thrill out of reading it, as if he were two places at once—impossible as that was for any but an Old One.

Jubal and the first man walked toward the pool, with Anne close behind. Smith relaxed his time sense to let them move faster, keeping it stretched just enough so that he could comfortably watch all the men at once. Two men closed in and flanked the group.

The first man stopped near Smith's friends by the pool, looked at them, took a picture from his pocket, looked at it, looked at Jill. Smith felt her fear mount and he became very alert. Jubal had told him, "Protect Jill. Don't worry about wasting food. Don't worry about anything else. Protect Jill."

He would protect Jill in any case, even at the risk of acting wrongly. But it was good to have Jubal's reassurance; it left his mind undivided and untroubled.

When the man pointed at Jill and the two men flanking him hurried toward her with their guns of great wrongness, Smith reached out through his Doppelgänger and gave them each that tiny twist which causes to topple away.

The first man stared at where they had been and reached for his gun—and he was gone, too.

The other four started to close in. Smith did not want

to twist them. He felt that Jubal would be pleased if he simply stopped them. But stopping a thing, even an ash tray, is work—and Smith did not have his body. An Old One could have managed it, but Smith did what he could, what he had to do.

Four feather touches—they were gone.

He felt intense wrongness from the car on the ground and went to it—grokked a quick decision, car and pilot were gone.

He almost overlooked the car riding cover patrol. Smith started to relax—when suddenly he felt wrongness increase, and looked up.

The second car was coming in for landing.

Smith stretched time to his limit and went to the car in the air, inspected it carefully, grokked that it was choked with wrongness . . . tilted it into neverness. Then he returned to the group by the pool.

His friends seemed excited; Dorcas was sobbing and Jill was holding and soothing her. Anne alone seemed untouched by emotions Smith felt seething around him. But wrongness was gone, all of it, and with it the trouble that had disturbed his meditations. Dorcas, he knew, would be healed faster by Jill than by anyone—Jill always grokked a hurting fully and at once. Disturbed by emotions around him, uneasy that he might not have acted in all ways rightly at cusp—or that Jubal might so grok—Smith decided that he was now free to leave. He slipped back into the pool, found his body, grokked that it was as he had left it—slipped it back on.

He considered contemplating events at cusp. But they were too new; he was not ready to enfold them, not ready to praise and cherish the men he had been forced to move. Instead he returned happily to the task he had been on. "Sherbet" . . . "Sherbetlee" . . . "Sherbetzide"—

He had reached "Tinwork" and was about to consider "Tiny" when he felt Jill approaching. He unswallowed his tongue and made himself ready, knowing that his brother Jill could not remain long under water without distress.

As she touched him, he took her face in his hands and kissed her. It was a thing he had learned quite lately and did not grok perfectly. It had the growing-closer of water ceremony. But it had something else, too . . . something he wanted to grok in perfect fullness.

XVI

HARSHAW DID NOT wait for Gillian to dig her problem child out of the pool; he left orders for Dorcas to be given a sedative and hurried to his study, leaving Anne to explain (or not) the events of the last ten minutes. *"Front!"* he called over his shoulder.

Miriam caught up with him. "I must be 'front,'" she said breathlessly. "But, Boss, what in the—"

"Girl, not one word."

"But, Boss—"

"Zip it, I said. Miriam, a week from now we'll sit down and get Anne to tell us what happened. But right now everybody and his cousins will be phoning and reporters will crawl out of trees—and I've got to make some calls first. Are you the sort of female who comes unstuck when she's needed? That reminds me—Make a note to dock Dorcas's pay for the time she spent having hysterics."

Miriam gasped. "Boss! You just dare and every single one of us will quit!"

"Nonsense."

"Quit picking on Dorcas. Why, I would have had hysterics myself if she hadn't beaten me to it." She added, "I think I'll have hysterics now."

Harshaw grinned. "You do and I'll spank you. All right, put Dorcas down for a bonus for 'hazardous duty.' Put all of you down for a bonus. Me, especially. *I* earned it."

"All right. Who pays your bonus?"

"The taxpayers. We'll find a way to clip—Damn!" They had reached his study; the telephone was already demanding attention. He slid into the seat and keyed in. "Harshaw speaking. Who the devil are you?"

"Skip it, Doc," a face answered. "You haven't frightened me in years. How's everything?"

Harshaw recognized Thomas Mackenzie, production manager-in-chief for New World Networks; he mellowed slightly. "Well enough, Tom. But I'm rushed as can be, so—"

"*You're* rushed? Try my forty-eight-hour day. Do you still think you are going to have something for us? I don't mind the equipment; I can overhead that. But I have to pay three crews just to stand by for your signal. I want to do you any favor I can. We've used lots of your script and we expect to use more in the future—but I wonder what to tell our comptroller."

Harshaw stared. "Don't you think that spot coverage was enough?"

"What spot coverage?"

Shortly Harshaw knew that New World Networks had seen nothing of recent events at his home. He stalled Mackenzie's questions, because he was certain that truthful answers would convince Mackenzie that poor old Harshaw had gone to pieces.

Instead they agreed that, if nothing worth picking up happened in twenty-four hours, New World could remove cameras and equipment.

As the screen cleared Harshaw ordered, "Get Larry. Have him fetch that panic button—Anne has it." He made two more calls. By the time Larry arrived Harshaw knew that no network had been watching when the Special Service squads attempted to raid his home. It was not necessary to check on the "hold" messages; their delivery depended on the same signal that had failed to reach the networks.

Larry offered him the "panic button" portable radio link. "You wanted this, Boss?"

"I wanted to sneer at it. Larry, let this be a lesson: never trust machinery more complicated than a knife and fork."

"Okay. Anything else?"

"Is there a way to check that dingus? Without hauling three networks out of bed?"

"Sure. The transceiver they set up down in the shop has a switch for that. Throw the switch, push the panic button; a light comes on. To test on through, you call 'em, right from the transceiver, and tell 'em you want a hot test to the cameras and back to the stations."

"Suppose the test shows that we aren't getting through? Can you spot what's wrong?"

"Maybe," Larry said doubtfully, "if it was just a loose connection. But Duke is the electron pusher—I'm more the intellectual type."

"I know, son—I'm not bright about practical matters, either. Well, do the best you can."

"Anything else, Jubal?"

"If you see the man who invented the wheel, send him up. *Meddler!*"

Jubal considered the possibility that Duke had sabotaged the "panic button" but rejected the thought. He allowed himself to wonder what had really happened in his garden and how the lad had done it—from ten feet under water. He had no doubt that Mike had been behind those impossible shenanigans.

What he had seen the day before in this very room was just as intellectually stupefying—but the emotional impact was not. A mouse was as much a miracle of biology as was an elephant; nevertheless there was a difference—an elephant was bigger.

To see an empty carton, just rubbish, disappear in midair implied that a squad car full of men could vanish. But one event kicked your teeth in—the other didn't.

Well, he wouldn't waste tears on Cossacks. Jubal conceded that cops *qua* cops were all right; he had met honest cops . . . and even a fee-splitting constable did not deserve to be snuffed out. The Coast Guard was an example of what cops ought to be and frequently were.

But to be in the S.S. a man had to have larceny in his heart and sadism in his soul. Gestapo. Storm troopers for whatever politico was in power. Jubal longed for the days when a lawyer could cite the Bill of Rights and not have some over-riding Federation trickery defeat him.

Never mind—What would happen now? Heinrich's force certainly had had radio contact with its base; ergo, its loss would be noted. More S.S. troopers would come looking—already headed this way if that second car had been chopped off in the middle of an action report. "Miriam—"

"Yes, Boss."

"I want Mike, Jill, and Anne at once. Then find Larry—in the shop, probably—and both of you come back, lock all doors and ground-floor windows."

"More trouble?"

"Get movin', gal."

If the apes showed up—no, *when* they showed up—if their leader chose to break into a locked house, well, he might have to turn Mike loose on them. But this warfare had to stop—which meant that Jubal must get through to the Secretary General.

How?

Call the Palace? Heinrich had probably been telling the truth when he said that a renewed attempt would simply be referred to Heinrich—or whatever S.S. boss was warming that chair. Well? It would surprise them to have a man they had sent a squad to arrest blandly phoning in, face to face—he might be able to bull his way to the top. Commandant What's-his-name, chap with a face like a well-fed ferret. Twitchell. The commanding officer of the S.S. buckos would have access to the boss.

No good. It would be a waste of breath to tell a man who believes in guns that you've got something better. Twitchell would keep on throwing men and guns till he ran out of both—but he would never admit he couldn't bring in a man whose location was known.

Well, when you couldn't use the front door you slipped in through the back—elementary politics. Damn it, he needed Ben Caxton—Ben would know who had keys to the back door.

But Ben's absence was the reason for this donkey derby. Since he couldn't ask Ben, whom did he know who would know?

Hell's halfwit, he had been talking to one! Jubal turned to the phone and tried to raise Tom Mackenzie, running into three layers of interference, all of whom knew him and passed him along. While he was doing this, his staff and the Man from Mars came in; they sat down, Miriam stopping to write on a pad: *"Doors and windows locked."*

Jubal nodded and wrote below it: *"Larry—panic button?"* then said to the screen, "Tom, sorry to bother you again."

"A pleasure, Jubal."

"Tom, if you wanted to talk to Secretary General Douglas, how would you go about it?"

"Eh? I'd phone his press secretary, Jim Sanforth. I wouldn't talk to the Secretary General; Jim would handle it."

"But suppose you wanted to talk to Douglas himself."

"Why, I'd let Jim arrange it. Be quicker to tell Jim my problem, though. Look, Jubal, the network is useful to the administration—and they know it. But we don't presume on it."

"Tom, suppose you just *had* to speak to Douglas. In the next ten minutes."

Mackenzie's eyebrows went up. "Well . . . if I had to, I would explain to Jim why it was—"

"No."

"Be reasonable."

"That's what I can't be. Assume that you had caught Sanforth stealing the spoons, so you couldn't tell *him* what the emergency was. But you had to speak to Douglas immediately."

Mackenzie sighed. "I would tell Jim that I had to talk to the boss—and that if I wasn't through to him right away, the administration would never get another trace of support from the network."

"Okay, Tom, do it."

"Huh?"

"Call the Palace on another instrument—and be ready to cut me in instantly. I've *got* to talk to the Secretary General *right now*!"

Mackenzie looked pained. "Jubal, old friend—"

"Meaning you won't."

"Meaning I *can't*. You've dreamed up a hypothetical situation in which a—pardon me—major executive of a global network could speak to the Secretary General. But I can't hand this entree to somebody else. Look, Jubal, I respect you. The network would hate to lose you and we are painfully aware that you won't let us tie you down to a contract. But I *can't* do it. One does not telephone the World chief of government unless *he* wants to speak to *you*."

"Suppose I sign an exclusive seven-year contract?"

Mackenzie looked as if his teeth hurt. "I still couldn't. I'd lose *my* job—and you would have to carry out your contract."

Jubal considered calling Mike into pickup and naming him. But Mackenzie's own programs had run the fake "Man from Mars" interviews—and Mackenzie was either in on the hoax—or he was honest, as Jubal thought, and would not believe that he had been hoaxed. "All right, Tom. But you know your way around in the government. Who calls Douglas whenever he likes—and gets him? I don't mean Sanforth."

"No one."

"Damn it, no man lives in a vacuum! There must be

people who can phone him and not get brushed off by a secretary."

"Some of his cabinet, I suppose. Not all of them."

"I don't know any of *them*, either. I don't mean politicos. Who can call him on a private line and invite him to play poker?"

"Um . . . you don't want much, do you? Well, there's Jake Allenby."

"I've met him. He doesn't like me. I don't like him. He knows it."

"Douglas doesn't have many intimate friends. His wife rather discourages—Say, Jubal . . . how do you feel about astrology?"

"Never touch the stuff. Prefer brandy."

"Well, that's a matter of taste. But—see here, Jubal, if you ever let on I told you this, I'll cut your lying throat."

"Noted. Agreed. Proceed."

"Well, Agnes Douglas *does* touch the stuff . . . and I know where she gets it. Her astrologer can call Mrs. Douglas any time—and, believe you me, Mrs. Douglas has the ear of the Secretary General. You can call her astrologer . . . and the rest is up to you."

"I don't recall any astrologers on my Christmas card list," Jubal answered dubiously. "What's his name?"

"Her. Her name is Madame Alexandra Vesant, Washington Exchange. That's V, E, S, A, N, T."

"I've got it," Jubal said happily. "Tom, you've done me a world of good!"

"Hope so. Anything for the network?"

"Hold it." Jubal glanced at a note Miriam had placed at his elbow. It read: *"Larry says the transceiver won't trans—he doesn't know why."* Jubal went on, "That spot coverage failed through a transceiver failure."

"I'll send somebody."

"Thanks. Thanks twice."

Jubal switched off, placed the call by name, and instructed the operator to use hush and scramble if the number was equipped for it. It was, not to his surprise. Soon Madame Vesant's dignified features appeared in his screen. He grinned at her and called, "Hey, Rube!"

She looked startled, then stared. "Why, Doc Harshaw, you old scoundrel! Lord love you, it's good to see you. Where have you been hiding?"

"Just that, Becky—hiding. The clowns are after me."

Becky Vesey answered instantly, "What can I do to help? Do you need money?"

"I've got plenty of money, Becky. I'm in much more serious trouble than that—and nobody can help me but the Secretary General himself. I need to talk to him— right away."

She looked blank. "That's a tall order, Doc."

"Becky, I know. I've been trying to get through to him . . . and I can't. But don't you get mixed up in it . . . girl, I'm hotter than a smoky bearing. I took a chance that you might be able to advise me—a phone number, maybe, where I could reach him. But I don't want you in it personally. You'd get hurt—and I'd never be able to look the Professor in the eye . . . God rest his soul."

"I know what the Professor would want me to do!" she said sharply. "Knock off the nonsense, Doc. The Professor always swore that you were the only sawbones fit to carve people. He never forgot that time in Elkton."

"Now, Becky, we won't bring that up. I was paid."

"You saved his life."

"I did no such thing. It was his will to fight—and your nursing."

"Uh . . . Doc, we're wasting time. Just how hot are you?"

"They're throwing the book . . . and anybody near me will get splashed. There's a warrant out—a Federation warrant—and they know where I am and I *can't* run. It will be served any minute . . . and Mr. Douglas is the *only* person who can stop it."

"You'll be sprung. I guarantee that."

"Becky . . . I'm sure you would. But it might take a few hours. It's that 'back room,' Becky. I'm too old for a session in the back room."

"But—Oh, goodness! Doc, can't you give me some details? I ought to cast a horoscope, then I'd know what to do. You're Mercury, of course, since you're a doctor. But if I knew what house to look in, I could do better."

"Girl, there isn't time." Jubal thought rapidly. Whom to trust? "Becky, just knowing could put you in as much trouble as I am in."

"Tell me, Doc. I've never taken a powder at a clem yet—and you know it."

"All right. So I'm 'Mercury.' But the trouble lies in Mars."

She looked at him sharply. "How?"

"You've seen the news. The Man from Mars is supposed to be in the Andes. Well, he's not. That's just to hoax the yokels."

Becky seemed not as startled as Jubal had expected. "Where do you figure in this, Doc?"

"Becky, there are people all over this sorry planet who want to lay hands on that boy. They want to use him, make him geek. He's my client and I won't hold still for it. But my only chance is to talk with Mr. Douglas."

"The Man from Mars is your client? You can turn him up?"

"Only to Mr. Douglas. You know how it is, Becky—the mayor can be a good Joe, kind to children and dogs. But he doesn't know everything his town clowns do—especially if they haul a man in and take him into that back room."

She nodded. "Cops!"

"So I need to dicker with Mr. Douglas before they haul me in."

"All you want is to talk to him?"

"Yes. Let me give you my number—and I'll sit here, hoping for a call . . . until they pick me up. If you can't swing it . . . thanks anyway, Becky. I'll know you tried."

"Don't switch off!"

"Eh?"

"Keep the circuit, Doc. If I have any luck, they can patch through this phone and save time. So hold on." Madame Vesant left the screen, called Agnes Douglas. She spoke with calm confidence, pointing out that this was the development foretold by the stars—exactly on schedule. Now had come the critical instant when Agnes must guide her husband, using her womanly wit and wisdom to see that he acted wisely and without delay. "Agnes dear, this configuration will not be repeated in a thousand years—Mars, Venus, and Mercury in perfect trine, just as Venus reaches meridian, making Venus dominant. Thus you see—"

"Allie, what do the Stars tell me to do? You know I don't understand the scientific part."

This was hardly surprising, since the described relationship did not obtain. Madame Vesant had not had time to compute a horoscope and was improvising. She was untroubled by it; she was speaking a "higher truth," giving good advice and helping her friends. To help two friends at once made Becky Vesey especially happy. "Dear, you do understand it, you have born talent. You are Venus, as always, and Mars is reinforced, being both your husband and that young man Smith for the duration of this crisis. Mercury is Dr. Harshaw. To offset the imbalance caused by the reinforcement of Mars, Venus must sustain Mercury until the crisis is past. But you have very little time; Venus waxes in influence until reaching meridian, only seven minutes from now—after that your influence will decline. You must act quickly."

"You should have warned me."

"My dear, I have been waiting by my phone all day, ready to act instantly. The Stars tell us the nature of each crisis; they never tell details. But there is still time. I have Dr. Harshaw on the telephone; all that is necessary is to bring them face to face—before Venus reaches meridian."

"Well—All right, Allie. I must dig Joseph out of some silly conference. Give me the number of the phone you have this Doctor Rackshaw on—or can you transfer the call?"

"I can switch it here. Just get Mr. Douglas. Hurry, dear."

"I will."

When Agnes Douglas left the screen, Becky went to another phone. Her profession required ample phone service; it was her largest business expense. Humming happily she called her broker.

XVII

AS BECKY LEFT the screen Jubal leaned back. "Front," he said.

"Okay, Boss," Miriam acknowledged.

"This is for the 'Real-Experiences' group. Specify that the narrator must have a sexy contralto voice—"

"Maybe I should try for it."

"Not that sexy. Dig out that list of null surnames we got from the Census Bureau, pick one and put an innocent, mammalian first name with it, for pen name. A girl's name ending in 'a' that always suggests a 'C' cup."

"Huh! And not one of us with a name ending in 'a.' You louse!"

"Flat-chested bunch, aren't you? 'Angela.' Her name is 'Angela.' Title: 'I Married a Martian.' Start: All my life I had longed to become an astronaut. Paragraph. When I was just a tiny thing, with freckles on my nose and stars in my eyes, I saved box tops just like my brothers—and cried when Mummy wouldn't let me wear my Space Cadet helmet to bed. Paragraph. In those carefree childhood days I did not dream to what strange, bittersweet fate my tomboy ambition would—"

"Boss!"

"Yes, Dorcas?"

"Here come two more loads."

"Hold for continuation. Miriam, sit at the phone." Jubal went to the window, saw two air cars about to land. "Larry, bolt this door. Anne, your robe. Jill, stick close to Mike. Mike, do what Jill tells you to."

"Yes, Jubal. I will do."

"Jill, don't turn him loose unless you have to. And I'd much rather he snatched guns and not men."

"Yes, Jubal."

"This indiscriminate liquidation of cops must stop."

"Telephone, Boss!"

"All of you stay out of pickup. Miriam, note another title: 'I Married a Human.'" Jubal slid into the seat and said, "Yes?"

A bland face looked at him. "Doctor Harshaw?"

"Yes."

"The Secretary General will speak with you."

"Okay."

The screen changed to the tousled image of His Excellency the Honorable Joseph Edgerton Douglas, Secretary General of the World Federation of Free Nations. "Dr. Harshaw? Understand you need to speak with me."

"No, sir."

"Eh?"

"Let me rephrase it, Mr. Secretary. *You* need to speak with *me*."

Douglas looked surprised, then grinned. "Doctor, you have ten seconds to prove that."

"Very well, sir. I am attorney for the Man from Mars."

Douglas stopped looking tousled. "Repeat?"

"I am attorney for Valentine Michael Smith. It may help to think of me as *de-facto* Ambassador from Mars . . . in the spirit of the Larkin Decision."

"You must be out of your mind!"

"Nevertheless I am acting for the Man from Mars. And he is prepared to negotiate."

"The Man from Mars is in Ecuador."

"Please, Mr. Secretary, Smith—the real Valentine Michael Smith, not the one who appeared in newscasts—escaped from Bethesda Medical Center on Thursday last, in company with Nurse Gillian Boardman. He kept his freedom—and will continue to keep it. If your staff has told you anything else, then someone has been lying."

Douglas looked thoughtful. Someone spoke to him from off screen. At last he said, "Even if what you said were true, Doctor, you can't speak for young Smith. He's a ward of the State."

Jubal shook his head. "Impossible. The Larkin Decision."

"Now see here, as a lawyer, I assure you—"

"As a lawyer myself, I must follow my own opinion—and protect my client."

"You are a lawyer? I thought you claimed to be attorney-in-fact, rather than counsellor."

"Both. I am an attorney, admitted to practice before the High Court." Jubal heard a dull boom from below and glanced aside. Larry whispered, *"The front door, I think, Boss—Shall I go look?"*

Jubal shook his head. "Mr. Secretary, time is running out. Your men—your S.S. hooligans—are breaking into my house. Will you abate this nuisance? So that we can negotiate? Or shall we fight it out in the High Court with all the stink that would ensue?"

Again the Secretary appeared to consult off screen. "Doctor, if Special Service police are trying to arrest you, it is news to me. I—"

"If you'll listen, you'll hear them tromping up my staircase, sir! Mike! Anne! Come here." Jubal shoved his chair back to allow the angle to include them. "Mr. Secretary

General—the Man from Mars!" He could not introduce Anne, but she and her white cloak of probity were in view.

Douglas stared at Smith; Smith looked back and seemed uneasy. "Jubal—"

"Just a moment, Mike. Well, Mr. Secretary? Your men have broken into my house—I hear them pounding on my study door." Jubal turned his head. "Larry, open the door." He put a hand on Mike. "Don't get excited, lad."

"Yes, Jubal. That man. I have know him."

"And he knows you." Over his shoulder Jubal called out, "Come in, Sergeant."

An S.S. sergeant stood in the doorway, mob gun at ready. He called out, "Major! Here they are!"

Douglas said, "Let me speak to the officer commanding them, Doctor."

Jubal was relieved to see that the major showed up with his sidearm holstered; Mike had been trembling ever since the sergeant's gun had come into view—Jubal lavished no love on these troopers but he did not want Smith to display his powers.

The major glanced around. "You're Jubal Harshaw?"

"Yes. Come here. Your boss wants you."

"None of that. Come along. I'm also looking for—"

"Come *here*! The Secretary General wants a word with you."

The S.S. major looked startled, came into the study, and in sight of the screen—looked at it, snapped to attention, and saluted. Douglas nodded. "Name, rank, and duty."

"Sir, Major C. D. Bloch, Special Service Squadron Cheerio, Enclave Barracks."

"Tell me what you are doing."

"Sir, that's rather complicated. I—"

"Then unravel it. Speak up, Major."

"Yes, sir. I came here pursuant to orders. You see—"

"I don't see."

"Well, sir, an hour and a half ago a flying squad was sent here to make several arrests. When we couldn't raise them by radio, I was sent to find them and render assistance."

"Whose orders?"

"Uh, the Commandant's, sir."

"And did you find them?"

"No, sir. Not a trace."

Douglas looked at Harshaw. "Counsellor, did you see anything of another squad?"

"It's not my duty to keep track of your servants, Mr. Secretary."

"That is hardly an answer to my question."

"You are correct, sir. I am not being interrogated. Nor will I be, other than by due process. I am acting for my client; I am not nursemaid to these uniformed, uh, persons. But I suggest, from what I have seen, that they could not find a pig in a bath tub."

"Mmm . . . possibly. Major, round up your men and return."

"Yes, sir!" The major saluted.

"Just a moment!" Harshaw interrupted. "These men broke into my house, I demand to see their warrant."

"Oh. Major, show him your warrant."

Major Bloch turned red. "Sir, the officer ahead of me had the warrants."

Douglas stared. "Young man . . . are you telling me that you broke into a citizen's home *without a warrant*?"

"But—Sir, you don't understand! There *are* warrants. Captain Heinrich has them. Sir."

Douglas looked disgusted. "Get on back. Place yourself under arrest. I'll see you later."

"Yes, sir."

"Hold it," Harshaw demanded. "I exercise my right to make citizen's arrest. I shall have him placed in our local lockup. 'Armed breaking and entering.'"

Douglas blinked. "Is this necessary?"

"*I* think it is. These fellows seem awfully hard to find— I don't want this one to leave our local jurisdiction. Aside from criminal matters, I haven't had opportunity to assess property damage."

"You have my assurance, sir, that you will be fully compensated."

"Thank you, sir. But what is to keep another uniformed joker from coming along later? He wouldn't even need to break down the door! My castle stands violated, open to any intruder. Mr. Secretary, only the moments of delay afforded by my once-stout door kept this scoundrel from dragging me away before I could reach you . . . and you heard him say that there is another like him at large— with, so *he* says, warrants."

"Doctor, I know nothing of any such warrant."

"Warrants, sir. He said 'warrants for several arrests.' Perhaps a better term would be 'lettres de cachet.'"

"That's a serious imputation."

"This is a serious matter."

"Doctor, I know nothing of these warrants, if they exist. But I give you my personal assurance that I will look into it at once, find out why they were issued, and act as the merits may appear. Can I say more?"

"You can say a great deal more, sir. I can reconstruct why those warrants were issued. Someone in your service, in an excess of zeal, caused a pliant judge to issue them . . . for the purpose of seizing the persons of myself and my guests in order to question us, out of your sight. Out of *anyone's* sight, sir! We will discuss issues with *you* . . . but we will not be questioned by such as *this*—" Jubal hooked a thumb at the major. "—in some windowless back room! Sir, I hope for justice at your hands . . . but if those warrants are not canceled at once, if I am not assured beyond quibble that the Man from Mars, Nurse Boardman, and myself will be undisturbed, free to come and go, then—" Jubal shrugged helplessly. "—I must seek a champion. There are persons and powers outside the administration who hold deep interest in the affairs of the Man from Mars."

"You threaten me."

"No, sir. I plead with you. We wish to negotiate. But we cannot while being hounded. I beg you, sir—call off your dogs!"

Douglas glanced aside. "Those warrants, if any, will not be served. As soon as I can track them down they will be canceled."

"Thank you, sir."

Douglas looked at Major Bloch. "You insist on booking him?"

"Him? Oh, he's merely a fool in uniform. Let's forget damages, too. You and I have serious matters to discuss."

"You may go, Major." The S.S. officer saluted and left abruptly. Douglas continued, "Counsellor, the matters you raise cannot be settled over the telephone."

"I agree."

"You and your, uh, client will be my guests at the Palace. I'll send my yacht. Can you be ready in an hour?"

Harshaw shook his head. "Thank you, Mr. Secretary. We'll sleep here . . . and when it comes time I'll dig up a dog sled, or something. No need to send your yacht."

Mr. Douglas frowned. "Come, Doctor! As you pointed out, conversations will be quasi-diplomatic. In proffering protocol I have conceded this. Therefore I must be allowed to provide official hospitality."

"Well, sir, my client has had too much official hospitality—he had the Devil's own time getting shut of it."

Douglas's face became rigid. "Sir, are you implying—"

"I'm not implying anything. Smith has been through a lot and is not used to high-level ceremony. He'll sleep sounder here. And so shall I. I am an old man, sir; I prefer my own bed. I might point out that talks may break down and my client would be forced to look elsewhere—in which case we would find it embarrassing to be guests under your roof."

The Secretary General looked grim. "Threats again. I thought you trusted me, sir? I distinctly heard you say that you were 'ready to negotiate.'"

"I do trust you, sir." (—*as far as I could throw a fit!*) "And we are ready to negotiate. But I use 'negotiate' in its original sense, not in this new-fangled meaning of 'appeasement.' However, we will be reasonable. But we can't start talks at once; we're shy one factor and must wait. How long, I don't know."

"What do you mean?"

"We expect the administration to be represented by whatever delegation you choose—and we have the same privilege."

"Surely. But let's keep it small. I shall handle this myself, with an assistant or two. The Solicitor General . . . our experts in space law. To transact business requires a small group—the smaller the better."

"Most certainly. Our group will be small. Smith—myself—I'll bring a Fair Witness—"

"Oh, come now!"

"A Witness does not hamper. We'll have one or two others—but we lack one man. I have instructions that a fellow named Ben Caxton must be present . . . and I can't find the beggar."

Jubal, having spent hours of maneuvering in order to toss in this one remark, waited. Douglas stared. "'Ben Caxton?' Surely you don't mean that cheap winchell?"

"The Caxton I refer to has a column with one of the syndicates."

"Out of the question!"

Harshaw shook his head. "Then that's all, Mr. Secretary. My instructions give me no leeway. I'm sorry to have wasted your time. I beg to be excused." He reached out as if to switch off.

"Hold it!"

"Sir?"

"I'm not through speaking to you!"

"I beg the Secretary General's pardon. We will wait until he excuses us."

"Yes, yes, never mind, Doctor, do you read the tripe that comes out of this Capitol labeled news?"

"Good Heavens, no!"

"I wish I didn't have to. It's preposterous to talk about having journalists present. We'll see them after everything is settled. But even if we were to admit them, Caxton would not be one. The man is poisonous . . . a keyhole sniffer of the worst sort."

"Mr. Secretary, *we* have no objection to publicity. In fact, we insist on it."

"Ridiculous!"

"Possibly. But I serve my client as I think best. If we reach agreement affecting the Man from Mars and the planet which is his home, I want every person on this planet to know how it was done and what was agreed. Contrariwise, if we fail, people must hear how the talks broke down. There will be no star chamber, Mr. Secretary."

"Damn it, I wasn't speaking of a star chamber and you know it! I mean quiet, orderly talks without elbows jostled!"

"Then let the press in, sir, through cameras and microphones . . . but with elbows outside. Which reminds me—we will be interviewed, my client and I, over the networks later today—and I shall announce that we want public talks."

"*What*? You mustn't give out interviews *now*—why, that's contrary to the whole spirit of this discussion."

"I can't see that it is. Are you suggesting that a citizen must have your permission to speak to the press?"

"No, of course not, but—"

"I'm afraid it's too late. Arrangements have been made and the only way you could stop it would be by sending more carloads of thugs. My reason for mentioning it is that you might wish to give out a news release—in advance—telling the public that the Man from Mars has returned and is vacationing in the Poconos. So as to avoid any appearance that the government was taken by surprise. You follow me?"

"I follow you." The Secretary General stared at Harshaw. "Please wait." He left the screen.

Harshaw motioned Larry to him while his other hand

covered the sound pickup. "Look, son," he whispered, "with that transceiver out I'm bluffing on a busted flush. I don't know whether he left to issue that release . . . or has gone to set the dogs on us again. You high-tail out, get Tom Mackenzie on another phone, tell him that if he doesn't get the setup working, he's going to miss the biggest story since the Fall of Troy. Then be careful coming home—there may be cops."

"How do I call Mackenzie?"

"Uh—" Douglas was back on screen. "Speak to Miriam."

"Dr. Harshaw, I took your suggestion. A release much as you worded it . . . plus substantiating details." Douglas smiled in his homespun *persona*. "I added that the administration will discuss interplanetary relations with the Man from Mars—as soon as he had rested from his trip—and would do so publicly . . . *quite* publicly." His smile became chilly and he stopped looking like good old Joe Douglas.

Harshaw grinned in admiration—why, the old thief had rolled with the punch and turned a defeat into a coup for the administration. "That's perfect, Mr. Secretary! We'll back you right down the line!"

"Thank you. Now about this Caxton person—Letting the press in does not apply to him. He can watch it over stereovision and make up his lies from that. But he will not be present."

"Then there will be no talks, Mr. Secretary, no matter what you told the press."

"I don't believe you understand me, Counsellor. This man is offensive to me. Personal privilege."

"You are correct, sir. It is a matter of personal privilege."

"Then we'll say no more about it."

"*You* misunderstand *me*. It is indeed personal privilege. But not yours. Smith's."

"Eh?"

"You are privileged to select your advisers—and you can fetch the Devil himself and we shall not complain. Smith is privileged to select his advisers and have them present. If Caxton is not present, we will not be there. We will be at some quite different conference. One where you won't be welcome. Even if you speak Hindi."

Harshaw thought clinically that a man of Douglas's age should not indulge in rage. At last Douglas spoke—to the Man from Mars.

Mike had stayed on screen, as silently and as patiently as the Witness. Douglas said, "Smith, why do you insist on this ridiculous condition?"

Harshaw said instantly, "Don't answer, Mike!"—then to Douglas: "Tut, tut, Mr. Secretary! The Canons! You may not inquire why my client has instructed me. And the Canons are violated with exceptional grievance in that my client has but lately learned English and cannot hold his own against you. If you will learn Martian, I may permit you to put the question . . . in *his* language. But not today."

Douglas frowned. "I might inquire what Canons *you* have played fast and loose with—but I haven't time; I have a government to run. I yield. But don't expect me to shake hands with this Caxton!"

"As you wish, sir. Now back to the first point, I haven't been able to find Caxton."

Douglas laughed. "You insisted on a privilege—one I find offensive. Bring whom you like. But round them up yourself."

"Reasonable, sir. But would you do the Man from Mars a favor?"

"Eh? What favor?"

"Talks will not begin until Caxton is located—that is not subject to argument. But I have not been able to find him. I am merely a private citizen."

"What do you mean?"

"I spoke disparagingly of the Special Service squadrons—check it off to the irk of a man who has had his door broken down. But I know that they can be amazingly efficient . . . and they have the cooperation of police forces everywhere. Mr. Secretary, if you were to call in your S.S. Commandant and tell him that you wanted to locate a man at once—well, sir, it would produce more activity in an hour than I could in a century."

"Why on Earth should I alert police forces everywhere to find one scandal-mongering reporter?"

"Not 'on Earth,' my dear sir—on Mars. I ask you this as a favor to the Man from Mars."

"Well . . . it's preposterous but I'll go along." Douglas looked at Mike. "As a favor to Smith. I expect similar cooperation when we get down to cases."

"You have my assurance that it will ease the situation enormously."

"Well, I can't promise anything. You say the man is missing. He may have fallen in front of a truck, he may be dead."

Harshaw looked grave. "Let us hope not, for all our sakes."

"What do you mean?"

"I've tried to point out that possibility to my client— but he won't listen to the idea." Harshaw sighed. "A shambles, sir. If we can't find this Caxton, that is what we will have: a shambles."

"Well . . . I'll try. Don't expect miracles, Doctor."

"Not I, sir. My client. He has the Martian viewpoint . . . and *does* expect miracles. Let's pray for one."

"You'll hear from me. That's all I can say."

Harshaw bowed without getting up. "Your servant, sir."

As Douglas's image cleared Jubal stood up—and found Gillian's arms around his neck. "Oh, Jubal, you were *wonderful*!"

"We aren't out of the woods, child."

"But if anything can save Ben, you've just done it." She kissed him.

"Hey, none of that! I swore off before you were born. Kindly show respect for my years." He kissed her carefully and thoroughly. "That's to take away the taste of Douglas—between kicking him and kissing him I was getting nauseated. Go smooch Mike. He deserves it—for holding still to my lies."

"Oh, I shall!" Jill let go of Harshaw, put her arms around the Man from Mars. "Such wonderful lies, Jubal!" She kissed Mike.

Jubal watched as Mike initiated a second section of the kiss himself, performing it solemnly but not quite as a novice. Harshaw awarded him B-minus, with A for effort.

"Son," he said, "you amaze me. I would have expected you to curl up in one of your faints."

"I so did," Mike answered seriously, without letting go, "on first kissing time."

"Well! Congratulations, Jill. A.C., or D.C.?"

"Jubal, you're a tease but I love you anyhow and refuse

to let you get my goat. Mike got a little upset once—but no longer, as you can see."

"Yes," Mike agreed, "it is a goodness. For water brothers it is a growing-closer. I will show you." He let go of Jill.

Jubal put up a palm. "No."

"No?"

"You'd be disappointed, son. It's a growing-closer for water brothers only if they are young girls and pretty—such as Jill."

"My brother Jubal, you speak rightly?"

"I speak very rightly. Kiss girls all you want to—it beats the hell out of card games."

"Beg pardon?"

"It's a fine way to grow closer . . . with girls. Hmm . . ." Jubal looked around. "I wonder if that first-time phenomenon would repeat? Dorcas, I want your help in a scientific experiment."

"Boss, I am not a guinea pig! You go to hell."

"In due course, I shall. Don't be difficult, girl; Mike has no communicable diseases or I wouldn't let him use the pool—which reminds me: Miriam, when Larry gets back, tell him I want the pool cleaned—we're through with murkiness. Well, Dorcas?"

"How do you know it would be our *first* time?"

"Mmm, there's that. Mike, have you ever kissed Dorcas?"

"No, Jubal. Only today did I learn that Dorcas is my water brother."

"She is?"

"Yes. Dorcas and Anne and Miriam and Larry. They are your water brothers, my brother Jubal."

"Mmm, yes. Correct in essence."

"Yes. It is essence, the grokking—not sharing of water. I speak rightly?"

"Very rightly, Mike."

"They are your water brothers." Mike paused to think words. "In catenative assemblage, they are my brothers." Mike looked at Dorcas. "For brothers, growing-closer is good."

Jubal said, "Well, Dorcas?"

"Huh? Oh, Heavens! Boss, you're the world's worst tease. But Mike isn't teasing. He's sweet." She went to him, stood on tiptoes, held up her arms. "Kiss me, Mike."

Mike did. For some seconds they "grew closer."

Dorcas fainted.

Jubal kept her from falling. Jill had to speak sharply to Mike to keep him from trembling into withdrawal. Dorcas came out of it and assured Mike that she was all right and would happily grow closer again—but needed to catch her breath. *"Whew!"*

Miriam had watched round-eyed. "I wonder if I dare risk it?"

Anne said, "By seniority, please. Boss, are you through with me as a Witness?"

"For the time being."

"Then hold my cloak. Want to bet on it?"

"Which way?"

"Seven-to-two I *don't* faint—but I wouldn't mind losing."

"Done."

"Dollars, not hundreds. Mike dear . . . let's grow *lots* closer."

Anne was forced to give up through hypoxia; Mike,

with Martian training, could have gone without oxygen much longer. She gasped for air and said, "I wasn't set right. Boss, I'm going to give you another chance."

She started to offer her face again but Miriam tapped her shoulder. "Out."

"Don't be so eager."

"'Out,' I said. The foot of the line, wench."

"Oh, well!" Anne gave way. Miriam moved in, smiled, and said nothing. They grew close and continued to grow closer.

"Front!"

Miriam looked around. "Boss, can't you see I'm *busy?*"

"All right! Get out of the way—I'll answer the phone myself."

"Honest, I didn't hear it."

"Obviously. But we've got to pretend to a modicum of dignity—it might be the Secretary General."

It was Mackenzie. "Jubal, what the devil is going on?"

"Trouble?"

"I got a call from a man who urged me to drop everything and get cracking, because you've got something for me. I had ordered a mobile unit to your place—"

"Never got here."

"I know. They called in, after wandering around north of you. Our despatcher straightened them out and they should be there any moment. I tried to call you, your circuit was busy. What have I missed?"

"Nothing yet." Damnation, he should have had someone monitor the babble box. Was Douglas committed? Or would a new passel of cops show up? While the kids played post office! Jubal, you're senile. "Has there been any special news flash this past hour?"

"Why, no—oh, one item: the Palace announced that the Man from Mars had returned and was vacationing in the—*Jubal!* Are you mixed up in *that*?"

"Just a moment. Mike, come here. Anne, grab your robe."

"Got it, Boss."

"Mr. Mackenzie—meet the Man from Mars."

Mackenzie's jaw dropped. "Hold it! Let me get a camera on this! We'll pick it up off the phone—and repeat in stereo as quick as those jokers of mine get there. Jubal . . . I'm safe on this? You wouldn't—"

"Would I swindle you with a Fair Witness at my elbow? I'm not forcing this on you. We should wait and tie in Argus and Trans-Planet."

"Jubal! You can't do this to me."

"I won't. The agreement with all of you was to monitor the cameras when I signalled. And use it if newsworthy. I didn't promise not to give interviews in addition." Jubal added, "Not only did you loan equipment but you've been helpful personally, Tom. I can't express how helpful."

"You mean, uh, that telephone number?"

"Correct! But no questions about *that*, Tom. Ask me privately—next year."

"Oh, I wouldn't think of it. You keep your lip buttoned and I'll keep mine. Now don't go away—"

"One more thing. Those messages you're holding. Send them back to me."

"Eh? All right—I've kept them in my desk, you were so fussy. Jubal, I've got a camera on you. Can we start?"

"Shoot."

"I'm going to do *this* one myself!" Mackenzie turned his face and apparently looked at the camera. "Flash news!

This is your NWNW reporter on the spot while it's hot! The Man from Mars just phoned and wants to talk to *you*! Cut. Monitor, insert flash-news acknowledgment to sponsor. Jubal, anything special I should ask?"

"Don't ask about South America. Swimming is your safest subject. You can ask me about his plans."

"End of cut. Friends, you are now face to face and voice to voice with Valentine Michael Smith the Man from Mars! As NWNW, always first with the burst, told you earlier, Mr. Smith has just returned from high in the Andes—and we welcome him back! Wave to your friends, Mr. Smith—"

("Wave at the telephone, son. Smile and wave.")

"Thank you, Valentine Michael Smith. We're happy to see you so healthy and tan. I understand you have been gathering strength by learning to swim?"

"*Boss!* Visitors. Or something."

"*Cut!*—after the word 'swim.' What the hell, Jubal?"

"I'll see. Jill, ride herd on Mike—it might be General Quarters."

But it was the NWNW unit landing—and again rose bushes were damaged—Larry returning from phoning Mackenzie, and Duke, returning. Mackenzie decided to finish the telephone interview quickly, since he was now assured of depth and color through his unit. In the meantime its crew would check equipment on loan to Jubal. Larry and Duke went with them.

The interview finished with inanities, Jubal fielding questions Mike failed to understand; Mackenzie signed off with a promise that a color and depth interview would follow. "Stay synched with this station!" He waited for his technicians to report.

Which the crew boss did, promptly. "Nothing wrong with this field setup, Mr. Mackenzie."

"Then what was wrong before?"

The technician glanced at Larry and Duke. "It works better with power. The breaker was open at the board."

Harshaw stopped a wrangle about whether Duke had, or had not, told Larry that a circuit breaker must be reset if the equipment was to be used. Jubal did not care who was to blame—it all confirmed his conviction that technology had reached its peak with the Model-T Ford and had been growing decadent ever since. They got through the depth and color interview. Mike sent greetings to his friends of the *Champion*, including one to Dr. Mahmoud delivered in throat-rasping Martian.

At last Jubal set the telephone for two hours' refusal, stretched and felt great weariness, wondered if he were getting old. "Where's dinner? Which one of you wenches was supposed to cook tonight? Gad, this household is falling to rack and ruin!"

"It was my turn tonight," Jill answered, "but—"

"Excuses, always excuses!"

"Boss," Anne interrupted sharply, "how do you expect anyone to cook when you've kept us penned up all afternoon?"

"That's the moose's problem," Jubal said dourly. "If Armageddon is held on these premises, I expect meals hot and on time right up to the final trump. Furthermore—"

"Furthermore," Anne completed, "it is only seven-forty and plenty of time to have dinner by eight. So quit yelping. Cry-baby."

"Only twenty minutes of eight? Seems like a week since

lunch. You haven't left a civilized amount of time for a pre-dinner drink."

"Poor you!"

"Somebody get me a drink. Get everybody a drink. Let's skip dinner; I feel like getting as tight as a tent rope in the rain. Anne, how are we fixed for smörgåsbord?"

"Plenty."

"Why not thaw out eighteen or nineteen kinds and let everybody eat when he feels like it? What's all the argument?"

"Right away," agreed Jill.

Anne stopped to kiss him on his bald spot. "Boss, you've done nobly. We'll feed you and get you drunk and put you to bed. Wait, Jill, I'll help."

"I may to help, too?" Smith said eagerly.

"Sure, Mike. You can carry trays. Boss, dinner will be by the pool. It's a hot night."

"How else?" When they left, Jubal said to Duke, "Where the hell have you been?"

"Thinking."

"Doesn't pay. Makes you discontented. Any results?"

"Yes," said Duke, "I've decided that what Mike eats is his business."

"Congratulations! A desire not to butt into other people's business is eighty percent of all human wisdom."

"You butt into other people's business."

"Who said *I* was wise?"

"Jubal, if I offered Mike a glass of water, would he go through that lodge routine?"

"I think he would. Duke, the only human characteristic Mike has is an overwhelming desire to be liked. But I want to make sure that you know how serious it is. I accepted water brotherhood with Mike before I understood it—and I've become deeply entangled with its responsibilities. You'll be committing yourself never to lie to him, never to mislead him, to stick by him come what may. Better think about it."

"I *have* been thinking about it. Jubal, there's something about Mike that makes you *want* to take care of him."

"I know. You've probably never encountered honesty before. Innocence. Mike has never tasted the fruit of the Tree of Knowledge of Good and Evil . . . so we don't understand what makes him tick. Well, I hope you never regret it." Jubal looked up. "I thought you had stopped to distill the stuff."

Larry answered, "Couldn't find a corkscrew."

"Machinery again. Duke, you'll find glasses behind 'The Anatomy of Melancholy' up there—"

"I know where you hide them."

"—and we'll have a quick one before we get down to serious drinking." Duke got glasses; Jubal poured and raised his own. "Here's to alcoholic brotherhood . . . more suited to the frail human soul than any other sort."

"Health."

"Cheers."

Jubal poured his down his throat. "Ah!" he said happily, and belched. "Offer some to Mike, Duke, and let him learn how good it is to be human. Makes me feel creative. Front! Why are those girls never around when I need them? *Front!*"

"I'm 'Front,'" Miriam answered, at the door, "but—"

"I was saying: '—to what strange, bittersweet fate my tomboy ambition—'"

"I finished *that* story while you were chatting with the Secretary General."

"Then you are no longer 'Front.' Send it off."

"Don't you want to read it? Anyhow, I've got to revise it—kissing Mike gave me new insight."

Jubal shuddered. "'*Read* it?' Good God! It's bad enough to write such a thing. And don't consider revising, certainly not to fit the facts. My child, a true-confession story should never be tarnished by any taint of truth."

"Okay, Boss. Anne says to come to the pool and have a bite before you eat."

"Can't think of a better time. Shall we adjourn, gentlemen?"

The party progressed liquidly, with bits of fish and other Scandinavian comestibles added to taste. At Jubal's invitation Mike tried brandy. Mike found the result disquieting, so he analyzed his trouble, added oxygen to ethanol in an inner process of reverse fermentation, and converted it to glucose and water.

Jubal had been observing the effect of liquor on the Man from Mars—saw him become drunk, saw him sober up even more quickly. In an attempt to understand, Jubal urged more brandy on Mike—which he accepted since his water brother offered it. Mike sopped up an extravagant quantity before Jubal conceded that it was impossible to get him drunk.

Such was not the case with Jubal, despite years of pickling; staying sociable with Mike during the experiment dulled his wits. So, when he asked Mike what he had done, Mike thought that he was inquiring about the raid by the S.S.—concerning which Mike felt latent guilt. He tried to explain and, if needed, receive Jubal's pardon.

Jubal interrupted when he realized what the boy was talking about. "Son, I don't want to know. You did what was needed—just perfect. But—" He blinked owlishly. "—don't tell me. Don't ever tell *anybody*."

"Not?"

"'Not.' Damnedest thing I've seen since my uncle with two heads debated free silver and refuted himself. An explanation would spoil it."

"I do not grok?"

"Nor I. So let's have another drink."

Reporters started arriving: Jubal received them with courtesy, invited them to eat, drink, and relax—but refrain from badgering himself or the Man from Mars.

Those who failed to heed were tossed into the pool.

Jubal kept Larry and Duke at flank to administer baptism. While some became angry, others added themselves to the dousing squad with the fanatic enthusiasm of proselytes—Jubal had to stop them from ducking the doyen lippmann of the *New York Times* a third time.

Late in the evening Dorcas sought out Jubal and whispered: "Telephone, Boss."

"Take a message."

"You must answer, Boss."

"I'll answer it with an ax! I've been intending to get rid of that Iron Maiden—and I'm in the mood. Duke, get me an ax."

"Boss! It's the man you spoke to for a long time this afternoon."

"Oh. Why didn't you say so?" Jubal lumbered upstairs, bolted his door, went to the phone. Another of Douglas's acolytes was on screen but was replaced by Douglas. "It took you long enough to answer your phone."

"It's my phone, Mr. Secretary. Sometimes I don't answer it at all."

"So it seems. Why didn't you tell me Caxton is an alcoholic?"

"Is he?"

"He certainly is! He's been on a bender. He was sleeping it off in a fleabag in Sonora."

"I'm glad to hear he has been found. Thank you, sir."

"He's been picked up for 'vagrancy.' The charge won't be pressed—we are releasing him to you."

"I am in your debt, sir."

"Oh, it's not entirely a favor! I'm having him delivered as he was found—filthy, unshaven, and, I understand, smelling like a brewery. I want you to see what a tramp he is."

"Very well, sir. When may I expect him?"

"A courier left Nogales some time ago. At Mach four it should be overhead soon. The pilot will deliver him and get a receipt."

"He shall have it."

"Now, Counsellor, I wash my hands of it. I expect you and your client to appear whether you bring that drunken libeller or not."

"Agreed. When?"

"Tomorrow at ten?"

"' 'Twere best done quickly.' Agreed."

Jubal went downstairs and outside. "*Jill!* Come here, child."

"Yes, Jubal." She trotted toward him, a reporter with her.

Jubal waved him back. "Private," he said firmly. "Family matter."

"Whose family?"

"A death in yours. Scat!" The newsman grinned and left. Jubal leaned over and said softly, "He's safe."

"Ben?"

"Yes. He'll be here soon."

"Oh, Jubal!" She started to bawl.

He took her shoulders. "Stop it. Go inside until you get control."

"Yes, Boss."

"Go cry in your pillow, then wash your face." He went out to the pool. "Quiet everybody! I have an announcement. We've enjoyed having you—but the party is over."

"Boo!"

"Toss him in the pool. I'm an old man and need my rest. And so does my family. Duke, cork those bottles. Girls, clear the food away."

There was grumbling, the more responsible quieted their colleagues. In ten minutes they were alone.

In twenty minutes Caxton arrived. The S.S. officer commanding the car accepted Harshaw's signature and print on a prepared receipt, left while Jill sobbed on Ben's shoulder.

Jubal looked him over. "Ben, I hear you've been drunk for a week."

Ben cursed, while continuing to pat Jill's back. "'M drunk, awri'—but haven't had a drink."

"What happened?"

"I don' know. I don't *know*!"

An hour later Ben's stomach had been pumped; Jubal had given him shots to offset alcohol and barbiturates; he was bathed, shaved, dressed in borrowed clothes, had met the Man from Mars, and was sketchily brought up to date, while ingesting milk and food.

But he was unable to bring them up to date. For Ben, the week had not happened—he had become unconscious in Washington; had been shaken into wakefulness in Mexico. "Of course I *know* what happened. They kept me doped and in a dark room . . . and wrung me out. But I can't prove *anything.* And there's the village *Jefe* and the madman of this dive—plus, I'm sure, other witnesses—to swear how this gringo spent his time. And there's nothing I can do about it."

"Then don't," Jubal advised. "Relax and be happy."

"The hell I will! I'll get that—"

"Tut, tut! Ben, you're alive . . . which I would have given long odds against. And Douglas is going to do exactly what we want him to—and like it."

"I want to talk about that. I think—"

"I think you're going to bed. With a glass of warm milk to conceal Old Doc Harshaw's Secret Ingredient for secret drinkers."

Soon Caxton was snoring. Jubal was heading for bed and encountered Anne in the upper hall. He shook his head tiredly. "Quite a day, lass."

"Yes. I wouldn't have missed it and don't want to repeat it. Go to bed, Boss."

"In a moment. Anne? What's so special about the way that lad kisses?"

Anne looked dreamy, then dimpled. "You should have tried it."

"I'm too old to change. But I'm interested in everything about the boy. Is this something different?"

Anne pondered it. "Yes."

"How?"

"Mike gives a kiss his whole attention."

"Oh, rats! I do myself. Or did."

Anne shook her head. "No. I've been kissed by men who did a very good job. But they don't give kissing their whole attention. They *can't*. No matter how hard they try parts of their minds are on something else. Missing the last bus—or their chances of making the gal—or their own techniques in kissing—or maybe worry about jobs, or money, or will husband or papa or the neighbors catch on. Mike doesn't have technique . . . but when Mike kisses you he isn't doing *anything* else. You're his whole universe . . . and the moment is eternal because he doesn't have any plans and isn't going anywhere. Just kissing you." She shivered. "It's overwhelming."

"Hmm—"

"Don't 'Hmm' at me, you old lecher! You don't understand."

"No. I'm sorry to say I never will. Well, goodnight—and, by the way . . . I told Mike to bolt his door."

She made a face at him. "Spoilsport!"

"He's learning fast enough. Mustn't rush him."

XVIII

THE CONFERENCE WAS postponed twenty-four hours, which gave Caxton time to recuperate, to hear about his missing week, and to "grow closer" with the Man from Mars—for Mike grokked that Jill and Ben were "water brothers," consulted Jill, and solemnly offered water to Ben.

Ben had been briefed by Jill. It caused him much soul

searching. Ben was bothered by an uneasy feeling: he felt irked at the closeness between Mike and Jill. His bachelor attitudes had been changed by a week of undead oblivion; he proposed to Jill again, as soon as he got her alone.

Jill looked away. "Please, Ben."

"Why not? I've got a steady job, I'm in good health— or will be, as soon as I get their 'truth' drugs out of my system . . . and since I haven't, I feel a compulsion to tell the truth. I love you. I want to marry you and rub your poor tired feet. Am I too old? Or are you planning to marry somebody else?"

"No, neither one! Dear Ben . . . Ben, I love you. But don't ask me this now, I have . . . responsibilities."

He could not budge her.

He finally realized that the Man from Mars wasn't a rival—he was Jill's patient—and a man who marries a nurse must accept the fact that nurses feel maternal toward their charges—accept it and like it, for if Gillian had not had the character that made her a nurse, he would not love her. It was not the figure eight in which her pert fanny moved when she walked, nor the lush view from the other direction—he was not the infantile type, interested solely in the size of mammary glands! No, it was herself he loved.

Since what she was would make it necessary for him to take second place to patients who needed her, then he was bloody-be-damned not going to be jealous! Mike was a nice kid—as innocent and guileless as Jill had described him.

And he wasn't offering Jill a bed of roses; the wife of a newspaperman had things to put up with. He might be gone for weeks at times and his hours were always irregular. He wouldn't like it if Jill bitched. But Jill wouldn't.

Having reached this summing up, Ben accepted water from Mike whole-heartedly.

Jubal needed the extra day to plan. "Ben, when you dumped this in my lap I told Gillian that I would not lift a finger to get this boy his so-called 'rights.' I've changed my mind. We're not going to let the government have the swag."

"Certainly not *this* administration!"

"Nor any, the next will be worse. Ben, you undervalue Joe Douglas."

"He's a cheap politician, with morals to match!"

"Yes. And ignorant to six decimal places. But he is also a fairly conscientious world chief—better than we deserve. I would enjoy poker with him . . . he wouldn't cheat and he would pay up with a smile. Oh, he's an S.O.B.—but that reads 'Swell Old Boy,' too. He's middlin' decent."

"Jubal, I'm damned if I understand you. You told me that you had been fairly certain that Douglas had had me killed . . . and it wasn't far from it! You juggled eggs to get me out alive and God knows I'm grateful! But do you expect me to forget that Douglas was behind it? It's none of his doing that I'm alive—he would rather see me dead."

"I suppose he would. But, yup, just that—forget it."

"I'm damned if I will!"

"You'll be silly not to. You can't prove anything. And there's no call to be grateful to me and I won't let you lay this burden on me. I didn't do it for *you*."

"Huh?"

"I did it for a little girl who was about to go charging out and maybe get herself killed. I did it because she was my guest and I stood in loco parentis. I did it because she was all guts and gallantry but too ignorant to monkey with such a buzz saw. But you, my cynical and sin-stained chum, know all about buzz saws. If your carelessness causes you to back into one, who am I to tamper with your karma?"

"Mmm . . . Okay, Jubal, you can go to hell—for monkeying with my karma. If I have one."

"A moot point. The predestinationers and free-willers were tied in the fourth quarter, last I heard. Either way, I have no wish to disturb a man sleeping in a gutter. Dogooding is like treating hemophilia—the real cure is to let hemophiliacs bleed to death . . . before they breed more hemophiliacs."

"You could sterilize them."

"You would have me play God? But we're off the subject. Douglas didn't try to have you assassinated."

"Says who?"

"Says the infallible Jubal Harshaw, speaking ex cathedra from his belly button. Son, if a deputy sheriff beats a prisoner to death, it's sweepstakes odds that the county commissioners wouldn't have permitted it had they known. At worst they shut their eyes—afterwards—rather than upset applecarts. Assassination has never been a policy in this country."

"I'll show you backgrounds of a number of deaths I've looked into."

Jubal waved it aside. "I said it wasn't a policy. We've always had assassination—from prominent ones like Huey Long to men beaten to death with hardly a page-eight story. But it's never been a policy and the reason you are alive is that it is not Joe Douglas's policy. They snatched you clean, they squeezed you dry and they could have disposed of you as quietly as flushing a dead mouse down a toilet. But their boss doesn't like them to play that rough and if he became convinced that they had, it would cost their jobs if not their necks."

Jubal paused for a swig. "Those thugs are just a tool; they aren't a Praetorian Guard that picks the Caesar. So whom do you want for Caesar? Courthouse Joe whose indoctrination goes back to when this country was a nation and not a satrapy in a polyglot empire . . . Douglas, who can't stomach assassination? Or do you want to toss him out—we can, just by double-crossing him—toss him out and put in a Secretary General from a land where life is cheap and assassination a tradition? If you do, Ben— what happens to the next snoopy newsman who walks down a dark alley?"

Caxton didn't answer.

"As I said, the S.S. is just a tool. Men are always for hire who *like* dirty work. How dirty will that work become if you nudge Douglas out of his majority?"

"Jubal, are you saying I ought *not* to criticize the administration?"

"Nope. Gadflies are necessary. But it's well to look at the new rascals before you turn your present rascals out. Democracy is a poor system; the only thing that can be said for it is that it's eight times as good as any other method. Its worst fault is that its leaders reflect their constituents—a low level, but what can you expect? So look at Douglas and ponder that, in his ignorance, stupidity, and self-seeking, he resembles his fellow Americans but is a notch or two above average. Then look at the man who will replace him if his government topples."

"There's little difference."

"There's always a difference! This is between 'bad' and

'worse'—which is much sharper than between 'good' and 'better.'"

"Well? What do you want me to do?"

"Nothing," Harshaw answered. "I'll run this show myself. I expect you to refrain from chewing out Joe Douglas over this coming settlement—maybe praise him for 'statesmanlike restraint—'"

"You're making me vomit!"

"Use your hat. I'm going to tell you what I'm going to do. The first principle in riding a tiger is to hang on tight to its ears."

"Quit being pompous. What's the deal?"

"Quit being obtuse and listen. Mike has the misfortune to be heir to more wealth than Croesus dreamed of . . . plus a claim to political power under a politico-judicial precedent unparalleled in jug-headedness since Secretary Fall was convicted of receiving a bribe that Doheny was acquitted of paying. I have no interest in 'True Prince' nonsense. Nor do I regard that wealth as 'his'; he didn't produce it. Even if he had earned it, 'property' is not the natural and obvious concept that most people think it is."

"Come again?"

"Ownership is a sophisticated abstraction, a mystical relationship. God knows our legal theorists make this mystery complicated—but I didn't dream how subtle it was until I got the Martian slant. Martians don't own *anything* . . . not even their bodies."

"Wait a minute, Jubal. Even animals have property. And the Martians aren't animals; they're a civilization, with cities and all sorts of things."

"Yes. 'Foxes have holes and the birds of the air have

nests.' Nobody understands 'meus-et-tuus' better than a watch dog. But not Martians. Unless you regard joint ownership of everything by millions or billions of senior citizens—'ghosts' to you, my friend—as 'property.'"

"Say, Jubal, how about these 'Old Ones'?"

"You want the official version?"

"No. Your opinion."

"I think it is pious poppycock, suitable for enriching lawns—superstition burned into the boy's brain so early that he stands no chance of breaking loose."

"Jill talks as if she believed it."

"You will hear me talk as if I did, too. Ordinary politeness. One of my most valued friends believes in astrology; I would never offend her by telling her what *I* think. The capacity of humans to believe in what seems to me highly improbable—from table tapping to the superiority of their children—has never been plumbed. Faith strikes me as intellectual laziness but Mike's faith in his 'Old Ones' is no more irrational than a conviction that the dynamics of the universe can be set aside through prayers for rain."

"Mmm, Jubal, I confess to a suspicion that immortality is a fact—but I'm glad my grandfather's ghost doesn't boss me. He was a cranky old devil."

"And so was mine. And so am I. But is there any reason why a citizen's franchise should be voided simply because he is dead? The precinct I was raised in had a large graveyard vote—almost Martian. As may be, our lad Mike *can't* own anything because the 'Old Ones' already own everything. So I have trouble explaining to him that he owns over a million shares of Lunar Enterprises, plus the Lyle Drive, plus assorted chattels and securities. It doesn't help that the original owners are dead; that makes them 'Old

Ones'—Mike never would stick his nose into the business of 'Old Ones.'"

"Uh . . . damn it, he's incompetent."

"Of course. He can't manage property because he doesn't believe in its mystique—any more than I believe in his ghosts. Ben, all that Mike owns is a toothbrush—and he doesn't know he owns that. If you took it, he would assume that the 'Old Ones' had authorized the change."

Jubal shrugged. "He is incompetent. So I shan't allow his competency to be tried—for what guardian would be appointed?"

"Huh! Douglas. Or one of his stooges."

"Are you certain, Ben? Consider the makeup of the High Court. Might not the appointee be named Savvona-vong? Or Nadi? Or Kee?"

"Uh . . . you could be right."

"In which case the lad might not live long. Or he might live to a ripe age in some pleasant garden more difficult to escape from than Bethesda Hospital."

"What do you plan to do?"

"The power the boy nominally owns is too dangerous. So we give it away."

"How do you give away that much money?"

"You don't. Giving it away would change the balance of power—any attempt would cause the boy to be examined on his competence. So, instead, we let the tiger run like hell while hanging onto its ears for dear life. Ben, let me outline what I intend to do . . . then you do your damned-est to pick holes in it. Not the legality; Douglas's legal staff will write the double-talk and I'll check it. I want you to sniff it for political feasibility. Now here's what we are going to do—"

XIX

THE MARTIAN DIPLOMATIC delegation went to the Executive Palace the next morning. The unpretentious pretender to the Martian throne, Mike Smith, did not worry about the purpose of the trip; he simply enjoyed it. They rode a chartered Flying Greyhound; Mike sat in the astrodome, Jill on one side and Dorcas on his other, and stared and stared as the girls pointed out sights and chattered. The seat was intended for two; a warming growing-closer resulted. He sat with an arm around each, and looked and listened and tried to grok and could not have been happier if he had been ten feet under water.

It was his first view of Terran civilization. He had seen nothing in being removed from the *Champion*; he had spent a few minutes in a taxi ten days earlier but had grokked none of it. Since then his world had been bounded by house and pool, garden and grass and trees—he had not been as far as Jubal's gate.

But now he was sophisticated; he understood windows, realized that the bubble surrounding him was for looking out of and that the sights he saw were cities. He picked out, with the help of the girls, where they were on the map flowing across the lap board. He had not known until recently that humans knew about maps. It had given him a twinge of happy homesickness the first time he had grokked a human map. It was static and dead compared with maps used by his people—but it was a map. Even human maps were Martian in essence—he liked them.

He saw almost two hundred miles of countryside, most

of it sprawling world metropolis, and savored every inch, tried to grok it. He was startled by the size of human cities and their bustling activity, so different from the monastery-garden cities of his own people. It seemed to him that a human city must wear out almost at once, so choked with experience that only the strongest Old Ones could bear to visit its deserted streets and grok in contemplation events and emotions piled layer on endless layer in it. He had visited abandoned cities at home on a few wonderful and dreadful occasions, then his teachers had stopped it, grokking that he was not strong enough.

Questions to Jill and Dorcas enabled him to grok the city's age; it had been founded a little over two Earth centuries ago. Since Earth time units had no favor for him, he converted to Martian years and numbers—three-filled-plus-three-waiting years ($3^4 + 3^3 = 08$ Martian years).

Terrifying and beautiful! Why, these people must be preparing to abandon the city to its thoughts before it shattered under the strain and became *not* . . . yet, by mere time, the city was only-an-egg.

Mike looked forward to returning to Washington in a century or two to walk its empty streets and try to grow close to its endless pain and beauty, grokking thirstily until he was Washington and the city was himself—if he were strong enough by then. He filed the thought as he must grow and grow and grow before he would be able to praise and cherish the city's mighty anguish.

The Greyhound driver swung east in response to re-routing of unscheduled traffic (caused, unknown to Mike, by Mike's presence), and Mike saw the sea.

Jill had to tell him that it was water; Dorcas added that it was the Atlantic Ocean and traced the shore line on the map. Mike had known since he was a nestling that the planet next nearer the Sun was almost covered with the water of life and lately he had learned that these people accepted this richness casually. He had taken the more difficult hurdle of grokking the Martian orthodoxy that water ceremony did not require water; water was symbol for essence—beautiful but not indispensable.

But Mike discovered that knowing in abstract was not the same as physical reality; the Atlantic filled him with such awe that Jill said sharply, "Mike! Don't you dare!"

Mike chopped off his emotion and stored it. Then he stared at water stretching to horizon, and tried to measure it until his head was buzzing with threes and powers of threes and superpowers of powers.

As they landed on the Palace Jubal called out, "Remember, girls, form a square around him and don't be backward about planting a heel or jabbing an elbow. Anne, you'll be cloaked but that's no reason not to step on a foot if you're crowded. Or is it?"

"Quit fretting, Boss; nobody crowds a Witness—and I'm wearing spike heels and weigh more than you do."

"Okay. Duke, send Larry back with the bus as soon as possible."

"I grok it, Boss. Quit jittering."

"I'll jitter as I please. Let's go." Harshaw, the four girls with Mike, and Caxton got out; the bus took off. The landing flat was not crowded but it was far from empty. A man stepped forward and said heartily, "Dr. Harshaw? I'm Tom Bradley, senior executive assistant to the Secretary General. You are to go to Mr. Douglas's office. He will see you before the conference starts."

"No."

Bradley blinked. "I don't think you understood. These are instructions from the Secretary General. Oh, he said that it was all right for Mr. Smith to come with you—the Man from Mars, I mean."

"No. We're going to the conference room. Have somebody lead the way. In the meantime, I have an errand for you. Miriam, that letter."

"But. Dr. Harshaw—"

"I said, '*No!*' You are to deliver this to Mr. Douglas *at once*—and fetch his receipt to me." Harshaw signed across the flap of an envelope Miriam handed to him, pressed his thumb print over the signature, handed it to Bradley. "Tell him that he must read this at once—before the meeting."

"But the Secretary General desires—"

"The Secretary desires to see that letter. Young man, I am endowed with second sight. I prophesy that you won't be here tomorrow if you waste time getting it to him."

Bradley said, "Jim, take over," and left, with the letter. Jubal sighed. He had sweated over that letter; Anne and he had been up most of the night preparing draft after draft. Jubal intended to arrive at an open settlement—but he had no intention of taking Douglas by surprise.

A man stepped forward in answer to Bradley's order; Jubal sized him up as one of the clever young-men-on-the-make who gravitate to those in power and do their dirty work. The man smiled and said, "The name's Jim Sanforth, Doctor—I'm the Chief's press secretary. I'll be buffering for you from now on—arranging press interviews and so forth. I'm sorry to say that the conference is not ready; at the last minute we've had to move to a larger room. It's my thought that—"

"It's my thought that we'll go to that conference room right now."

"Doctor, you don't understand. They are stringing wires and things, the room is swarming with reporters and—"

"Very well. We'll chat with 'em."

"No, Doctor. I have instructions—"

"Youngster, you can take your instructions, fold them until they are all corners—and shove them in your oubliette. We are here for one purpose: a public conference. If the conference is not ready, we'll see the press—in the conference room."

"But—"

"You're keeping the Man from Mars standing on a windy roof." Harshaw raised his voice. "Is there anyone smart enough to lead us to this conference room?"

Sanforth swallowed and said, "Follow me, Doctor."

The conference room was alive with newsmen and technicians but there was a big oval table, chairs, and several smaller tables. Mike was spotted and Sanforth's protest did not keep the crowd back. Mike's flying wedge of Amazons got him to the big table; Jubal sat him against it with Dorcas and Jill flanking him and the Fair Witness and Miriam seated behind him. Then Jubal made no attempt to fend off questions or pictures. Mike had been told that people would do strange things and Jubal had warned him to take no sudden actions (such as causing persons or things to go away, or stop) unless Jill told him to.

Mike took the confusion gravely; Jill was holding his hand and her touch reassured him.

Jubal wanted pictures, the more the better; as for questions, he did not fear them. A week of talking with Mike had convinced him that no reporter could get anything out of Mike without expert help. Mike's habit of answering literally and stopping would nullify attempts to pump him.

Most questions Mike answered with: "I do not know," or "Beg pardon?"

A Reuters correspondent, anticipating a fight over Mike's status as an heir, tried to sneak in his own test of Mike's competence: "Mr. Smith? What do you know about the laws of inheritance?"

Mike knew that he was having trouble grokking the human concept of property and, in particular, the ideas of bequest and inheritance. So he stuck to the book—which Jubal recognized as "Ely on Inheritance and Bequest," chapter one.

Mike recited what he had read, with precision and no expression, for page after page, while the room settled into silence and his interrogator gulped.

Jubal let it go on until every newsman there knew more than he wanted to know about dower and curtesy, consanguinean and uterine, *per stirpes* and *per capita*. At last Jubal said, "That's enough, Mike."

Mike looked puzzled. "There is more."

"Later. Does someone have a question on another subject?"

A reporter for a London Sunday paper jumped in with one close to his employer's pocketbook: "Mr. Smith, we understand you like girls. Have you ever kissed a girl?"

"Yes."

"Did you like it?"

"Yes."

"How did you like it?"

Mike hardly hesitated. "Kissing girls is a goodness," he explained. "It beats the hell out of card games."

Their applause frightened him. But he could feel that Jill and Dorcas were not frightened; they were trying to restrain that noisy expression of pleasure which he could not learn. So he calmed his fright and waited.

He was saved from further questions and was granted a great joy; he saw a familiar figure entering by a side door. "My brother Dr. Mahmoud!" Mike went on in overpowering excitement—in Martian.

The *Champion*'s semantician waved and smiled, answered in the same jarring language while hurrying to Mike. The two continued talking in unhuman symbols, Mike in eager torrent, Mahmoud not as rapidly, with sounds like a rhinoceros ramming a steel shed.

The newsmen stood it for some time, those who used sound recording it and writers noting it as color. At last one interrupted. "Dr. Mahmoud! What are you saying?"

Mahmoud answered in clipped Oxonian, "For the most part I've been saying, 'Slow down, my dear boy—do, please.'"

"And what does *he* say?"

"The rest is personal, private, of no possible int'rest. Greetings, y'know. Old friends." He continued to chat—in Martian.

Mike was telling his brother all that had happened since he had last seen him, so that they might grok closer—but Mike's abstraction of what to tell was Martian in concept, it being concerned primarily with new water brothers and the flavor of each . . . the gentle water that was Jill . . . the depth of Anne . . . the strange not-yet-fully-grokked fact that Jubal tasted now like an egg, then like an Old One, but was neither—the ungrokkable vastness of ocean—

Mahmoud had less to tell since less had happened to him, by Martian standards—one Dionysian excess of which he was not proud, one long day spent lying face down in Washington's Suleiman Mosque, the results of which he had not yet grokked and would not discuss. No new water brothers.

He stopped Mike presently and offered his hand to Jubal. "You're Dr. Harshaw. Valentine Michael thinks he has introduced me—and he has, by his rules."

Harshaw looked him over as he shook hands. Chap looked like a huntin', shootin', sportin' Britisher, from tweedy, expensively casual clothes to clipped grey mustache . . . but his skin was swarthy and the genes for that nose came from somewhere near the Levant. Harshaw did not like fakes and would choose cold cornpone over the most perfect syntho "sirloin."

But Mike treated him as a friend, so "friend" he was, until proved otherwise.

To Mahmoud, Harshaw looked like a museum exhibit of what he thought of as a "Yank"—vulgar, dressed too informally for the occasion, loud, probably ignorant, and almost certainly provincial. A professional man, too, which made it worse, as in Dr. Mahmoud's experience American professional men were under-educated and narrow, mere technicians. He held a vast distaste for all things American. Their incredible polytheistic babel of religions, their cooking (*cooking!!!*), their manners, their bastard architecture and sickly arts—and their blind, arrogant belief in their superiority long after their sun had set. Their women.

Their women most of all, their immodest, assertive women, with gaunt, starved bodies which nevertheless reminded him disturbingly of houris. Four of them crowded around Valentine Michael—at a meeting which should be all male—

But Valentine Michael offered these people—including these ubiquitous female creatures—offered them proudly and eagerly as his water brothers, thereby laying on Mahmoud an obligation more binding than that owed to the sons of one's father's brother—since Mahmoud understood the Martian term for such accretive relationships from observation of Martians and did not need to translate it inadequately as "catenative assemblage," nor even as "things equal to the same thing are equal to each other." He had seen Martians at home; he knew their poverty (by Earth standards); he had dipped into—and had guessed at far more of—their cultural wealth; and grokked the supreme value that Martians placed on inter-personal relationships.

Well, there was nothing else for it—he had shared water with Valentine Michael and now he must justify his friend's faith in him . . . he hoped that these Yanks were not complete bounders.

So he smiled warmly. "Yes. Valentine Michael has explained to me—most proudly—that you are all in—" (Mahmoud used one word of Martian.) "—to him."

"Eh?"

"Water brotherhood. You understand?"

"I grok it."

Mahmoud doubted if Harshaw did, but went on smoothly, "Since I am in that relationship to him, I must ask to be considered a member of the family. I know your name, Doctor, and I have guessed that this must be Mr. Caxton—I have seen your face pictured at the head of your column, Mr. Caxton— but let me see if I have the young ladies straight. This must be Anne."

"Yes. But she's cloaked."

"Yes, of course. I'll pay my respects to her later."

Harshaw introduced him to the others . . . and Jill startled him by addressing him with the correct honorific for a water brother, pronouncing it three octaves higher than any Martian would talk but with sore-throat purity of accent. It was one of a dozen words she could speak out of a hundred-odd that she was beginning to understand—but this one she had down pat because it was used to her and by her many times each day.

Dr. Mahmoud's eyes widened—perhaps these people were not mere uncircumcised barbarians . . . his young friend *did* have strong intuition. Instantly he offered Jill the correct honorific in response and bowed over her hand.

Jill saw that Mike was delighted; she managed to croak the shortest of nine forms by which a water brother may return the response—although she did not grok it and would not have considered suggesting (in English) the nearest human biological equivalent . . . certainly not to a man she had just met!

Mahmoud, who did understand it, took its symbolic meaning rather than its (humanly impossible) literal meaning, and spoke rightly in response. Jill had passed her limit; she did not understand his answer and could not reply even in English.

But she got an inspiration. At intervals around the table were water pitchers each with its clump of glasses. She got a pitcher and tumbler, filled the latter.

She looked Mahmoud in the eye, said earnestly, "Water. Our nest is yours." She touched it to her lips and handed it to Mahmoud.

He answered in Martian, saw that she did not understand and translated, "Who shares water shares all." He took a sip and started to return it—checked himself and offered Harshaw the glass.

Jubal said, "I can't speak Martian, son—but thanks for water. May you never be thirsty." He drank a third of it. *"Ah!"* He passed it to Ben.

Caxton looked at Mahmoud and said soberly, "Grow closer. With water of life we grow closer." He sipped it and passed it to Dorcas.

In spite of precedents already set Dorcas hesitated. "Dr. Mahmoud? You do know how serious this is to Mike?"

"I do, miss."

"Well . . . it's just as serious to us. You understand? You . . . grok?"

"I grok its fullness . . . or I would have refused to drink."

"All right. May you always drink deep. May our eggs share a nest." Tears started down her cheeks; she drank and passed the glass hastily to Miriam.

Miriam whispered, "Pull yourself together, kid," then spoke to Mike, "With water we welcome our brother,"— then added to Mahmoud, "Nest, water, life." She drank. "Our brother." She offered him the glass.

Mahmoud drank what was left and spoke, but in Arabic: *"And if ye mingle your affairs with theirs, then they are your brothers.'"*

"Amen," Jubal agreed.

Dr. Mahmoud looked quickly at him, decided not to

inquire whether Harshaw had understood; this was not the place to say anything which might lead to unbottling his own troubles, his doubts. Nevertheless he felt warmed in his soul—as always—by water ritual . . . even though it reeked of heresy.

His thoughts were cut short by the assistant chief of protocol bustling up. "You're Dr. Mahmoud. You belong on the far side, Doctor. Follow me."

Mahmoud smiled. "No, I belong here. Dorcas, may I pull up a chair and sit between you and Valentine Michael?"

"Certainly, Doctor. I'll scrunch over."

The a.c. of p. was almost tapping his foot. "Dr. Mahmoud, *please*! The chart places you on the other side of the room! The Secretary General will be here any moment— and the place is still simply *swarming* with *reporters* and goodness knows who else . . . and I don't know *what* I'm going to do!"

"Then do it someplace else, bub," Jubal suggested.

"What? Who are you? Are you on the list?" He worriedly consulted a seating chart.

"Who are *you*?" Jubal answered. "The head waiter? I'm Jubal Harshaw. If my name is not on that list, you can tear it up. Look, buster, if the Man from Mars wants Dr. Mahmoud by him, that settles it."

"But he *can't* sit here! Seats at the conference table are reserved for High Ministers, Chiefs of Delegations, High Court Justices, and equal ranks—and I don't know *how* I can squeeze them in if any more show up—and the Man from Mars, of course."

"'Of course,'" Jubal agreed.

"And of course Dr. Mahmoud has to be near the

Secretary General—just back of him, so that he'll be ready to interpret. I must say you're not being helpful."

"I'll help." Jubal plucked the paper out of the official's hand. "Mmm . . . lemme see now. The Man from Mars will sit opposite the Secretary General, near where he happens to be. Then—" Jubal took a pencil and attacked the chart. "—this half, from *here* to *here*, belongs to the Man from Mars." Jubal scratched cross marks and joined them with a thick black arc, then began scratching out names assigned to that side of the table. "That takes care of half of your work . . . because I'll seat anybody on our side."

The protocol officer was too shocked to talk. His mouth worked but only noises came out. Jubal looked at him mildly. "Something the matter? Oh—I forgot to make it official." He scrawled under his amendments: *"J. Harshaw for V. M. Smith."* "Trot back to your top sergeant, son, and show him that. Tell him to check his rule book on official visits from heads of friendly planets."

The man opened his mouth—left without stopping to close it. He returned on the heels of an older man. The newcomer said in a no-nonsense manner, "Dr. Harshaw, I'm LaRue, Chief of Protocol. Do you actually need half the main table? I understood that your delegation was quite small."

"That's beside the point."

LaRue smiled briefly. "I'm afraid it's not beside the point. I'm at my wit's end for space. Almost every official of first rank has elected to be present. If you are expecting more people—though I do wish you had notified me—I'll have a table placed behind these two seats reserved for Mr. Smith and yourself."

"No."

"I'm afraid that's the way it must be. I'm sorry."

"So am I—for you. Because if half the main table is not reserved for Mars, we are leaving. Tell the Secretary General you busted up his conference by being rude to the Man from Mars."

"Surely you don't mean that?"

"Didn't you get my message?"

"Uh . . . well, I took it as a jest."

"I can't afford to joke, son. Smith is either top man from another planet paying an official visit to the top man of this planet—in which case he is entitled to all the side boys and dancing girls you can dig up—or he is just a tourist and gets no official courtesies of any sort. You can't have it both ways. Look around you, count the 'officials of first rank' as you call them, and guess whether they would be here if, in *their* minds, Smith is just a tourist."

LaRue said slowly, "There's no precedent."

Jubal snorted. "I saw the Chief of Delegation from the Lunar Republic come in—go tell *him* there's no precedent. Then duck!— I hear he's got a quick temper. But, son, I'm an old man and I had a short night and it's none of my business to teach you your job. Tell Mr. Douglas that we'll see him another day . . . when he's ready to receive us properly. Come on, Mike." He started to pry himself painfully out of his chair.

LaRue said hastily, "No, no, Dr. Harshaw! We'll clear this side of the table. I'll—Well, I'll do something. It's yours."

"That's better." Harshaw remained poised to get up. "But where's the Flag of Mars? And how about honors?"

"I'm afraid I don't understand."

"Never seen a day when I had so much trouble with

plain English. Look—See that Federation Banner back of where the Secretary is going to sit? Where's the one over here, for Mars?"

LaRue blinked. "I must admit you've taken me by surprise. I didn't know the Martians used flags."

"They don't. But you couldn't possibly whop up what *they* use for high state occasions." (Nor could I, boy, but that's beside the point!) "So we'll let you off easy and take an attempt for the deed. Piece of paper, Miriam—now. Like this." Harshaw drew a rectangle, sketched in it the traditional human symbol for Mars, a circle with an arrow leading out to upper right. "Make the field in white and the sigil of Mars in red—should be sewed in silk of course, but with a sheet and some paint any Boy Scout could improvise one. Were you a Scout?"

"Uh, some time ago."

"Good. You know the Scout's motto. Now about honors—You expect to play 'Hail to Sovereign Peace' as the Secretary comes in?"

"Oh, we must."

"Then you'll want to follow it with the anthem for Mars."

"I don't see how I can. Even if there *is* one . . . we don't have it. Dr. Harshaw, be reasonable!"

"Look, son. I *am* being reasonable. We came here for a small, informal meeting. We find you've turned it into a circus. Well, if you're going to have a circus, you've got to have elephants. Now we realize you can't play Martian music, any more than a boy with a tin whistle can play a symphony. But you *can* play a symphony—'The Nine Planets Symphony.' Grok it? I mean, 'Do you catch on?' Have the tape cut in at the beginning of the Mars movement; play that . . . or enough bars to let the theme be recognized."

LaRue looked thoughtful. "Yes, I suppose we could— but, Dr. Harshaw, I don't see how I can promise sovereign honors even on this improvised scale. I—I don't think I have the authority."

"Nor the guts," Harshaw said bitterly. "Well, *we* didn't want a circus—so tell Mr. Douglas that we'll be back when he's not so busy. Been nice chatting with you, son. Stop by the Secretary's office and say hello when we come back—if you're still here." He again went through the slow, apparently painful act of being too old and feeble to get out of a chair easily.

LaRue said, "Dr. Harshaw, *please* don't leave! Uh the Secretary won't come in until I send word that we are ready—so let me see what I can do. Yes?"

Harshaw relaxed with a grunt. "Suit yourself. But one more thing, while you're here. I heard a ruckus a moment ago—what I could catch, some crew members of the *Champion* wanted in. They're friends of Smith, so let 'em in. We'll accommodate 'em. Help to fill up this side of the table." Harshaw sighed and rubbed a kidney.

"Very well, sir," LaRue agreed stiffly and left.

Miriam whispered: "Boss—did you sprain your back doing those hand stands night before last?"

"Quiet, girl, or I'll paddle you." With satisfaction Jubal surveyed the room, which was continuing to fill with high officials. He had told Douglas that he wanted a "small, informal" talk—knowing that the announcement would fetch the powerful and power-hungry as light attracts moths. And now (he felt sure) Mike was about to be treated as a sovereign by those nabobs—with the world watching. Let 'em try to roust the boy around after this!

Sanforth was shooing out newsmen and the unfortunate assistant chief of protocol was jittering like a nervous babysitter in his attempt to play musical chairs with too few chairs and too many notables. They continued pouring in and Jubal concluded that Douglas had never intended to convene earlier than eleven and that everyone else had been informed—the hour given Jubal was to permit the private pre-conference meeting that he had refused. Well, the delay suited Jubal.

The leader of the Eastern Coalition came in. Mr. Kung was, by choice, not Chief of Delegation for his nation; his status under strict protocol was merely that of Assemblyman—but Jubal was not surprised to see the assistant chief of protocol drop everything and rush to seat Douglas's chief political enemy at the main table near the seat reserved for the Secretary General; it reinforced Jubal's opinion that Douglas was no fool.

Dr. Nelson, surgeon of the *Champion*, and Captain van Tromp, her skipper, came in together and were greeted with delight by Mike. Jubal was pleased, as it gave the boy something to do under the cameras, instead of sitting like a dummy. Jubal made use of the disturbance to rearrange seating. He placed Mike opposite the Secretary General's chair and himself took the chair on Mike's left—where he could touch Mike. Since Mike had foggy notions of human manners, Jubal had arranged signals as imperceptible as those used in putting a high-school horse through dressage—"stand up," "sit down," "bow," "shake hands"— except that Mike was not a horse and his training had required only five minutes to achieve perfection.

Mahmoud broke away from his shipmates and spoke to Jubal. "Doctor, the Skipper and the Surgeon are also water brothers of our brother—and Valentine Michael wanted to confirm it by again using ritual, all of us. I told him to wait. Do you approve?"

"Eh? Yes, certainly. Not in this mob." Damn it, how many water brothers did Mike have? "Maybe you three can come with us when we leave? And have a bite and a talk in private."

"I shall be honored. I feel sure the other two will come also."

"Good. Dr. Mahmoud, do you know of any other brothers of our young brother who are likely to show up?"

"No. Not from the *Champion*, there are no more." Mahmoud decided not to ask the complementary question, as it would hint at how disconcerted he had been—at first—to discover his own conjugational commitments. "I'll tell Sven and the Old Man."

Harshaw saw the Papal Nuncio come in, saw him seated at the main table, and smiled inwardly—if that long-eared debit, LaRue, had any lingering doubt about the official nature of this meeting, he would do well to forget them!

A man tapped Harshaw on the shoulder. "Is this where the Man from Mars hangs out?"

"Yes," agreed Jubal.

"I'm Tom Boone—Senator Boone, that is—and I've got a message for him from Supreme Bishop Digby."

Jubal put his cortex into emergency high speed. "I'm Jubal Harshaw, Senator—" He signalled Mike to stand and shake hands. "—and this is Mr. Smith. Mike, this is Senator Boone."

"How do you do, Senator Boone," Mike said in perfect

dancing-school form. He looked at Boone with interest. He had it straightened out for him that "Senator" did not mean "Old One" as the words seemed to shape; nevertheless he was interested in seeing a "Senator." He decided that he did not grok it.

"Pretty well, thank you, Mr. Smith. I won't take up your time; they seem about to get this shindig started. Mr. Smith, Supreme Bishop Digby sent me to give you a personal invite to attend services at Archangel Foster Tabernacle of the New Revelation."

"Beg pardon?"

Jubal moved in. "Senator, as you know, many things here—everything—is new to the Man from Mars. But it happens that Mr. Smith has seen one of your services by stereovision—"

"Not the same thing."

"I know. He expressed great interest and asked many questions—many of which I could not answer."

Boone looked keenly at him. "You're not one of the faithful?"

"I must admit I am not."

"Come along yourself. Always hope for a sinner."

"Thank you, I will." (I surely will, friend!—I won't let Mike go into your trap alone!)

"Next Sunday—I'll tell Bishop Digby."

"Next Sunday if possible," Jubal corrected. "We might be in jail."

Boone grinned. "There's always that, ain't th'r? Send word around to me or the Supreme Bishop and you won't stay in long." He looked around the room. "Kind o' short on chairs. Not much chance for a plain senator with all those muckamucks elbowing each other."

"Perhaps you would honor us by joining us, Senator," Jubal answered smoothly, "at this table?"

"Eh? Why, thank you, sir! Don't mind if I do—ringside seat."

"That is," Harshaw added, "if you don't mind the implications of being seen seated with the Mars delegation. We aren't trying to crowd you into an embarrassing situation."

Boone barely hesitated. "Not at all! Matter of fact, between you and I, the Bishop is very, *very* interested in this young fellow."

"Fine. There's a chair by Captain van Tromp—probably you know him."

"Van Tromp? Sure, sure, old friends, know him well—met him at the reception." Senator Boone nodded at Smith, swaggered down and seated himself.

Fewer were getting past the guards. Jubal watched one argument over seating and the longer he watched the more he fidgeted. At last he could not sit still and watch this indecency go on. So he spoke with Mike, made sure that, if Mike did not understand why, at least he knew what Jubal wanted.

"Jubal, I will do."

"Thanks, son." Jubal got up and approached a group of three: the assistant chief of protocol, the Chief of the Uruguayan Delegation, and a man who seemed angry and baffled. The Uruguayan was saying: "—seat him, then you must find seats for all local chiefs of state—eighty or more. This is Federation soil and no chief of state has precedence over any other. If exceptions are made—"

Jubal interrupted by addressing the third man. "Sir—" He waited long enough to gain attention, plunged on.

"—the Man from Mars has instructed me to ask you to do him the great honor of sitting with him . . . if your presence is not required elsewhere."

The man looked startled, then smiled broadly. "Why, yes, that would be satisfactory."

The other two, palace official and Uruguayan dignitary, started to object; Jubal turned his back. "Let's hurry, sir—we have very little time." He had seen men coming in with what appeared to be a stand for a Christmas tree and a bloody sheet—but what was certainly the "Martian Flag." As they hurried, Mike stood up and was waiting.

Jubal said, "Sir, permit me to present Valentine Michael Smith. Michael—the President of the United States!"

Mike bowed very low.

There was barely time to seat him on Mike's right while the improvised flag was being set up. Music sounded, everyone stood, and a voice proclaimed:

"The Secretary General!"

XX

JUBAL HAD CONSIDERED having Mike remain seated while Douglas came in, but had rejected the idea; he was not trying to place Mike higher than Douglas but merely to establish that the meeting was between equals. So, when he stood up, he signalled Mike to do so. Great doors at the back of the hall opened at the first strains of "Hail to Sovereign Peace" and Douglas came in. He went to his chair and started to sit down.

Instantly Jubal signalled Mike to sit down, the result

being that Mike and the Secretary General sat down simultaneously—with a respectful pause before anyone else did so.

Jubal held his breath. Had LaRue done it? He hadn't quite promised—

The fortissimo tocsin of the "Mars" movement filled the room—the "War God" theme that startles even an audience expecting it. With his eyes on Douglas and Douglas looking back at him, Jubal was up out of his chair like a recruit snapping to attention.

Douglas stood, not as quickly but promptly.

But Mike did not; Jubal had not signalled him. He sat, unembarrassed by the fact that everyone else got back on his feet when the Secretary General did. Mike did not understand any of it and was content to do what his water brother wanted.

Jubal had puzzled over this, after he had demanded the "Martian Anthem." If the demand was met, what should Mike do? The answer depended on what role Mike was playing in this comedy—

The music stopped. On Jubal's signals Mike stood up, bowed quickly, and sat down, seating himself about as the Secretary General and the rest were seated. They all sat down more quickly this time, as no one missed the glaring point that Mike had remained seated through the "anthem."

Jubal sighed with relief. He had gotten away with it. Many years earlier he had seen one of the vanishing tribe of royalty (a reigning queen) receive a parade—and he had noticed that the royal lady bowed *after* her anthem was played, i.e., she had acknowledged a salute offered to her sovereign self.

But the head of a democracy stands for his nation's anthem like any citizen—he is not a sovereign.

As Jubal had pointed out, one couldn't have it two ways. Either Mike was a private citizen, in which case this gymkhana should never have been held—or, by the theory inherent in the Larkin Decision, the kid was sovereign all by his lonesome.

Jubal felt tempted to offer LaRue a pinch of snuff. Well, the point had not been missed by one—the Papal Nuncio kept his face straight but his eyes were twinkling.

Douglas started to speak: "Mr. Smith, we are honored and happy to have you as our guest. We hope that you will consider Earth your home quite as much as the planet of your birth, our neighbor—our good neighbor—Mars—" He went on in rounded, pleasant periods. Mike was welcomed—but whether as a sovereign, as a tourist, or as a citizen returning home, was impossible to tell.

Jubal watched Douglas, looking for some sign that would show how Douglas had taken the letter Jubal had sent to him. But Douglas never looked at him. Presently Douglas concluded, having said nothing and said it very well.

Jubal said, "Now, Mike."

Smith addressed the Secretary General—in Martian.

He cut it off and said gravely: "Mr. Secretary General of the Federation of Free Nations of the Planet Earth—" then went on again in Martian.

Then in English: "—we thank you for our welcome here today. We bring greetings to the peoples of Earth from the Ancient Ones of Mars—" and shifted again into Martian.

Jubal felt that "Ancient Ones" was a good touch; it

carried more bulge than "Old Ones" and Mike had not objected. It had been Jill's idea to alternate a Martian version with the English one—and Jubal admitted with warm pleasure that her gimmick puffed up a formal little speech as devoid of content as a campaign promise into something as rollingly impressive as Wagnerian opera. (And as hard to figure out!)

It didn't matter to Mike. He could insert the Martian as easily as he could memorize and recite the English. If it would please his water brothers to say these sayings, it made Mike happy.

Someone touched Jubal's shoulder, shoved an envelope in his hand, and whispered, "From the Secretary General." Jubal looked up, saw that it was Bradley, hurrying silently away. Jubal opened the envelope, glanced inside.

The note was one word: "Yes," and had been signed with "J.E.D."—in the famous green ink.

Jubal looked up, found Douglas's eyes on him; Jubal nodded and Douglas looked away. The conference was over; all that remained was to let the world know it.

Mike concluded the sonorous nullities; Jubal heard his own words: "—growing-closer, with mutual benefit to both worlds—" and "each race according to its own nature—" Douglas then thanked the Man from Mars, briefly but warmly.

Jubal stood up. "Mr. Secretary General—"

"Yes, Dr. Harshaw?"

"Mr. Smith is here in a dual role. Like some visiting prince in the history of our own great race, traveling by caravan and sail across uncharted vastnesses to a distant realm, he brings the good wishes of the Ancient Powers of Mars. But he is also a human being, a citizen of the

Federation of the United States of America. As such, he has rights and properties and obligations." Jubal shook his head. "Pesky ones. As attorney for his capacity as a citizen and a human being, I have been puzzling over his affairs and I have not even managed a complete list of what he owns—much less decide what to tell tax collectors."

Jubal stopped to wheeze. "I'm an old man, I might not live to complete the task. You know that my client has no business experience in the human sense—Martians do these things differently. But he is a young man of great intelligence—the whole world knows that his parents were geniuses—and blood will tell. There's no doubt that in a few years he could, if he wished, do nicely on his own without the aid of one old, broken-down lawyer. But his affairs need attention *today*; business won't wait.

"But, he is more eager to learn the history and arts and ways of the people of this, his second home, than he is to bury himself in debentures and stock issues and royalties—and I think in this he is wise. Mr. Smith possesses a direct wisdom that continues to astonish me . . . and astonishes all who meet him. When I explained the trouble, he looked at me with a clear gaze and said, 'That's no problem, Jubal—we'll ask Mr. Douglas.'" Jubal paused and said anxiously, "The rest is personal business, Mr. Secretary. Should I see you privately? And let these ladies and gentlemen go home?"

"Go ahead, Dr. Harshaw." Douglas added, "Protocol is dispensed with. Anyone who wishes to leave please feel free to do so."

No one left. "All right," Jubal went on. "I can wrap it up in one sentence. Mr. Smith wants to appoint you his attorney-in-fact, with full power to handle all his business affairs."

Douglas looked convincingly astonished. "That's a tall order, Doctor."

"I know it is, sir. I pointed out to him that you are the busiest man on this planet and didn't have *time* for his affairs." Jubal shook his head and smiled. "I'm afraid I didn't impress him—seems on Mars the busier a person is the more is expected of him. Mr. Smith simply said, 'We can ask him.' So I'm asking you. Of course we don't expect an answer off-hand—that's another Martian trait; Martians are never in a hurry. Nor are they inclined to make things complicated. No bond, no auditing, none of that claptrap—a written power of attorney if you want it. But it does not matter to him; he would do it just as readily, orally and right now. That's another Martian trait; if a Martian trusts you, he trusts you all the way. Oh, I should add: Mr. Smith is *not* making this request of the Secretary General; he's asking a favor of Joseph Edgerton Douglas, you personally. If you retire from public life, it will not affect this. Your successor in office doesn't figure in it. It's *you* he trusts . . . not just whoever happens to occupy the Octagon Office in this Palace."

Douglas nodded. "Regardless of my answer, I feel honored . . . and humble."

"Because if you decline to serve, or can't serve, or take on this chore and want to drop it later, or anything, Mr. Smith has his second choice—Ben Caxton, it is. Stand up, Ben; let people see you. And if both you and Caxton can't or won't, his next choice is—well, I guess we'll reserve that for the moment; just let it rest that there are successive choices. Uh, let me see now—" Jubal looked fuddled. "I'm out of the habit of talking on my feet. Miriam, where is that paper we listed things on?"

Jubal accepted a sheet from her and added, "Better give me the other copies, too." She passed over a thick stack of sheets. "This is a memo we prepared for you, sir—or for Caxton, if it turns out that way. Mmm, lemme see—oh yes, steward to pay himself what he thinks the job is worth but not less than—well, a considerable sum, nobody else's business, really. Steward to deposit monies in a drawing account for living expenses of party of the first part—uh, oh yes, I thought maybe you would want to use the Bank of Shanghai, say, as depository, and say, Lloyd's as your business agent—or the other way around—just to protect your name and fame. But Mr. Smith won't hear of fixed instructions— just an unlimited assignment of power, revocable by either side. But I won't read all this; that's why we wrote it out." Jubal peered vacantly around. "Uh, Miriam—trot around and give this to the Secretary General, that's a good girl. Um, these other copies, I'll leave them here. You may want to pass 'em out . . . or you may need them yourself. Oh, I'd better give one to Mr. Caxton—here, Ben."

Jubal looked anxiously around. "Uh, I guess that's all, Mr. Secretary. Did you have anything to say to us?"

"Just a moment. Mr. Smith?"

"Yes, Mr. Douglas?"

"Is this what you want? Do *you* want *me* to do what it says on this paper?"

Jubal held his breath, avoided glancing at his client. Mike had been coached to expect such a question . . . but there had been no telling what form it would take, nor any way to tell how Mike's literal interpretations could trip them.

"Yes, Mr. Douglas." Mike's voice rang out in the room—and in a billion rooms around the planet.

"You want me to handle your business affairs?"

"Please, Mr. Douglas. It would be a goodness. I thank you."

Douglas blinked. "Well, that's clear enough. Doctor, I'll reserve my answer—but you shall have it promptly."

"Thank you, sir. For myself as well as for my client."

Douglas started to stand up. Assemblyman Kung's voice interrupted. "One moment! How about the Larkin Decision?"

Jubal grabbed it. "Ah, yes, the Larkin Decision. I've heard a lot of nonsense about the Larkin Decision—mostly from irresponsible persons. Mr. Kung, what about it?"

"I'm asking *you*. Or your . . . client. Or the Secretary General."

Jubal said gently, "Shall I speak, Mr. Secretary?"

"Please do."

"Very well." Jubal took out a handkerchief and blew his nose in a prolonged blast, a minor chord three octaves below middle C. He fixed Kung with his eye and said solemnly, "Mr. Assemblyman, I'll address *you*—because I know it is unnecessary to address it to the government in the person of the Secretary. A long time ago, when I was a little boy, another boy and I formed a club. Since we had a club, we had to have rules . . . and the first rule we passed—unanimously—was that henceforth we could call our mothers 'Crosspatch.' Silly, of course . . . but we were very young. Mr. Kung, can you deduce the outcome?"

"I won't guess, Dr. Harshaw."

"I implemented our 'Crosspatch' decision just once. Once was enough and it saved my chum from the same mistake. All it got *me* was my bottom warmed with a peach switch. And that was the end of the 'Crosspatch' decision."

Jubal cleared his throat. "Knowing that someone was certain to raise this non-existent issue I tried to explain the Larkin Decision to my client. He had trouble realizing that anyone could think that this legal fiction would apply to Mars. After all, Mars is inhabited, by an old and wise race—much older than yours, sir, and possibly wiser. But when he did understand it, he was amused. Just that, sir—tolerantly amused. Once—just once—I underrated my mother's power to punish impudence. That lesson was cheap. But this planet cannot afford such a lesson on a planetary scale. Before we parcel out lands which do not belong to us, it behooves us to be very sure what peach switches are hanging in the Martian kitchen."

Kung looked unconvinced. "Dr. Harshaw, if the Larkin Decision is no more than a small boy's folly . . . *why were sovereign honors rendered to Mr. Smith?*"

Jubal shrugged. "That should be put to the government, not to me. But I can tell you how *I* interpreted them—as elementary politeness . . . to the Ancient Ones of Mars."

"Please?"

"Mr. Kung, those honors were no hollow echo of the Larkin Decision. In a fashion beyond human experience, Mr. Smith is the Planet Mars!"

Kung did not blink. "Continue."

"Or, rather, the Martian race. In Smith's person, the Ancient Ones of Mars are visiting us. Honors to him are honors to them—and harm done to him is harm to them. This is true in a literal but utterly unhuman sense. It was prudent for us to render honors to our neighbors today—but the wisdom has nothing to do with the Larkin Decision. No responsible person has argued that the Larkin precedent applies to an inhabited planet—I venture to say that none ever will." Jubal looked up, as if asking Heaven for help. "But, Mr. Kung, be assured that the ancient rulers of Mars notice how we treat their ambassador. Honors rendered them through him were a gracious symbol. I am certain that the government of this planet showed wisdom thereby. In time, *you* will learn that it was a prudent act as well."

Kung answered blandly, "Doctor, if you are trying to frighten me, you have not succeeded."

"I did not expect to. But, fortunately for the welfare of this planet, *your* opinion did not control." Jubal turned to Douglas. "Mr. Secretary, this is the longest public appearance I have made in years . . . and I am fatigued. Could we recess? While we await your decision?"

XXI

THE MEETING ADJOURNED. Jubal found his intention of getting his flock quickly away balked by the American President and Senator Boone; both realized the enhanced value of being seen on intimate terms with the Man from Mars—and both were aware that the eyes of the world were on them.

Other hungry politicos were closing in.

Jubal said quickly, "Mr. President, Senator—we're leaving at once to have lunch. Can you join us?" He reflected that two in private would be easier to handle than two dozen in public—and he had to get Mike away before anything came unstuck.

To his relief both had duties elsewhere. Jubal found himself promising not only to fetch Mike to that obscene Fosterite service but also to bring him to the White House—well, the boy could get sick, if necessary. "Please, girls!"

Mike was convoyed to the roof, Anne creating a bow wave with her height, her Valkyrie beauty, her impressive cloak. Jubal, Ben, and the officers from the *Champion* covered the rear. Larry and the bus were waiting; minutes later the driver left them on the roof of the New Mayflower. Newsmen caught up with them there, but the girls guarded Mike on down to a suite Duke had taken. They were enjoying it; Miriam and Dorcas displayed ferocity that reminded Jubal of a cat defending her young. A reporter that closed within three feet courted a spiked instep.

They found their corridor patrolled by S.S. troopers and an officer outside their suite.

Jubal's back hair rose, but he realized that their presence meant that Douglas was carrying out the bargain. The letter Jubal had sent before the conference had included a plea to Douglas to use his power to protect Mike's privacy—so that the unfortunate lad could lead a normal life.

So Jubal called out, "Jill! Keep Mike under control. It's okay."

"Right, Boss."

The officer at the door saluted, Jubal glanced at him. "Well! Howdy, Major. Busted down any doors lately?"

Major Bloch turned red and did not answer. Jubal wondered if the assignment was punishment. Duke was waiting inside. Jubal said, "Sit down, gentlemen. How about it, Duke?"

Duke shrugged. "Nobody has bugged this suite since I took it. But, Boss, *any* dump can be bugged so you can't find it."

"Yes, yes—I didn't mean that. I mean, 'How about our supplies?' I'm hungry, boy, and thirsty—and we've got three more for lunch."

"Oh, that. The stuff was unloaded under my eyes; I put it in the pantry. You've got a suspicious nature, Boss."

"You'd better acquire one if you want to live as long as I have."

"I don't hanker to."

"Matter of taste. I've had a good time, on the whole. Get crackin', girls. First one back with a drink for me skips her next turn at 'Front.' After our guests, I mean. Do sit down, gentlemen. Sven, what's your favorite poison? Akvavit? Larry, duck out and buy a couple of bottles. And Bols gin for the captain."

"Hold it, Jubal," Nelson said. "I'd rather have Scotch."

"Me, too," agreed van Tromp.

"Got enough to drown a horse. Dr. Mahmoud? If you prefer soft drinks, I'm sure the girls tucked some in."

Mahmoud looked wistful. "I should not be tempted by strong drink."

"Allow me." Jubal looked him over. "Son, you've been under nervous strain. Having no meprobamate, I'm forced to substitute two ounces of ninety-proof ethanol, repeat as needed. Any particular flavor?"

Mahmoud smiled. "Thank you, Doctor—but I'll sin my own sins. Gin, please, with water on the side. Or vodka. Or whatever is available."

"Or medicinal alcohol," Nelson added. "Don't let him kid you, Jubal. Stinky drinks anything—and regrets it."

"I do regret it," Mahmoud said earnestly. "It is sinful."

"Don't needle him, Sven," Jubal said brusquely. "If Stinky gets more mileage out of his sins by regretting, that's his business. To each his own. How about victuals, Stinky? Anne stuffed a ham into one of those hampers—and there may be other unclean items. Shall I check?"

Mahmoud shook his head. "I'm not a traditionalist, Jubal. That legislation was given long ago, for the needs of the time. The times are different now."

Jubal suddenly looked sad. "Yes. But for the better? Never mind, this too shall pass. Eat what you will, my brother—God forgives necessity."

"Thank you. But I often do not eat in the middle of the day."

"Better eat or ethanol will do more than relax you. Besides, these kids who work for me may sometimes misspell words . . . but they are all superb cooks."

Miriam was entering with a tray of drinks, orders filled while Jubal ranted. "Boss," she broke in, "will you put that in writing?"

"*What?*" He whirled around. "*Snooping!* Stay after school and write one thousand times: 'I will not flap my ears at private conversations.'"

"Yes, Boss. This is for you, Captain . . . and you, Dr. Nelson . . . and yours, Dr. Mahmoud. Water on the side, you said?"

"Yes, Miriam. Thank you."

"Usual Harshaw service—sloppy but fast. Here's yours, Boss."

"You put water in it!"

"Anne's orders. You're too tired to have it on the rocks."

Jubal looked long-suffering. "See what I put up with, gentlemen? We should never have put shoes on 'em. Miriam, make that 'one thousand times' in Sanskrit."

"Yes, Boss." She patted him on the head. "Go ahead and have your tizzy, dear; you've earned it. We're proud of you."

"Back to the kitchen, woman. Has everybody got a drink? Where's Ben?"

"They have by now. Ben is phoning in his column, his drink is at his elbow."

"Very well. You may back out quietly—and send Mike in. Gentlemen! Me ke aloha pau ole!" He drank, they joined him.

"Mike's helping. I think he's going to be a butler when he grows up."

"I thought you had left. Send him in anyhow; Dr. Nelson wants to examine him."

"No hurry," put in the ship's surgeon. "Jubal, this is excellent Scotch—but what was the toast?"

"Sorry. Polynesian. 'May our friendship be everlasting.' Call it a footnote to the water ceremony. By the way, gentlemen, Larry and Duke are water brothers to Mike, too, but don't let it fret you. They can't cook . . . but they're the sort to have at your back in a dark alley."

"If you vouch for them, Jubal," van Tromp assured him, "admit them and tyle the door. But let's drink to the girls. Sven, what's that toast to the flickas?"

"The one to pretty girls everywhere? Let's drink to the four who are here. *Skaal!*" They drank to their female water brothers and Nelson continued, "Jubal, where do you *find* them?"

"Raise 'em in my own cellar. Then when I've got 'em

trained, some city slicker comes along and marries them. It's a losing game."

"I see how you suffer," Nelson said sympathetically.

"I do. I trust all you gentlemen are married?"

Two were, Mahmoud was not. Jubal looked at him bleakly. "Would you have the grace to discorporate? After lunch—I wouldn't want you to do it on an empty stomach."

"I'm no threat, I'm a permanent bachelor."

"Come, sir! I saw Dorcas making eyes at you . . . and you were purring."

"I'm safe, I assure you." Mahmoud thought of telling Jubal that he would never marry out of his faith, decided that a gentile would take it amiss. "But, Jubal, don't make a suggestion like that to Mike. He wouldn't grok that you were joking—and you might have a corpse on your hands. I don't *know* that Mike can think himself dead. But he would try."

"I'm sure he can," Nelson said firmly. "Doctor—'Jubal' I mean—have you noticed anything odd about Mike's metabolism?"

"Uh, let me put it this way. I haven't noticed anything about his metabolism that is *not* odd."

"Exactly."

Jubal turned to Mahmoud. "Don't worry that I might invite Mike to suicide. I grok that he doesn't grok joking." Jubal blinked. "But *I* don't grok 'grok.' Stinky, you speak Martian."

"A little."

"You speak it fluently, I heard you. Do *you* grok 'grok'?"

Mahmoud looked thoughtful. "No. 'Grok' is the most important word in the language—and I expect to spend years trying to understand it. But I don't expect to be successful. You need to *think* in Martian to grok the word 'grok.' Perhaps you have noticed that Mike takes a veering approach to some ideas?"

"Have I! My throbbing head!"

"Mine, too."

"FOOD," ANNOUNCED JUBAL. "Lunch, and about time! Girls, put it where we can reach it and maintain a respectful silence. Go on, Doctor. Or does Mike's presence make it better to postpone it?"

"Not at all." Mahmoud spoke in Martian to Mike. Mike answered, smiled sunnily; his expression became blank again and he applied himself to food. "I told him what I was trying to do and he told me that I would speak rightly; this was not opinion but a fact, a necessity. I hope that if I fail to, he will notice and tell me. But I doubt if he will. Mike thinks in Martian—and this gives him a different 'map.' You follow me?"

"I grok it," agreed Jubal. "Language itself shapes a man's basic ideas."

"Yes, but—Doctor, you speak Arabic?"

"Eh? Badly," admitted Jubal. "Put in a while as an army surgeon in North Africa. I still read it because I prefer the words of the Prophet in the original."

"Proper. The Koran cannot be translated—the 'map' changes no matter how one tries. You understand, then, how difficult *I* found English. It was not alone that my native language has simpler inflections; the 'map' changed. English is the largest human tongue; its variety, subtlety, and irrational idiomatic complexity make it possible to say things in English which cannot be said in any other language. It almost drove me crazy . . . until I learned to think in it—and that put a new 'map' of the world on top of the one I grew up with. A better one, perhaps—certainly a more detailed one.

"But there are things which can be said in Arabic that *cannot* be said in English."

Jubal nodded. "That's why I've kept up my reading."

"Yes. But Martian is so much *more* complex than is English—and so wildly different in how it abstracts its picture of the universe—that English and Arabic might as well be one language. An Englishman and an Arab can learn to think each other's language. But I'm not certain that it will ever be possible for us to *think* in Martian (other than the way Mike learned it)—oh, we can learn 'pidgin' Martian— that is what I speak.

"Take this word: 'grok.' Its literal meaning, one which I suspect goes back to the origin of the Martian race as thinking creatures—and which throws light on their whole 'map'—is easy. 'Grok' means 'to drink.'"

"Huh?" said Jubal. "Mike never says 'grok' when he's just talking about drinking. He—"

"Just a moment." Mahmoud spoke to Mike in Martian. Mike looked faintly surprised. "'Grok' is drink."

"But Mike would have agreed," Mahmoud went on, "if I had named a hundred other English words, words which we think of as different concepts, even antithetical concepts. 'Grok' means *all* of these. It means 'fear,' it means 'love,' it means 'hate'—proper hate, for by the Martian 'map' you cannot hate anything unless you grok it, understand it so thoroughly that you merge with it and it merges with you—then can you hate. By hating yourself. But this implies that you love it, too, and cherish it and would not have it otherwise. Then you can *hate*—and (I think) Martian hate is an emotion so black that the nearest human equivalent could only be called mild distaste."

Mahmoud screwed up his face. "'Grok' means 'identically equal.' The human cliché. 'This hurts me worse than it does you' has a Martian flavor. The Martians seem to know instinctively what we learned painfully from modern physics, that observer interacts with observed through the process of observation. 'Grok' means to understand so thoroughly that the observer becomes a part of the observed—to merge, blend, intermarry, lose identity in group experience. It means almost everything that we mean by religion, philosophy, and science and it means as little to us as color means to a blind man." Mahmoud paused. "Jubal, if I chopped you up and made a stew, you and the stew, whatever was in it, would grok—and when I ate you, we would grok together and nothing would be lost and it would not matter which one of us did the eating."

"It would to me!" Jubal said firmly.

"You aren't a Martian." Mahmoud stopped to talk to Mike in Martian.

Mike nodded. "You spoke rightly, my brother. Dr. Mahmoud. I am been saying so. Thou art God."

Mahmoud shrugged helplessly. "You see how hopeless it is? All I got was a blasphemy. We don't think in Martian. We *can't*."

"Thou are God," Mike said agreeably. "God groks."

"Let's change the subject! Jubal, could I impose on brotherhood for more gin?"

"I'll get it!" said Dorcas.

* * *

IT WAS A family picnic, made easy by Jubal's informality, plus the fact that the newcomers were the same sort—each learned, acclaimed, and with no need to strive. Even Dr. Mahmoud, rarely off guard with those who did not share the one true faith in submission to the Will of God, always beneficent, merciful, found himself relaxed. It had pleased him greatly that Jubal read the words of the Prophet . . . and, now that he stopped to notice, the women of Jubal's household were plumper than he had thought. That dark one—He put the thought out of his mind; he was a guest.

But it pleased him that these women did not chatter, did not intrude into sober talk of men, but were quick with food and drink in warm hospitality. He had been shocked at Miriam's disrespect toward her master—then recognized it: a liberty permitted cats and favorite children in the privacy of the home.

Jubal explained that they were simply waiting on the Secretary General. "If he means business, we will hear from him soon. If we had stayed in the Palace, he might have been tempted to dicker. Here we can refuse to dicker."

"Dicker for what?" asked Captain van Tromp. "You gave him what he wanted."

"Not all he wanted. Douglas would rather have it be irrevocable . . . instead of on good behavior, with the power reverting to a man he detests—namely that scoundrel with the innocent smile, our brother Ben. But others would want to dicker, too. That bland buddha Kung— hates my guts, I snatched the rug out from under him. But if he could figure a deal that might tempt us, he would offer it. So we stay out of *his* way, too. Kung is one reason why we are eating and drinking nothing that we did not fetch."

"You feel that's something to worry about?" asked Nelson. "Jubal, I assumed that you were a gourmet who demanded his own cuisine. I can't imagine being poisoned in a hotel such as this."

Jubal shook his head sorrowfully. "Sven, nobody wants to poison *you*—but your wife might collect your insurance because you shared a dish with Mike."

"You really think so?"

"Sven, I'll call room service for anything you want. But I won't touch it and won't let Mike touch it. They know where we are and they've had a couple of hours in which to act—so I must assume that any waiter is on Kung's payroll . . . and maybe two or three others. My prime worry is to keep this lad alive while we sterilize the power he represents."

Jubal frowned. "Consider the black widow spider. A timid little beastie, useful, and the prettiest of the arachnids, with its patent-leather finish and its hourglass trademark. But the poor thing has the misfortune of too much power for its size. So everybody kills it.

"The black widow can't help it, it has no way to avoid its venomous power."

"Mike is in the same dilemma. He isn't as pretty as a black widow—"

"Why, Jubal!" Dorcas said indignantly. "What a mean thing to say! And how *untrue*!"

"Child, I don't have your glandular bias. Pretty or not, Mike can't get rid of that money, nor is it safe for him to have it. Not just Kung. The High Court is not as 'non-political' as it might be . . . although their methods would make a prisoner out of him rather than kill him—a fate which, for my taste, is worse. Not to mention other interested parties, in and out of office, who have turned over in their minds how it would affect *their* fortunes if Mike were guest of honor at a funeral. I—"

"Telephone, Boss."

"Anne, you hail from Porlock."

"No, Dallas."

"I will not answer the phone."

"She said to tell you it was Becky."

"Why didn't you say so?" Jubal hurried out of the room, found Madame Vesant's face in the screen. "Becky! I'm glad to see you, girl!"

"Hi, Doc. I caught your act."

"How'd it look?"

"I've never seen a tip turned more expertly. Doc, the profession lost a great talker when you weren't born twins."

"That's high praise, Becky." Jubal thought rapidly. "But you set up the act; I just cashed in on it—and there's plenty of cash. So name your fee, Becky."

Madame Vesant frowned. "You've hurt my feelings."

"Becky! Anybody can clap and cheer—but applause worth while will be found in a pile of soft, green folding money. The Man from Mars picks up this tab and, believe me, he can afford it." He grinned. "All you'll get from me is a hug and kiss that will crack your ribs."

She relaxed and smiled. "I remember how you used to pat my fanny while you assured me that the Professor was sure to get well—you always could make a body feel better."

"Surely I never did anything so unprofessional."

"You know you did. You weren't fatherly about it, either."

"Maybe it was the treatment you needed. I've given up fanny-patting—but I'll make an exception in your case."

"You'd better."

"And you'd better figure out that fee. Don't forget the zeroes."

"Doc, there are more ways of collecting a fee than by making a fast count on the change. Have you been watching the market today?"

"No, and don't tell me. Come have a drink instead."

"Uh, I'd better not. I promised, well, a rather important client that I would be available."

"I see. Becky, would the stars show that this matter would turn out best for everybody if it were signed and sealed today? Maybe just after the market closes?"

She looked thoughtful. "I'll look into it."

"Do. And come visit us. You'll like the boy. He's as weird as snake's suspenders but sweet as a stolen kiss."

"Uh . . . I will. Thanks, Doc."

They said good-by. Jubal found that Dr. Nelson had taken Mike into a bedroom to examine him. The surgeon was looking baffled. "Doctor," Nelson said, "I saw this patient only ten days ago. Tell me where he got those muscles?"

"Why, he sent in a coupon from 'Rut: The Magazine for He-Men.' You know, the ad that tells how a ninety-pound weakling can—"

"Doctor, please!"

"Why not ask *him*?"

Nelson did so. "I thinked them," Mike answered.

"That's right," Jubal agreed. "He 'thinked' 'em. When I got him, last week, he was a mess, slight, flabby, and pale. Looked as if he had been raised in a cave—I gather he was. So I told him to grow strong. He did."

"Exercises?" Nelson said doubtfully.

"Some swimming."

"A few days' swimming won't make a man look as if he had been sweating over bar bells for years!" Nelson frowned. "I know Mike has control of the so-called 'involuntary' muscles. But that has precedent. This, however, requires one to assume—"

"Doctor," Jubal said gently, "why not admit you don't grok it?"

Nelson sighed. "I might as well. Put on your clothes, Michael."

LATER, JUBAL UNBURDENED himself privately to the three officers of the *Champion*. "The financial end was simple: just tie up Mike's money so that a struggle couldn't take place. Not even if he dies, because I've told Douglas that Mike's death ends his stewardship whereas a rumor from a usually reliable source—me—has reached Kung and others that Mike's death gives Douglas permanent control. Of course, if I had magic powers, I would have stripped the boy of every penny. That—"

"Why, Jubal?" the captain interrupted.

Harshaw stared. "Are you wealthy, Skipper? I mean *rich*."

"*Me?*" Van Tromp snorted. "I've my salary, a pension someday, a mortgaged house—and two girls in college. I'd like to be wealthy!"

"You wouldn't like it."

"*Huh!* You wouldn't say that if you had daughters in school."

"I put four through college—and went in debt to my armpits. One is a star in her profession . . . under her married name because I'm an old bum instead of a revered memory. The others remember my birthday and don't bother me; education didn't harm them. I mention my offspring only to prove that I know that a father often needs more than he has. But you can go with some firm that will pay you several times what you're getting just for your name on their letterhead. You've had offers?"

"That's beside the point," Captain van Tromp answered stiffly. "I'm a professional man."

"Meaning that money can't tempt you into giving up commanding space ships."

"I wouldn't mind having money, too!"

"A little is no good. Daughters can spend ten percent more than a man can make in any usual occupation. That's a law of nature, to be known henceforth as 'Harshaw's Law.' But, Captain, *real* wealth, on the scale that calls for a battery of finaglers to hold down taxes, would ground you as certainly as resigning would."

"Nonsense! I'd put it into bonds and just clip coupons."

"Not if you were the type who acquires great wealth in the first place. Big money isn't hard to come by. All it costs is a lifetime of devotion. But no ballerina ever works harder. Captain, that's not your style; you don't want to make money, you simply want to *spend* money."

"Correct, sir! So I can't see why you would want to take Mike's wealth away from him."

"Because great wealth is a curse—unless you enjoy

money-making for its own sake. Even then it has serious drawbacks."

"Oh, piffle! Jubal, you talk like a harem guard trying to sell a whole man on the advantages of being a eunuch."

"Possibly," agreed Jubal. "The mind's ability to rationalize its own shortcomings is unlimited; I am no exception. Since I, like yourself, sir, have no interest in money other than to spend it, it is impossible for me to get rich. Conversely, there has never been any danger that I would fail to scrounge the modest amount needed to feed my vices, since anyone with the savvy not to draw to a small pair can do that. But great wealth? You saw that farce. Could I have rewritten it so that I acquired the plunder—become its manager and defacto owner while milking off any income I coveted—and still have rigged it so that Douglas would have supported the outcome? Mike trusts me; I am his water brother. Could I have stolen his fortune?"

"Uh . . . damn you, Jubal, I suppose so."

"A certainty. Because our Secretary General is no more a money-seeker than you are. *His* drive is power—a drum whose beat I do not hear. Had I guaranteed (oh, gracefully!) that the Smith estate would continue to bulwark his administration, then I would have been left with the boodle."

Jubal shuddered. "I thought I was going to have to do that, to protect Mike from vultures—and I was panic-stricken. Captain, you don't *know* what an Old Man of the Sea great wealth is. Its owner is beset on every side, like beggars in Bombay, each demanding that he invest or give away part of his wealth. He becomes suspicious—honest friendship is rarely offered him; those who could have been friends are too fastidious to be jostled by beggars, too proud to risk being mistaken for one.

"Worse yet, his family is always in danger. Captain, have your daughters ever been threatened with kidnapping?"

"What? Good Lord, no!"

"If you possessed the wealth Mike had thrust on him, you would have those girls guarded night and day—still you would not rest, because you would never be sure of the guards. Look at the last hundred or so kidnappings and note how many involved a trusted employee . . . and how few victims escaped alive. Is there anything money can buy which is worth having your daughters' necks in a noose?"

Van Tromp looked thoughtful. "I'll keep my mortgaged house, Jubal."

"Amen. I want to live my own life, sleep in my own bed—and not be *bothered*! Yet I thought I was going to be forced to spend my last years in an office, barricaded by buffers, working long hours as Mike's man of business.

"Then I had an inspiration. Douglas lives behind such barricades, has such a staff. Since we were surrendering the power to insure Mike's freedom, why not make Douglas pay by assuming the headaches? I was not afraid that he would steal; only second-rate politicians are money hungry—and Douglas is no pipsqueak. Quit scowling, Ben, and hope that he never dumps the load on *you*.

"So I dumped it on Douglas—and now I can go back to my garden. But that was simple, once I figured it out. It was the Larkin Decision that fretted me."

Caxton said, "I think you lost your wits on that, Jubal. That silly business of letting them give Mike sovereign 'honors.' You should simply have had Mike sign over all interest, if any, under that ridiculous Larkin theory."

"Ben m'boy," Jubal said gently, "as a reporter you are sometimes readable."

"Gee, thanks! My fan."

"But your concepts of strategy are Neanderthal."

Caxton sighed. "That's better. For a moment I thought you had gone soft."

"When I do, please shoot me. Captain, how many men did you leave on Mars?"

"Twenty-three."

"And what is their status under the Larkin Decision?"

Van Tromp frowned. "I'm not supposed to talk."

"Then don't," Jubal advised. "We can deduce it."

Dr. Nelson said, "Skipper, Stinky and I are civilians again. I shall talk as I please—"

"And I," agreed Mahmoud.

"—and they know what they can do with my reserve commission. What business has the government, telling us *we* can't talk? Those chair-warmers didn't go to Mars."

"Stow it, Sven. I intend to talk—these are our water brothers. But, Ben, I would rather not see this in print."

"Captain, if you'll feel easier, I'll join Mike and the girls."

"Please don't leave. The government is in a stew about that colony. Every man signed away his Larkin rights—to the government. Mike's presence on Mars confused things. I'm no lawyer, but I understood that, if Mike did waive his rights, that would put the administration in the driver's seat when it came to parceling out things of value."

"*What* things of value?" demanded Caxton. "Look, Skipper, I'm not running down your achievement, but from all I've heard, Mars isn't valuable real estate for human beings. Or are there assets still classified 'drop dead before reading'?"

Van Tromp shook his head. "No, the technical reports are all de-classified. But, Ben, the Moon was a worthless hunk of rock when we got it."

"Touché," Caxton admitted. "I wish my grandpappy had bought Lunar Enterprises." He added, "But Mars is inhabited."

Van Tromp looked unhappy. "Yes. But—Stinky, you tell him."

Mahmoud said, "Ben, there is plenty of room on Mars for human colonization and, so far as I was able to find out, the Martians would not interfere. We're flying our flag and claiming extraterritoriality right now. But our status may be like that of one of those ant cities under glass one sees in school rooms. I don't know where we stand."

Jubal nodded. "Nor I. I had no idea of the situation . . . except that the government was anxious to get those so-called rights. So I assumed that the government was equally ignorant and went ahead. 'Audacity, always audacity.'"

Jubal grinned. "When I was in high school, I won a debate by quoting an argument from the British Colonial Shipping Board. The opposition was unable to refute me—because there never was a 'British Colonial Shipping Board.'

"I was equally shameless this morning. The administration wanted Mike's 'Larkin rights' and was scared silly that we might make a deal with somebody else. So I used their greed and worry to force that ultimate logical absurdity of their fantastic legal theory, acknowledgment in unmistakable protocol that Mike was a sovereign—and must be treated accordingly!" Jubal looked smug.

"Thereby," Ben said dryly, "putting yourself up the well-known creek."

"Ben, Ben," Jubal said chidingly, "by their own logic they had crowned Mike. Need I point out that, despite the old saw about heads and crowns, it is safer to be publicly a king than a pretender in hiding? Mike's position was much improved by a few bars of music and an old sheet. But it was still not an easy one. Mike was, for the nonce, the acknowledged sovereign of Mars under the legalistic malarky of the Larkin precedent . . . and empowered to hand out concessions, trading rights, enclaves, ad nauseam. He must either do these things and be subjected to pressures even worse than those attendant on great wealth—or he must abdicate and allow his Larkin rights to devolve on those men now on Mars, i.e., to Douglas."

Jubal looked pained. "I detested both alternatives. Gentlemen, I could not permit my client to be trapped into such a farce. The Larkin Decision itself had to be nullified with respect to Mars—without giving the High Court a chance to rule."

Jubal grinned. "So I lied myself blue in the face to create a theory. Sovereign honors had been rendered Mike; the world had seen it. But sovereign honors may be rendered to a sovereign's alter ego, his ambassador. So I asserted that Mike was no cardboard king under a precedent not in point—but the ambassador of the great Martian nation!"

Jubal shrugged. "Sheer bluff. But I was staking my bluff on my belief that others—Douglas, and Kung—would be no more certain of the facts than was *I*." Jubal looked around. "I risked that bluff because you three were with us, Mike's water brethren. If you did not challenge me, then Mike *must* be accepted as Martian ambassador—and the Larkin Decision was dead."

"I hope so," Captain van Tromp said soberly, "but I did not take your statements as lies, Jubal."

"Eh? I was spinning fancy words, extemporizing."

"No matter. I think you told the truth." The skipper of the *Champion* hesitated. "Except that I would not call Mike an ambassador—an invasion force is probably closer."

Caxton's jaw dropped. Harshaw answered, "In what way, sir?"

Van Tromp said, "I'll amend that. I think he's a scout, reconnoitering for his Martian masters. Don't mistake me—I'm as fond of the boy as you are. But there's no reason for him to be loyal to us —to Earth, I mean." The captain frowned. "Everybody assumes that a man found on Mars would jump at the chance to go 'home'—but it wasn't that way. Eh, Sven?"

"Mike hated the idea," agreed Nelson. "We couldn't get close to him; he was afraid. Then the Martians told him to go with us . . . and he behaved like a soldier carrying out orders that scared him silly."

"Just a moment," Caxton protested. "Captain—Mars invade us? *Mars?* Wouldn't that be like us attacking Jupiter? We have two and a half times the surface gravity that Mars has; Jupiter has two and a half times ours. Analogous differences on pressure, temperature, atmosphere, and so forth. *We* couldn't live on Jupiter . . . and I don't see how Martians could stand our conditions. Isn't that true?"

"Close enough," admitted van Tromp.

"Why should we attack Jupiter? Or Mars attack us?"

"Ben, have you seen the proposals for a beachhead on Jupiter?"

"Nothing has gone beyond the dream stage. It isn't practical."

"Space flight wasn't practical a few years ago. Engineers calculate that, by using all we've learned from ocean exploration, plus equipping men with powered suits, it is possible to tackle Jupiter. Don't think that Martians are less clever than we are. You should see their cities."

"Uh—" said Caxton. "Okay, I still don't see why they would bother."

"Captain?"

"Yes, Jubal?"

"I see another objection. You know the classification of cultures into 'Apollonian' and 'Dionysian.'"

"I know in general."

"Well, it seems to me that even Zuni culture would be called 'Dionysian' on Mars. You've been there—but I've been talking with Mike. That boy was raised in an Apollonian culture—such cultures are not aggressive."

"Mmm . . . I wouldn't count on it."

Mahmoud said suddenly, "Skipper, there's evidence to support Jubal. You can analyse a culture from its language—and there isn't any Martian word for 'war.' At least, I don't think there is. Nor for 'weapon' . . . nor 'fighting.' If a word isn't in a language, then its culture never has the referent."

"Oh, twaddle, Stinky! Animals fight—ants conduct wars. Do they have *words* for it?"

"They would have," Mahmoud insisted, "in any verbalizing race. A verbalizing race has words for every concept and creates new ones or new definitions whenever a new concept evolves. A nervous system able to verbalize cannot avoid verbalizing. If the Martians know what 'war' is, they have a word for it."

"There's a way to settle it," Jubal suggested. "Call in Mike."

"Just a moment," van Tromp objected. "I learned years ago never to argue with a specialist. But I also learned that history is a long list of specialists who were dead wrong—sorry, Stinky."

"You're right, Captain—only I'm not wrong this time."

"All Mike can settle is whether he *knows* a certain word . . . which might be like asking a two-year-old to define 'calculus.' Let's stick to facts. Sven? About Agnew?"

Nelson answered, "It's up to you, Captain."

"Well . . . this is among water brothers, Gentlemen. Lieutenant Agnew was our junior medical officer. Brilliant, Sven tells me. But he couldn't stand Martians. I had given orders against going armed once it appeared that Martians were peaceful.

"Agnew disobeyed me—at least we were never able to find his side arm and the men who saw him alive say that he was wearing it. But all my log shows is: 'Missing and presumed dead.'

"Two crewmen saw Agnew go into a passage between two large rocks. Then they saw a Martian enter the same way—whereupon they hurried, as Dr. Agnew's peculiarity was well known.

"Both heard a shot. One says that he reached this opening in time to glimpse Agnew past the Martian. And then he didn't see Agnew. The second man says that when he got there the Martian was just exiting, sailed on past and went his way. With the Martian out of the way they could see the space between the rocks . . . and it was a dead end, empty.

"That's all, gentlemen. Agnew might have jumped that rock wall, under Mars' low gravity and the impetus of fear—but I could not and I tried—and to mention that these crewmen were wearing breathing gear—have to, on Mars—and hypoxia makes a man's senses unreliable. I don't know that the first crewman was drunk through oxygen shortage; I mention it because it is easier to believe than what he reported—which is that Agnew vanished in the blink of an eye. I suggested that he had suffered hypoxia and ordered him to check his breather gear.

"I thought Agnew would show up and I was looking forward to chewing him out for going armed.

"But we never found him. My misgivings about Martians date to that incident. They never again seemed to be just big, gentle, harmless, rather comical creatures, even though we never had trouble and they always gave us anything we wanted, once Stinky figured out how to ask for it. I played down the incident—can't let men panic when you're a hundred million miles from home. I couldn't play down the fact that Dr. Agnew was missing; the ship's company searched for him. But I squelched any suggestion of anything mysterious—Agnew got lost among those rocks, died when his oxygen ran out . . . was buried under sand drift. I used it to clamp down on always traveling in company, staying in radio contact, checking breather gear. I did not tell that crewman to keep his mouth shut; I simply hinted that his story was ridiculous since his mate did not confirm it. I think the official version prevailed."

Mahmoud said slowly, "Captain, this is the first I've

heard that there was any mystery. And I prefer your 'official' version—I'm not superstitious."

Van Tromp nodded. "That's what I wanted. Only Sven and myself heard that wild tale. But, just the same—" The captain suddenly looked old. "—I wake up in the night and ask myself: *'What became of Agnew?'*"

Jubal listened without comment. Had Jill told Ben about Berquist and that other fellow—Johnson? Had anyone told Ben about the battle of the swimming pool? It seemed unlikely; the kids knew that the "official" version was that the first task force had never showed up, they had all heard his phone call with Douglas.

Damn it, the only course was to keep quiet and keep on trying to impress the boy that he must *not* make unpleasant strangers disappear!

Jubal was saved from further soul-searching by Anne's arrival. "Boss, Mr. Bradley is at the door. The one who called himself 'senior executive assistant to the Secretary General.'"

"You didn't let him in?"

"No. We talked through the speakie. He says he has papers to deliver to you and that he will wait for an answer."

"Have him pass them through the flap. This is still the Martian Embassy."

"Just let him stand outside?"

"Anne, I know you were gently reared—but this is a situation in which rudeness pays off. We don't give an inch, until we get what we want."

"Yes, Boss."

The package was bulky with copies; there was only one document. Jubal called in everyone and passed them around. "I am offering one lollipop for each loophole, boobytrap, or ambiguity."

Presently Jubal broke the silence. "He's an honest politician—he stays bought."

"Looks that way," admitted Caxton.

"Anybody?" No one claimed a prize; Douglas had merely implemented the agreement. "Okay," said Jubal, "everybody witness every copy. Get your seal, Miriam. Hell, let Bradley in and have him witness, too—then give him a drink. Duke, tell the desk we're checking out. Call Greyhound and get our go-buggy. Sven, Skipper, Stinky— we're leaving the way Lot left Sodom . . . why don't you come up in the country and relax? Plenty of beds, home cooking, no worries."

The married men asked for rain checks; Dr. Mahmoud accepted. The signing took rather long because Mike enjoyed signing his name, drawing each letter with artistic satisfaction. The remains of the picnic had been loaded by the time all copies were signed and sealed, and the hotel bill had arrived.

Jubal glanced at the fat total, wrote on it: "Approved for payment—J. Harshaw for V. M. Smith," and handed it to Bradley.

"This is your boss's worry."

Bradley blinked. "Sir?"

"Oh, Mr. Douglas will doubtless turn it over to the Chief of Protocol. I'm rather green about these things."

Bradley accepted the bill. "Yes," he said slowly, "LaRue will voucher it—I'll give it to him."

"Thank you, Mr. Bradley—for *every*thing!"

PART THREE

His Eccentric Education

XXII

IN ONE LIMB of a spiral galaxy, close to a star known as "Sol" to some, another star became nova. Its glory would be seen on Mars in three-replenished (729) years, or 1370 Terran years. The Old Ones noted it as useful, shortly, for instruction of the young, while never ceasing the exciting discussion of esthetic problems concerning the new epic woven around the death of the Fifth Planet.

The departure of the *Champion* they noted without comment. A watch was kept on the strange nestling sent back in it, but nothing more, since there would be waiting before it would be fruitful to grok the outcome. The humans left on Mars struggled with environment lethal to naked humans but less difficult than that in the Free State of Antarctica. One discorporated through an illness some times called "homesickness." The Old Ones cherished the wounded spirit and sent it where it belonged for further healing; aside from that Martians left Terrans alone.

On Earth the exploding star was not noticed, human astronomers then being limited by speed of light. The Man from Mars was briefly in the news. The Federation Senate minority leader called for "a bold, new approach" to problems of population and malnutrition in southeast

Asia, starting with increased grants-in-aid to families with more than five children. Mrs. Percy B. S. Souchek sued the Los Angeles City-County supervisors over the death of her pet poodle Piddle which had taken place during a five-day stationary inversion. Cynthia Duchess announced that she was going to have the Perfect Baby by a scientifically selected donor and an equally perfect host-mother as soon as experts completed calculating the instant for conception to insure that the wonder child would be equally a genius in music, art, and statesmanship—and that she would (with the aid of hormonal treatments) nurse her child herself. She gave an interview on the psychological benefits of natural feeding and permitted (insisted) that the press take pictures to prove that she was endowed for this.

Supreme Bishop Digby denounced her as the Harlot of Babylon and forbade any Fosterite to accept the commission, either as donor or host-mother. Alice Douglas was quoted: "While I do not know Miss Duchess, one cannot help but admire her. Her brave example should be an inspiration to mothers everywhere."

Jubal Harshaw saw one of her pictures in a magazine. He posted it in the kitchen, then noted that it did not stay up long, which made him chuckle.

He did not have many chuckles that week; the world was too much with him. The press ceased bothering Mike when the story was over—but thousands of people did not forget Mike. Douglas tried to insure Mike's privacy; S.S. troopers patrolled Harshaw's fence and an S.S. car circled overhead and challenged any car that tried to land. Harshaw resented needing guards.

The telephone Jubal routed through an answering service to which was given a short list from whom Harshaw would accept calls—and kept the house instrument on "refuse & record" most of the time.

But mail always comes through.

Harshaw told Jill that Mike had to grow up; he could start by handling his mail. She could help him. "But don't bother *me*; I have enough screwball mail."

Jubal could not make it stick; there was too much and Jill did not know how.

Just sorting was a headache. Jubal called the local postmaster (which got no results), then called Bradley, which caused a "suggestion" to trickle down; thereafter Mike's mail arrived sacked as first, second, third, and fourth class, with mail for everyone else in another sack. Second and third class was used to insulate a root cellar. Once the cellar was over-insulated, Jubal told Duke to use such mail to check erosion in gullies.

Fourth class mail was a problem. One package exploded in the village post office, blowing down several years of "Wanted" announcements and one "Use Next Window" sign—by luck the postmaster was out for coffee and his assistant, an elderly lady with weak kidneys, was in the washroom. Jubal considered having parcels processed by bomb specialists.

This turned out not to be necessary; Mike could spot a "wrongness" about a package without opening it. Thereafter fourth class mail was left at the gate; Mike pried through it from a distance, caused to disappear any harmful parcel; Larry trucked the remainder to the house.

Mike loved opening packages although the plunder might not interest him. Anything nobody wanted wound up in a gully; this included gifts of food, as Jubal was not certain that Mike's nose for "wrongness" extended to poisons—Mike had drunk a poisonous solution used for photography which Duke had left in the refrigerator; Mike said mildly that the "iced tea" had a flavor he was not sure he liked.

Jubal told Jill that it was all right to keep anything provided nothing was (a) paid for, (b) acknowledged, nor (c) returned no matter how marked. Some items were gifts; more was unordered merchandise. Either way, Jubal assumed that unsolicited chattels represented efforts to use the Man from Mars and merited no thanks.

An exception was livestock, which Jubal advised Jill to return—unless she guaranteed care and feeding, and keeping same from falling into the pool.

First class mail was the biggest headache. After looking over a bushel or so, Jubal set up categories:

A. Begging letters—erosion fill.

B. Threatening letters—file unanswered. Later letters from same source—turn over to S.S.

C. Business "opportunities"—forward to Douglas.

D. Crackpot letters—pass around any dillies; the rest to a gully.

E. Friendly letters—answer if accompanied by stamped self-addressed envelope, using form letters signed by Jill. (Jubal pointed out that letters signed by the Man from Mars were valuable, and an invitation to more useless mail.)

F. Scatological letters—pass to Jubal (who had a bet with himself that none would show the faintest literary novelty) for disposition, i.e., gully.

G. Proposals of marriage and propositions less formal—file.

H. Letters from scientific and educational

institutions—handle as under "E." If answered, use form letter explaining that the Man from Mars was not available for *anything*; if Jill felt that a brush-off would not do, pass to Jubal.

I. Letters from persons who knew Mike, such as the crew of the *Champion*, the President of the United States, and others—let Mike answer as he pleased; exercise in penmanship would be good and exercise in human relations even better (if he wanted advice, let him ask).

This cut the answers to a few for Jill, seldom even one for Mike. Jill found that she could skim and classify in about one hour each day. The first four categories remained large; category "G" was very large following the stereocast from the Palace, then dwindled. Jubal cautioned Jill that, while Mike should answer letters only from acquaintances, mail addressed to him was his.

The third morning after the system was installed Jill brought a letter, category "G," to Jubal. The ladies and other females (plus misguided males) who supplied this category usually included pictures alleged to be of themselves; some left little to the imagination.

This letter enclosed a picture which left nothing to the imagination, then stimulated fresh imaginings. Jill said, "Look at this, Boss! I ask you!"

Jubal read the letter. "She knows what she wants. What does Mike think?"

"He hasn't seen it."

Jubal glanced at the picture. "A type which, in my youth, we called 'stacked.' Well, her sex is not in doubt, nor her agility. Why show it to *me*? I've seen better."

"What should I *do*! The letter is bad enough . . . but that *disgusting* picture—should I tear it up?"

"What's on the envelope?"

"Just the address and return address."

"How does the address read?"

"Huh? 'Mr. Valentine Michael Smith, the Man from'—"

"*Oh!* Then it's not addressed to *you*."

"Why, no, of course—"

"Let's get something straight. You are neither Mike's mother nor his chaperone. If Mike wants to read everything addressed to him, including junk mail, he is free to do so."

"He does read most of those ads. But you don't want him to see filth! He's *innocent*."

"So? How many men has he killed?"

Jill looked unhappy.

Jubal went on: "If you want to help him, you will concentrate on teaching him that killing is frowned on in this society. Otherwise he will be conspicuous when he goes out into the world."

"Uh, I don't think he wants to 'go out into the world.'"

"I'm going to push him out of the nest as soon as he can fly. I shan't make it possible for him to live out his life as an arrested infant. For one thing, I *can't* . . . Mike will outlive me by many years. But you are correct; Mike is innocent. Nurse, have you seen that sterile laboratory at Notre Dame?"

"I've read about it."

"Healthiest animals in the world—but they can't leave the laboratory. Child, Mike has got to get acquainted with 'filth'—and get immunized. Someday he'll meet the gal who wrote this, or her spiritual sisters—he'll meet her by the hundreds—shucks, with his notoriety and looks he could spend his life skipping from one bed to another. You can't stop it, I can't stop it; it's up to Mike. Furthermore, *I* wouldn't want to stop it, although it's a silly way to spend one's life—the same exercises over and over again, I mean. What do *you* think?"

"I—" Jill blushed.

"Maybe you don't find them monotonous—none of my business, either way. But if you don't want Mike's feet kicked out from under him by the first five hundred women who get him alone, then don't intercept his mail. Letters like that may put him on guard. Just pass it along in the stack, answer his questions—and try not to blush."

"Boss, you're infuriating when you're logical!"

"A most uncouth way to argue."

"I'm going to tear up that picture after Mike has seen it!"

"Oh, don't do that!"

"What? Do *you* want it?"

"Heaven forbid! But Duke collects such pictures. If Mike doesn't want it, give it to Duke."

"*Duke* collects such trash? He seems such a nice person."

"He is."

"But—I don't understand."

Jubal sighed. "I could explain it all day and you still wouldn't. My dear, there are aspects of sex on which it is impossible to communicate between the two sexes of our race. They are sometimes grokked by intuition across the gulf that separates us, by exceptionally gifted individuals. But words are useless. Just believe me: Duke is a perfect knight—and he will like that picture."

"I won't hand it to Duke myself—he might get ideas."

"Sissy. Anything startling in the mail?"

"No. The usual crop who want Mike to endorse things, or peddle 'Official Man-from-Mars' junk—one character asked for a five-year royalty-free monopoly—and wants Mike to finance it, too."

"I admire a whole-hearted thief. Tell him that Mike needs tax losses—so how much guarantee would he like?"

"Are you serious, Boss?"

"No, the gonif would show up, with his family. But you've given me an idea for a story. *Front!*"

Mike was interested in the "disgusting" picture. He grokked (theoretically) what the letter and picture symbolized, and studied the picture with the delight with which he studied each butterfly. He found butterflies and women tremendously interesting—all the grokking world was enchanting and he wanted to drink so deep that his own grokking would be perfect.

He understood the mechanical and biological processes being offered in these letters but wondered why strangers wanted his help in quickening eggs? Mike knew (without grokking) that these people made ritual of this necessity, a "growing-closer" somewhat like water ceremony. He was eager to grok it.

But he was not in a hurry, "hurry" he failed to grok. He was sensitive to correct timing—but with Martian approach: timing was accomplished by waiting. He noticed that his human brothers lacked his discrimination of time and often were forced to wait faster than a Martian would—but he did not hold their awkwardness against them; he learned to wait faster to cover their lack—he sometimes waited faster so efficiently that a human would have concluded that he was hurrying at breakneck speed.

He accepted Jill's edict that he was not to reply to these brotherly offers from female humans, but accepted it as a waiting—possibly a century hence would be better; in any case now was not the time since his brother Jill spoke rightly.

Mike agreed when Jill suggested that he give this picture to Duke. He would have anyhow; Mike had seen Duke's collection, looked through it with interest, trying to grok why Duke said, "That one ain't much in the face, but look at those legs—*brother*!" It made Mike feel good to be called "brother" by one of his own but legs were legs, save that his people had three each while humans had only two—without being crippled, he reminded himself.

As for faces, Jubal had the most beautiful face Mike had ever seen, distinctly his own. These human females in Duke's picture collection could hardly be said to have faces. All young human females had the same face—how could it be otherwise?

He had never had trouble recognizing Jill's face; she was the first woman he had ever seen and his first female water brother—Mike knew every pore on her nose, every incipient wrinkle in her face, and had praised each one in happy meditation. But, while he now knew Anne from Dorcas and Dorcas from Miriam by faces, it had not been so at first. Mike had distinguished by size and coloration—and by voice, since voices were never alike. When, as sometimes *did* happen, all three females were quiet at once, it was well that Anne was so much bigger, Dorcas so small, and that Miriam, bigger than Dorcas but smaller than Anne, nevertheless need not be mistaken for another if Anne or Dorcas was absent, because Miriam had hair called "red" even though it was not the color called "red" when speaking of anything but hair.

Mike knew that every English word held more than one meaning. It was a fact one got used to, just as the sameness of girl faces one could get used to . . . and, after waiting, they were no longer the same. Mike now could call up Anne's face and count the pores in her nose as readily as Jill's. In essence, even an egg was uniquely self, different from all other eggs any where and when. So each girl had potentially her own face, no matter how small the difference.

Mike gave the picture to Duke and was warmed by Duke's pleasure. Mike was not depriving himself; he could see it in his mind whenever he wished—even the face, as it had glowed with an unusual expression of beautiful pain.

He accepted Duke's thanks and went happily back to his mail.

Mike did not share Jubal's annoyance at the postal avalanche; he reveled in it, insurance ads and marriage proposals. His trip to the Palace had opened his eyes to enormous variety in this world and he resolved to grok it all. It would take centuries and he must grow and grow and grow, but he was in no hurry—he grokked that eternity and the ever-beautifully-changing now were identical.

He decided not to reread the Encyclopedia Britannica; mail gave him brighter glimpses of the world. He read it, grokked what he could, remembered the rest for contemplation while the household slept. He was beginning, he thought, to grok "business," "buying," "selling," and related unMartian activities—the Encyclopedia had left him unfilled, as (he now grokked) each article had assumed that he knew things that he did not.

There arrived in the mail, from Mr. Secretary General Joseph Edgerton Douglas, a checkbook and papers; his brother Jubal took pains to explain what money was and how it was used. Mike failed to understand, even though Jubal showed him how to make out a check, gave him "money" in exchange for it, taught him to count it.

Then suddenly, with grokking so blinding that he trembled, he understood money. These pretty pictures and bright medallions were not "money"; they were symbols for an idea which spread through these people, all through their world. But *things* were not money, any more than water shared was growing-closer. Money was an *idea*, as abstract as an Old One's thoughts—money was a great structured symbol for balancing and healing and growing-closer.

Mike was dazzled with the magnificent beauty of money.

The flow and change and countermarching of symbols was beautiful in small, reminding him of games taught nestlings to encourage them to reason and grow, but it was the totality that dazzled him, an entire world reflected in one dynamic symbol structure. Mike then grokked that the Old Ones of this race were very old indeed to have composed such beauty; he wished humbly to be allowed to meet one.

Jubal encouraged him to spend money and Mike did so, with the timid eagerness of a bride being brought to bed. Jubal suggested that he "buy presents for friends" and Jill helped, starting by placing limits: one per friend and a total cost not even a reciprocal filled-three of the sum in his account—Mike had intended to spend *all*.

He learned how difficult it was to spend money. There were so many things, all wonderful and incomprehensible. Surrounded by catalogs from Marshall Field's and the Ginza, Bombay and Copenhagen, he felt smothered in riches. Even the Sears & Montgomery catalog was too much.

Jill helped. "No. Duke would not want a tractor."

"Duke likes tractors."

"He's got one, or Jubal has, which is the same thing. He might like one of those cute little Belgian unicycles— he could take it apart and put it together all day long. But even that is too expensive. Mike dear, a present ought not to be expensive—unless you are trying to get a girl to marry you—or something. A present should show that you considered that person's tastes. Something he would enjoy but probably would not buy."

"How?"

"That's the problem. Wait, I just remembered something in this morning's mail." She was back quickly. "Found it! Listen to this: 'Living Aphrodite: A deluxe Album of Femi- nine Beauty in Gorgeous Stereo-Color by the World's Greatest Artists of the Camera. Notice: this item cannot be mailed. Orders cannot be accepted from addresses in the following states—' Um, Pennsylvania is on the list—but we'll find a way—for if I know Duke's tastes, this is what he likes."

It was delivered via S.S. patrol car—and the next ad boasted: "—as supplied to the Man from Mars, by special appointment," which pleased Mike and annoyed Jill.

Picking a present for Jubal stumped Jill. What does one buy for a man who has everything he wants that money can buy? Three Wishes? The fountain that Ponce de Leon failed to find? Oil for his ancient bones, or one golden day of youth? Jubal had long forsworn pets, because he out- lived them, or (worse yet) it was now possible that a pet would outlive him, be orphaned.

They consulted others. "Shucks," Duke told them, "didn't you know? The boss likes statues."

"Really?" Jill answered. "I don't see any sculpture around."

"The stuff he likes mostly isn't for sale. He says the crud they make nowdays looks like disaster in a junk yard and any idiot with a blow torch and astigmatism calls himself a sculptor."

Anne nodded. "Duke is right. You can tell by looking at books in Jubal's study."

Anne picked out three books as bearing evidence (to her eyes) of having been looked at most often. "Hmm . . ." she said. "The Boss likes anything by Rodin. Mike, if you could buy one of these, which would you pick? Here's a pretty one—'Eternal Springtime.'"

Mike glanced at it and turned pages. "This one."

"What?" Jill shuddered. "Mike, that's *dreadful*! I hope I die long before I look like that."

"That is beauty," Mike said firmly.

"Mike!" Jill protested. "You've got a depraved taste—you're worse than Duke."

Ordinarily such a rebuke, especially from Jill, would shut Mike up, force him to spend the night in trying to grok his fault. But in this he was sure of himself. The portrayed figure felt like a breath of home. Although it pictured a human woman it gave him a feeling that a Martian Old One should be near, responsible for its creation. "It is beauty," he insisted. "She has her own face. I grok."

"Jill," Anne said slowly, "Mike is right."

"Huh? Anne! Surely you don't *like* that?"

"It frightens me. But the book falls open in three places; this page has been handled more than the other two. This other one—'The Caryatid Fallen under Her Stone'—Jubal looks at almost as often. But Mike's choice is Jubal's pet."

"I buy it," Mike said decisively.

Anne telephoned the Rodin Museum in Paris and only Gallic gallantry kept them from laughing. *Sell* one of the Master's works? My dear lady, they are not only not for sale but may not be reproduced. Non, non, non! Quelle Idée!

But for the Man from Mars unlikely things are possible. Anne called Bradley; two days later he called back. As a compliment from the French government—with a request that the present never be exhibited—Mike would receive a full-size, microscopically-exact bronze photo-pantogram of "She Who Used to Be the Beautiful Heaulmière."

Jill helped select presents for the girls but when Mike asked what he should buy for *her*, she insisted that he not buy anything.

Mike was beginning to realize that, while water brothers spoke rightly, sometimes they spoke more rightly than others. He consulted Anne.

"She has to tell you that, dear, but you give her a present anyhow. Hmm . . ." Anne selected one which puzzled him—Jill already smelled the way Jill should smell.

When the present arrived, its size and apparent unimportance added to his misgivings—and when Anne had him whiff it before giving it to Jill, Mike was more in doubt than ever; the odor was very strong and not at all like Jill.

Jill was delighted with the perfume and insisted on kissing him at once. In kissing her he grokked that this gift was what she wanted and that it made them grow closer.

When she wore it at dinner that night, he discovered that in some unclear fashion it made Jill smell more deliciously Jill than ever. Still stranger, it caused Dorcas to kiss him and whisper, "Mike hon . . . the negligee is just lovely—but perhaps someday you'll give *me* perfume?"

Mike could not grok why Dorcas would want it; Dorcas did not smell like Jill, so perfume would not be proper for her . . . nor would he want Dorcas to smell like Jill; he wanted Dorcas to smell like Dorcas.

Jubal interrupted: "Quit nuzzling the lad and let him eat! Dorcas, you reek like a Marseilles cat house; don't wheedle Mike for more stinkum."

"Boss, mind your own business."

It was puzzling—that Jill could smell still more like Jill . . . but Dorcas should wish to smell like Jill when she smelled like herself . . . that Jubal would say that Dorcas smelled like a cat. There was a cat on the place (not a pet, but co-owner); on occasion it came to the house and deigned to accept a handout. The cat and Mike grokked each other; Mike found its carnivorous thoughts most pleasing and quite Martian. He discovered that the cat's name (Friedrich Wilhelm Nietzsche) was not the cat's name, but he had not told anyone because he could not pronounce the cat's real name; he could only hear it in his head.

The cat did not smell like Dorcas.

Giving presents was a great goodness and taught Mike the true value of money. But he did not forget other things he was eager to grok. Jubal put off Senator Boone twice without mentioning it and Mike did not notice; his grasp of time made "next Sunday" no particular date. But the next invitation came addressed to Mike; Boone was under pressure from Supreme Bishop Digby and sensed that Harshaw was stalling.

Mike took it to Jubal. "Well?" Jubal growled. "Do you

want to go? You don't have to. We can tell 'em to go to hell."

A Checker Cab with a human pilot (Harshaw refused to trust a robocab) called next Sunday morning to deliver Mike, Jill, and Jubal to the Archangel Foster Tabernacle of the Church of the New Revelation.

XXIII

ALL THE WAY to church Jubal was trying to warn Mike—of what, Mike was not certain. He listened—but the landscape tugged for attention; he compromised by storing what Jubal said. "Look, boy," Jubal admonished, "these Fosterites are after your money. And the prestige of having the Man from Mars join their church. They'll work on you—you'll have to be firm."

"Beg pardon?"

"Damn it, you're not listening."

"I am sorry, Jubal."

"Well . . . look at it this way. Religion is a solace to many and it is conceivable that some religion, somewhere, is Ultimate Truth. But being religious is often a form of conceit. The faith in which I was brought up assured me that I was better than other people; I was 'saved,' they were 'damned'— we were in a state of grace and the rest were 'heathens.' By 'heathen' they meant such as our brother Mahmoud. Ignorant louts who seldom bathed and planted corn by the Moon claimed to know the final answers of the Universe. That entitled them to look down on outsiders. Our hymns were loaded with arrogance—self-congratulation on how cozy we were with the Almighty and what a high opinion he had of us, what hell everybody else would catch some Judgment Day. We peddled the only authentic brand of Lydia Pinkham's—"

"Jubal!" Jill protested. "He doesn't grok it."

"Uh? Sorry. My folks tried to make a preacher of me; I guess it shows."

"It does."

"Don't scoff, girl. I would have made a good one if I hadn't fallen into the fatal folly of reading. With a touch more confidence and a liberal helping of ignorance I would have been a famous evangelist. Shucks, this place we're headed for would be known as 'Archangel Jubal Tabernacle.'"

Jill shuddered. "Jubal, please! Not so soon after breakfast."

"I mean it. A confident man knows he's lying; that limits his scope. But a successful shaman believes what he says—and belief is contagious; there is no limit to *his* scope. But I lacked the necessary confidence in my own infallibility; I could never become a prophet . . . just a critic—a sort of fourth-rate prophet with delusions of grandeur." Jubal frowned. "That's what worries me about Fosterites, Jill. I think they are sincere. Mike is a sucker for sincerity."

"What do you think they'll try to do?"

"Convert him. Then get their hands on his fortune."

"I thought you had things fixed so that nobody could?"

"No, just so that nobody can grab it against his will. Ordinarily he couldn't give it away without the government stepping in. But giving it to a politically powerful church is another matter."

"I don't see why."

Jubal scowled. "My dear, religion is a null area in the law. A church can do anything any organization can do—and has no restrictions. It pays no taxes, need not publish records, is effectively immune to search, inspection, or control—and a church is *anything* that calls itself a church. Attempts have been made to distinguish between 'real' religions entitled to immunities, and 'cults.' It can't be done, short of establishing a state religion . . . a cure worse than the disease. Both under what's left of the United States Constitution and under the Treaty of Federation, all churches are equally immune—especially if they swing a bloc of votes. If Mike is converted to Fosterism . . . and makes a will in favor of his church . . . then 'goes to Heaven' some sunrise, it will be, in the correct tautology, 'as legal as church on Sunday.'"

"Oh, dear! I thought we had him safe at last."

"There is no safety this side of the grave."

"Well . . . what are you going to do, Jubal?"

"Nothing. Just fret."

Mike stored their conversation without trying to grok it. He recognized the subject as one of utter simplicity in his own language but amazingly slippery in English. Since his failure to achieve mutual grokking even with his brother Mahmoud, through imperfect translation of the all-embracing Martian concept as: "Thou art God," he had waited. Waiting would fructify at its time; his brother Jill was learning his language and he would explain it to her. They would grok together.

SENATOR BOONE MET them at the Tabernacle's landing flat. "Howdy, folks! May the Good Lord bless you this beautiful Sabbath. Mr. Smith, I'm happy to see you again.

And you, too, Doctor." He took his cigar out of his mouth and looked at Jill. "And this little lady—didn't I see you at the Palace?"

"Yes, Senator. I'm Gillian Boardman."

"Thought so, m'dear. Are you saved?"

"Uh, I guess not, Senator."

"It's never too late. We'll be happy to have you attend seekers' service in the Outer Tabernacle—I'll find a Guardian to guide you. Mr. Smith and the Doc will be going into the Sanctuary."

"Senator—"

"Uh, what, Doc?"

"If Miss Boardman can't go into the Sanctuary, we had better attend seekers' service. She's his nurse."

Boone looked perturbed. "Is he ill?"

Jubal shrugged. "As his physician, I prefer to have a nurse with us. Mr. Smith is not acclimated to this planet. Why don't you ask *him*? Mike, do you want Jill with you?"

"Yes, Jubal."

"But—Very well, Mr. Smith." Boone again removed his cigar, put fingers between his lips and whistled. "Cherub here!"

A youngster in his teens came dashing up. He was dressed in short full robe, tights, slippers, and pigeon's wings. He had golden curls and a sunny smile. Jill thought he was as cute as a ginger ale ad.

Boone ordered, "Fly up to the Sanctum office and tell the Warden on duty that I want another pilgrim's badge at the Sanctuary gate right away. The word is Mars."

"'Mars,'" the kid repeated, threw Boone a Scout salute, and made a sixty-foot leap over the crowd. Jill realized why the robe looked bulky; it concealed a jump harness.

"Have to watch those badges," Boone remarked. "Be surprised how many sinners would like to sample God's Joy without having their sins washed away. We'll mosey along and sightsee while we wait for the third badge."

They pushed through the crowd and entered the Tabernacle, into a long high hall. Boone stopped. "I want you to notice. There is salesmanship in everything, even the Lord's work. Any tourist, whether he attends seekers' service or not—and services run twenty-four hours a day—has to come through here. What does he see? These happy chances." Boone waved at slot machines lining both walls. "The bar and quick lunch is at the far end, he can't even get a drink without running this gauntlet. I tell you, it's a remarkable sinner who gets that far without shedding his change.

"But we don't take his money and give him nothing. Take a look—" Boone shouldered his way to a machine, tapped the woman playing it. "Please, Daughter."

She looked up, annoyance changed to a smile. "Certainly, Bishop."

"Bless you. You'll note," Boone went on, as he fed a quarter into the machine, "that whether it pays off in worldly goods or not, a sinner is rewarded with a blessing and a souvenir text."

The machine stopped; lined up in the window was: GOD—WATCHES—YOU.

"That pays three for one," Boone said and fished the pay-off out of the receptacle, "and here's your text." He tore off a paper tab and handed it to Jill. "Keep it, little lady, and ponder it."

Jill sneaked a glance before putting it into her purse: "*But the Sinner's belly is filled with filth*—N.R. XXII 17"

"You'll note," Boone went on, "that the pay-off is to-kens, not cash—and the bursar's cage is back past the bar . . . plenty of opportunity there to make love offerings for charity and other good works. So the sinner probably feeds them back in . . . with a blessing each time and another text. The cumulative effect is tremendous! Why, some of our most faithful sheep got their start right in this room."

"I don't doubt it," agreed Jubal.

"Especially if they hit a jackpot. You understand, every combination is a blessing. But the jackpot, that's the three Holy Eyes. I tell you, when they see those eyes lined up and starin' at 'em, all that manna from Heaven coming down, it really makes 'em think. Sometimes they faint. Here, Mr. Smith—" Boone offered Mike one of the tokens. "Give it a whirl."

Mike hesitated. Jubal took the token himself—damn it, he didn't want the boy hooked by a one-armed bandit! "I'll try it, Senator." He fed the machine.

Mike had extended his time sense a little and was feeling around inside the machine, trying to discover what it did. He was too timid to play it himself.

But when Jubal did so, Mike watched the cylinders spin, noted the eye pictured on each, and wondered what this "jackpot" was. The word had three meanings, so far as he knew; none of them seemed to apply. Without intending to cause excitement, he slowed and stopped each wheel so that the eyes looked out through the window.

A bell tolled, a choir sang hosannas, the machine lighted up and started spewing slugs. Boone looked delighted. "Well, bless you! Doc, this is your day! Here—put one back to take the jackpot off." He picked up one of the flood and fed it back in.

Mike was wondering why this was happening, so he lined up the eyes again. Events repeated, save that the flood was a trickle. Boone stared. "Well, I'll be—blessed! It's not supposed to hit twice in a row. But I'll see that you're paid on both." Quickly he put a slug back in.

Mike still wanted to see why this was a "jackpot." The eyes lined up again.

Boone stared. Jill squeezed Mike's hand and whispered, "Mike . . . stop it!"

"But, Jill, I was seeing—"

"Don't talk. Just stop. Oh, wait till I get you home!"

Boone said slowly, "I'd hesitate to call this a miracle. Probably needs a repairman." He shouted, "Cherub here!" and added, "We'd better take the last one off, anyhow," and fed in another slug.

Without Mike's intercession, the wheels slowed down and announced: "FOSTER—LOVES—YOU." A Cherub came up and said, "Happy day. You need help?"

"Three jackpots," Boone told him.

"'Three'?"

"Didn't you hear the music? Are you deaf? We'll be at the bar; fetch the money there. And have somebody check this machine."

"Yes, Bishop."

Boone hurried them to the bar. "Got to get you out of here," he said jovially, "before you bankrupt the Church. Doc, are you always that lucky?"

"Always," Harshaw said solemnly. He told himself that he did not *know* that the boy had anything to do with it . . . but he wished that this ordeal were over.

Boone took them to a counter marked "Reserved" and said, "This'll do—or would the little lady like to sit?"

"This is fine." (—you call me "little lady" once more and I'll turn Mike loose on you!)

A bartender hurried up. "Happy day. Your usual, Bishop?"

"Double. What'll it be, Doc? And Mr. Smith? Don't be bashful; you're the Supreme Bishop's guests."

"Brandy, thank you. Water on the side."

"Brandy, thank you," Mike repeated and added, "No water for me, please." Water was not the essence; nevertheless he did not wish to drink water here.

"That's the spirit!" Boone said heartily. "That's the spirit with spirits! No water. Get it? It's a joke." He dug Jubal in the ribs. "What'll it be for the little lady? Cola? Milk for your rosy cheeks? Or a real Happy Day drink with the big folks?"

"Senator," Jill said carefully, "would your hospitality extend to a martini?"

"Would it! Best martinis in the world—we don't use vermouth. We bless 'em instead. Double martini for the little lady. Bless you, son, and make it fast. We've time for a quick one, then pay our respects to Archangel Foster and on into the Sanctuary to hear the Supreme Bishop."

The drinks arrived and the jackpots' pay-off. They drank with Boone's blessing, then he wrangled over the three hundred dollars, insisting that all prizes belonged to Jubal. Jubal settled it by depositing it all in a love-offering bowl.

Boone nodded approvingly. "That's a mark of grace, Doc. We'll save you yet. Another round, folks?"

Jill hoped that someone would say yes—The gin was watered but it was starting a flame of tolerance in her middle. Nobody spoke up, so Boone led them away, up a flight, past a sign reading: POSITIVELY NO SEEKERS NOR SINNERS—THIS MEANS *YOU*!

Beyond was a gate. Boone said to it: "Bishop Boone and three pilgrims, guests of the Supreme Bishop."

The gate opened. He led them around a curved passage into a room. It was large, luxurious in a style that reminded Jill of undertakers' parlors but was filled with cheerful music. The theme was *Jingle Bells* with a Congo beat added; Jill found that it made her want to dance.

The far wall was glass and appeared to be not even that. Boone said briskly, "Here we are, folks—in the Presence. You don't have to kneel—but do so if it makes you feel better. Most pilgrims do. And there *he* is . . . just as he was when he was called up to Heaven."

Boone gestured with his cigar. "Don't he look natural? Preserved by a miracle, flesh incorruptible. That's the very chair he used when he wrote his Messages . . . and that's the pose he was in when he went to Heaven. He's never been moved—we built the Tabernacle right around him . . . removing the old church, naturally, and preserving its sacred stones."

Facing them about twenty feet away, seated in a chair remarkably like a throne, was an old man. He looked as if he were alive . . . and he reminded Jill of an old goat on the farm where she had spent childhood summers—out-thrust lower lip, the whiskers, the fierce, brooding eyes. Jill felt her skin prickle; Archangel Foster made her uneasy.

Mike said in Martian, *"My brother, this is an Old One?"*

"I don't know, Mike. They say he is."

He answered, *"I do not grok an Old One."*

"I don't know, I tell you."

"I grok wrongness."

"Mike! Remember!"

"Yes, Jill."

Boone said, "What's he saying, little lady? What was your question, Mr. Smith?"

Jill said quickly, "It wasn't anything. Senator, can I get out of here? I feel faint." She glanced at the corpse. Billowing clouds were above it; one shaft of light cut through and sought out the face. As lighting changed the face seemed to change, the eyes seemed bright and alive.

Boone said soothingly, "It has that effect, first time. You ought to try the seekers' gallery below us—looking up and with different music. Heavy music, with subsonics, I believe it is—reminds 'em of their sins. Now *this* room is a Happy Thoughts meditation chamber for high officials of the Church—I come here and sit and smoke a cigar if I'm feeling a bit low."

"Please, Senator!"

"Oh, certainly. Wait outside, m'dear. Mr. Smith, you stay as long as you like."

Jubal said, "Senator, hadn't we best get on into the services?"

They left. Jill was shaking—she had been scared silly that Mike might do something to that grisly exhibit—get them all lynched.

Two guards thrust crossed spears in their path at the portal of the Sanctuary. Boone said reprovingly, "Come, come! These pilgrims are the Supreme Bishop's personal guests. Where are their badges?"

Badges were produced and with them door prize numbers. A respectful usher said, "This way, Bishop," and led them up wide stairs to a center box facing the stage.

Boone stood back. "You first, little lady." Boone wanted

to sit next to Mike: Harshaw won and Mike sat between Jill and Jubal, with Boone on the aisle.

The box was luxurious—self-adjusting seats, ash trays, drop tables for refreshments. They were above the congregation and less than a hundred feet from the altar. In front of it a young priest was warming up the crowd, shuffling to music and shoving heavily muscled arms back and forth, fists clenched. His strong bass voice joined the choir from time to time, then he would lift it in exhortation:

"Up off your behinds! Gonna let the Devil catch you napping?"

A snake dance was weaving down the right aisle, across in front, and back up the center aisle, feet stomping in time with the priest's piston-like jabs and the syncopated chant of the choir. Clump, clump, *moan*! . . . Clump, clump, *moan*! Jill felt the beat and realized sheepishly that it would be fun to get into that dance—as more and more people were doing under the brawny young priest's taunts.

"That boy's a comer," Boone said approvingly. "I've team-preached with him and I can testify he turns the crowd over to you sizzlin'. Reverend 'Jug' Jackerman—used to play left tackle for the Rams. You've seen him."

"I'm afraid not," Jubal admitted. "I don't follow football."

"Really? Why, during the season most of the faithful stay after services, eat lunch in their pews, and watch the game. The wall behind the altar slides away and you're looking into the biggest stereo tank ever built. Puts the plays right in your lap. Better reception than you get at home—and it's more thrill with a crowd around you." He whistled. "Cherub! Over here!"

Their usher hurried over. "Yes, Bishop?"

"Son, you ran away so fast I didn't have time to put in my order."

"I'm sorry, Bishop."

"Being sorry won't get you into Heaven. Get happy, son. Get that old spring into your step and stay on your toes. Same thing all around, folks?" He gave the order and added, "Bring me a handful of my cigars—see the chief barkeep."

"Right away, Bishop."

"Bless you, son. Hold it—" The snake dance was about to pass under them; Boone leaned over, made a megaphone of hands, and cut through the noise. "Dawn! Hey, *Dawn*!" A woman looked up, he beckoned to her. She smiled. "Add a whiskey sour to that. Fly."

The woman showed up quickly, as did the drinks. Boone swung a seat out of the back row for her. "Folks, meet Miss Dawn Ardent. M'dear, that's Miss Boardman, the little lady down in the corner—and this is the famous Doctor Jubal Harshaw here by me—"

"Really? Doctor, I think your stories are simply divine!"

"Thank you."

"Oh, I do! I put one of your tapes on and let it lull me to sleep almost every night."

"Higher praise a writer cannot expect," Jubal said with a straight face.

"That's enough, Dawn," put in Boone. "The young man between them is . . . Mr. Valentine Smith, the Man from Mars."

Her eyes got big. "Oh, my goodness!"

Boone roared. "Bless you, child! I really snuck up on you."

She said, "Are you *really* the Man from Mars?"

"Yes, Miss Dawn Ardent."

"Just call me 'Dawn.' Oh goodness!"

Boone patted her hand. "Don't you know it's a sin to doubt the word of a Bishop? M'dear, how would you like to help lead the Man from Mars to the light?"

"Oh, I'd love it!"

(You would, you sleek bitch! Jill said to herself.) She had been growing angry ever since Miss Ardent joined them. The woman's dress was long sleeved, high necked, and opaque—and covered nothing. It was a knit fabric the shade of her tanned skin and Jill was certain that skin was all there was under it—other than Miss Ardent, which was plenty. The dress was ostentatiously modest compared with the clothes of most females in the congregation, some of whom seemed about to jounce out.

Jill thought that Miss Ardent looked as if she had just wiggled out of bed and was anxious to crawl back in. With Mike. Quit squirming your carcass at him, you cheap hussy!

Boone said, "I'll speak to the Supreme Bishop, m'dear. Now get back and lead that parade. Jug needs you."

"Yes, Bishop. Pleased to meet you, Doctor, and Miss Broad. I hope I'll see you again, Mr. Smith. I'll pray for you." She undulated away.

"A fine girl, that," Boone said happily. "Ever catch her act, Doc?"

"I think not. What does she do?"

"You don't *know*?"

"No."

"Didn't you hear her *name*? That's Dawn Ardent—she's the highest paid peeler in all Baja California, that's who. Works under an irised spot and by the time she's down to her shoes, the light is just on her face and you really can't see anything else. Very effective. Highly spiritual. Would you believe, looking at that sweet face now, that she used to be a most immoral woman?"

"I can't believe it."

"Well, she was. Ask her. She'll tell you. Better yet, come to a cleansing for seekers—I'll let you know when she's going to be on. When she confesses, it gives other women courage to tell *their* sins. She doesn't hold back—it does *her* good, too, to know she's helping people. Very dedicated— flies up every Saturday night after her last show, to teach Sunday School. She teaches the Young Men's Happiness Class and attendance has tripled since she took over."

"I can believe *that*," Jubal agreed. "How old are these lucky 'Young Men'?"

Boone laughed. "You're not fooling me, you old devil— somebody told you the motto of Dawn's class: 'Never too old to be young.'"

"No, truly."

"You can't attend until you've seen the light and gone through cleansing. This is the One True Church, Pilgrim, not like those traps of Satan, those foul pits of iniquity that call themselves 'churches' to lure the unwary into idolatry and other abominations. You can't walk in to kill a couple hours out of the rain—you gotta be *saved* first. In fact—oh, oh, camera warning." Lights were blinking in each corner of the great hall. "And Jug's got 'em done to a turn. Now you'll see action!"

The snake dance gained recruits while the few left seated clapped cadence and bounced up and down. Ushers hurried to pick up the fallen, some of whom, mostly women, were writhing and foaming. These they dumped at the altar and left to flop like fish. Boone pointed his cigar at a gaunt red-head about forty whose dress was badly torn. "See that woman? It has been fully a year since she has gone through a service without being possessed by the Spirit. Sometimes Archangel Foster uses her mouth to talk to us . . . when that happens it takes four husky acolytes to hold her. She could go to Heaven any time, she's ready. Anybody need a refill? Bar service is slow once the cameras are on and things get lively."

Mike let his glass be replenished. He shared none of Jill's disgust with the scene. He had been deeply troubled when he discovered that the "Old One" was mere spoiled food, but he tabled that matter and was drinking deep of the frenzy below. It was so Martian in flavor that he felt both homesick and warmly at home. No detail was Martian, all was wildly different, yet he grokked a growing-closer as real as water ceremony, in numbers and intensity that he had never met outside his own nest. He wished forlornly that someone would invite him to join that jumping up and down. His feet tingled with an urge to merge with them.

He spotted Miss Dawn Ardent—perhaps she would invite him. He did not have to recognize her by size and proportions even though she was exactly as tall as his brother Jill with almost the same shapings. But Miss Dawn Ardent had her own face, her pains and sorrows and growings graved on it under her warm smile. He wondered if Miss Dawn Ardent might some day be willing to share water. Senator Bishop Boone made him feel wary and he was glad that Jubal had not seated them side by side. But he was sorry that Miss Dawn Ardent had been sent away.

Miss Dawn Ardent did not look up. The procession carried her away.

The man on the platform raised both arms; the great

cave became quieter. Suddenly he brought them down. "Who's *happy?*"

"WE'RE HAPPY!"

"Why?"

"God . . . LOVES US!"

"How d'you *know?*"

"FOSTER TOLD US!"

He dropped to his knees, raised one fist. "Let's hear that Lion *ROAR!*"

They roared and shrieked and screamed while he used his fist as a baton, raising the volume, lowering it, squeezing it to subvocal growl, then driving it to crescendo that shook the balcony. Mike wallowed in it, with ecstasy so painful that he feared he must withdraw. But Jill had told him that he must not, except in his own room; he controlled it and let the waves wash over him.

The man stood up. "Our first hymn," he said briskly, "is sponsored by Manna Bakeries, makers of Angel Bread, the loaf of love with our Supreme Bishop's smiling face on every wrapper and containing a valuable premium coupon redeemable at your nearest neighborhood Church of the New Revelation. Brothers and Sisters, tomorrow Manna Bakeries with branches throughout the land start a giant, price-slashing sale of pre-equinox goodies. Send your child to school with a bulging box of Archangel Foster cookies, each one blessed and wrapped in an appropriate text—and pray that each goodie he gives away may lead a child of sinners nearer to the light.

"And now let's live it up with the holy words of that old favorite: 'Forward, Foster's Children!' All together—"

"Forward, Foster's Chil—*dren!*

Smash apart your foes . . .

Faith our Shield and Ar—*mor*!
Strike them down by rows—!"
"Second verse!"
"Make no peace with sin—*ners*!
God is *on* our side!"

Mike was so joyed that he did not try to grok words. He grokked that words were not of essence; it was a growing-closer. The dance started moving again, marchers chanting potent sounds with the choir.

After the hymn there were announcements, Heavenly messages, another commercial, and awarding of door prizes. A second hymn. "Happy Faces Uplifted" was sponsored by Dattelbaum's Department Stores where the Saved Shop in Safety since no merchandise is offered which competes with a sponsored brand—a children's Happy Room in each branch supervised by a Saved sister.

The priest moved to the front of the platform and cupped his ear.

"We . . . want . . . *Digby*!"

"Who?"

"We—Want—DIG—BY!"

"Louder! Make him hear you!"

"We—WANT—DIG—*BY*!" Clap, clap, stomp, stomp! "WE—WANT—DIG—BY!" Clap, clap, stomp, stomp—

It went on and on, until the building rocked. Jubal leaned to Boone. "Much of that and you'll do what Samson did."

"Never fear," Boone told him, around his cigar. "Reinforced, sustained by faith. It's built to shake, designed that way. Helps."

Lights went down, curtains parted; a blinding radiance

picked out the Supreme Bishop, waving clasped hands over his head and smiling at them.

They answered with the lion's roar and he threw them kisses. On his way to the pulpit he stopped, raised one of the possessed women still writhing slowly, kissed her, lowered her gently, started on—stopped and knelt by the bony red-head. He reached behind him and a microphone was placed in his hand.

He put an arm around her shoulders, placed the pickup near her lips.

Mike could not understand her words. He did not think they were English.

The Supreme Bishop translated, interjecting it at each pause in the foaming spate.

"Archangel Foster is with us—

"He is pleased with you. Kiss the sister on your right—

"Archangel Foster loves you. Kiss the sister on your left—

"He has a message for one of you."

The woman spoke again; Digby hesitated. "What was that? Louder, I pray you." She muttered and screamed.

Digby looked up and smiled. "His message is for a pilgrim from another planet—Valentine Michael Smith the Man from Mars! Where are you, Valentine Michael! Stand up!"

Jill tried to stop him but Jubal growled, "Easier not to fight it. Let him stand. Wave, Mike. Sit down." Mike did so, amazed that they were now chanting: "Man from *Mars*! . . . Man from *Mars*!"

The sermon seemed to be directed at him, too, but he could not understand it. The words were English, but they seemed to be put together wrongly and there was so much noise, so much clapping, so many shouts of "Hallelujah!" and "Happy Day!" that he grew quite confused.

The sermon ended, Digby turned the service back to the young priest and left; Boone stood up. "Come, folks. We'll sneak out ahead of the crowd."

Mike followed, Jill's hand in his. Presently they were going through an elaborately arched tunnel. Jubal said, "Does this lead to the parking lot? I told my driver to wait."

"Eh?" Boone answered. "Yes, straight ahead. But we're going to see the Supreme Bishop."

"What?" Jubal replied. "No, it's time for us to go."

Boone stared. "Doctor, the Supreme Bishop is waiting. You must pay your respects. You're his guests."

Jubal gave in. "Well—There won't be a lot of people? This boy has had enough excitement."

"Just the Supreme Bishop." Boone ushered them into an elevator; moments later they were in a parlor of Digby's apartments.

A door opened, Digby hurried in. He had removed his vestments and was dressed in flowing robes. He smiled. "Sorry to keep you waiting, folks—I have to shower as soon as I come off. You've no notion how it makes you sweat to punch Satan. So this is the Man from Mars? God bless you, son. Welcome to the Lord's House. Archangel Foster wants you to feel at home. He's watching over you."

Mike did not answer. Jubal was surprised to see how short Digby was. Lifts in his shoes on stage? Or the lighting? Aside from the goatee he wore in imitation of Foster the man reminded Jubal of a used car salesman—the same smile and warm manner. But he reminded Jubal of someone in particular—Got it! "Professor" Simon Magus, Becky

Vesey's long-dead husband. Jubal felt friendlier toward the clergyman. Simon had been as likeable a scoundrel as he had ever known—

Digby turned his charm on Jill. "Don't kneel, daughter; we're just friends in private here." He spoke with her, startling Jill with knowledge of her background and adding earnestly, "I have deep respect for your calling, daughter. In the blessed words of Archangel Foster, God commands us to minister to the body in order that the soul may seek the light untroubled by the flesh. I know that you are not yet one of us . . . but your service is blessed by the Lord. We are fellow travelers on the road to Heaven."

He turned to Jubal. "You, too, Doctor. Archangel Foster tells us that the Lord commands us to be happy . . . and many is the time I have put down my crook, weary unto death, and enjoyed a happy hour over one of your stories . . . stood up refreshed, ready to fight again."

"Uh, thank you, Bishop."

"I mean it deeply. I've had your record searched in Heaven—now, now, never mind; I know that you are an unbeliever. Even Satan has a purpose in God's Great Plan. It is not time for you to believe. Out of your sorrow and heartache and pain you spin happiness for others. This is credited on your page of the Great Ledger. Now please! I did not bring you here to argue theology. We never argue, we wait until you see the light and then welcome you. Today we shall just enjoy a happy hour together."

Jubal conceded that the glib fraud was a good host; his coffee and liquor and food were excellent. Mike seemed jumpy, especially when Digby got him aside and spoke with him alone—but, confound it, the boy had to get used to meeting people.

Boone was showing Jill relics of Foster in a case on the other side of the room; Jubal watched with amusement while he spread pâté de foie gras on toast. He heard a door click and looked around; Digby and Mike were missing. "Where did they go, Senator?"

"Eh? What was that, Doctor?"

"Bishop Digby and Mr. Smith. Where are they?"

Boone seemed to notice the closed door. "Oh, they've stepped in there for a moment. That's a retiring room for private audiences. Weren't you in it? When the Supreme Bishop was showing you around?"

"Um, yes." It was a room with a chair on a dais—a "Throne," Jubal corrected himself with a grin—and a kneeler. Jubal wondered which one would use the throne and which would be stuck with the kneeler—if this tinsel bishop tried to argue religion with Mike he was in for shocks. "I hope they don't stay long."

"I doubt if they will. Probably Mr. Smith wanted a word in private. Look, I'll have your cab wait at the end of that passageway where we took the elevator—that's the Supreme Bishop's private entrance. Save you a good ten minutes."

"That's very kind."

"So if Mr. Smith has something on his soul he wants to confess we won't have to hurry him. I'll step outside and phone." Boone left.

Jill said, "Jubal, I don't like this. I think we were deliberately maneuvered so that Digby could get Mike alone."

"Obviously."

"They haven't any business doing that! I'm going to bust in and tell Mike it's time to leave."

"Suit yourself," Jubal answered, "but you're acting like

a broody hen. If Digby tries to convert Mike, they'll wind up with Mike converting him. Mike's ideas are hard to shake."

"I still don't like it."

"Relax. Help yourself to chow."

"I'm not hungry."

"If I turned down a free feed, they'd toss me out of the Authors' Guild." He piled Virginia ham on buttered bread, added other items in an unsteady ziggurat, munched it.

Ten minutes later Boone had not returned. Jill said sharply, "Jubal, I'm going to get Mike out of there."

"Go ahead."

She strode to the door. "It's locked!"

"Thought it might be."

"What do we do? Break it down?"

Jubal looked it over. "Mmm, with a battering ram and twenty stout men I might try. Jill, that door would do credit to a vault."

"What do we do?"

"Beat on it, if you want to. I'm going to see what's keeping Boone."

When Jubal looked out into the hallway he saw Boone returning. "Sorry," Boone said. "Had to have the Cherubim find your driver. He was in the Happiness Room, having lunch."

"Senator," Jubal said, "we've got to leave. Will you be so kind as to tell Bishop Digby?"

Boone looked perturbed. "I could phone, if you insist. But I can't walk in on a private audience."

"Then phone him."

Boone was saved embarrassment; the door opened and

Mike walked out. Jill looked at his face and shrilled, "Mike! Are you all right?"

"Yes, Jill."

"I'll tell the Supreme Bishop you're leaving," said Boone and went into the smaller room. He reappeared at once. "He's left," he announced. "There's a back way into his study." Boone smiled. "Like cats and cooks, the Supreme Bishop goes without saying. That's a joke. He says that 'good-bys' add nothing to happiness. Don't be offended."

"We aren't. Thank you for a *most* interesting experience. No, don't bother; we can find our way out."

XXIV

ONCE IN THE air Jubal said, "Mike, what did you think of it?"

Mike frowned. "I do not grok."

"You aren't alone, son. What did the Bishop have to say?"

Mike hesitated a long time. "My brother Jubal, I need to ponder until grokking is."

"Ponder ahead, son."

Jill said, "Jubal? How do they get away with it?"

"With what?"

"Everything. That's not a church—it's a madhouse."

"No, Jill. It *is* a church . . . and the logical eclecticism of our time."

"Huh?"

"The New Revelation is old stuff. Neither Foster nor Digby ever had an original thought. They pieced together time-worn tricks, gave them a new paint job, and were in business. A booming business. The thing that bothers me is that I might live to see it made compulsory for everybody."

"Oh, no!"

"Oh, yes. Hitler started with less and all he peddled was hate. For repeat trade happiness is sounder merchandise. I know; I'm in the same grift. As Digby reminded me." Jubal grimaced. "I should have punched him. Instead, he made me like it. That's why I'm afraid of him, he's clever. He knows what people want. Happiness. The world has suffered a long century of guilt and fear—now Digby tells them that they have nothing to fear, this life or hereafter, and that God commands them to be happy. Day in, day out, he keeps pushing it: Don't be afraid, be *happy*."

"Well, that's all right," Jill admitted, "and he does work hard. But—"

"Piffle! He *plays* hard."

"No, he gave me the impression that he really is devoted, that he had sacrificed everything to—"

"'Piffle!' I said. Jill, of all the nonsense that twists the world, the concept of 'altruism' is the worst. People do what they want to, every time. If it pains them to make a choice—if the choice looks like a 'sacrifice'—you can be sure that it is no nobler than the discomfort caused by greediness . . . the necessity of deciding between two things you want when you can't have both. The ordinary bloke suffers every time he chooses between spending a buck on beer or tucking it away for his kids, between getting up to go to work or losing his job. But he always chooses what hurts least or pleasures most. The scoundrel and the saint make the same choices on a larger scale. As

Digby does. Saint or scoundrel, he's not one of the harried chumps."

"Which do you think he is, Jubal?"

"There's a difference?"

"Oh, Jubal, your cynicism is a pose! Of course there's a difference."

"Mmm, yes, there is. I hope he's a scoundrel . . . because a saint can stir up ten times as much mischief. Strike that last; you would tag it 'cynicism'—as if tagging it proved it wrong. Jill, what troubled you about those services?"

"Well . . . *everything*. You can't tell *me* that *that* is worship."

"Meaning they didn't do things that way in the Little Brown Church you attended as a kid? Brace yourself, Jill—they don't do it your way in St. Peter's either. Nor in Mecca."

"Yes, but—Well, none of them do it *that* way! Snake dances . . . slot machines . . . even a bar! That's not even dignified!"

"I don't suppose temple prostitution was dignified, either."

"Huh?"

"I imagine the two-backed beast is as comical in the service of a god as it is under other circumstances. As for snake dances, have you ever seen a Shaker service? Neither have I; a church that is agin sexual intercourse doesn't last. But dancing to the glory of God has a long history. It doesn't have to be artistic—the Shakers could never have made the Bolshoi—it merely has to be enthusiastic. Do you find Indian Rain Dances irreverent?"

"That's different."

"Everything always is—and the more it changes, the

more it is the same. Now slot machines—Ever see a Bingo game in church?"

"Well . . . yes. Our parish used them to raise the mortgage. But only on Friday nights; we didn't do such things during *church* services."

"So? Minds me of a wife who was proud of her virtue. Slept with other men only when her husband was away."

"Jubal, the two cases are miles apart!"

"Probably. Analogy is even slipperier than logic. But, 'little lady'—"

"Smile when you say that!"

"'It's a joke.' Jill, if a thing is sinful on Sunday, it is sinful on Friday—at least it groks that way to me—and perhaps to a man from Mars. The only difference I see is that the Fosterites give away, absolutely free, a scriptural text even if you lose. Could your Bingo games make that claim?"

"Fake scripture! A text from the New Revelation. Boss, have you read the thing?"

"I've read it."

"Then you know. It's just dressed up in Biblical language. Part is icky-sweet, more is nonsense . . . and some is just hateful."

Jubal was silent a long time. At last he said, "Jill, are you familiar with Hindu sacred writings?"

"I'm afraid not."

"The Koran? Any other major scripture? I could illustrate my point from the Bible but do not wish to hurt your feelings."

"You won't hurt my feelings."

"Well, I'll use the Old Testament, picking it to pieces usually doesn't upset people as much. You know about

Sodom and Gomorra? How Lot was saved from these wicked cities when Yahweh smote 'em?"

"Oh, of course. His wife was turned into a pillar of salt."

"Always seemed to me a stiff punishment. But we were speaking of Lot. Peter describes him as a just, Godly, and righteous man, vexed by the filthy conversation of the wicked. Saint Peter must be an authority on virtue, since to him were given the keys to the Kingdom of Heaven. But it is hard to see what made Lot such a paragon. He divided a cattle range at his brother's suggestion. He got captured in battle. He lammed out of town to save his skin. He fed and sheltered two strangers but his conduct shows that he knew them to be V.I.P.s—and by the Koran and by my own lights, his hospitality would count more if he had thought they were mere beggars. Aside from these items and Saint Peter's character reference there is only one thing in the Bible on which we can judge Lot's virtue—virtue so great that Heavenly intercession saved his life. See Genesis nineteen, verse eight."

"What does it say?"

"Look it up. I don't expect you to believe *me*."

"Jubal! You're the most infuriating man I've ever met."

"And you're a very pretty girl, so I don't mind your ignorance. All right—but look it up later. Lot's neighbors beat on his door and wanted to meet these blokes from out of town. Lot didn't argue; he offered a deal. He had two daughters, virgins, so he said—he told this mob that he would give them these girls and they could use them any way they liked—a gang shagging. He *pleaded* with them to do any damn thing they pleased . . . only quit beating on his door."

"Jubal . . . does it *really* say that?"

"I've modernized the language but the meaning is as unmistakable as a whore's wink. Lot offered to let a gang of men—'young and old,' the Bible says—abuse two young virgins if only they wouldn't break down his door. Say!" Jubal beamed. "I should have tried that when the S.S. was breaking down *my* door! Maybe it would have got *me* into Heaven." He frowned. "No, the recipe calls for 'virginis intactac'—and I wouldn't have known which of you gals to offer."

"*Hmmph!* You won't find out from *me*."

"Well, even Lot might have been mistaken. But that's what he promised—his virgin daughters, young and tender and scared—urged this gang to rape them . . . if only they would leave *him* in peace!" Jubal snorted. "The Bible cites this scum as a '*righteous*' man."

Jill said slowly, "I don't think that's the way we were taught it in Sunday School."

"Damn it, look it up! That's not the only shock in store for anybody who *reads* the Bible. Consider Elisha. Elisha was so all-fired holy that touching his bones restored a dead man to life. He was a bald-headed old coot, like myself. One day children made fun of his baldness, just as you girls do. So God sent bears to tear forty-two children into bloody bits. That's what it says—second chapter of Second Kings."

"Boss, I never make fun of your bald head."

"Who sent my name to those hair-restorer quacks? Whoever it was, *God* knows—and she had better keep a sharp eye for bears. The Bible is loaded with such stuff. Crimes that turn your stomach are asserted to be divinely ordered or divinely condoned . . . along with, I must add, hard common sense and workable rules for social behavior. I am not running down the Bible. It isn't a patch on the pornographic trash that passes as sacred writings among Hindus. Or a dozen other religions. But I'm not condemning *them*, either; it is conceivable that one of these mythologies is the word of God . . . that God is in truth the sort of paranoid Who rends to bits forty-two children for sassing His priest. Don't ask *me* about the Front Office; I just work here. My point is that Foster's New Revelation is sweetness-and-light as scripture goes. Bishop Digby's Patron is a good Joe; He wants people to be happy—happy on Earth plus eternal bliss in Heaven. He doesn't expect you to chastise the flesh. Oh no! this is the giant-economy package. If you like to drink and gamble and dance and wench—come to church and do it under holy auspices. Do it with your conscience free. Have fun at it. Live it up! Get happy!"

Jubal failed to look happy. "Of course there's a charge; Digby's God expects to be acknowledged. Anyone stupid enough to refuse to get happy on His terms is a sinner and deserves anything that happens to him. But this rule is common to all gods; don't blame Foster and Digby. Their snake oil is orthodox in all respects."

"Boss, you sound halfway converted."

"Not me! I don't enjoy snake dances, I despise crowds, and I do not let slobs tell me where to go on Sundays. I simply object to your criticizing them for the wrong things. As literature, the New Revelation stacks up about average— it should; it was composed by plagiarizing other scriptures. As for internal logic, mundane rules do not apply to sacred writings—but here the New Revelation must be rated superior; it hardly ever bites its own tail. Try reconciling the

Old Testament with the New, or Buddhist doctrine with Buddhist apocrypha. As morals, Fosterism is the Freudian ethic sugar-coated for people who can't take psychology straight, although I doubt if the old lecher who wrote it—pardon me, 'was inspired to write it'—knew this; he was no scholar. But he *was* in tune with his times, he tapped the Zeitgeist. Fear and guilt and loss of faith—How could he *miss*? Pipe down, I'm going to nap."

"Who's talking?"

"'The woman tempted me.'" Jubal closed his eyes.

On reaching home they found that Caxton and Mahmoud had flown in for the day. Ben had been disappointed to find Jill away but had managed to bear up through the company of Anne, Miriam, and Dorcas. Mahmoud always visited for the avowed purpose of seeing Mike and Dr. Harshaw; however, he too had shown fortitude at having only Jubal's food, liquor, garden—and odalisques—to entertain him. Miriam was rubbing his back while Dorcas rubbed his head.

Jubal looked at him. "Don't get up."

"I can't, she's sitting on me. Hi, Mike."

"Hi, my brother Stinky Dr. Mahmoud." Mike then gravely greeted Ben, and asked to be excused.

"Run along, son," Jubal told him.

Anne said, "Mike, have you had lunch?"

He said solemnly, "Anne, I am not hungry. Thank you," turned, and went into the house.

Mahmoud twisted, almost unseating Miriam. "Jubal? What's troubling our son?"

"Yeah," said Ben. "He looks seasick."

"Let him be. An overdose of religion." Jubal sketched the morning's events.

Mahmoud frowned. "Was it necessary to leave him alone with Digby? This seems to me—pardon me, my brother!—unwise."

"Stinky, he's got to take such things in stride. You've preached theology at him—he's told me. Can you name one reason why Digby shouldn't have his innings? Answer as a scientist, not as a Muslim."

"I am unable to answer anything other than as a Muslim," Dr. Mahmoud said quietly.

"Sorry. I recognize your necessity, even though I disagree."

"Jubal, I used the word 'Muslim' in its exact sense, not as a sectarian which Maryam incorrectly terms 'Mohammedan.'"

"Which I'll go on calling you until you learn to pronounce 'Miriam'! Quit squirming."

"Yes, Maryam. *Ouch!* Women should not be muscular. Jubal, as a scientist, I find Michael the prize of my career. As a Muslim, I find in him a willingness to submit to the will of God . . . and this makes me happy for his sake although there are difficulties and as yet he does not grok what the English word 'God' means." He shrugged. "Nor the Arabic word 'Allah.' But as a man—and always a Slave of God—I love this lad, our foster son and water brother, and would not have him under bad influences. Aside from creed, this Digby strikes me as a bad influence. What do *you* think?"

"*Ole!*" Ben applauded. "He's a slimy bastard—I haven't exposed his racket in my column simply because the Syndicate is afraid to print it. Stinky, keep talking and you'll have me studying Arabic and buying a rug."

"I hope so. The rug is not necessary."

Jubal sighed. "I agree with you. I'd rather see Mike smoking marijuana than converted by Digby. But I don't think there is any danger of Mike's being taken in by that syncretic hodgepodge . . . and he's got to learn to stand up to bad influences. I consider *you* a good influence—but I don't think you stand much more chance—the boy has an amazingly strong mind. Muhammad may have to make way for a new prophet."

"If God so wills," Mahmoud answered.

"That leaves no room for argument," Jubal agreed.

"We were discussing religion before you got home," Dorcas said softly. "Boss, did you know that women have souls?"

"They *do*?"

"So Stinky says."

"Maryam," Mahmoud explained, "wanted to know why we 'Mohammedans' thought only men had souls."

"Miriam, that's as vulgar a misconception as the notion that Jews sacrifice Christian babies. The Koran states that entire families enter into Paradise, men and women together. For example, see 'Ornaments of Gold'—verse seventy, isn't it, Stinky?"

"'Enter the Garden, ye and your wives, to be made glad.' That's as well as it can be translated," agreed Mahmoud.

"Well," said Miriam, "I had heard about the beautiful houris that Mohammedan men have for playthings in Paradise and that didn't seem to leave room for wives."

"Houris," said Jubal, "are separate creations, like djinni and angels. They don't need souls, they are spirits to start with, eternal, unchanging, and beautiful. There are male houris, too, or equivalents. Houris don't earn their way into Paradise; they're on the staff. They serve delicious foods and pass around drinks that never give hangovers and entertain as requested. But the souls of wives don't have to work. Correct, Stinky?"

"Close enough, aside from your flippant choice of words. The houris—" He sat up so suddenly that he dumped Miriam. "Say! Perhaps you girls *don't* have souls!"

Miriam said bitterly, "Why, you ungrateful dog of an infidel! Take that back!"

"Peace, Maryam. If you don't have a soul, then you're immortal anyhow. Jubal . . . is it possible for a man to die and not notice it?"

"Can't say. Never tried it."

"Could I have died on Mars and just dreamed that I came home? Look around you! A garden the Prophet himself would envy. Four beautiful houris, serving lovely food and delicious drinks at all hours. Even their male counterparts, if you want to be fussy. Is this Paradise?"

"I guarantee it ain't," Jubal assured him. "My taxes are due."

"Still, that doesn't affect *me*."

"And take these houris—Even if we stipulate that they are of adequate beauty—after all, beauty is in the eye of the beholder—"

"They pass."

"And you'll pay for that, Boss," Miriam added.

"—there still remains," Jubal pointed out, "one requisite attribute of houris."

"Mmmm—" said Mahmoud, "we need not go into that. In Paradise, rather than a temporary physical condition, it would be a permanent spiritual attribute. Yes?"

"In that case," Jubal said emphatically, "I am *certain* that these are not houris."

Mahmoud sighed. "Then I'll have to convert one."

"Why one? There are places where you can have the full quota."

"No, my brother. In the wise words of the Prophet, while the Legislations permit four, it is impossible to deal justly with more than one."

"That's some relief. Which one?"

"We'll see. Maryam, are you feeling spiritual?"

"You go to hell! 'Houris' indeed!"

"Jill?"

"Give me a break," Ben protested. "I'm working on Jill."

"Later, Jill. Anne?"

"Sorry. I've got a date."

"Dorcas? You're my last chance."

"Stinky," she said softly, "just how spiritual do you want me to feel?"

MIKE WENT UPSTAIRS to his room, closed the door, got on the bed, assumed the fetal position, rolled up his eyes, swallowed his tongue, and slowed his heart. Jill did not like him to do this in the daytime but did not object as long as he did not do it publicly—so *many* things he must not do publicly but only this one aroused her ire. He had been waiting since leaving that room of terrible wrongness; he needed very badly to withdraw and try to grok.

He had done something that Jill had told him not to—

He felt a human urge to tell himself that it had been forced on him, but his Martian training did not permit this escape. He had arrived at cusp, right action had been required, the choice had been his. He grokked that he had chosen correctly. But his water brother Jill had forbidden this choice—

But that would have left *no* choice. This was contradiction; at cusp, choice is. By choice, spirit grows.

Would Jill have approved had he taken other action, not wasting food?

No, he grokked that Jill's injunction covered that variant.

At this point the being sprung from human genes and shaped by Martian thought, who could never be either, completed one stage of his growth, burst out and ceased to be a nestling. The solitary loneliness of predestined free will was then his and with it Martian serenity to embrace, cherish, savor its bitterness, accept its consequences. With tragic joy he knew that this cusp was his, not Jill's. His water brother could teach, admonish, guide—but choice at cusp was not shared. Here was "ownership" beyond sale, gift, hypothecation; owner and owned grokked inseparable. He eternally *was* the action he had taken at cusp.

Now that he knew himself to be self he was free to grok ever closer to his brothers, merge without let. Self's integrity was and is and ever had been. Mike stopped to cherish all his brother selves, the many threes-fulfilled on Mars, corporate and discorporate, the precious few on Earth— the unknown powers of three on Earth that would be his to merge with and cherish now that at last long waiting he grokked and cherished himself.

Mike remained in trance; there was much to grok, loose ends to puzzle over and fit into his growing—all that he had seen and heard and been at the Archangel Foster Tabernacle (not just cusp when he and Digby had come face to face alone) . . . why Bishop Senator Boone made him warily uneasy, how Miss Dawn Ardent tasted like a water brother when she was not, the smell of goodness he had incompletely grokked in the jumping up and down and wailing—

Jubal's conversations coming and going—Jubal's words troubled him most; he studied them, compared them with what he had been taught as a nestling, struggling to bridge between languages, the one he thought with and the one he was learning to think in. The word "church" which turned up over and over again among Jubal's words gave him knotty difficulty; there was no Martian concept to match it—unless one took "church" and "worship" and "God" and "congregation" and many other words and equated them to the totality of the only world he had known during growing-waiting   then forced the concept back into English in that phrase which had been rejected (by each differently) by Jubal, by Mahmoud, by Digby.

"Thou art God." He was closer to understanding it in English now, although it could never have the inevitability of the Martian concept it stood for. In his mind he spoke simultaneously the English sentence and the Martian word and felt closer grokking. Repeating it like a student telling himself that the jewel is in the lotus he sank into nirvana.

Before midnight he speeded his heart, resumed normal breathing, ran down his check list, uncurled, and sat up. He had been weary; now he felt light and gay and clearheaded, ready for the many actions he saw spreading out before him.

He felt a puppyish need for company as strong as his earlier necessity for quiet. He stepped out into the hall, was delighted to encounter a water brother. *"Hi!"*

"Oh. Hello, Mike. My, you look chipper."

"I feel fine! Where is everybody?"

"Asleep. Ben and Stinky went home an hour ago and people started going to bed."

"Oh." Mike felt disappointed that Mahmoud had left; he wanted to explain his new grokking.

"I ought to be asleep, too, but I felt like a snack. Are you hungry?"

"Sure, I'm hungry!"

"Come on, there's some cold chicken and we'll see what else." They went downstairs, loaded a tray lavishly. "Let's take it outside. It's plenty warm."

"A fine idea," Mike agreed.

"Warm enough to swim—real Indian summer. I'll switch on the floods."

"Don't bother," Mike answered. "I'll carry the tray." He could see in almost total darkness. Jubal said that his night-sight probably came from the conditions in which he had grown up, and Mike grokked this was true but grokked that there was more to it; his foster parents had taught him to see. As for the night being warm, he would have been comfortable naked on Mount Everest but his water brothers had little tolerance for changes in temperature and pressure; he was considerate of their weakness, once he learned of it. But he was looking forward to snow—seeing for himself that each tiny crystal of the water of life was a unique individual, as he had read—walking barefoot, rolling in it.

In the meantime he was pleased with the warm night and the still more pleasing company of his water brother.

"Okay, take the tray. I'll switch on the underwater lights. That'll be plenty to eat by."

"Fine." Mike liked having light up through the ripples; it was a goodness, beauty. They picnicked by the pool, then lay back on the grass and looked at stars.

"Mike, there's Mars. It is Mars, isn't it? Or Antares?"

"It is Mars."

"Mike? What are they doing on Mars?"

He hesitated; the question was too wide for the sparse English language. "On the side toward the horizon—the southern hemisphere—it is spring; plants are being taught to grow."

"'Taught to grow'?"

He hesitated. "Larry teaches plants to grow. I have helped him. But my people—Martians, I mean; I now grok *you* are my people—teach plants another way. In the other hemisphere it is growing colder and nymphs, those who stayed alive through the summer, are being brought into nests for quickening and more growing." He thought. "Of the humans we left at the equator, one has discorporated and the others are sad."

"Yes, I heard it in the news."

Mike had not heard it; he had not known it until asked. "They should not be sad. Mr. Booker T W Jones Food Technician First Class is not sad; the Old Ones have cherished him."

"You knew him?"

"Yes. He had his own face, dark and beautiful. But he was homesick."

"Oh, dear! Mike . . . do you ever get homesick? For Mars?"

"At first I was homesick," he answered. "I was lonely always." He rolled toward her and took her in his arms. "But now I am not lonely. I grok I shall never be lonely again."

"Mike darling—" They kissed, and went on kissing.

Presently his water brother said breathlessly, "Oh, my! That was almost worse than the first time."

"You are all right, my brother?"

"Yes. Yes indeed. Kiss me again."

A long time later, by cosmic clock, she said, "Mike? Is that—I mean, 'Do you know—'"

"I know. It is for growing-closer. Now we grow closer."

"Well . . . I've been ready a long time—goodness, we *all* have, but . . . never mind, dear; turn just a little. I'll help."

As they merged, grokking together, Mike said softly and triumphantly: "Thou art God."

Her answer was not in words. Then, as their grokking made them ever closer and Mike felt himself almost ready to discorporate her voice called him back: "Oh! . . . *Oh! Thou* art God!"

"We grok God."

XXV

ON MARS HUMANS were building pressure domes for the male and female party that would arrive by next ship. This went faster than scheduled as the Martians were helpful. Part of the time saved was spent on a preliminary estimate for a long-distance plan to free bound oxygen in the sands of Mars to make the planet more friendly to future human generations.

The Old Ones neither helped nor hindered this plan; time was not yet. Their meditations were approaching a violent cusp that would shape Martian art for many millennia. On Earth elections continued and a very advanced poet published a limited edition of verse consisting entirely of punctuation marks and spaces; *Time* magazine reviewed it and suggested that the Federation Assembly Daily Record should be translated into the medium.

A colossal campaign opened to sell more sexual organs of plants and Mrs. Joseph ("Shadow of Greatness") Douglas was quoted as saying: "I would no more sit down without flowers on my table than without serviettes." A Tibetan swami from Palermo, Sicily, announced in Beverly Hills a newly discovered, ancient yoga discipline for ripple breathing which increased both pranha and cosmic attraction between sexes. His chelas were required to assume the matsyendra posture dressed in hand-woven diapers while he read aloud from Rig-Veda and an assistant guru examined their purses in another room—nothing was stolen; the purpose was less immediate.

The President of the United States proclaimed the first Sunday in November as "National Grandmothers' Day" and urged America to say it with flowers. A funeral parlor chain was indicted for price-cutting. Fosterite bishops, after secret conclave, announced the Church's second Major Miracle: Supreme Bishop Digby had been translated bodily to Heaven and spot-promoted to Archangel, ranking with-but-after Archangel Foster. The glorious news had been held up pending Heavenly confirmation of the elevation of a new Supreme Bishop, Huey Short—a candidate accepted by the Boone faction after lots had been cast repeatedly.

L'Unita and Hoy published identical denunciations of Short's elevation, l'Osservatore Romano and the Christian Science Monitor ignored it, Times of India snickered at it, and the Manchester Guardian simply reported it—the Fosterites in England were few but extremely militant.

Digby was not pleased with his promotion. The Man from Mars had interrupted him with his work half finished—and that stupid jackass Short was certain to louse it up. Foster listened with angelic patience until Digby ran down, then said, "Listen, junior, you're an angel now—so forget it. Eternity is no time for recriminations. You too were a stupid jackass until you poisoned me. Afterwards you did well enough. Now that Short is Supreme Bishop he'll do all right, he can't help it. Same as with the Popes. Some of them were warts until they got promoted. Check with one of them, go ahead—there's no professional jealousy here."

Digby calmed down, but made one request.

Foster shook his halo. "You can't touch him. You shouldn't have tried to. Oh, you can submit a requisition for a miracle if you want to make a fool of yourself. But, I'm telling you, it'll be turned down—you don't understand the System yet. The Martians have their own setup, different from ours, and as long as they need him, we can't touch him. They run their show their way—the Universe has variety, something for everybody—a fact you field workers often miss."

"You mean this punk can brush me aside and I've got to hold still for it?"

"I held still for the same thing, didn't I? I'm helping you now, am I not? Now look, there's work to be done and lots of it. The Boss wants performance, not gripes. If you need a day off to calm down, duck over to the Muslim Paradise and take it. Otherwise, straighten your halo, square your wings, and dig in. The sooner you act like an angel the quicker you'll feel angelic. Get Happy, junior!"

Digby heaved a deep ethereal sigh. "Okay, I'm Happy. Where do I start?"

Jubal did not hear of Digby's disappearance when it was

announced, and, when he did, while he had a fleeting suspicion, he dismissed it; if Mike had had a finger in it, he
had gotten away with it—and what happened to supreme
bishops worried Jubal not at all as long as he wasn't
bothered.

His household had gone through an upset. Jubal de-
duced what had happened but did not know with whom—
and didn't want to inquire. Mike was of legal age and
presumed able to defend himself in the clinches. Anyhow,
it was high time the boy was salted.

Jubal couldn't reconstruct the crime from the way the
girls behaved because patterns kept shifting—ABC *vs* D,
then BCD *vs* A . . . or AB *vs* CD, or AD *vs* CB, through all
ways that four women can gang up on each other.

This continued most of the week following that ill-
starred trip to church, during which period Mike stayed in
his room and usually in a trance so deep that Jubal would
have pronounced him dead had he not seen it before. Jubal
would not have minded it if service had not gone to pieces.
The girls seemed to spend half their time tiptoeing in "to
see if Mike was all right" and they were too preoccupied
to cook, much less be secretaries. Even rock-steady Anne—
Hell, Anne was the worst! Absent-minded, subject to un-
explained tears . . . Jubal would have bet his life that if
Anne were to witness the Second Coming, she would
memorize date, time, personae, events, and barometric
pressure without batting her calm blue eyes.

Late Thursday Mike woke himself and suddenly it was
ABCD in the service of Mike, "less than the dust beneath
his chariot wheels." The girls resumed giving Jubal service, so he counted his blessings and let it lie . . . except for
a wry thought that, if he demanded a showdown, Mike

could quintuple their salaries by a post card to Douglas—
but the girls would just as readily support Mike.

With domestic tranquility restored Jubal did not mind
that his kingdom was ruled by a mayor of the palace. Meals
were on time and better than ever; when he shouted
"Front!" the girl who appeared was bright-eyed, happy,
and efficient—such being the case, Jubal did not give a
hoot who rated the most side boys. Or girls.

Besides, the change in Mike was interesting. Before
that week Mike had been docile in a fashion that Jubal
classed as neurotic; now he was so self-confident that Jubal
would have described it as cocky had it not been that Mike
continued to be unfailingly polite and considerate.

He accepted homage from the girls as if a natural right,
he seemed older than his age rather than younger, his
voice deepened, he spoke with forcefulness rather than
timidly. Jubal decided that Mike had joined the human
race; he could discharge this patient.

Except (Jubal reminded himself) on one point: Mike
still did not laugh. He could smile at a joke and sometimes
did not ask to have them explained. Mike was cheerful,
even merry—but he never laughed.

Jubal decided that it was not important. This patient
was sane, healthy—and human. Short weeks earlier Jubal
would have given odds against a cure. He was humble
enough not to claim credit; the girls had had more to do
with it. Or should he say "girl"?

From the first week of his stay Jubal had told Mike almost daily that he was welcome . . . but that he should stir
out and see the world as soon as he felt able. Jubal should
not have been surprised when Mike announced one

breakfast that he was leaving. But he was surprised and, to his greater surprise, hurt.

He covered it by using his napkin unnecessarily. "So? When?"

"We're leaving today."

"Um. Plural. Are Larry and Duke and I going to have to put up with our own cooking?"

"We've talked that over," Mike answered. "I need somebody, Jubal; I don't know how people do things yet—I make mistakes. It ought to be Jill because she wants to go on learning Martian. But it could be Duke or Larry if you can't spare one of the girls."

"I get a vote?"

"Jubal, you must decide. We know that."

(Son, you've probably told your first lie. I doubt if I could hold even Duke if you set your mind.) "I guess it should be Jill. But look, kids –This is your home."

"We know that—we'll be back. Again we will share water."

"We will, son."

"Yes, Father."

"*Huh*?"

"Jubal, there is no Martian word for 'father.' But lately I grokked that you are my father. And Jill's father."

Jubal glanced at Jill. "Mmm, I grok. Take care of yourselves."

"Yes. Come, Jill." They were gone before he left the table.

XXVI

IT WAS THE usual carnival—rides, cotton candy, the same flat joints separating marks from dollars. The sex lecture deferred to local opinion concerning Darwin's opinions, the posing show wore what local lawmen decreed, Fearless Fenton did his Death-Defying Dive before the last bally. The ten-in-one did not have a mentalist, it had a magician; it had no bearded lady, it had a half-man-half-woman; no sword swallower but a fire eater, no tattooed man but a tattooed lady who was also a snake charmer, and for the blow-off she appeared "absolutely *nude*! . . . clothed only in bare living flesh in exotic designs!"—any mark who found one square inch untattooed below her neckline would win twenty dollars.

The prize went unclaimed. Mrs. Paiwonski posed in "bare living flesh"—her own and a fourteen-foot boa constrictor named "Honey Bun"—with the snake looped so strategically that the ministerial alliance could not complain. As further protection (for the boa) she stood on a stool in a canvas tank containing a dozen cobras.

Besides, the lighting was poor.

But Mrs. Paiwonski's claim was honest. Until his death her husband had a tattooing studio in San Pedro; when trade was slack they decorated each other. Eventually the art work on her was so complete from neck down that there was no room for an encore. She took pride in being the most decorated woman in the world, by the world's greatest artist—such being her opinion of her husband.

Patricia Paiwonski associated with grifters and sinners

unharmed; she and her husband had been converted by Foster himself, she attended the nearest Church of the New Revelation wherever she was. She would gladly have dispensed with any covering in the blow-off because she was clothed in conviction that she was canvas for religious art greater than any in museum or cathedral. When she and George saw the light, there was about three square feet of Patricia untouched; before he died she carried a pictorial life of Foster, from his crib with angels hovering around to the day of glory when he had taken his appointed place.

Regrettably much of this sacred history had to be covered. But she could show it in closed Happiness meetings of the churches she attended if the shepherd wanted her to, which he almost always did. Patricia couldn't preach, she couldn't sing, she was never inspired to speak in tongues—but she was a living witness to the light.

Her act came next to last; this left time to put away her photographs, then slip behind the rear canvas for the blow-off. Meanwhile the magician performed.

Dr. Apollo passed out steel rings and invited the audience to make sure that each was solid; then he had them hold the rings so that they overlapped—tapped each overlap with his wand. The links formed a chain. He laid his wand in the air, accepted a bowl of eggs from his assistant, juggled half a dozen. His juggling did not attract many eyes, his assistant got more stares. She wore more than the young ladies in the posing show; nevertheless there seemed slight chance that she was tattooed anywhere. The marks hardly noticed six eggs become five, then four . . . three, two—at last Dr. Apollo was tossing one egg in the air.

He said, "Eggs are scarcer every year," and tossed it

into the crowd. He turned away and no one seemed to note that the egg never reached a destination.

Dr. Apollo called a boy to the platform. "Son, I know what you are thinking. You think I'm not a real magician. For that you win a dollar." He handed the kid a dollar bill. It disappeared.

"Oh, dear! We'll give you one more chance. Got it? Get out of here fast—you should be home in bed." The kid dashed away with the money. The magician frowned. "Madame Merlin, what should we do now?"

His assistant whispered to him, he shook his head. "Not in front of all these people?"

She whispered again; he sighed. "Friends, Madame Merlin wants to go to bed. Will any of you gentlemen help her?"

He blinked at the rush. "Oh, too many! Were any of you in the Army?"

There were still many volunteers; Dr. Apollo picked two and said, "There's an army cot under the platform, just lift the canvas—now, will you set it up on the platform? Madame Merlin, face this way, please."

While the men set up the cot, Dr. Apollo made passes in the air. "Sleep . . . sleep . . . you are asleep. Friends, she is in deep trance. Will you gentlemen who prepared her bed now place her on it? Careful—" In corpselike rigidity the girl was transferred to the cot.

"Thank you, gentlemen." The magician recovered his wand from the air, pointed to a table at the end of his platform; a sheet detached itself from piled props and came to him. "Spread this over her. Cover her head, a lady should not be stared at while sleeping. Thank you. If you will step down—Fine! Madame Merlin . . . can you hear me?"

"Yes, Doctor Apollo."

"You were heavy with sleep. Now you feel lighter. You are sleeping on clouds. You are floating—" The sheet-covered form raised about a foot. "Wups! Don't get too light."

A boy explained in a whisper, "When they put the sheet over her, she went down through a trap door. That's just a wire framework. He'll flip the sheet away and the framework collapses and disappears. Anybody could do it."

Dr. Apollo ignored him. "Higher, Madame Merlin. Higher. There—" The draped form floated six feet above the platform.

The youngster whispered. "There's a steel rod you can't see. It's where that corner of the sheet hangs down and touches the cot."

Dr. Apollo requested volunteers to remove the cot. "She doesn't need it, she sleeps on clouds." He faced the floating form and appeared to listen. "Louder, please. Oh? She says she doesn't want the sheet."

("Here's where the framework disappears.")

The magician snatched the sheet away; the audience hardly noticed that it disappeared; they were looking at Madame Merlin, sleeping six feet above the platform. A companion of the boy who knew all about magic said, "Where's the steel rod?"

The kid said, "You have to look where he doesn't want you to. It's the way they've got those lights fixed to shine in your eyes."

Dr. Apollo said, "That's enough, fair princess. Give me

your hand. Wake up!" He pulled her erect and helped her step down to the platform.

("You saw where she put her foot? *That's* where the rod went." The kid added with satisfaction, "Just a gimmick.")

The magician went on, "And now, friends, kindly give your attention to our learned lecturer, Professor Timoshenko—"

The talker cut in. "Don't go 'way! For this one performance only by arrangement with the Council of Universities and the Department of Safety of this wonderful city, we offer this twenty-dollar bill absolutely free to any one of you—"

The tip was turned into the blow-off; carnies started packing for tear-down. There was a train jump in the morning, living tops would remain up for sleep, but canvas boys were loosening stakes on the sideshow top.

The talker-owner-manager came back into the top, having rushed the blow-off and spilled the marks out the rear. "Smitty, don't go 'way." He handed the magician an envelope and added, "Kid, I hate to tell you—but you and your wife ain't going to Paducah."

"I know."

"Look, it's nothing personal—I got to think of the show. We're getting a mentalist team. They do a top reading act, then she runs a phrenology and mitt camp while he makes with the mad ball. You know you didn't have no season's guarantee."

"I know," agreed the magician. "No hard feelings, Tim."

"Well, I'm glad you feel that way." The talker hesitated. "Smitty, want some advice?"

"I would like to have your advice," the magician said simply.

"Okay. Smitty, your tricks are good. But tricks don't make a magician. You're not really with it. You behave like a carnie—you mind your own business and never crab anybody's act and you're helpful. But you're not a carnie. You don't have any feeling for what makes a chump a chump. A real magician can make the marks open their mouths by picking a quarter out of the air. That levitation you do—I've never seen it done better but the marks don't warm to it. No psychology. Now take me, I can't even pick a quarter out of the air. I got no act—except that one that counts. I know marks. I know what he hungers for, even if he don't. That's showmanship, son, whether you're a politician, a preacher pounding a pulpit—or a magician. Find out what the chumps want and you can leave half your props in your trunk."

"I'm sure you're right."

"I know I am. He wants sex and blood and money. We don't give him blood—but we let him hope that a fire eater or a knife thrower will make a mistake. We don't give him money; we encourage his larceny while we take a little. We don't give him sex. But why do seven out of ten buy the blow-off? To see a nekkid broad. So he don't see one and still we send him out happy.

"What else does a chump want? Mystery! He wants to think the world is a romantic place when it damn well ain't. That's your job . . . only you ain't learned how. Shucks, son, the marks know your tricks are fake . . . only they'd like to believe they're real, and it's up to you to help 'em. That's what you lack."

"How do I get it, Tim?"

"Hell, you have to learn for yourself. But—Well, this notion you had of billing yourself as 'The Man from Mars.'

You *mustn't* offer the chump what he can't swallow. They've *seen* the Man from Mars, in pictures or on stereo. You look a bit like him—but even if you were his twin, the marks *know* they won't find him in a ten-in-one. It's like billing a sword swallower as 'President of the United States.' A chump *wants* to believe—but he won't let you insult what intelligence he has. Even a chump has brains of a sort."

"I will remember."

"I talk too much—a talker gets the habit. Are you kids going to be all right? How's the grouch bag? Hell, I oughtn't to—but do you need a loan?"

"Thanks, Tim. We're not hurtin'."

"Well, take care of yourself. Bye, Jill." He hurried out.

Patricia Paiwonski came in through the rear, wearing a robe. "Kids? Tim sloughed your act."

"We were leaving anyhow, Pat."

"I'm so mad I'm tempted to jump the show."

"Now, Pat—"

"Leave him without a blow-off! He can get acts . . . but a blow-off the clowns won't clobber is hard to find."

"Pat, Tim is right. I don't have showmanship."

"Well . . . I'm going to miss you. Oh, dear! Look, the show doesn't roll until morning—come back to my top and set awhile."

Jill said, "Better yet, Patty, come with us. How would you like to soak in a big, hot tub?"

"Uh . . . I'll bring a bottle."

"No," Mike objected, "I know what you drink and we've got it."

"Well—you're at the Imperial, aren't you? I've got to be sure my babies are all right and tell Honey Bun I'll be gone. I'll catch a cab. Half an hour, maybe."

They drove with Mike at the controls. It was a small town, without robot traffic guidance; Mike drove exactly at zone maximum, sliding into holes Jill did not see until they were through them. He did it without effort. Jill was learning to do it; Mike stretched his time sense until juggling eggs or speeding through traffic was easy, everything in slow motion. She reflected that it was odd in a man who, only months earlier, had been baffled by shoelaces.

They did not talk; it was awkward to converse with minds on different time rates. Instead Jill thought about the life they were leaving, calling it up and cherishing it, in Martian concepts and English. All her life, until she met Mike, she had been under the tyranny of the clock, as a girl in school, then as a big girl in a harder school, then the pressures of hospital routine.

Carnival life was nothing like that. Aside from standing around looking pretty several times a day, she never had to do anything at any set time. Mike did not care whether they ate once a day or six times, whatever housekeeping she did suited him. They had their own living top; in many towns they never left the lot from arrival to teardown. The carnival was a nest where troubles of the outside world did not reach.

To be sure, every lot was crawling with marks—but she had learned the carnie viewpoint; marks weren't people; they were blobs whose sole function was to cough up cash.

The carnie had been a happy home. Things had not been that way when first they had gone out into the world to increase Mike's education. They were spotted repeatedly and sometimes had trouble getting away, not only from the press but from endless people who seemed to feel that they had a right to demand things of Mike.

Presently Mike thought his features into mature lines and made other changes. That, plus the fact that they frequented places where the Man from Mars would not be expected to go, got them privacy. About that time, while Jill was phoning home a new mailing address, Jubal suggested a cover-up story—and a few days later Jill read that the Man from Mars had gone into retreat, in a Tibetan monastery.

The retreat had been "Hank's Grill" in a "nowhere" town, with Jill as a waitress and Mike as dishwasher. Mike had a quick way of cleaning dishes when the boss was not watching. They kept that job a week, moved on, sometimes working, sometimes not. They visited public libraries almost daily once Mike found out about them—Mike had thought that Jubal's library contained a copy of every book on Earth. When he learned the marvelous truth, they remained in Akron a month—Jill did a lot of shopping, Mike with a book was almost no company.

But Baxter's Combined Shows and Riot of Fun had been the nicest part of their meandering. Jill recalled with a giggle the time in—what town?—when the posing show had been pinched. It wasn't fair; they always worked under prearrangement: bras or no bras; blue lights or bright lights; whatever the fix was. Nevertheless the sheriff hauled them in and the justice of peace had seemed disposed to jail the girls. The lot closed down and the carnies went to the hearing, along with chumps slavering to catch sight of "shameless women." Mike and Jill had crowded into the back of the courtroom.

Jill had impressed on Mike that he must never do anything out of the ordinary where it might be noticed. But Mike grokked a cusp—

The sheriff was testifying to "public lewdness"—and enjoying it—when suddenly sheriff and judge were stripped bare.

Jill and Mike ducked out during the excitement; all the accused left, too. The show tore down and moved to a more honest town. No one connected the miracle with Mike.

Jill would treasure forever the expression on the sheriff's face. She started to speak to Mike in her mind, to remind him of how funny that hick sheriff had looked. But Martian had no concept for funny; she could not say it. They shared a growing telepathic bond—but in Martian only.

(*"Yes, Jill?"*) his mind answered.

(*"Later."*)

They neared the hotel, she felt his mind slow down as he parked the car. Jill preferred camping on the lot—except for one thing: bath tubs. Showers were all right, but nothing could beat a big tub of hot water, climb in and *soak*! So sometimes they checked into a hotel and rented a car. Mike did not, by early training, share her hatred for dirt. He was now as clean as she was—but only because she had retrained him. He could keep himself immaculate without washing, just as he never had to see a barber once he knew how Jill wanted his hair to grow. But Mike enjoyed immersing himself in the water of life as much as ever.

The Imperial was old and shabby but the tub in the "Bridal Suite" was big. Jill went to it as they came in, started to fill it—was unsurprised to find herself stripped for her bath. Dear Mike! He knew she liked to shop; he forced her to indulge her weakness by sending to never-never any outfit which he sensed no longer delighted her. He would do so daily had she not warned him that too many new clothes would be conspicuous around the carnival.

"Thanks, dear!" she called out. "Let's climb in."

He had either undressed or vanished his clothes—the former she decided; Mike found buying clothes without interest. He could see no sense in clothes other than for protection against weather, a weakness he did not share. They got in facing each other; she scooped up water, touched it to her lips, offered it to him. The ritual was not necessary; it simply pleased Jill to remind them of something for which no reminder could ever be necessary, through eternity.

Then she said, "I was thinking how funny that horrid sheriff looked in his skin."

"Did he look funny?"

"Oh, yes indeed!"

"Explain why he was funny. I do not see the joke."

"Uh . . . I don't think I can. It was not a joke—not like puns and things which can be explained."

"I did not grok he was funny," Mike said. "In both men—the judge and the lawman—I grokked wrongness. Had I not known that it would displease you, I would have sent them away."

"Dear Mike." She touched his cheek. "Good Mike. It was better to do what you did. They'll never live it down—there won't be another arrest for indecent exposure there for fifty years. Let's talk about something else. I have been wanting to say that I'm sorry our act flopped. I did my best in writing the patter—but I'm no showman, either."

"It was my fault, Jill. Tim speaks rightly—I don't grok chumps. But it has helped me to be with the carnie . . . I have grokked closer to chumps each day."

"You must not call them chumps, nor marks, now that we are no longer with it. Just people—not 'chumps.'"

"I grok they are chumps."

"Yes, dear. But it isn't polite."

"I will remember."

"Have you decided where we are going?"

"No. When the time comes, I will know."

True, Mike always did know. From his first change from docility to dominance he had grown steadily in strength and sureness. The boy who had found it tiring to hold an ash tray in the air could now not only hold her in the air while doing other things, but could exert any strength needed—she recalled one muddy lot where a truck had bogged down. Twenty men were trying to get it free— Mike added his shoulder; the sunken hind wheel lifted itself. Mike, more sophisticated now, did not allow anyone to guess.

She recalled when he had at last grokked that "wrongness" being necessary before he could make things go away applied only to living, grokking things—her dress did not have to have "wrongness." The rule was for nestlings; an adult was free to do as he grokked.

She wondered what his next change would be? But she did not worry; Mike was good and wise. "Mike, wouldn't it be nice to have Dorcas and Anne and Miriam here in the tub, too? And Father Jubal and the boys and—oh, our whole family!"

"Need a bigger tub."

"Who minds crowding? When are we making another visit home, Mike?"

"I grok it will be soon."

"Martian 'soon'? Or Earth 'soon'? Never mind,

darling, it will be when waiting is filled. That reminds me that Aunt Patty will be here soon and I mean Earth 'soon.' Wash me?"

She stood; soap lifted out of the dish, traveled all over her, replaced itself and the soapy layer slathered into bubbles. "Oooh! You tickle."

"Rinse?"

"I'll dunk." She squatted, sloshed off, stood up. "Just in time, too."

Someone was knocking. "Dearie? Are you decent?"

"Coming, Pat!" Jill shouted, and added as she stepped out of the tub, "Dry me, please?"

At once she was dry, not even wet footprints. "Dear? You'll remember to put on clothes? Patty's a lady—not like me."

"I will remember."

XXVII

JILL GRABBED A negligee, hurried into the living room. "Come in, dear. We were bathing; he'll be right out. I'll get you a drink—then you'll have your second drink in the tub. Loads of hot water."

"I had a shower after I put Honey Bun to bed, but—yes, I'd love a tub bath. But, Jill baby, I didn't come here to borrow your tub; I came because I'm heartsick that you kids are leaving."

"We won't lose track of you." Jill got busy with glasses. "Tim was right. Mike and I need to slick up our act."

"Your act is okay. Needs some laughs, maybe, but—Hi, Smitty." She offered him a gloved hand. Away from the lot Mrs. Paiwonski always wore gloves, high-necked dresses, and stockings. She looked like (and was) a middle-aged, respectable widow who had kept her figure trim.

"I was telling Jill," she went on, "that you've got a good act."

Mike smiled. "Pat, don't kid us. It stinks."

"No, it doesn't dearie. Oh, it could use some zing. A few jokes. Or you could cut down on Jill's costume a little. You've got a cute figure, hon."

Jill shook her head. "That wouldn't do it."

"Well, I knew a magician that used to dress his assistant as Gay 'Nineties—eighteen-nineties, that is—not even her legs showing. Then he would disappear one garment after another. The marks loved it. Don't get me wrong, dear—nothing unrefined. She finished in as much as you wear now."

"Patty," Jill said, "I'd do our act stark naked if the clowns wouldn't close the show."

"You couldn't, honey. The marks would riot. But if you've got a figure, why not use it? How far would I get as a tattooed lady if I didn't peel all they'll let me?"

"Speaking of clothes," Mike said, "you don't look comfortable, Pat. The aircooling in this dump has gone sour—must be at least ninety." He dressed in a light robe, enough for easy-going carnie manners. Heat affected him only slightly; he sometimes had to adjust his metabolism. But their friend was used to the comfort of almost nothing and affected clothes to cover her tattoos when out among marks. "Why not get comfortable? 'Ain't nobody here but just us chickens.'" The latter was a joke, appropriate for emphasizing that friends were in private—Jubal had explained it to him.

"Sure, Patty," Jill agreed. "If you're raw underneath, I can get you something."

"Uh . . . well, I did slip into one of my costumes."

"Then don't be stiff with friends. I'll get your zippers."

"Le'me get these stockings and shoes." She went on talking while trying to think how she could get around to religion. Bless them, these kids were ready to be seekers, she was certain—but she had counted on the whole season to bring them to the light. "The point about show business, Smitty, is that you have to understand marks. If you were a *real* magician—oh, I don't mean you aren't skillful, dearie, you *are*." She tucked hose in her shoes, let Jill get her zippers. "I mean like you had a pact with the Devil. But the marks know it's sleight-of-hand. So you need a light-hearted routine. Did you ever see a fire eater with a pretty assistant? Heavens, a pretty girl would just clutter *his* act; the marks are hoping he'll set fire to hisself."

She snaked the dress over her head; Jill took it and kissed her. "You look more natural, Aunt Patty. Sit back and enjoy your drink."

"Just a second, dearie." Mrs. Paiwonski prayed for guidance. Well, her pictures would speak for themselves— that was why George had put them there. "Now *this* is what I've got for the marks. Have you ever looked, really *looked*, at my pictures?"

"No," Jill admitted, "we didn't want to stare at you, like a couple of marks."

"Then stare now, dears—that's why George, bless his

sweet soul in Heaven, put them on me. To be stared at and studied. Here under my chin is the birth of our prophet, the holy Archangel Foster—just an innocent babe and not knowing what Heaven had in store for him. But the angels knew—see 'em there around him? The next scene is his first miracle, when a younger sinner in the country school he went to shot a poor little birdie . . . and he picked it up and stroked it and it flew away unharmed. Now I have to turn my back." She explained that George had not had a bare canvas when the great opus was started—how with inspired genius George had turned "Attack on Pearl Harbor" into "Armageddon," and "Skyline of New York" into "The Holy City."

"But," she admitted, "even though every inch is sacred pictures now, it did force George to skip around to record in living flesh each milestone in the earthly life of our prophet. Here you see him preaching on the steps of the ungodly theological seminary that turned him down—that was the first time he was arrested, the beginning of the Persecution. And on around, on my spine, you see him smashing idolatrous images . . . and next you see him in jail, with holy light streaming down. Then the Faithful Few bust into the jail—"

(The Reverend Foster had realized that, in upholding religious freedom, brass knucks, clubs, and a willingness to tangle with cops outweighed passive resistance. His was a church militant from scratch. But he had been a tactician; battles were fought where the heavy artillery was on the side of the Lord.)

"—and rescue him and tar and feather the false judge who put him there. Around in front—Uh, you can't see much; my bra covers it. A shame."

(*"Michael, what does she want?"*)

(*"Thou knowest. Tell her."*)

"Aunt Patty," Jill said gently, "you want us to look at all your pictures. Don't you?"

"Well . . . it's just as Tim says in the bally, George used all the skin I have in making the story complete."

"If George went to all that work, he meant them to be seen. Take off your costume. I told you that I wouldn't mind working our act stark naked—and ours is just entertainment. *Yours* has a purpose . . . a holy purpose."

"Well . . . If you want me to." She sang a silent hallelujah! Foster was sustaining her—with blessed luck and George's pictures she would have these dear kids seeking the light.

"I'll unhook you."

(*"Jill—"*)

(*"No, Michael?"*)

(*"Wait."*)

With stunned astonishment Mrs. Paiwonski found that her spangled briefies and bra were gone! Jill was unsurprised when her negligee vanished and only mildly surprised when Mike's robe disappeared; she chalked it up to his catlike good manners.

Mrs. Paiwonski gasped. Jill put her arms around her. "There, dear! It's all right. Mike, you must tell her."

"Yes, Jill. Pat—"

"Yes, Smitty?"

"You said my tricks were sleight-of-hand. You were about to take off your costume—so I did it for you."

"But *how?* Where is it?"

"Same place Jill's wrapper is—and my robe. Gone."

"Don't worry, Patty," put in Jill. "We'll replace it. Mike, you shouldn't have done it."

"I'm sorry, Jill. I grokked it was all right."

"Well . . . perhaps it is." Aunt Patty wasn't too upset—and would never tell; she was carnie.

Mrs. Paiwonski was not worried over two scraps of costume, nor by nudity, hers or theirs. But she was greatly troubled by a theological problem. "Smitty? That was *real* magic?"

"I guess you would call it that," he agreed, using words exactly.

"I'd rather call it a miracle," she said bluntly.

"Call it that if you like. It wasn't sleight-of-hand."

"I know that." She was not afraid. Patricia Paiwonski was not afraid of anything, being sustained by faith. But she was uneasy for her friends. "Smitty—look me in the eye. Have you made a pact with the Devil?"

"No, Pat, I have not."

She continued to search his eyes. "You aren't lying—"

"He doesn't know how to lie, Aunt Patty."

"—so it's a miracle. Smitty . . . you *are* a holy man!"

"I don't know, Pat."

"Archangel Foster didn't know until his teens . . . even though he performed miracles before then. You are a holy man; I can feel it. I think I felt it when I first met you."

"I don't know, Pat."

"I think he may be," admitted Jill. "But he doesn't know. Michael . . . we've told too much not to tell more."

"'Michael!'" Patty repeated suddenly. "Archangel Michael, sent to us in human form."

"Patty, please! If he is, he doesn't know it—"

"He wouldn't necessarily know. God performs His wonders in His own way."

"Aunt Patty, will you *please* let me talk?"

Shortly Mrs. Paiwonski knew that Mike was the Man from Mars. She agreed to treat him as a man—while stating that she kept her own opinion as to his nature and why he was on Earth—Foster had been truly a man while on Earth but had been also and *always* an archangel. If Jill and Michael insisted that they were not saved, she would treat them as they asked to be treated—God moves in mysterious ways.

"I think you could call us 'seekers,'" Mike told her.

"That's enough, dears! I'm sure you're saved—but Foster himself was a seeker in his early years. I'll help."

She participated in another miracle. They were seated on the rug; Jill lay back and suggested it to Mike in her mind. With no patter, no props, Mike lifted her. Patricia watched with serene happiness. "Pat," Mike then said. "Lie flat."

She obeyed as readily as if he had been Foster. Jill turned her head. "Hadn't you better put me down, Mike?"

"No, I can do it."

Mrs. Paiwonski felt herself gently lifted. She was not frightened; she felt overpowering religious ecstasy like heat lightning in her loins, making tears come to her eyes; such power she had not felt since Holy Foster had touched her. Mike moved them closer and Jill hugged; her tears increased with gentle sobs of happiness.

Mike lowered them to the floor and was not tired—he could not recall when last he had been tired.

Jill said, "Mike . . . we need water."

("????")

(*"Yes,"* her mind answered.)

(*"And?"*)

(*"Of elegant* necessity. Why do you think she came here?"*)

(*"I* knew. I was not sure that you knew . . . or would approve. My brother. My self."*)

(*"My brother."*)

Mike sent a glass into the bathroom, had the tap fill it, return it to Jill. Mrs Paiwonski watched with interest; she was beyond being astonished. Jill said to her, "Aunt Patty this is like being baptized . . . and like getting married. It's . . . a Martian thing. It means you trust us and we trust you . . . we can tell you anything and you can tell us anything . . . and that we are partners, now and forever. But once done it can never be broken. If you broke it, we would die—at once. Saved or not. If we broke it But we won't. But don't share water with us if you don't want to—we'll still be friends. If this interferes with your faith, don't do it. We don't belong to your church. We may never belong. 'Seekers' is the most you can call us. Mike?"

"We grok," he agreed. "Pat, Jill speaks rightly. I wish we could tell you in Martian, it would be clearer. But this is everything that getting married is—and much more. We are free to offer water . . . but if there is any reason, in your religion or your heart, not to accept—*don't drink it!*"

Patricia Paiwonski took a deep breath. She had made such a decision before . . . with her husband watching . . . had not funked it. Who was she to refuse a holy man? And this blessed bride? "I want it," she said firmly.

Jill took a sip. "We grow ever closer." She passed the glass to Mike.

"I thank you for water, my brother." He took a sip.

"Pat, I give you the water of life. May you always drink deep." He passed the glass to her.

Patricia took it. "Thank you. Thank you, oh my dears! The 'water of life'—I love you both!" She drank thirstily.

Jill took the glass, finished it. "Now we grow closer, my brothers."

("*Jill?*")

("*Now!!!*")

Michael lifted his new brother, wafted her in and placed her gently on the bed.

Valentine Michael Smith grokked that physical human love—very human and very physical—was not simply a quickening of eggs, nor was it ritual through which one grew closer; the act *itself* was a growing-closer. He was still grokking it, trying at every opportunity to grok its fullness. He had long since quit shying away from his strong suspicion that even the Old Ones did not know *this* ecstasy—he grokked that his new people held spiritual depths unique. Happily he tried to sound them, with no childhood inhibitions to cause him guilt nor reluctance of any sort.

His human teachers, gentle and generous, had instructed his innocence without bruising it. The result was as unique as he was.

Jill was unsurprised to find that Patty accepted with forthright fullness that sharing water with Mike in a very ancient Martian ceremony led at once to sharing Mike himself in an ancient human rite. Jill was somewhat surprised at Pat's calm acceptance when Mike proved capable of miracles here, too. But Jill did not know that Patricia had met a holy man before—she *expected* more of holy men. Jill was serenely happy that a cusp had been met with right action . . . then was ecstatically happy to grow closer herself.

When they rested, Jill had Mike treat Patty to a bath by telekinesis, and squealed and giggled when the older woman did. Mike had done it playfully for Jill on the initial occasion; it had become a family custom, one that Jill knew Patty would like. It tickled Jill to see Patty's face when she found herself scrubbed by invisible hands, then dried with neither towel nor air blast.

Patricia blinked. "After that I need a drink."

"Certainly, darling."

"And I *still* want to show you kids my pictures." They went into the living room and Patty stood in the middle of the rug. "First look at me. At *me*, not my pictures. What do you see?"

Mike stripped off her tattoos in his mind and looked at his new brother without her decorations. He liked her tattoos; they set her apart and made her a self. They gave her a slightly Martian flavor, she did not have the bland sameness of most humans. He thought of having himself tattooed all over, once he grokked what should be pictured. The life of his father, water brother Jubal? He would ponder it. Jill might wish to be tattooed, too. What designs would make Jill more beautifully Jill?

What he saw when he looked at Pat without tattoos pleased him not as much; she looked as a woman must look to be woman. Mike still did not grok Duke's collection of pictures; they had taught him that there was variety in sizes, shapes, and colors of women and some variety in the acrobatics of love—but beyond this he seemed to grok nothing to learn from Duke's prized pictures. Mike's training had made him an exact observer, but that same training had left him unresponsive to the subtle pleasures of voyeurism. It was not that he did not find women (including, emphatically, Patricia Paiwonski) sexually stimulating, but it lay not in seeing them. Smell and touch counted more—in which he was quasi-human, quasi-Martian; the parallel Martian reflex (as unsubtle as a sneeze) was triggered by those senses but could activate only in season—"sex" in a Martian was as romantic as intravenous feeding.

With her pictures gone, Mike noted more sharply one thing: Patricia had her own face, marked in beauty by her life. She had, he saw with wonder, her own face even more than Jill had. It made him feel toward Pat even more of an emotion he did not as yet call love.

She had her own odor, too, and her own voice. Her voice was husky, he liked hearing it even when he did not grok her meaning; her odor was mixed with a trace of bitter muskiness from handling snakes. Mike liked her snakes and could handle the poisonous ones—not alone by stretching time to avoid their strikes. They grokked with him; he savored their innocent merciless thoughts—they reminded him of home. Mike was the only other person who could handle Honey Bun with pleasure to the boa constrictor. Her torpor was such that others could handle her—but Mike she accepted as a substitute for Pat.

Mike let the pictures reappear.

Jill wondered why Aunt Patty had let herself be tattooed? She would look rather nice—if she weren't a living comic strip. But she loved Patty herself, not the way she looked—and it did give her a steady living . . . until she got so old that marks wouldn't pay to see her even if those pictures had been by Rembrandt. She hoped that Patty was tucking away plenty in the grouch bag—then remembered that Aunt Patty was now a water brother and shared Mike's endless fortune. Jill felt warmed by it.

"Well?" repeated Mrs. Paiwonski. "What do you see? How old am I, Michael?"

"I don't know."

"Guess."

"I can't, Pat."

"Oh, go ahead!"

"Patty," Jill put in, "he really can't. He hasn't learned to judge ages—you know how short a time he's been on Earth. And Mike thinks in Martian years and Martian arithmetic. If it's time or figures, I do it for him."

"Well . . . you guess, hon. Be truthful."

Jill looked Patty over, noting her trim figure but also hands and throat and eyes—then discounted by five years despite the honesty owed a water brother. "Mmm, thirtyish, give or take a year."

Mrs. Paiwonski chortled. "That's one bonus of the True Faith, my dears! Jill hon, I'm crowding fifty."

"You don't look it!"

"That's what Happiness does, dearie. After my first kid, I let my figure go to pot—they invented the word 'broad' just for me. My belly looked like six months gone. My busts hung down—and I've never had 'em lifted. You can see for yourself—sure, a good surgeon doesn't leave a scar . . . but on *me* it would *show*, dear; it would chop holes in two pictures.

"Then I seen the light! Nope, not exercise, not diet—I eat like a pig. Happiness, dear. Perfect Happiness in the Lord through the help of Blessed Foster."

"It's amazing," said Jill. Aunt Patty certainly had not dieted nor exercised during the time she had known her, and Jill knew what was excised in breast-lifting; those tattoos had never known a knife.

Mike assumed that Pat had learned to think her body as she wished it, whether she attributed it to Foster or not. He was teaching this control to Jill, but she would have to perfect her knowledge of Martian before it could be perfect. No hurry, waiting would do it. Pat went on:

"I wanted you to *see* what Faith can do. But the real change is inside. Happiness. The good Lord knows I'm not gifted with tongues but I'll try to tell you. First you've got to realize that all other so-called churches are traps of the Devil. Our dear Jesus preached the True Faith, so Foster said and I truly believe. But in the Dark Ages his words were twisted and changed until Jesus wouldn't recognize 'em. So Foster was sent to proclaim a New Revelation and make it clear again."

Patricia Paiwonski pointed her finger and suddenly was a priestess clothed in holy dignity and mystic symbols. "God wants us to be Happy. He filled the world with things to make us Happy. Would God let grape juice turn to wine if He didn't want us to drink and be joyful? He could let it stay grape juice . . . or turn it into vinegar that nobody could get a giggle out of. Ain't that *true*? Of course He don't mean we should get roaring drunk and beat your wife and neglect your kids . . . He gave us good things to *use*, not abuse. If you feel like a drink or six, among friends who have seen the light, and it makes you want to dance and give thanks to the Lord for His goodness—why not? God made alcohol and God made feet—He made 'em so you could put 'em together and be Happy!"

She paused. "Fill 'er up again, honey; preaching is

thirsty work—not much ginger ale; that's good rye. And that ain't all. If God didn't want women to be looked at, He would have made 'em ugly—that's reasonable, isn't it? God isn't a cheat; He set up the game Himself—He wouldn't rig it so that the marks can't win, like a flat joint wheel in a town with a fix on. He wouldn't send anybody to Hell for losing in a crooked game.

"All right! God wants us to be Happy and He told us how: 'Love one another!' Love a snake if the poor thing needs love. Love thy neighbor . . . and the back of your hand only to Satan's corruptors who want to lead you away from the appointed path and down into the pit. And by 'love' He didn't mean nambypamby old-maid love that's scared to look up from a hymn book for fear of seeing a temptation of the flesh. If God hated flesh, *why did He make so much of it*? God is no sissy. He made the Grand Canyon and comets coursing through the sky and cyclones and stallions and earthquakes—can a God who can do all that turn around and practically wet His pants just because some little sheila leans over a mite and a man catches sight of a tit? You know better, hon—and so do I! When God told us to love, He wasn't holding out a card on us; He *meant* it. Love little babies that always need changing and love strong, smelly men so that there will be more babies to love—and in between go on loving because it's so *good* to love!

"Of course that don't mean to peddle it any more than a bottle of rye means I gotta get fighting drunk and clobber a cop. You can't sell love and you can't buy Happiness, no price tags on either . . . and if you think there is, the way to Hell lies open. But if you give with an open heart and receive what God has an unlimited supply of, the

Devil can't touch you. Money?" She looked at Jill. "Hon, would you do that water-sharing thing with somebody, say for a million dollars? Make it ten million, tax free."

"Of course not." (*"Michael*, do you grok this?")

(*"Almost in fullness, Jill. Waiting is."*)

"You see, dearie? I knew love was in that water. You're seekers, very near the light. But since you two, from the love that is in you, did 'share water and grow closer,' as Michael says, I can tell you things I couldn't ordinarily tell a seeker—"

THE REVEREND FOSTER, self-ordained—or ordained by God, depending on authority cited—had an instinct for the pulse of his times stronger than that of a skilled carnie sizing up a mark. The culture known as "America" had a split personality throughout its history. Its laws were puritanical; its covert behavior tended to be Rabelaisian; its major religions were Apollonian; its revivals were almost Dionysian. In the twentieth century (Terran Christian Era) nowhere on Earth was sex so vigorously suppressed—and nowhere was there such deep interest in it.

Foster had in common with every great religious leader of that planet two traits: he had an extremely magnetic personality, and sexually he did not fall near the human norm. On Earth great religious leaders were always either celibate or the antithesis. Foster was not celibate.

Nor were his wives and priestesses—the clincher for rebirth under the New Revelation included a ritual uniquely suited for growing-closer.

In Terran history, many cults had used the same technique—but not on a major scale in America before Foster's time. Foster was run out of town more than once before he perfected a method that permitted him to expand his capric cult. He borrowed from Freemasonry, Catholicism, the Communist Party, and Madison Avenue just as he borrowed from earlier scriptures in composing his New Revelation. He sugar-coated it all as a return to primitive Christianity. He set up an outer church which anybody could attend. Then there was a middle church, which to outward appearance was "The Church of the New Revelation," the happy saved, who paid tithes, enjoyed all benefits of the church's ever-widening business tie-ins, and whooped it up in an endless carnival of Happiness, Happiness, Happiness! Their sins were forgiven— and very little was sinful as long as they supported their church, dealt honestly with fellow Fosterites, condemned sinners, and stayed Happy. The New Revelation did not specifically encourage lechery, but it got quite mystical in discussing sexual conduct.

The middle church supplied shock troops. Foster borrowed a trick from early-twentieth-century Wobblies; if a community tried to suppress a Fosterite movement, Fosterites converged on that town until neither jails nor cops could handle them—cops had ribs kicked in and jails were smashed.

If a prosecutor was rash enough to push an indictment, it was impossible to make it stick. Foster (after learning under fire) saw to it that prosecutions were persecution under the letter of the law; no conviction of a Fosterite *qua* Fosterite was ever upheld by the Supreme Court—nor, later, by the High Court.

Inside the overt church was the Inner Church—a hard core of fully dedicated who made up the priesthood, the lay leaders, all keepers of keys and makers of policy. They were "reborn," beyond sin, certain of Heaven, and sole celebrants of the inner mysteries.

Foster selected these with great care, personally until the operation got too big. He looked for men like himself and for women like his priestess-wives—dynamic, utterly convinced, stubborn, and free (or able to be freed, once guilt and insecurity were purged) of jealousy in its most human meaning—and all of them potential satyrs and nymphs, as the secret church was that Dionysian cult that America had lacked and for which there was enormous potential market.

He was most cautious—if candidates were married, it had to be both spouses. Unmarried candidates had to be sexually attractive and aggressive—and he impressed on his priests that males must equal or exceed in number the females. Nowhere was it recorded that Foster studied earlier, similar cults in America—but he knew or sensed that most such had foundered because possessive concupiscence of their priests led to jealousy. Foster never made this error; not once did he keep a woman to himself, not even those he married.

Nor was he too eager in expanding his core group; the middle church offered plenty to slake the milder needs of the masses. If a revival produced two couples capable of "Heavenly Marriage" Foster was content. If it produced none, he let the seeds grow and sent in a salted priest and priestess to nurture them.

So far as possible, he tested candidate couples himself, with a priestess. Since such a couple was already "saved" insofar as the middle church was concerned, he ran little risk—none with the woman and he always sized up the man before letting his priestess go ahead.

Before she was saved, Patricia Paiwonski was young, married, and "very happy." She had one child, she looked up to and admired her much older husband. George Paiwonski was a generous, affectionate man with only one weakness—but one which often left him too drunk to show his affection after a long day. Patty counted herself a lucky woman—true, George occasionally got affectionate with a female client . . . quite affectionate if it was early in the day—and, of course, tattooing required privacy, especially with ladies. Patty was tolerant; she sometimes made a date with a male client, after George got to hitting the bottle more and more.

But there was a lack in her life, one not filled even when a grateful client gave her a snake—shipping out, he said, and couldn't keep it. She liked pets and had no snake phobia; she made a home for it in their show window and George made a beautiful four-color picture to back it: "Don't Tread on Me!" This design turned out to be popular.

She acquired more snakes and they were a comfort. But she was the daughter of an Ulsterman and a girl from Cork; the armed truce between her parents had left her with no religion.

She was already a "seeker" when Foster preached in San Pedro; she had managed to get George to go a few Sundays but he had not seen the light.

Foster brought them the light, they made their confessions together. When Foster returned six months later, the Paiwonskis were so dedicated that he gave them personal attention.

"I never had a minute's trouble from the day George saw the light," she told Mike and Jill. "He still drank . . . but only in church and never too much. When our holy leader returned, George had started his Great Project.

Naturally we wanted to show it to Foster—" Mrs. Paiwon-ski hesitated. "Kids, I ought not to tell this."

"Then don't," Jill said emphatically. "Patty darling, we don't want you *ever* to do anything you don't feel easy about. 'Sharing water' has to be easy."

"Uh . . . I *do* want to! But remember this is Church things, so you mustn't tell anyone . . . just as I wouldn't tell anything about *you*."

Mike nodded. "Here on Earth we call it 'water brother' business. On Mars there's no problem . . . but here I grok there sometimes is. 'Water brother' business you don't repeat."

"I . . . I 'grok.' That's a funny word, but I'm learning it. All right, darlings, this is 'water brother' business. Did you know that *all* Fosterites are tattooed? *Real* Church members, I mean, the ones who are eternally saved forever and a day—like me? Oh, I don't mean tattooed all over but—see that? Right over my heart? That's Foster's holy kiss. George worked it in so that it looks like part of the picture . . . so that nobody could guess. But it's his kiss—and *Foster put it there hisself*!" She looked ecstatically proud.

They examined it. "It is a kiss mark," Jill said wonder-ingly, "like somebody had kissed you there wearing lip-stick. I thought it was part of that sunset."

"Yes, indeedy, that's how George fixed it. Because you don't show Foster's kiss to anyone who doesn't wear Fos-ter's kiss—and I never have, up to now. But," she insisted, "you're going to wear one, both of you, someday—and when you do, I want to tattoo 'em on."

Jill said, "I don't understand, Patty. How can he kiss *us*? After all, he's—up in Heaven."

"Yes, dearie, he is. Let me explain. Any priest or priestess can give you Foster's kiss. It means God's in your heart, God is part of you . . . forever."

Mike was suddenly intent. "Thou art God!"

"Huh, Michael? Well—I've never heard it put that way. But that does express it . . . God is in you and of you and with you, and the Devil can't get at you."

"Yes," agreed Mike. "You grok God." He thought happily that this was nearer to putting the concept across than he had ever managed before . . . except that Jill was learning it, in Martian. Which was inevitable.

"That's the idea, Michael. God . . . groks you—and you are married in Holy Love and Eternal Happiness to His Church. The priest or priestess kisses you and the mark is tattooed on to show it's forever. It doesn't have to be this big—mine is exactly the size and shape of Foster's blessed lips—and it can be placed anywhere to shield from sinful eyes. Any spot where it won't be noticed. Then you show it when you go into a Happiness gathering of the eternally saved."

"I've heard of happiness meetings," Jill commented, "but I've never known quite what they are."

"Well," Mrs. Paiwonski said judicially, "there are Happiness meetings and Happiness meetings. The ones for ordinary members, who are saved but might backslide, are fun—grand parties with only the amount of praying that comes happily, and plenty of whoop-it-up that makes a good party. Maybe a little real lovin'—but you'd better be mighty careful who and how, because you mustn't be a seed of dissension among the brethren. The Church is *very* strict about keeping things in their proper places.

"But a Happiness meeting for the eternally saved—well,

you don't have to be careful because there won't be *any-body* there who can sin—all past and done with. If you want to drink and pass out . . . okay, it's God's will or you wouldn't want to. You want to kneel down and pray, or lift up your voice in song—or tear off your clothes and dance; it's God's will. There can't possibly be anybody there who would see anything wrong in it."

"It sounds like quite a party," said Jill.

"Oh, it is—always! And you're filled with Heavenly bliss. If you wake up in the morning with one of the eternally saved brethren, he's there because God willed it to make you all blessedly Happy. They've all got Foster's kiss—they're *yours*." She frowned thoughtfully. "It feels a little like 'sharing water.' You understand?"

"I grok," agreed Mike.

(*"Mike?????"*)

(*"Wait, Jill. Wait for fullness."*)

"But don't think," Patricia said earnestly, "that a person can get into an Inner Temple Happiness meeting just with a tattoo mark. A visiting brother or sister—Well, take me. As soon as I know where the carnie is going, I write the local churches and send my fingerprints so they can check 'em against the file of eternally saved at Archangel Foster Tabernacle. I give 'em my address care of Billboard. Then when I do—and I always go Sundays and *never* miss a Happiness meeting even if Tim has to slough the blow-off—I am identified. They're glad to see me; I'm an added attraction, with my unique and unsurpassed sacred pictures—I often spend an evening just letting people examine me . . . every minute of it bliss. Sometimes the priest has me bring Honey Bun to do Eve and the Serpent—that takes body make-up, of course. Some brother plays Adam and we get scourged out of the Garden of Eden, and the priest explains the *real* meaning, not the twisted lies—and we end by regaining our blessed innocence, and that gets the party rolling. Joy!"

She added, "But everybody is interested in my Foster's kiss . . . because, since he went back to Heaven twenty years ago, not many have a Foster's kiss that wasn't laid on by proxy—I have the Tabernacle testify to *that*, too. And I tell them about it. Uh—"

Mrs. Paiwonski hesitated, then told them, in explicit detail—and Jill wondered where her limited ability to blush had gone? Then she grokked that Mike and Patty were two of a kind—God's innocents, unable to sin no matter what they did. She wished, for Patty's sake, that Foster had really been a holy prophet who had saved her for eternal bliss.

But *Foster*! God's Wounds, what a travesty!

Suddenly, through her greatly improved recall, Jill was back in a room with a glass wall, looking into Foster's dead eyes. But he seemed alive . . . and she felt a shiver in her loins and wondered what *she* would have done if Foster had offered her his holy kiss—and his holy self?

She shut it out of her mind, but not before Mike caught it. She felt him smile, with knowing innocence.

She stood up, "Pattycake darling, what time do you have to be at the lot?"

"Oh, dear! I should be back this blessed minute!"

"Why? The show doesn't roll until nine-thirty."

"Well . . . Honey Bun misses me. She's jealous if I stay out late."

"Can't you tell her that it's a Happiness meeting?"

"Uh . . ." The older woman gathered Jill in her arms. "It is! It certainly is!"

"Good. I'm going to sleep—Jill is bushed. What time do you have to be up?"

"Uh, if I'm back by eight, I can get Sam to tear down my top and have time to make sure my babies are loaded safely."

"Breakfast?"

"I'll get it on the train. Just coffee when I wake up, usually."

"I make that here. You dears stay up as long as you like; I won't let you oversleep—if you sleep. Mike doesn't sleep."

"Not at all?"

"Never. He curls up and thinks a while, usually—but he doesn't sleep."

Mrs. Paiwonski nodded solemnly. "Another sign. I know—and, Michael, some day you will know. Your call will come."

"Maybe," agreed Jill. "Mike, I'm falling asleep. Pop me into bed. Please?" She was lifted, wafted into the bedroom, covers rolled themselves back—she slept.

Jill woke at seven, slipped out of bed, put her head into the other room. Lights were out and shades were tight, but they were not asleep. Jill heard Mike say with soft certainty:

"Thou art God."

"'Thou art God'—" Patricia whispered in a voice as heavy as if drugged.

"Yes. Jill is God."

"Jill . . . is God. Yes, Michael."

"And thou art God."

"*Thou*—art God! Now, Michael, *now*!"

Jill went quietly away and brushed her teeth. Presently she let Mike know that she was awake and found that he knew it. When she came back into the living room, sunlight was streaming in. "Good morning, darlings!" She kissed them.

"Thou art God," Patty said simply.

"Yes, Patty. And thou art God. God is in all of us." She looked at Patty in the harsh morning light and noted that she did not look tired. Well, she knew that effect—if Mike wanted her to stay up all night, Jill never found it any trouble. She suspected that her sleepiness the night before had been Mike's idea . . . and heard Mike agree in his mind.

"Now coffee, darlings. And I happen to have stashed away a redipak of orange juice, too."

They breakfasted lightly, replete with happiness. Jill saw Patty looking thoughtful. "What is it, dear?"

"Uh, I hate to mention this—but what are you kids going to eat on? Aunt Patty has a pretty well stuffed grouch bag and I thought—"

Jill laughed. "Oh, darling, I shouldn't laugh. But the Man from Mars is *rich!* Surely you know?"

Mrs. Paiwonski looked baffled. "Well, I guess I knew. But you can't trust anything you hear over the news."

"Patty, you're an utter darling. Believe me, now that we're water brothers, we wouldn't hesitate—'sharing the nest' isn't just poetry. But it's the other way around. If you *ever* need money, just say so. Any amount. Any time. Write us—better yet, call me; Mike doesn't have the foggiest idea about money. Why, dear, I'm keeping a couple of hundred thousand in my name right now. Want some?"

Mrs. Paiwonski looked startled. "Bless me! I don't need money."

Jill shrugged. "If you ever do, just holler. If you want a yacht—Mike would enjoy giving you a yacht."

"I certainly would, Pat. I've never seen a yacht."

Mrs. Paiwonski shook her head. "Don't take me up on a tall mountain, dearie—all I want from you two is your love—"

"You have that," Jill told her.

"I don't grok 'love,'" Mike said. "But Jill always speaks rightly. If we've got it, it's yours."

"—and to know that you're saved. But I'm no longer worried about that. Mike has told me about waiting, and why waiting is. You understand, Jill?"

"I grok. I'm no longer impatient about anything."

"But I have something for you two." The tattooed lady got her purse, took a book out. "My dear ones . . . this is the very copy of the New Revelation that Blessed Foster gave me . . . the night he placed his kiss on me. I want you to have it."

Jill's eyes filled with tears. "But, Aunt Patty—Patty our brother! We *can't* take this one. We'll buy one."

"No. It's . . . it's 'water' I'm sharing with you. For growing-closer."

"Oh—" Jill jumped up. "We'll share it. It's ours now—all of us." She kissed her.

Mike tapped her shoulder. "Greedy little brother. My turn."

"I'll always be greedy, that way."

The Man from Mars kissed his new brother first on her mouth, then kissed the spot Foster had kissed. He pondered, briefly by Earth time, picked a corresponding spot on the other side where George's design could be matched—kissed her there while he thought by stretched-out time and in great detail. It was necessary to grok the capillaries—

To the other two, he briefly pressed his lips to skin. But Jill caught a hint of his effort. "Patty! *See!*"

Mrs. Paiwonski looked down. Marked on her, paired stigmata in blood red, were his lips. She started to faint—then showed her staunch faith. "Yes. *Yes!* Michael—"

Shortly the tattooed lady was replaced by a mousy housewife in high neck, long sleeves, and gloves. "I won't cry," she said soberly, "and there are no good-bys in eternity. I will be waiting." She kissed them, left without looking back.

XXVIII

"BLASPHEMY!"

Foster looked up. "Something bite you, Junior?" This annex had been run up in a hurry and Things did get in—swarms of almost invisible imps usually . . . harmless, but a bite from one left an itch on the ego.

"Uh . . . you'd have to see it to believe it—here, I'll run the omniscio back a touch."

"You'd be surprised at what I can believe, Junior." Nevertheless Digby's supervisor shifted part of his attention. Three temporals—humans, he saw they were; a man and two women—speculating about the eternal. Nothing odd about that. "Yes?"

"You heard what she said! 'Archangel Michael' indeed!"

"What about it?"

"'What about it?' Oh, for God's sake!"

"Very possibly."

Digby's halo quivered. "Foster, you must not have

taken a good look! She meant that over-age juvenile delin-quent that sent me to the showers. Scan it again."

Foster let the gain increase, noted that the angel-in-training had spoken rightly—and noticed something else and smiled his angelic smile. "How do you know he isn't, Junior?"

"Huh?"

"I haven't seen Mike around the Club lately and his name has been scratched on the Millennial Solipsist Tournament—that's a Sign that he's likely away on de-tached duty; Mike is one of the most eager Solipsism play-ers in this sector."

"But the notion's obscene!"

"You'd be surprised how many of the Boss's best ideas have been called 'obscene' in some quarters—or, rather, *you* should not be surprised, in view of your field work. But 'obscene' is a null concept; it has no theological meaning. 'To the pure all things are pure.'"

"But—"

"I'm still Witnessing, Junior. In addition to the fact that our brother Michael seems to be away at this micro-instant—I don't keep track of him; we're not on the same Watch list—that tattooed lady who made that oracular pronouncement is not likely to be mistaken; she's a very holy temporal herself."

"Who says?"

"I say. I know." Foster smiled again with angelic sweet-ness. Dear little Patricia! Getting a little long in the tooth but still Earthily desirable—and shining with an inner light that made her look like a stained glass window. He noted without temporal pride that George had finished his great dedication since he had last looked at Patricia—that picture of his being called up to Heaven wasn't bad, not bad at all, in the Higher sense. He must remember to look up George and compliment him on it, and tell him he had seen Patricia—hmm, where was George? A creative artist in the universe design section, working right under the Architect, as he recalled—no matter, the master file would dig him out in a split millennium.

What a delicious little butterball Patricia had been and such holy frenzy! If she had had just a touch more assertiveness and a touch less humility he could have made her a priestess. But such was Patricia's need to accept God according to her own nature that she could have qualified only among the Lingayats . . . where she wasn't needed. Foster considered scanning back and seeing her as she had been, decided against it with angelic restraint; there was work to be done—

"Forget the omniscio, Junior. I want a Word with you." Digby did so and waited. Foster twanged his halo, an annoying habit he had when he was meditating. "Junior, you aren't shaping up too angelically."

"I'm sorry."

"Sorrow is not for eternity. But the Truth is you've been preoccupied with that young fellow who may or may not be our brother Michael. Now wait—In the first place it is not for you to Judge the instrument used to call you from the pasture. In the second place it is not he who vexes you—you hardly knew him—what's bothering you is that little brunette secretary you had. She had earned my Kiss quite some temporal period before you were called. Hadn't she?"

"I was still testing her."

"Then no doubt you have been angelically pleased to

note that Supreme Bishop Short, after giving her a thorough examination himself—oh, most thorough; I told you he would measure up—has passed her and she now enjoys the wider Happiness she deserves. Mmmm, a Shepherd should take joy in his work . . . but when he's promoted, he should take joy in that, too. Now it happens there is a spot open for a Guardian-in-Training in a new sector being opened up—a job under your nominal rank, I concede, but good angelic experience. This planet—well, you think of it as a planet; you'll see—is occupied by a race of tripolarity instead of bipolarity and I have it on High Authority that Don Juan himself could not manage to take Earthly interest in *any* of their three polarities . . . that's not opinion; he was borrowed as a test. He screamed and prayed to be returned to the solitary hell he has created for himself."

"Going to send me to Flatbush, huh? So I won't interfere!"

"Tut, tut! You *can't* interfere—the one Impossibility that permits all else to be possible; I tried to tell you that when you arrived. But don't let it fret you; you are eternally permitted to try. Your orders will include a loop so that you will check back here-now without loss of temporality. Now fly away and get cracking; I have work to do." Foster turned back to where he had been interrupted. Oh, yes, a poor soul temporally designated as "Alice Douglas"— to be a goad was a hard assignment and she had met it unflaggingly. But her job was complete and now she would need rest and rehabilitation from the inescapable battle fatigue . . . she'd be kicking and screaming and foaming ectoplasm at all orifices.

Oh, she would need exorcism after a job that rough!

But they were all rough; they couldn't be anything else. And "Alice Douglas" was an utterly reliable field operative; she could take any left-hand assignment as long as it was essentially virginal—burn her at the stake or put her in a nunnery; she always delivered.

Not that he cared much for virgins, other than with professional respect for any job well done. Foster sneaked a last look at Mrs. Paiwonski. *There* was a fellow worker he could appreciate. Darling little Patricia! What a blessed, lusty benison—

XXIX

AS THE DOOR closed behind Patricia, Jill said, "What now, Mike?"

"We're leaving. Jill, you've read some abnormal psychology."

"Yes. Not as much as you have."

"You know the symbolism of tattooing? And snakes?"

"Of course. I knew that about Patty as soon as I met her. I had been hoping that you would find a way."

"I couldn't, until we were water brothers. Sex is a helpful goodness—but only if it is sharing and growing-closer. I grok that if I did it without growing-closer—well, I'm not sure."

"I grok you couldn't, Mike. That is one reason—one of many reasons—I love you."

"I still don't grok 'love.' Jill, I don't grok 'people.' But I didn't want Pat to leave."

"Stop her. Keep her with us."

("*Waiting is, Jill.*")

("*I know.*")

He added, "I doubt if we could give her all she needs. She wants to give herself all the time, to everybody. Happiness meetings and snakes and marks aren't enough for Pat. She wants to offer herself on an altar to everybody in the world, always—and make them happy. This New Revelation . . . I grok it is other things to other people. But that is what it is to Pat."

"Yes, Mike. Dear Mike."

"Time to leave. Pick a dress and get your purse. I'll dispose of the trash."

Jill thought wistfully that she would like to take one or two things. Mike always moved on with just the clothes on his back—and seemed to grok that she preferred it that way. "I'll wear that pretty blue one."

It floated out, posed over her, wriggled onto her as she held up her hands; the zipper closed. Shoes walked toward her, she stepped into them. "I'm ready."

Mike had caught the flavor of her thought but not the concept; it was too alien to Martian ideas. "Jill? Do you want to stop and get married?"

She thought about it. "It's Sunday, we couldn't get a license."

"Tomorrow, then. I grok you would like it."

"No, Mike."

"Why not, Jill?"

"We wouldn't be any closer, we already share water. That's true both in English and Martian."

"Yes."

"And a reason just in English. I wouldn't have Dorcas

and Anne and Miriam—and Patty—think that I was trying to crowd them out."

"Jill, none of them would think so."

"I won't chance it, because I don't need it. Because you
married me in a hospital room ages and ages ago." She
hesitated. "But there is something you might do for me."

"What, Jill?"

"Well, you might call me pet names! The way *I* do *you*."

"Yes, Jill. What pet names?"

"Oh!" She kissed him quickly. "Mike, you're the sweetest, most lovable man I've ever met—and the most infuriating creature on two planets! Don't bother. Just call me
'little brother' occasionally . . . it makes me all quivery
inside."

"Yes, Little Brother."

"Oh, my! Let's get out of here—before I take you back
to bed. Meet me downstairs; I'll be paying the bill." She
left suddenly.

They caught the first Greyhound going anywhere. A
week later they stopped at home, shared water for a few
days, left without saying good-by—good-by was one human custom Mike resisted; he used it only with strangers.

Shortly they were in Las Vegas, stopping in a hotel off
the Strip. Mike tried the games while Jill killed time as a
show girl. She couldn't sing or dance; parading in a tall
improbable hat, a smile, and a scrap of tinsel was the job
suited to her in the Babylon of the West. She preferred to
work if Mike was busy and, somehow, Mike always got her
the job she picked. Since casinos never closed, Mike was
busy almost all the time.

Mike was careful not to win much, keeping to limits Jill

set. After he had milked each casino for a few thousand he put it all back, never letting himself be the big-money player. Then he took a job as a croupier, letting the little ball roll without interference and studying people, trying to grok why they gambled. He grokked a drive that felt intensely sexual—but he seemed to grok wrongness in this.

Jill assumed that the customers in the palatial theater-restaurant where she worked were just marks—and, as such, did not count. But to her surprise she actively enjoyed displaying herself in front of them. With increasing Martian honesty she examined this feeling. She had always enjoyed being looked at with admiration by men whom she found attractive enough to want to touch—she had been irked that the sight of her body meant nothing to Mike even though he was as devoted to her body as a woman could dream of—

—if he wasn't preoccupied. But he was generous even then; he would let her call him out of trance, shift gears without complaint and be smiling and eager and loving.

Nevertheless, there it was—one of his strangenesses, like his inability to laugh. Jill decided, after her initiation as a show girl, that she enjoyed being visually admired by strangers because this was the one thing Mike did not give her.

Her perfecting self-honesty soon washed out that theory. The men in the audience were mostly too old, too fat, too bald for Jill to find them attractive—and Jill had always been scornful of "lecherous old wolves"—although not of old men, she reminded herself; Jubal could look at her, even use crude language, and not give her any feeling that he wanted to get her alone and grope her.

But now she found that these "lecherous old wolves" did not set her teeth on edge. When she felt their admiring stares or outright lust—and she did feel it, could identify the sources—she did not resent it; it warmed her and made her smugly pleased.

"Exhibitionism" had been to her just a technical term—a weakness she held in contempt. Now, in digging out her own and looking at it, she decided that either this form of narcissism was normal, or she was abnormal. But she didn't *feel* abnormal; she felt healthier than ever. She had always been of rugged health—nurses need to be—but she hadn't had a sniffle or an upset stomach in she couldn't remember when . . . why, not even cramps.

Okay, if a healthy woman liked to be looked at, then it follows as the night the day that healthy men should like to look, else there was just no darn sense to it! At which point she finally understood, intellectually, Duke and his pictures.

She discussed it with Mike—but Mike could not understand why Jill had ever minded being looked at. He understood not wishing to be touched; Mike avoided shaking hands, he wanted to be touched only by water brothers. (Jill wasn't sure how far this went; she had explained homosexuality, after Mike had read about it and failed to grok—and had given him rules for avoiding passes; she knew that Mike, pretty as he was, would attract such. He had followed her advice and had made his face more masculine, instead of the androgynous beauty he had had. But Jill was not sure that Mike would refuse a pass, say, from Duke—fortunately Mike's male water brothers were decidedly masculine, just as his others were very female women. Jill suspected that Mike would grok a "wrongness" in the poor in-betweeners anyhow—they would never be offered water.)

Nor could Mike understand why it now pleased her to be stared at. The only time their attitudes had been roughly similar had been as they left the carnival, when Jill had become indifferent to stares. She saw now that her present self-knowledge had been nascent then; she had not been truly indifferent to masculine stares. Under the stresses of adjusting to the Man from Mars she had shucked off part of her cultural conditioning, that degree of prissiness a nurse can retain despite a no-nonsense profession.

But Jill hadn't known that she had *any* prissiness until she lost it. At last she was able to admit to herself that there was something inside her as happily shameless as a tabby in heat.

She tried to explain this to Mike, giving her theory of the complementary functions of narcissist display and voyeurism. "The truth is, Mike, I get a kick out of having men stare at me . . . lots of men and almost any man. So now I grok why Duke likes pictures of women, the sexier the better. It doesn't mean that I want to go to bed with them, any more than Duke wants to go to bed with a photograph. But when they look at me and tell me—think at me—that I'm desirable, it gives me a warm tingle right in my middle." She frowned slightly. "I ought to get a real naughty picture taken of me and send it to Duke . . . to tell him I'm sorry I failed to grok what I thought was a weakness in him. If it's a weakness, I've got it, too—girl style. If it *is* a weakness—I grok it isn't."

"All right. We'll find a photographer."

She shook her head. "I'll apologize instead. I won't

send such a picture; Duke has never made a pass at me—
and I don't want him getting ideas."

"Jill, you would not want Duke?"

She heard an echo of "water brother" in his mind.
"Hmm . . . I've never thought about it. I guess I've been
'being faithful' to you. But I grok you speak rightly; I
wouldn't turn Duke down—and I would *enjoy* it, too!
What do you think of *that*, darling?"

"I grok a goodness," Mike said seriously.

"Hmm . . . my gallant Martian, there are times when
human females appreciate a semblance of jealousy—but I
don't think there is any chance that you will ever grok
'jealousy.' Darling, what would you grok if one of those
marks made a pass at me?"

Mike barely smiled. "I grok he would be missing."

"I grok he might. But, Mike—listen, dear. You promised you wouldn't do anything of that sort except in utter
emergency. If you hear me scream, and reach into my
mind and I'm in real trouble, that's another matter. But I
was coping with wolves when you were still on Mars. Nine
times out of ten, if a girl gets raped, it's partly her fault. So
don't be hasty."

"I will remember. I wish you were sending that naughty
picture to Duke."

"What, dear? If I make a pass at Duke—and I may, now
that you've put the idea in my head—I'd rather grab his
shoulders and say, 'Duke, how about it?—I'm willing.' I
don't want to do it by sending him a picture like those
nasty women used to send to you. But if you want me to,
okay."

Mike frowned. "If you wish to send Duke a naughty
picture, do so. If you not wish, then not. But I had hoped

to see the naughty picture taken. Jill, what is a 'naughty' picture?"

Mike was baffled by Jill's reversal in attitude, plus long-standing bafflement at Duke's "art" collection. But the pale Martian thing which parallels tumultuous human sexuality gave him no foundation for grokking either narcissism or voyeurism, modesty or display. He added, "'Naughty' means a small wrongness, but I grok you did not mean a wrongness, but a goodness."

"Uh, a naughty picture could be either, I guess—depending on who it's for—now that I'm over my prejudice. But—Mike, I'll have to show you; I can't tell you. Close those slats, will you?"

Venetian blinds flipped themselves shut. "All right," she said. "This pose is just a little naughty—any show girl would use it as a professional pic . . . and this is a bit more so, some girls would use it. But this is unmistakably naughty . . . and this one is *quite* naughty . . . and *this* is so extremely naughty that I wouldn't pose with my face wrapped in a towel—unless you wanted it."

"If your face was covered, why would I want it?"

"Ask Duke. That's all I can say."

"I grok not wrongness, I grok not goodness. I grok—" He used a Martian word indicating a null state of all emotions.

Because he was baffled, they went on discussing it, in Martian when possible because of its extremely fine discriminations for emotions and values—and in English because Martian couldn't cope with the concepts. To pursue this mystery, Mike took a ringside table that night, Jill having coached him in how to bribe the maître d'hôtel. Jill came strutting out in the first number, her smile for everyone but a wink for Mike. She discovered that, with Mike present, the warm, pleased sensation she had been enjoying nightly was greatly amplified—she suspected that she would glow in the dark.

When the girls formed a tableau, Mike was about ten feet from Jill—she had been promoted to a front position. The director had shifted her on her fourth day, saying, "I don't know what it is, kid. We've got girls with twice your build—but you've got what customers look at."

She posed, and talked with Mike in her mind (*"Feel anything?"*)

(*"I grok but not in fullness."*)

(*"Look where I am looking, my brother. The small one. He quivers. He thirsts for me."*)

(*"I grok his thirst."*)

(*"Can you see him?"*) Jill stared into the customer's eyes both to increase his interest and to let Mike use her eyes. As her grokking of Martian thought had increased and as they had grown steadily closer they had begun to use this common Martian convenience. Jill had little control as yet; Mike could see through her eyes simply by calling to her, she could see through his only if he gave it his attention.

(*"We grok him together,"*) Mike agreed. (*"Great thirst for Little Brother."*)

(*"!!!!"*)

(*"Yes. Beautiful agony."*)

A music cue told Jill to resume her slow strut. She did so, moving with proud sensuousness and feeling lust boil up in response to emotions both from Mike and the stranger. The routine caused her to walk toward the rutty little stranger; she continued to lock eyes with him.

Something happened which was totally unexpected to

her because Mike had never explained that it was possible. She had been letting herself receive the stranger's emotions, teasing him with eyes and body, and relaying what she felt to Mike—when suddenly she was seeing herself through strange eyes and feeling all the primitive need with which that stranger saw her.

She stumbled and would have fallen had not Mike caught her, lifted her, steadied her until she could walk unassisted, second-sight gone.

The parade of beauties continued through the exit. Off stage the girl behind her said, "What happened, Jill?"

"Caught my heel."

"That was the wildest recover I ever saw. You looked like a puppet on strings."

(—and so I was, dear!) "I'm going to ask the stage manager to check that spot. I think there's a loose board."

For the rest of the show Mike gave her glimpses of how she looked to various men while making sure that she was not again taken by surprise. Jill was startled at how varied were the images: one noticed her legs, another was fascinated by undulations of her torso, a third saw only her proud bosom. Then Mike let her look at other girls in the tableaux. She was relieved to find that Mike saw them as she did—but sharper.

But she was amazed to find that her excitement increased as she looked through his eyes at other girls.

Mike left during the finale, ahead of the crowd. She did not expect to see him again that night since he had asked for time off only to see her show. But when she returned to their hotel, she felt him before she reached the room. The door opened, closed behind her. "Hello, darling!" she called out. "How nice you came home!"

He smiled gently. "I now grok naughty pictures." Her clothes vanished. "Make naughty pictures."

"Huh? Yes, dear, of course." She ran through poses as she had earlier. With each one Mike let her use his eyes to see herself. She looked, and felt his emotions . . . and felt her own swell in mutually amplified re-echoing. At last she placed herself in a pose as randy as her imagination could devise.

"Naughty pictures are a great goodness," Mike said gravely.

"*Yes!* And now *I* grok them, too! *What are you waiting for?*"

They quit their jobs and saw every revue on the Strip. Jill found that she "grokked naughty pictures" only through a man's eyes. If Mike watched, she shared his mood, from sensuous pleasure to full rut—but if Mike's attention wandered, the model, dancer, or peeler was just another woman. She decided that this was fortunate; to have discovered in herself Lesbian tendencies would have been too much.

But it was fun—"great goodness"—to see girls through his eyes—and ecstatic goodness to know that, at last, he looked at her the same way.

THEY MOVED ON to Palo Alto, where Mike tried to swallow the Hoover Library. But scanners could not spin that fast, nor could Mike turn pages fast enough to read them all. At last he admitted that he was taking in data faster than he could grok it, even spending all hours the library was closed in contemplation. With relief Jill moved them to San Francisco and he embarked on systematic research.

She came back to their flat one day to find him doing nothing, surrounded by books—many books: The Talmud, the Kama-Sutra, Bibles in several versions, the Book of the Dead, the Book of Mormon, Patty's precious copy of the New Revelation, various Apocrypha, the Koran, the unabridged Golden Bough, The Way, Science and Health with key to the Scriptures, sacred writings of a dozen other religions major and minor—even such oddities as Crowley's Book of the Law.

"Trouble, dear?"

"Jill, I don't grok."

(*"Waiting, Michael. Waiting for fullness is."*)

"I don't think waiting will fill it. I know what's wrong; I'm not a man, I'm a Martian—a Martian in a body of the wrong shape."

"You're plenty of man for me, dear—and I love the way your body is shaped."

"Oh, you grok what I'm talking about. I don't grok *people*. I don't understand this multiplicity of religions. Now among my people—"

"*Your* people, Mike?"

"Sorry. I should have said that, among Martians, there is only one religion—and it is not a faith, it's a certainty. You grok it. 'Thou art God!'"

"Yes," she agreed. "I do grok . . . in Martian. But, dearest, it doesn't say the same thing in English. I don't know why."

"Mmmm . . . on Mars, when we needed to know anything, we asked the Old Ones and the answer was never wrong. Jill, is it possible that we humans don't have 'Old Ones'? No souls, I mean. When we discorporate—*die*—do we die *dead* . . . die all over and nothing left? Do we live in ignorance because it doesn't matter? Because we are gone and not a rack behind in time so short that a Martian would use it for one long contemplation? Tell me, Jill. You're human."

She smiled with sober serenity. "You yourself have told *me*. You have taught me to know eternity and you can't take it away from me. You can't die, Mike—you can only discorporate." She gestured at herself with both hands. "This body that you have taught me to see through your eyes . . . and that you have loved so well, someday it will be gone. But *I* shall not be gone . . . *I am that I am!* Thou art God and I am God and we are God, eternally. I am not sure where I will be, or whether I will remember that I was once Jill Boardman who was happy trotting bedpans and equally happy strutting her stuff in her buff under bright lights. I have liked this body—"

With a most uncustomary gesture of impatience Mike threw away her clothes.

"Thank you, dear," she said. "It has been a nice body to me—and to you—to both of us who thought of it. But I don't expect to miss it when I am through with it. I hope that you will eat it when I discorporate."

"Oh, I'll eat you, all right—unless I discorporate first."

"I don't suppose you will. With your much greater control over your sweet body I suspect that you can live several centuries at least. Unless you choose to discorporate sooner."

"I might. But not now. Jill, I've tried and tried. How many churches have we attended?"

"All the sorts in San Francisco, I think. I don't recall how many times we have been to seekers' services."

"That's just to comfort Pat—I'd never go again if you

weren't sure that she needs to know that we haven't given up."

"She does need to. We can't lie—you don't know how and I can't, not to Patty."

"Actually," he admitted, "the Fosterites have quite a lot. All twisted, of course. They are groping—the way I did as a carnie. They'll never correct their mistakes, because this—" He caused Patty's book to lift. "—is mostly crap!"

"Yes. But Patty doesn't see those parts. She is wrapped in innocence. She is God and behaves accordingly . . . only She doesn't know She is."

"Uh, huh," he agreed. "That's our Pat. She believes it only when I tell her—with proper emphasis. But, Jill, there are only three places to look. Science—and I was taught more about how the universe ticks while I was still in the nest than human scientists can yet handle. So much that I can't talk to them, even about as elementary a gimmick as levitation. I'm not disparaging scientists. What they do is as it should be; I grok that fully. But what they are after is *not* what *I* am looking for—you don't grok a desert by counting its grains of sand. Then there's philosophy—supposed to tackle everything. Does it? All any philosopher ever comes out with is what he walked in with—except for self-deluders who prove their assumptions by their conclusions. Like Kant. Like other tail-chasers. So the answer ought to be *here*." He waved at piles of books. "Only it's *not*. Bits that grok true, but never a pattern—or if there is, they ask you to take the hard part on *faith*! Faith! What a dirty monosyllable—Jill, why didn't you mention that one when you were teaching me the short words that mustn't be used in polite company?"

She smiled. "Mike, you made a joke."

"I didn't mean it as a joke . . . and I can't see that it's funny. Jill, I haven't even been good for *you*—you used to laugh. I haven't learned to laugh; instead you've forgotten. Instead of my becoming human . . . you're becoming Martian."

"I'm happy, dear. You probably just haven't noticed me laughing."

"If you laughed clear down on Market Street, I would hear. I grok. Once I quit being frightened by it I always noticed it—you, especially. If I grokked it, I would grok people—I think. Then I could help somebody like Pat . . . teach her what I know and learn what she knows. We could understand each other."

"Mike, all you need to do for Patty is to see her occasionally. Why don't we, dear? Let's get out of this dreary fog. She's home now; the carnie is closed for the season. Drop south and see her . . . and I've always wanted to see Baja California; we could go on south into warmer weather—and take her with us, that would be fun!"

"All right."

She stood up. "Let me get a dress. Do you want to save those books? I could ship them to Jubal."

He flipped his fingers and all were gone but Patricia's gift. "We'll take that one; Pat would notice. But, Jill, right now I need to go to the zoo."

"All right."

"I want to spit back at a camel and ask him what he's sour about. Maybe camels are the 'Old Ones' on this planet . . . and that's what's wrong with the place."

"Two jokes in one day, Mike."

"I ain't laughing. Neither are you. Nor the camel.

Maybe he groks why. Is this dress all right? Do you want underclothes?"

"Please, dear. It's chilly."

"Up easy." He levitated her a couple of feet. "Pants. Stockings. Garter belt. Shoes. Down you go and lift your arms. Bra? You don't need one. Now the dress—and you're decent. And pretty, whatever that is. You look good. Maybe I can get a job as lady's maid if I'm not good for anything else. Baths, shampoos, massages, hair styling, make-up, dressing for all occasions—I've even learned to do your nails so it suits you. Will that be all, Madame?"

"You're a perfect lady's maid, dear."

"Yes, I grok I am. You look so good I think I'll toss it away and give you a massage. The growing-closer kind."

"Yes, Michael!"

"I thought you had learned waiting? First you have to take me to the zoo and buy me peanuts."

"Yes, Mike."

It was windy cold at Golden Gate Park but Mike did not notice and Jill had learned how not to be cold. But it was pleasant to relax control in the warm monkey house. Aside from its heat Jill did not like the monkey house—monkeys and apes were depressingly human. She was, she thought, finished forever with prissiness; she had grown to cherish an ascetic, almost Martian joy in all things physical. The public copulations and evacuations of these simians did not offend her; these poor penned people possessed no privacy, they were not at fault. She could watch without repugnance, her own fastidiousness untouched. No, it was that they were "Human, All Too Human"—every action, every expression, every puzzled troubled look reminded her of what she liked least about her own race.

Jill preferred the Lion House—the great males arrogant even in captivity, the placid motherliness of the big females, the lordly beauty of Bengal tigers with jungle staring out of their eyes, little leopards swift and deadly, reek of musk that air-conditioning could not purge. Mike shared her tastes; they would spend hours there or in the aviary or the reptile house or in watching seals— once he told her that, if one had to be hatched on this planet, to be a sea lion would be of greatest goodness.

When first he saw a zoo, Mike was much upset; Jill was forced to order him to wait and grok, as he had been about to free the animals. He conceded presently that most of them could not live where he proposed to turn them loose—a zoo was a nest, of a sort. He followed this with hours of withdrawal, after which he never again threatened to remove bars and glass and grills. He explained to Jill that bars were to keep people out more than to keep animals in, which he had failed to grok at first. After that Mike never missed a zoo wherever they went.

But today even the misanthropy of camels could not shake Mike's moodiness. Nor did monkeys and apes cheer him up. They stood in front of a cage containing a family of capuchins, watching them eat, sleep, court, nurse, groom, and swarm aimlessly around, while Jill tossed them peanuts.

She tossed one to a monk; before he could eat it a larger male not only stole his peanut but gave him a beating. The little fellow made no attempt to pursue his tormentor; he pounded his knucks against the floor and chattered helpless rage. Mike watched solemnly.

Suddenly the mistreated monkey rushed across the cage, picked a monkey still smaller, bowled it over and gave it a dubbing worse than the one he had suffered. The third monk crawled away, whimpering. The other monkeys paid no attention.

Mike threw back his head and laughed—and went on laughing, uncontrollably. He gasped for breath, started to tremble and sink to the floor, still laughing.

"Stop it, Mike!"

He did cease folding up but his guffaws went on. An attendant hurried over. "Lady, do you need help?"

"Can you call us a cab? Ground, air, anything—I've got to get him out of here." She added, "He's not well."

"Ambulance? Looks like he's having a fit."

"Anything!" A few minutes later she led Mike into a piloted air cab. She gave their address, then said urgently, "Mike, listen to me! Quiet down."

He became somewhat quiet but continued to chuckle, laugh aloud, chuckle again, while she wiped his eyes, all the minutes it took to get home. She got him inside, got his clothes off, made him lie down. "All right, dear. Withdraw if you need to."

"I'm all right. At last I'm all right."

"I hope so." She sighed. "You scared me, Mike."

"I'm sorry, Little Brother. I was scared, too, the first time I heard laughing."

"Mike, what happened?"

"Jill . . . I grok people!"

"Huh?" ("????")

(*I speak rightly, Little Brother. I grok.*") "I grok people now, Jill . . . Little Brother . . . precious darling . . . little imp with lively legs and lovely lewd lascivious lecherous licentious libido . . . beautiful bumps and pert posterior . . . soft voice and gentle hands. My baby darling."

"Why, Michael!"

"Oh, I knew the words; I simply didn't know when or why to say them . . . nor why you wanted me to. I love you, sweetheart—I grok 'love' now, too."

"You always have. And I love you . . . you smooth ape. My darling."

"'Ape,' yes. Come here, she ape, put your head on my shoulder and tell me a joke."

"Just tell you a joke?"

"Well, nothing more than snuggling. Tell me a joke I've never heard and see if I laugh at the right place. I will, I'm sure of it—and I'll tell you *why* it's funny. Jill . . . *I grok people!*"

"But how, darling? Can you tell me? Does it need Martian? Or mind-talk?"

"No, that's the point. I grok people. I *am* people . . . so now I can say it in people talk. I've found out why people laugh. They laugh because it hurts . . . because it's the only thing that'll make it stop hurting."

Jill looked puzzled. "Maybe I'm the one who isn't people. I don't understand."

"Ah, but you *are* people, little she ape. You grok it so automatically that you don't have to think about it. Because you grew up with people. But I didn't. I've been like a puppy raised apart from dogs—who couldn't be like his masters and had never learned how to be a dog. So I had to be taught. Brother Mahmoud taught me, Jubal taught me, lots of people taught me . . . and you taught me most of all. Today I got my diploma—and I laughed. That poor little monk."

"Which one, dear? I thought that big one was just mean . . . and the one I flipped the peanut to turned out to be just as mean. There certainly wasn't anything funny."

"Jill, Jill my darling! Too much Martian has rubbed off on you. Of course it wasn't funny; it was tragic. That's why I had to laugh. I looked at a cageful of monkeys and suddenly I saw all the mean and cruel and utterly unexplainable things I've seen and heard and read about in the time I've been with my own people—and suddenly it hurt so much I found myself laughing."

"But—Mike dear, laughing is what you do when something is nice . . . not when it's horrid."

"Is it? Think back to Las Vegas—When you girls came out on stage, did people laugh?"

"Well . . . no."

"But you girls were the nicest part of the show. I grok now, that if they had laughed, you would have been hurt. No, they laughed when a comic tripped over his feet and fell down . . . or something else that is not a goodness."

"But that's not *all* people laugh at."

"Isn't it? Perhaps I don't grok its fullness yet. But find me something that makes you laugh, sweetheart . . . a joke, anything—but something that gave you a belly laugh, not a smile. Then we'll see if there isn't a wrongness somewhere and whether you would laugh if the wrongness wasn't there." He thought. "I grok when apes learn to laugh, they'll be people."

"Maybe." Doubtfully but earnestly Jill started digging into her memory for jokes that had struck her as irresistably funny, ones which had jerked a laugh out of her:

"—her entire bridge club." . . . "Should I bow?" . . . "Neither one, you idiot—*instead!*" . . . "—the Chinaman objects." . . . "—broke her leg." . . . "—make trouble for *me*!" . . . "—but it'll spoil the ride for me." . . . "—and his mother-in-law fainted." . . . "Stop you? I bet three to one you could do it!" . . . "—something has happened to Ole." . . . "—and so are you, you clumsy ox!"

She gave up on "funny" stories, pointing out that such were just fantasies, and tried to recall real incidents. Practical jokes? All practical jokes supported Mike's thesis, even ones as mild as a dribble glass—and when it came to an intern's notion of a joke—interns should be kept in cages. What else? The time Elsa Mae lost her panties? It hadn't been funny to Elsa Mae. Or the—

She said grimly, "Apparently the pratt fall is the peak of all humor. It's not a pretty picture of the human race, Mike."

"Oh, but it is!"

"Huh?"

"I had thought—I had been told—that a 'funny' thing is a thing of goodness. It isn't. Not ever is it funny to the person it happens to. Like that sheriff without his pants. The goodness is in the laughing. I grok it is a bravery . . . and a sharing . . . against pain and sorrow and defeat."

"But—Mike, it is not a goodness to laugh *at* people."

"No. But I was not laughing at the little monkey. I was laughing at *us*. People. And suddenly I knew I was people and could not stop laughing." He paused. "This is hard to explain, because you have never lived as a Martian, for all that I've told you about it. On Mars there is *never* anything to laugh at. All the things that are funny to us humans either cannot happen on Mars or are not permitted to happen—sweetheart, what you call 'freedom' doesn't exist on Mars; everything is planned by the Old Ones—or the things that *do* happen on Mars which we laugh at here on Earth aren't funny because there is no wrongness about them. Death, for example."

"Death isn't funny."

"Then why are there so many jokes about death? Jill, with us—us humans—death is so sad that we *must* laugh at it. All those religions—they contradict each other on every other point but each one is filled with ways to help people be brave enough to laugh even though they know they are dying." He stopped and Jill could feel that he had almost gone into trance. "Jill? Is it possible that I was searching them the wrong way? Could it be that *every one* of *all* religions is true?"

"Huh? How could that be? Mike, if one is true, then the others are wrong."

"So? Point to the shortest direction around the universe. It doesn't matter where you point, it's the shortest . . . and you're pointing back at yourself."

"Well, what does that prove? You taught me the true answer, Mike. 'Thou art God.'"

"And Thou art God, my lovely. But that prime fact which doesn't depend on faith may mean that *all* faiths are true."

"Well . . . if they're all true, then right now I want to worship Siva." Jill changed the subject with emphatic action.

"Little pagan," he said softly. "They'll run you out of San Francisco."

"But we're going to Los Angeles . . . where it won't be noticed. *Oh!* Thou are Siva!"

"Dance, Kali, dance!"

During the night she woke and saw him standing at the window, looking out over the city. (*"Trouble, my brother?"*)

He turned. "There's no *need* for them to be so unhappy."

"Darling, darling! I had better take you home. The city is not good for you."

"But I would still know it. Pain and sickness and hunger and fighting—there's no need for *any* of it. It's as foolish as those little monkeys."

"Yes, darling. But it's not your fault—"

"Ah, but it *is*!"

"Well . . . that way—yes. But it's not just this one city; it's five billion people and more. You can't help five billion people."

"I wonder."

He came over and sat by her. "I grok them now, I can talk to them. Jill, I could set up our act and make the marks laugh every minute. I am certain."

"Then why not do it? Patty would be pleased—and so would I. I liked being 'with it'—and now that we've shared water with Patty, it would be like being home."

He didn't answer. Jill felt his mind and knew that he was contemplating, trying to grok. She waited.

"Jill? What do I have to do to be ordained?"

PART FOUR

His Scandalous Career

XXX

THE FIRST MIXED load of colonists reached Mars; six of seventeen survivors of twenty-three originals returned to Earth. Prospective colonists trained in Peru at sixteen thousand feet. The President of Argentina moved one night to Montevideo, taking two suitcases; the new President started an extradition process before the High Court to yank him back, or at least the suitcases. Last rites for Alice Douglas were held privately in the National Cathedral with two thousand attending; commentators praised the fortitude with which the Secretary General took his bereavement. A three-year-old named Inflation, carrying 126 pounds, won the Kentucky Derby paying fifty-four for one; two guests of the Colony Airotel, Louisville, discorporated, one voluntarily, one by heart failure.

A bootleg edition of the unauthorized biography *The Devil and Reverend Foster* appeared throughout the United States; by nightfall every copy was burned and plates destroyed, along with damage to chattels and real estate, plus mayhem, maiming, and simple assault. The British Museum was rumored to possess a copy of the first edition (untrue), and also the Vatican Library (true, but available only to church scholars).

In the Tennessee legislature a bill was introduced to make pi equal to three; it was reported out by the committee on public education and morals, passed without objection by the lower house, and died in the upper house. An interchurch fundamentalist group opened offices in Van Buren, Arkansas, to solicit funds to send missionaries to the Martians; Dr. Jubal Harshaw made a donation but sent it in the name (and with the address) of the editor of the *New Humanist*, rabid atheist and his close friend.

Otherwise Jubal had little to cheer him—too much news about Mike. He treasured the visits home of Jill and Mike and was most interested in Mike's progress, especially after Mike developed a sense of humor. But they seldom came home now and Jubal did not relish the latest developments.

It had not troubled Jubal when Mike was run out of Union Theological Seminary, pursued by a pack of enraged theologians, some of whom were angry because they believed in God and others because they did not—but unanimous in detesting the Man from Mars. Jubal reckoned anything that happened to a theologian short of breaking him on the wheel was no more than meet—and the experience was good for the boy; he'd know better next time.

Nor had he been troubled when Mike (with the help of Douglas) enlisted under an assumed name in the Federation armed forces. He had been sure that no sergeant could cause Mike permanent distress, and Jubal was not troubled by what might happen to Federation troops—an unreconciled old reactionary, Jubal had burned his honorable discharge and all that went with it the day the United States ceased having its own forces.

Jubal was surprised at how little shambles Mike created as "Private Jones" and how long he lasted—almost three weeks. Mike crowned his military career by grabbing the question period following a lecture to preach the uselessness of force (with comments on the desirability of reducing surplus population through cannibalism), then offered himself as a test animal for any weapon of any nature to prove that force was not only unnecessary but *impossible* when attempted against a self-disciplined person.

They did not take his offer; they kicked him out.

Douglas allowed Jubal to see a super-secret eyes-only numbered-one-of-three report after cautioning Jubal that no one, not even the Supreme Chief of Staff, knew that "Private Jones" was the Man from Mars. Jubal scanned the exhibits, mostly conflicting reports as to what happened when "Jones" had been "trained" in the uses of weapons; the surprising thing to Jubal was that some witnesses had the courage to state under oath that they had seen weapons disappear.

The last paragraph Jubal read carefully; "Conclusion: Subject man is a natural hypnotist and could conceivably be useful in intelligence, but he is unfitted for any combat branch. However, his low intelligence quotient (moron), his extremely low general classification score, and his paranoid tendencies (delusions of grandeur) make it inadvisable to exploit his *idiot-savant* talent. Recommendation: Discharge, Inaptitude—no pension credit, no benefits."

Mike had managed to have fun. At parade on his last day while Mike's platoon was passing in review, the commanding general and his staff were buried hip deep in a bucolic end-product symbolic to all soldiers but no longer common on parade grounds. This deposit vanished, leaving nothing but an odor and a belief in mass hypnosis. Jubal decided that Mike had atrocious taste in practical jokes. Then he recalled an incident in medical school involving a cadaver and the Dean—Jubal had worn rubber gloves and a good thing, too!

Jubal enjoyed Mike's inglorious military career because Jill spent the time at home. When Mike came home after it was over, he hadn't seemed hurt by it—he boasted to Jubal that he had obeyed Jill's wishes and hadn't disappeared *anybody*, merely a few dead things . . . although, as Mike grokked it, there had been times when Earth could have been made a better place if Jill didn't have this weakness. Jubal didn't argue; he had a lengthy "Better Dead" list himself.

Mike's unique ways of growing up were all right; Mike was unique. But this last thing—"The Reverend Doctor Valentine M. Smith, A.B., D.D., Ph.D., Founder and Pastor of the Church of All Worlds, Inc."—gad! It was bad enough that the boy had decided to be a Holy Joe instead of leaving other people's souls alone as a gentleman should. But those diploma-mill degrees—Jubal wanted to throw up.

The worst was that Mike claimed that he had hatched the idea from something Jubal had said, about what a church was and what it could do. Jubal admitted that it was something he could have said, although he did not recall it.

Mike had been cagey about the operation—some months of residence at a very small, very poor sectarian college, a bachelor's degree awarded by examination, a "call" to their ministry followed by ordination in this recognized though flat-headed sect, a doctor's dissertation on comparative religion which was a marvel of scholarship while

ducking any conclusions, the award of the "earned" doctorate coinciding with an endowment (anonymous) to this very
hungry school, the second doctorate (honorary) for "con-
tributions to interplanetary knowledge" from a university
that should have known better, when Mike let it be known
that such was his price for appearing at a conference on solar
system studies. The Man from Mars had turned down everybody from Cal-Tech to Kaiser Wilhelm Institute in the
past; Harvard could not resist the bait.

Well, they were as crimson as their banner now, Jubal
thought cynically. Mike put in a few weeks as assistant
chaplain at his churchmouse alma mater—then broke with
the sect in a schism and founded his own church. Completely kosher, legally airtight, as venerable in precedent as
Martin Luther—and as nauseating as last week's garbage.

Jubal was called out of his sour daydream by Miriam.
"Boss! Company!"

Jubal looked up to see a car about to land. "Larry, fetch
my shotgun—I swore I would shoot the next dolt who
landed on the rose bushes."

"He's landing on the grass, Boss."

"Tell him to try again. We'll get him on the next pass."

"Looks like Ben Caxton."

"So it is. Hi, Ben! What'll you drink?"

"Nothing, you professional bad influence. Need to talk
to you, Jubal."

"You're doing it. Dorcas, fetch Ben a glass of warm
milk; he's sick."

"Without much soda," amended Ben, "and milk the
bottle with the three dimples. Private talk, Jubal."

"All right, up to my study—although if you can keep
anything from the kids around here, let me in on your

method." After Ben finished greeting properly (and unsanitarily, in three cases) members of the family, they moseyed upstairs.

Ben said, "What the deuce? Am I lost?"

"Oh. You haven't seen the new wing. Two bedrooms and another bath downstairs—and up here, my gallery."

"Enough statues to fill a graveyard!"

"Please, Ben. 'Statues' are dead politicians. This is 'sculpture.' Please speak in a reverent tone lest I become violent. Here are replicas of some of the greatest sculpture this naughty globe has produced."

"Well, *that* hideous thing I've seen before . . . but when did you acquire the rest of this ballast?"

Jubal spoke to the replica La Belle Heaulmière. "Do not listen, ma petite chère—he is a barbarian and knows no better." He put his hand to her beautiful ravaged cheek, then gently touched one empty, shrunken dug. "I know how you feel . . . it can't be much longer. Patience, my lovely."

He turned to Caxton and said briskly, "Ben, you will have to wait while I give you a lesson in how to look at sculpture. You've been rude to a lady. I don't tolerate that."

"Huh? Don't be silly, Jubal; you're rude to ladies—*live ones*—a dozen times a day."

Jubal shouted, "*Anne!* Upstairs! Wear your cloak!"

"You know I wouldn't be rude to the old woman who posed for that. What I can't understand is a so-called artist having the gall to pose somebody's great grandmother in her skin . . . and you having the bad taste to want it around."

Anne came in, cloaked. Jubal said, "Anne, have I ever been rude to you? Or to any of the girls?"

"That calls for opinion."

"That's what I'm asking for. You're not in court."

"You have never been rude to any of us, Jubal."

"Have you ever known me to be rude to a lady?"

"I have seen you be intentionally rude to a woman. I have never seen you be rude to a lady."

"One more opinion. What do you think of this bronze?"

Anne looked at Rodin's masterpiece, said slowly, "When I first saw it, I thought it was horrible. But I have come to the conclusion that it may be the most beautiful thing I have ever seen."

"Thanks. That's all." She left. "Want to argue, Ben?"

"Huh? When I argue with Anne, that day I turn in my suit. But I don't grok it."

"Attend me, Ben. Anybody can see a pretty girl. An artist can look at a pretty girl and see the old woman she will become. A better artist can look at an old woman and see the pretty girl she used to be. A *great* artist can look at an old woman, portray her *exactly* as she is . . . and force the viewer to see the pretty girl she used to be . . . more than that, he can make anyone with the sensitivity of an armadillo see that this lovely young girl is still alive, prisoned inside her ruined body. He can make you feel the quiet, endless tragedy that there was never a girl born who ever grew older than eighteen in her heart . . . no matter what the merciless hours have done. Look at her, Ben. Growing old doesn't matter to you and me—but it *does* to them. *Look at her!*"

Ben looked at her. Presently Jubal said gruffly, "All right, blow your nose. Come sit down."

"No," Caxton answered. "How about this one? I see it's a girl. But why tie her up like a pretzel?"

Jubal looked at the replica "Caryatid Who Has Fallen under Her Stone." "I won't expect you to appreciate the masses which make that figure much more than a 'pretzel'—but you can appreciate what Rodin was saying. What do people get out of looking at a crucifix?"

"You know I don't go to church."

"Still, you must know that representations of the Crucifixion are usually atrocious—and ones in churches are the worst . . . blood like catsup and that ex-carpenter portrayed as if He were a pansy . . . which He certainly was *not*. He was a hearty man, muscular and healthy. But a poor portrayal is as effective as a good one for most people. They don't see defects; they see a symbol which inspires their deepest emotions; it recalls to them the Agony and Sacrifice of God."

"Jubal, I thought you weren't a Christian?"

"Does that make me blind to human emotion? The crummiest plaster crucifix can evoke emotions in the human heart so strong that many have died for them. The artistry with which such a symbol is wrought is irrelevant. Here we have another emotional symbol—but wrought with exquisite artistry. Ben, for three thousand years architects designed buildings with columns shaped as female figures. At last Rodin pointed out that this was work too heavy for a girl. He didn't say, 'Look, you jerks, if you must do this, make it a brawny male figure.' No, he *showed* it. This poor little caryatid has fallen under the load. She's a good girl—look at her face. Serious, unhappy at her failure, not blaming anyone, not even the gods . . . and still trying to shoulder her load, after she's crumpled under it.

"But she's more than good art denouncing bad art; she's a symbol for every woman who ever shouldered a load too heavy. But not alone women—this symbol means every man and woman who ever sweated out life in uncomplaining fortitude until they crumpled under their loads. It's courage, Ben, and victory."

"'Victory'?"

"Victory in defeat, there is none higher. She didn't give up, Ben; she's still trying to lift that stone after it has crushed her. She's a father working while cancer eats away his insides, to bring home one more pay check. She's a twelve-year-old trying to mother her brothers and sisters because mama had to go to Heaven. She's a switchboard operator sticking to her post while smoke chokes her and fire cuts off her escape. She's all the unsung heroes who couldn't make it but never quit. Come. Salute as you pass and come see my Little Mermaid."

Ben took him literally; Jubal made no comment. "Now this," he said, "is one Mike didn't give to me. I haven't told Mike why I got it . . . since it is self-evident that it's one of the most delightful compositions ever wrought by the eye and hand of man."

"This one I don't need explained—it's *pretty*!"

"Which is excuse enough, as with kittens and butterflies. But there is more. She's not quite a mermaid—see?— nor is she human. She sits on land, where she has chosen to stay . . . and stares eternally out to sea, forever lonely for what she left. You know the story?"

"Hans Christian Andersen."

"Yes. She sits by the haven of København—and she's

everybody who ever made a difficult choice. She doesn't regret it but she must pay for it; every choice must be paid for. The cost is not only endless homesickness. She can never be quite human; when she uses her dearly bought feet, every step is on sharp knives. Ben, I think that Mike walks always on knives—but don't tell him I said so."

"I won't. I'd rather look at her and not think about knives."

"She's a little darling, isn't she? How would you like to coax her into bed? She would be lively as a seal, and as slippery."

"Cripes! You're an evil old man, Jubal."

"And getting eviler each year. We won't look at any others—usually I ration myself to one a day."

"Suits. I feel as if I had had three quick drinks. Jubal, why isn't there stuff like this where a person can see it?"

"Because the world has gone nutty and art always paints the spirit of its times. Rodin died about the time the world started flipping its lid. His successors noted the amazing things he had done with light and shadow and mass and composition and they copied that part. What they failed to see was that the master told stories that laid bare the human heart. They became contemptuous of painting or sculpture that told stories—they dubbed such work 'literary.' They went all out for abstractions."

Jubal shrugged. "Abstract design is all right—for wallpaper or linoleum. But *art* is the process of evoking pity and terror. What modern artists do is pseudo-intellectual masturbation. Creative art is intercourse, in which the artist renders emotional his audience. These laddies who won't deign to do that—or can't—lost the public. The ordinary bloke will not buy 'art' that leaves him unmoved.

If he does pay, the money is conned out of him, by taxes or such."

"Jubal, I've always wondered why I didn't give a hoot for art. I thought it was something missing in *me*."

"Mmm, one does have to learn to look at art. But it's up to the artist to use language that can be understood. Most of these jokers don't *want* to use language you and I can learn; they would rather sneer because we 'fail' to see what they are driving at. If anything. Obscurity is the refuge of incompetence. Ben, would you call *me* an artist?"

"Huh? You write a fair stick."

"Thank you. 'Artist' is a word I avoid for the same reason I hate to be called 'Doctor.' But I *am* an artist. Most of my stuff is worth reading only once . . . and not even once by a person who knows the little I have to say. But I am an *honest* artist. What I write is intended to reach the customer—and affect him, if possible with pity and terror . . . or at least divert the tedium of his hours. I *never* hide from him in a private language, nor am I seeking praise from other writers for 'technique' or other balderdash. I want praise from the customer, given in cash because I've reached him—or I don't want anything. Support for the arts—*merde!* A government-supported artist is an incompetent whore! Damn it, you punched one of my buttons. Fill your glass and tell me what's on your mind."

"Jubal, I'm unhappy."

"This is news?"

"I've got a fresh set of troubles." Ben frowned. "I'm not sure I want to talk about them."

"Then listen to my troubles."

"*You* have troubles? Jubal, I thought you were the one man who had managed to beat the game."

"Hmm, sometime I must tell you about my married life. Yes, I've got troubles. Duke has left—or did you know?"

"I knew."

"Larry is a good gardener—but the gadgets that run this hogan are falling to pieces. Good mechanics are scarce. Ones that will fit into this household are almost non-existent. I'm limping along on repairmen—every visit a disturbance, all of them with larceny in their hearts, and most of them can't use a screw driver without cutting themselves. Nor can I, so I'm at their mercy."

"My heart aches for you, Jubal."

"Never mind the sarcasm. Mechanics and gardeners are convenient; secretaries are essential. Two of mine are pregnant, one is getting married."

Caxton looked flabbergasted. Jubal growled, "Oh, I'm not telling tales. They're sore because I took you up here without giving them time to boast. So be surprised when they tell you."

"Uh, which one is getting married?"

"Isn't that obvious? The happy man is that smooth-talking refugee from a sand storm, our esteemed water brother Stinky Mahmoud. I told him that they have to live *here* whenever they're in this country. Bastard laughed and pointed out that I had invited him to, long ago." Jubal sniffed. "Wouldn't be so bad if he would. I might get some work out of *her*."

"You probably would. She likes to work. The other two are pregnant?"

"Higher 'n a kite. I'm refreshing in O.B. because they say they're going to have 'em at home. What a crimp babies will put in my working habits! But why do you assume that neither turgescent tummy belongs to the bride?"

"Why, I assumed that Stinky was more conventional than that . . . or more cautious."

"Stinky wouldn't be given a ballot. Ben, in all the years I have studied this subject, trying to trace the meanderings of their twisty little minds, the only thing I have learned is that when a gal is gonna, she's gonna. All a man can do is cooperate with the inevitable."

"Well, which one isn't getting married or anything? Miriam? Or Anne?"

"Hold it, I didn't say the bride was pregnant . . . and you seem to be thinking that Dorcas is the prospective bride. It's Miriam who is studying Arabic."

"*Huh?* I'm a cross-eyed baboon!"

"Obviously."

"But Miriam was always snapping at Stinky—"

"And they trust you with a newspaper column—Ever watch a bunch of sixth-graders?"

"Yes, but—Dorcas did everything but a nautch dance."

"That is Dorcas's natural behavior. Be sure that when Miriam shows you her ring—size of a roc's egg and about as scarce—act surprised. I'm damned if I'll sort out which are spawning. Just remember that they are pleased . . . which is why I tipped you off, so that you wouldn't think *they* thought they were 'caught.' They don't. They weren't. They're smug." Jubal sighed. "I'm too old to enjoy the patter of little feet—but I *won't* lose perfect secretaries—and kids that I love—for *any* reason if I can induce them to stay. This household has become steadily disorganized ever since Jill kicked Mike's feet out from under him. Not that I blame her . . . and I don't think you do, either."

"No, but—Jubal, are you under the impression that *Jill* started Mike on his merry rounds?"

"Huh?" Jubal looked startled. "Then who was it?"

"'Don't be nosy, bub.' However, Jill straightened me out when I jumped to the same conclusion. As I understand it, which one scored first was more or less chance."

"Mmm . . . yes. I believe so."

"Jill thinks so. She thinks Mike was lucky in happening to seduce, or be seduced by, the one best fitted to start him off right. Which gives you a hint if you know how Jill's mind works."

"Hell, I don't even know how *mine* works. As for Jill, I would never have expected her to take up preaching no matter how love-struck she was—so I don't know how *her* mind works."

"She doesn't preach much—we'll get to that. Jubal, what do you read from the calendar?"

"Huh?"

"You think Mike did it—in both cases—if his visits home match up."

Jubal said guardedly, "Ben, I've said nothing to lead you to think so."

"The hell you haven't. You said they were smug. I know the effect that goddam superman has on women."

"Hold it, son—he's our water brother."

Ben said levelly, "I know it—and I love him, too. But that's all the more reason I understand why they are smug."

Jubal stared at his glass. "Ben, seems to me *your* name could be on the list easier than Mike's."

"Jubal, you're out of your mind!"

"Take it easy. While I really do so help me by all the Billion Names of God believe in not poking my nose into other people's business, nevertheless I have normal eyesight and hearing. If a brass band parades through my home, I notice. You've slept under this roof dozens of times. Did you ever sleep alone?"

"Why, you scoundrel! Uh, I slept alone the first night I was here."

"Dorcas must have been off her feed. No, you were under sedative that night—doesn't count. Some other night?"

"Your question is irrelevant, immaterial, and beneath my notice."

"That's an answer. Please note that the added bedrooms are as far from mine as possible. Soundproofing is never perfect."

"Jubal, wouldn't *your* name be higher up that list than mine?"

"*What?*"

"Not to mention Larry and Duke. Jubal, everybody assumes that you are keeping the fanciest harem since the Sultan. Don't misunderstand me—they *envy* you. But they think you're a lecherous old goat."

Jubal drummed on his chair arm. "Ben, I do not mind being treated flippantly by my juniors. But in this matter I insist that my years be treated with respect."

"Sorry," Ben said stiffly. "I thought if it was all right for you to kick *my* sex life around, you would not mind my being equally frank."

"No, no, Ben!—you misunderstand. I require the *girls* to treat me with respect—on this subject."

"Oh—"

"I am, as you pointed out, old—quite old. Privately, I am happy to say that I am still lecherous. But lechery does not command me. I prefer dignity to indulging in pastimes which, believe me, I have enjoyed in full measure and do not need to repeat. Ben, a man my age, who looks like a slum clearance in its grimmest stage, can bed a young girl—and possibly big her and thanks for the compliment; it might not be amiss—through three means: money . . . or the equivalent in terms of wills and community property and such . . . and—pause for question: Can you imagine any of these four bedding with a man for *those* reasons?"

"No. Not any of them."

"Thank you, sir. I associate only with ladies; I'm pleased that you know it. The third incentive is a most female one. A sweet young girl sometimes takes an old wreck to bed because she is fond of him, sorry for him, and wishes to make him happy. Would that apply?"

"Uh . . . Jubal, it might. With any of them."

"I think so, too. But this reason which any of these ladies might find sufficient is *not* sufficient for *me*. I have my dignity, sir—so please take my name off the list."

Caxton grinned. "Okay—you stiff-necked old coot. I hope that when I am your age I won't be so hard to tempt."

Jubal smiled. "Better to be tempted and resist, than be disappointed. Now about Duke and Larry: I don't know nor care. Whenever anyone comes here to live, I make it plain that this is neither a sweat shop nor a whore house, but a home . . . and, as such, it combines anarchy and tyranny without a trace of democracy, as in any well-run family, i.e., they are on their own except where I give orders, which orders are not subject to debate. My tyranny never extends to love life. The kids have always kept their private matters reasonably private. At least—" Jubal smiled ruefully. "—until the Martian influence got out of hand. Perhaps Duke and Larry have been dragging the gals behind every bush. But there have been no screams."

"Then you think it's Mike."

Jubal scowled. "Yes. That's all right—I told you the girls were smugly happy . . . and I'm not broke plus the fact that I could bleed Mike for any amount. Their babies won't lack. But, Ben, I'm troubled about Mike himself."

"So am I, Jubal."

"And about Jill."

"Uh . . . Jubal, Jill isn't the problem. It's Mike."

"Damn it, why can't the boy come home and quit this obscene pulpit pounding?"

"Mmm . . . Jubal, that's not quite what he's doing." Ben added, "I've just come from there."

"*Huh?* Why didn't you *say* so?"

Ben sighed. "First you talked art, then you sang the blues, then you wanted to gossip."

"Uh . . . you have the floor."

"Coming back from the Capetown conference, I visited them. What I saw worried the hell out of me—so I stopped by my office, then came here. Jubal, couldn't you rig it with Douglas to close down this operation?"

Jubal shook his head. "What Mike does with his life is his business."

"You would if you had seen what I saw."

"Not I! But in the second place I *can't*. Nor can Douglas."

"Jubal, Mike would accept any decision you made about his money. He probably wouldn't even understand it."

"Ah, but he *would*! Ben, recently Mike made his will and sent it to me to criticize. It was one of the shrewdest documents I've ever seen. He recognized that he had more wealth than his heirs could use—so he used part of his money to guard the rest. It is booby-trapped not only against heirs-claimants of both his legal and natural parents—he knows he's a bastard though I don't know how he found out—but also of every member of the *Envoy*'s company. *He* provided a way to settle out of court with any heir having a prima facie claim—and rigged it so that they would almost have to overthrow the government to break his will. The will showed that he knew every security and asset. I couldn't find *anything* to criticize." (—including, Jubal thought, his provision for you, my brother!) "Don't tell *me* that I could rig his money!"

Ben looked morose. "I wish you could."

"*I* don't. But it wouldn't help if we could. Mike hasn't drawn a dollar from his account for almost a year. Douglas called me about it—Mike hadn't answered his letters."

"No withdrawals? Jubal, he's spending a lot."

"Maybe the church racket pays well."

"That's the odd part. It's not really a church."

"What is it?"

"Uh, primarily a language school."

"Repeat?"

"To teach the Martian language."

"Well, then, I wish he wouldn't call it a church."

"Maybe it is a church, within the legal definition."

"Look, Ben, a skating rink is a church—as long as some sect claims that skating is essential to worship—or even that skating served a desirable function. If you can sing to the glory of God, you can skate to the same end. There are temples in Malaya which are nothing—to an outsider— but boarding houses for snakes . . . but the same High Court rules them to be 'churches' as protects our own sects."

"Well, Mike raises snakes, too. Jubal, isn't *anything* ruled out?"

"Mmm . . . a moot point. A church usually can't charge for fortune telling or calling up spirits of the dead—but it can accept offerings and let the 'offerings' be fees in fact. Human sacrifice is illegal—but it is done in several spots around the globe . . . probably right here in this former land of the free. The way to do anything that would otherwise be suppressed is to do it in the inner sanctum and keep the gentiles out. Why, Ben? Is Mike doing something that might get him jailed?"

"Uh, probably not."

"Well, if he's careful—the Fosterites have shown how to get by with almost anything. Much more than Joseph Smith was lynched for."

"Mike has lifted a lot from the Fosterites. That's part of what worries me."

"But what *does* worry you?"

"Uh, Jubal, this is a 'water brother' matter."

"Shall I carry poison in a hollow tooth?"

"Uh, the inner circle are supposed to be able to discorporate voluntarily—no poison needed."

"I never got that far, Ben. But I know ways to put up the only final defense. Let's have it."

"Jubal, I said Mike raises snakes. I meant figuratively and literally—the setup is a snake pit. Unhealthy. Mike's

Temple is a big place. An auditorium for public meetings, smaller ones for invitational meetings, many smaller rooms—and living quarters. Jill sent me a radiogram telling me where to go, so I was dropped at the private entrance on the back street. Quarters are above the auditorium, as private as you can be and still live in a city."

Jubal nodded. "Be your acts legal or illegal, nosy neighbors are noxious."

"In this case a *very* good idea. Outer doors let me in; I suppose I was scanned, although I didn't spot the scanner. Through two more automatic doors—then up a bounce tube. Jubal, it wasn't an ordinary one. Not controlled by the passenger, but by someone out of sight. Didn't feel like the usual bounce tube, either."

"I have never used them and never shall," Jubal said firmly.

"You wouldn't have minded this. I floated up gently as a feather. "

"Ben, I don't trust machinery. It bites." Jubal added, "However, Mike's mother was one of the great engineers and his father—his real father—was a competent engineer, or better. If Mike has improved bounce tubes until they are fit for humans, we ought not to be surprised."

"As may be. I got to the top and landed without having to grab for it, or depend on safety nets—didn't see any, to tell the truth. Through more automatic doors and into an enormous living room. Oddly furnished and rather austere. Jubal, people think you run an odd household."

"Nonsense! Just plain and comfortable."

"Well, your menage is Aunt Jane's Finishing School compared with Mike's weirdie. I'm just inside the joint when the first thing I see I don't believe. A babe, tattooed from chin to toes—and not a goddam stitch on. Hell, she was tattooed *everywhere*. Fantastic!"

"You're a big-city bumpkin, Ben. I knew a tattooed lady once. Very nice girl."

"Well . . ." Ben conceded, "this gal is nice, too, once you get adjusted to her pictorial supplement—and the fact that she usually has a snake with her."

"I was wondering if it was the same woman. Fully tattooed women are scarce. But the lady I knew, thirty years back, had the usual vulgar fear of snakes. However, I'm fond of snakes . . . I look forward to meeting your friend."

"You will when you visit Mike. She's sort of a major-domo for him. Patricia   but called 'Pat,' or 'Patty.'"

"Oh, yes! Jill thinks highly of her. Never mentioned her tattoos, however."

"But she's nearly the age to be your friend. When I said 'babe' I was giving a first impression. She looks to be in her twenties; she claims her oldest child is that old. Anyhow, she trotted up, all big smile, put her arms around me and kissed me. 'You're Ben. Welcome, brother! I give you water!'"

"Jubal, I've been in the newspaper racket for years— I've been around. But I had *never* been kissed by a strange babe dressed only in tattoos. I was *embarrassed*."

"Poor Ben."

"Damn it, you would have felt the same way."

"No. Remember, I've met one tattooed lady. They feel dressed in those tattoos. Or at least this was true of my friend Sadako. Japanese, she was. But Japanese are not body conscious the way we are."

"Well," Ben answered. "Pat isn't body conscious—just about her tattoos. She wants to be stuffed and mounted, nude, when she dies, as a tribute to George."

"'George'?"

"Sorry. Her husband. Up in Heaven, to my relief . . . although she talked as if he had just slipped out for a beer. But, essentially, Pat is a lady . . . and she didn't let me stay embarrassed—"

XXXI

PATRICIA PAIWONSKI GAVE Ben Caxton the all-out kiss of brotherhood before he knew what hit him. She felt his unease and was surprised. Michael had told her to expect him and placed Ben's face in her mind. She knew that Ben was a brother in all fullness, of the Inner Nest, and Jill was grown-closer with Ben second only to that with Michael.

But Patricia's nature was an endless wish to make other people as happy as she was; she slowed down. She invited Ben to get rid of his clothes but did not press the matter, except to ask him to remove his shoes—the Nest was soft, and clean as only Michael's powers could keep things clean.

She showed him where to hang clothes and hurried to fetch him a drink. She knew his preferences from Jill and decided on a double martini; the poor dear looked tired. When she came back with drinks, Ben was barefooted and had removed his jacket. "Brother, may you never thirst."

"We share water," he agreed and drank. "There's mighty little water in that."

"Enough," she answered. "Michael says that water could be in the thought; it is the sharing. I grok he speaks rightly."

"I grok. And just what I needed. Thanks, Patty."

"Ours is yours and you are ours. We're glad you're home. The others are at services or teaching. There's no hurry; they will come when waiting is filled. Would you like to look around your Nest?"

Ben let her lead him on a tour—a huge kitchen with a bar at one end, a library even more loaded than Jubal's, bathrooms ample and luxurious, bedrooms—Ben decided that they must be bedrooms although they contained no beds but simply floors that were even softer than elsewhere; Patty called them "little nests" and showed him the one she usually slept in.

It had been fitted on one side for her snakes. Ben suppressed his queasiness until he came to cobras. "It's all right," she assured him. "We did have glass in front of them. But Michael has taught them that they must not come past this line."

"I would rather trust glass."

"Okay, Ben." She lowered a glass barrier. He felt relieved and managed to stroke Honey Bun when invited to. Then Pat showed him one other room. It was very large, circular, had a floor as cushiony as the bedrooms; its center was a round swimming pool. "This," she told him, "is the Innermost Temple, where we receive new brothers into the Nest." She dabbled a foot in water. "Want to share water and grow closer? Or maybe just swim?"

"Uh, not right now."

"Waiting is," she agreed. They returned to the huge living room and Patricia went to get him another drink. Ben settled himself on a big couch—then got up. The place was warm, that drink was making him sweat, and a couch that adjusted to his contours made him hotter. He decided it was silly to dress the way he would in Washington—with Patty decked out in nothing but a bull snake she had left around her shoulders.

He compromised on jockey shorts and hung the rest in the foyer. There he noticed a sign on the entrance door: *"Did You Remember to Dress?"*

He decided that, in this household, the warning might be necessary. He saw nothing else that he had missed on coming in. On each side of the door was a huge brass bowl—filled with money.

More than filled—Federation notes of various denominations spilled out on the floor.

He was staring at this when Patricia returned. "Here's your drink, Brother Ben. Grow close in Happiness."

"Uh, thanks." His eyes returned to the money.

She followed his glance. "I'm a sloppy housekeeper, Ben. Michael makes it so easy, cleaning and such, that I forget." She retrieved the money, stuffed it into the less crowded bowl.

"Patty, why in the world?"

"Oh. We keep it here because this door leads to the street. If one of us is leaving the Nest—and I do, myself, almost every day for grocery shopping—we may need money. We keep it where you won't forget to take some."

"Just grab a handful and go?"

"Why, yes, dear. Oh, I see what you mean. There is never

anyone here but us. If we have friends outside—and all of us do—there are rooms lower down, the sort outsiders are used to, where we visit. This isn't where it can tempt a weak person."

"Huh! I'm pretty weak, myself!"

She chuckled. "How can it tempt you when it's yours?"

"Uh . . . how about burglars?" He tried to guess how much money those bowls contained. Most of the notes seemed to be larger than singles—hell, he could see one with three zeroes on the floor; Patty had missed it.

"One did get in, last week."

"So? How much did he steal?"

"Oh, he didn't. Michael sent him away."

"Called the cops?"

"Oh, no! Michael would never turn anybody over to cops. Michael just—" She shrugged. "—made him go away. Then Duke fixed the hole in the skylight in the garden room—did I show you that? It's lovely, a grass floor. You have a grass floor, Jill told me. That's where Michael first saw one. Is it grass all over?"

"Just my living room."

"If I ever get to Washington, can I walk on it? Lie down on it? Please?"

"Of course, Patty. Uh . . . it's yours."

"I know, dear. But it is good to ask. I'll lie on it and feel the grass against me and be filled with Happiness to be in my brother's 'little nest.'"

"You're most welcome, Patty." He hoped she would leave her snakes behind! "When will you be there?"

"I don't know. When waiting is filled. Maybe Michael knows."

"Well, warn me if possible, so I'll be in town. If not, Jill always knows my door code. Patty, doesn't anybody keep track of this money?"

"What for, Ben?"

"Uh, people usually do."

"We don't. Just help yourself—then put back any you have left when you come home, if you remember. Michael told me to keep the grouch bag filled. If it runs low I get more from him."

Ben dropped the matter, stonkered by its simplicity. He had some idea of the moneyless communism of Martian culture; he could see that Mike had set up an enclave of it here—these bowls marked transition from Martian to Terran economy. He wondered if Patty knew that it was fake . . . propped up by Mike's wealth.

"Patty, how many are there in the Nest?" He felt a mild worry, then shoved back the thought—why would they sponge on him?—*he* didn't have pots of gold inside his door.

"Let me see . . . almost twenty, counting novitiate brothers who don't think in Martian yet and aren't ordained."

"Are you ordained, Patty?"

"Oh, yes. Mostly I teach. Beginners' classes in Martian, and I help novitiates and such. And Dawn and I—Dawn and Jill are High Priestesses—Dawn and I are pretty well-known Fosterites, so we work together to show other Fosterites that the Church of All Worlds doesn't conflict with the Faith, any more than being a Baptist keeps a man from joining the Masons." She showed Ben Foster's kiss, explained it, and showed him its miraculous companion placed by Mike.

"They know what Foster's kiss means and how hard it is to win it . . . and they've seen some of Mike's miracles and are about ripe to buckle down and climb into a higher circle."

"It's an effort?"

"Of course, Ben—for them. In your case and mine, and Jill's, and a few others Michael called us straight into brotherhood. But to others Michael first teaches a discipline—not a faith but a way to realize faith in works. That means they've got to learn Martian. That's not easy; I'm not perfect in it. But it is Happiness to work and learn. You asked about the Nest—let me see, Duke and Jill and Michael . . . two Fosterites, Dawn and myself . . . one circumcised Jew and his wife and four children—"

"Kids in the Nest?"

"Oh, lots of them. In the nestlings' nest just off of here; nobody could meditate with kids hollering and raising Ned. Want to see it?"

"Uh, later."

"One Catholic couple with a little boy —excommunicated I'm sorry to say; their priest found out. Michael had to give them special help; it was a nasty shock—and utterly unnecessary. They were getting up early every Sunday to go to mass as usual—but kids will talk. One Mormon family of the new schism—that's three more, and their kids. The rest are Protestants and one atheist . . . that is, he thought he was until Michael opened his eyes. He came here to scoff; he stayed to learn . . . he'll be a priest soon. Uh, nineteen grown-ups, but we're hardly ever all in the Nest at once, except for our own services in the Innermost Temple. The Nest is built to hold eighty-one—'three-filled'—but Michael groks much waiting before we need a bigger nest and by then we will build other nests. Ben? Would you like to see an outer service, see how Michael makes the pitch? Michael is preaching now."

"Why, yes, if it's not too much trouble."

"Good. Just a sec, dearie, while I get decent."

"JUBAL, SHE CAME back in a robe like Anne's Witness robe but with angel-wing sleeves and a high neck and the trademark Mike uses—nine concentric circles and a conventionalized Sun—over her heart. This getup was vestments; Jill and the other priestesses wear the same, except that Patty's was high-necked to cover her cartoons. She had put on socks and was carrying sandals.

"Changed the hell out of her, Jubal. It gave her great dignity. I could see she was older than I had guessed although not within years of what she claims. She has an exquisite complexion—a shame ever to tattoo such skin.

"I had dressed again. She asked me to carry my shoes and led me back through the Nest and out into the corridor; we stopped to put on shoes and took a ramp that wound down a couple of floors. We reached a gallery overlooking the main auditorium. Mike was on the platform. No pulpit, just a lecture hall, with a big All-Worlds symbol on the back wall. A priestess was with him and, at that distance, I thought it was Jill—but it was the other high priestess, Dawn—Dawn Ardent."

"What was that name?"

"Dawn Ardent—née Higgins, if you want to be fussy."

"I've met her."

"I know you have, you allegedly-retired goat. She's got a crush on you."

Jubal shook his head. "The 'Dawn Ardent' I mean I just barely met, two years ago. She wouldn't remember me."

"She remembers you. She gets every one of your pieces of commercial crud, on tape, under every pseudonym she can track down. She goes to sleep by them; they give her beautiful dreams. She says. But they all know you, Jubal; that living room has exactly *one* ornament—a life-sized color-solly of your head. Looks as if you had been decapitated, with your face in a hideous grin. A shot Duke sneaked of you."

"Why that brat!"

"Jill asked him to."

"Double brat!"

"Mike put her up to it. Brace yourself, Jubal—you are the patron saint of the Church of All Worlds."

Jubal looked horrified. "They can't *do* that!"

"They already have. Mike gives you credit for having started the whole show by explaining things so well that he was able to figure out how to put over Martian theology to humans."

Jubal groaned. Ben went on, "In addition, Dawn thinks you're beautiful. Aside from that quirk, she is intelligent . . . and utterly charming. But I digress. Mike spotted us and called out, 'Hi, Ben! Later'—and went on with his spiel.

"Jubal, you'll have to hear it. He didn't sound preachy and didn't wear robes—just a smart, well-tailored white suit. He sounded like a damned good car salesman. He cracked jokes and told parables. The gist was a sort of pantheism . . . one parable was the oldy about the earthworm burrowing through the soil who encounters another earthworm and says, 'Oh, you're beautiful! Will you marry me?' and is answered: 'Don't be silly! I'm your other end.' You've heard it?"

"'Heard it'? I *wrote* it!"

"Hadn't realized it was *that* old. Mike made good use of it. His idea is that whenever you encounter any other grokking thing—man, woman, or stray cat . . . you are meeting your 'other end.' The universe is a thing we whipped up among us and agreed to forget the gag."

Jubal looked sour. "Solipsism and pantheism. Together they explain *anything.* Cancel out any inconvenient fact, reconcile all theories, include any facts or delusions you like. But it's cotton candy, all taste and no substance—as unsatisfactory as solving a story by saying: '—then the little boy fell out of bed and woke up.'"

"Don't crab at me; take it up with Mike. Believe me, he made it convincing. Once he stopped and said, 'You must be tired of so much talk—' and they yelled back, '*No!*' He really had them. He protested that his voice was tired and, anyhow it was time for miracles. Then he did amazing sleight-of-hand—did you know he had been a magician in a carnival?"

"I knew he had been with it. He never told me the nature of his shame."

"He's a crackerjack; he did stunts that had me fooled. But it would have been okay if he had used just kid tricks; it was his patter that had them spellbound. Finally he stopped and said, 'The Man from Mars is expected to do wonderful things . . . so I pass some miracles each meeting. I can't help being the Man from Mars; it's just something that happened. Miracles can happen for *you,* if you want them. However, for anything more than these narrow-gauge miracles, you must enter the Circle. Those who want to learn I will see later. Cards are being passed around.'

"Patty explained it. 'This crowd is just marks, dear— people here out of curiosity or maybe shilled in by people who have reached one of the inner circles.' Jubal, Mike has rigged the thing in nine circles, like lodge degrees—and nobody is told that there are circles farther in until they're ripe for it. 'This is Michael's bally,' Pat told me, 'which he does as easy as he breathes—while he's feeling them out and deciding which ones are possible. That's why he strings it out—Duke is up behind that grille and Michael tells him who might measure up, where he sits and everything. Michael's about to turn this tip . . . and spill the ones he doesn't want. Then Dawn takes over, after she gets the seating diagram from Duke.'"

"How did they work that?" asked Harshaw.

"I didn't see it, Jubal. There are a dozen ways they could cut from the herd as long as Mike knew which they were and had some way to signal Duke. Patty says Mike's clairvoyant—I won't deny the possibility. Then they took the collection. Mike doesn't do even this church style—you know, soft music and dignified ushers. He said nobody would believe this was a church if he didn't take a collection. Then, so help me, they passed collection baskets already loaded with money and Mike told them that this was what the last crowd had given, so help themselves—if they were broke or hungry and needed it. But if they felt like giving . . . give. Do one or the other—put something in, or take something out. I figured he had found one more way to get rid of too much money."

Jubal said thoughtfully, "That pitch, properly given, should result in people giving *more* . . . while a few take just a little. Probably *very* few."

"I don't know, Jubal. Patty whisked me away when Mike turned the service over to Dawn. She took me to a private auditorium where services were opening for the seventh circle—people who had belonged for months and had made progress. If it *is* progress.

"Jubal, we went straight from one to the other and it was hard to adjust. That outer meeting was half lecture, half entertainment—this one was almost a voodoo rite. Mike was in robes now; he looked taller, ascetic, and intense—his eyes gleamed. The place was dim, there was creepy music and yet it made you want to dance. Patty and I took a couch that was darn near a bed. What the service was I couldn't say. Mike would sing out in Martian, they would answer in Martian—except for chants of 'Thou art God! Thou art God!' echoed by some Martian word that would make my throat sore to pronounce."

Jubal made a croaking noise. "Was that it?"

"Huh? I believe so. Jubal . . . are *you* hooked? Have you been stringing me along?"

"No. Stinky taught it to me—he says it's heresy of the blackest sort. By his lights I mean. It's the word Mike translates as 'Thou are God.' Mahmoud says that isn't even close to a translation. It's the universe proclaiming its self-awareness . . . or it's 'peccavimus' with a total absence of contrition . . . or a dozen other things. Stinky says that he doesn't understand it even in Martian—except that it is a bad word, the worst possible in his opinion . . . and closer to Satan's defiance than to the blessing of God. Go on. Was that all? Just a bunch of fanatics yelling Martian?"

"Uh . . . Jubal, they didn't yell and it wasn't fanatical. Sometimes they barely whispered. Then it might climb a little. They did it in a rhythm, a pattern, like a cantata . . . yet it didn't feel rehearsed; it felt more as if they were all one person, humming whatever he felt. Jubal, you've seen Fosterites work themselves up—"

"Too much, I'm sorry to say."

"Well, this was not that sort of frenzy; this was quiet and easy, like dropping off to sleep. It was intense all right and got steadily more so, but—Jubal, ever try a spiritualist seance?"

"I have. I've tried everything I could, Ben."

"Then you know how tension can grow without anybody moving or saying a word. This was more like that than like a revival, or even the most sedate church service. But it wasn't mild; it packed terrific wallop."

"The word is 'Apollonian.'"

"Huh?"

"As opposed to 'Dionysian.' People simplify 'Apollonian' into 'mild,' and 'calm,' and 'cool.' But 'Apollonian' and 'Dionysian' are two sides of one coin—a nun kneeling in her cell, holding perfectly still, can be in ecstasy more frenzied than any priestess of Pan Priapus celebrating the vernal equinox. Ecstasy is in the skull, not the setting-up exercises." Jubal frowned. "Another error is to identify 'Apollonian' with 'good'—merely because our most respectable sects are Apollonian in ritual and precept. Mere prejudice. Proceed."

"Well . . . things weren't as quiet as a nun's devotions. They wandered about, swapped seats, and there was necking going on—nothing more, I believe, but the lighting was low. One gal started to join us, but Patty gave her some sign . . . so she kissed us and left." Ben grinned. "Kissed quite well, too. I was the only person not in a robe; I felt conspicuous. But she didn't seem to notice.

"The whole thing was casual . . . and yet as coordinated as a ballerina's muscles. Mike kept busy, sometimes in front, sometimes wandering among the others—once he squeezed my shoulder and kissed Patty, unhurriedly but quickly. He didn't speak. Back of where he stood when he seemed to be leading was a dingus like a big stereo tank; he used it for 'miracles,' only he never used the word—at least not in English. Jubal, every church promises miracles. But it's jam yesterday and jam tomorrow."

"Exception," Jubal interrupted. "Many of them deliver—exempli gratia among many: Christian Scientists and Roman Catholics."

"Catholics? You mean Lourdes?"

"I had in mind the Miracle of Transubstantiation."

"Hmm—I can't judge that subtle a miracle. As for Christian Scientists—if I break a leg, I want a sawbones."

"Then watch where you put your feet," Jubal growled. "Don't bother me."

"Wouldn't think of it. I don't want a classmate of William Harvey."

"Harvey could reduce a fracture."

"Yeah, but how about his classmates? Jubal, those cases you cited may be miracles—but Mike offers splashy ones. He's either an expert illusionist, or an amazing hypnotist—"

"He might be both."

"—or he's smoothed the bugs out of closed-circuit stereovision so that it cannot be told from reality."

"How can you rule out *real* miracles, Ben?"

"It's not a theory I like. Whatever he used, it was good theater. Once the lights came up and here was a black-maned lion, as stately as a guardian for library steps, and little lambs wobbling around him. The lion just blinked and yawned. Sure, Hollywood can tape such effects—but I smelled lion. However, that can be faked, too."

"Why insist on fakery?"

"Damn it. I'm *trying* to be judicial!"

"Then don't lean over backwards. Try to emulate Anne."

"I'm not Anne. I wasn't judicial at the time; I just enjoyed it, in a warm glow. Mike did a lot of gung-ho illusions. Levitation and such. Patty slipped away toward the end after whispering to me to stay. 'Michael just told them that any who do not feel ready for the next circle should now leave,' she told me.

"I said, 'I had better leave.'

"She said, 'Oh, no, dear! You're Ninth Circle. Stay seated, I'll be back.' And she left.

"I don't think anybody chickened out. This group was Seventh-Circlers supposed to be promoted. But I didn't notice as lights came up again . . . and there was Jill!

"Jubal, it did not feel like stereovision. Jill picked me out and smiled at me. Oh, if an actor looks directly at camera, his eyes meet yours no matter where you're seated. But if Mike has it smoothed out this well, he should patent it. Jill was in an outlandish costume. Mike started intoning something, partly in English . . . stuff about the Mother of All, the unity of many, and started calling her a series of names . . . and with each name her costume changed—"

BEN CAXTON CAME quickly alert when he saw Jill. He was not fooled by lighting and distance—this was Jill! She looked at him and smiled. He half listened to the invocation while thinking that he had been convinced that the space behind the Man from Mars was surely a stereo tank. But he would swear that he could walk up those steps and pinch her.

He was tempted to—but it would be a crummy trick to ruin Mike's show. Wait till Jill was free—

"Cybele!"

Jill's costume suddenly changed.

"Isis!"

—again.

"Frigg!" . . . *"Ge!"* . . . *"Devil!"* . . . *"Ishtar!"* . . . *"Maryam!"*

"Mother Eve! Mater Deum Magna! Loving and Beloved, Life undying—"

Caxton stopped hearing. Jill was Mother Eve, clothed in glory. Light spread and he saw that she was in a Garden, beside a tree on which was twined a great serpent.

Jill smiled, reached up and smoothed the serpent's head—turned back and opened her arms.

Candidates moved forward to enter the Garden.

Patty returned and touched Caxton on the shoulder. "Ben—Come, dear."

Caxton wanted to stay and drink in the glorious vision of Jill . . . he wanted to join that procession. But he got up and left. He looked back and saw Mike put his arms around the first woman in line . . . turned to follow Patricia and failed to see the candidate's robe vanish as Mike kissed her—did not see Jill kiss the first male candidate . . . and his robe vanished.

"We'll go around," Patty explained, "to give them time to get into the Temple. Oh, we could barge in, but it would waste Michael's time, getting them back in the mood—and he does work so very hard."

"Where are we going?"

"To pick up Honey Bun. Then back to the Nest. Unless you want to take part in the initiation. But you haven't learned Martian yet; you'd find it confusing."

"Well—I'd like to see Jill."

"Oh. She said to tell you she's going to duck upstairs and see you. Down this way, Ben."

A door opened, Ben found himself in that garden. The serpent raised her head as they came in. "There, dear!" Patricia said. "You were Mama's good girl!" She unwrapped the boa and flaked it down into a basket. "Duke brought her down but I have to arrange her on the tree and tell her not to wander off. You were lucky, Ben; a transition to Eighth happens very seldom."

Ben carried Honey Bun and learned that a fourteen-foot snake is a load; the basket had steel braces. When they reached the top, Patricia stopped. "Put her down, Ben." She took off her robe and handed it to him, then draped the snake around her. "This is Honey Bun's reward for being a good girl; she expects to cuddle up to Mama. I've got a class almost at once, so I'll carry her until the last moment. It's not a goodness to disappoint a snake; they're like babies, they can't grok in fullness."

They walked fifty yards to the entrance of the Nest proper. Ben took off her sandals and socks after he removed his shoes. They went inside and Patty stayed with him while Ben shucked down to shorts—stalling, trying to make up his mind to discard shorts, too. He was now fairly certain that clothing inside the Nest was as unconventional (and possibly as rude) as hobnailed boots on a dance floor. The warning on the exit door, the absence of windows, the womblike comfort of the Nest, Patricia's lack of attire plus the fact that she had suggested that he could do likewise—all added up to domestic nudity.

Patricia's behavior he discounted from a feeling that a tattooed lady might have odd habits about clothing, but coming into the living room they passed a man headed out toward the baths and "little nests"—and he wore less than Patricia by one snake and many pictures. He greeted them with "Thou art God" and went on. There was more evidence in the living room: a body sprawled on a couch—a woman.

Caxton knew that many families were casually naked in their homes—and this was a "family"—all water brothers. But he was unable to make up his mind between the urbanity of removing his symbolic fig leaf . . . and the certainty that if he did and strangers came in who were dressed, he would feel silly! Hell, he might blush!

"WHAT WOULD *YOU* have done, Jubal?"

Harshaw lifted his eyebrows. "Are you expecting me to be shocked, Ben? The human body is often pleasing, frequently depressing—and never significant per se. So Mike runs his household along nudist lines. Shall I cheer? Or must I cry?"

"Damn it, Jubal, it's easy to be Olympian. But I've never seen *you* take off your pants in company."

"Nor will you. But I grok you were not motivated by modesty. You were suffering from a morbid fear of appearing ridiculous—a neurosis with a long, pseudo-Greek name."

"Nonsense! I wasn't certain what was polite."

"Nonsense to you, sir—you knew what was polite . . . but were afraid of looking silly . . . or feared being surprised in the gallant reflex. But I grok Mike has reasons for this custom—Mike always has reasons."

"Oh, yes. Jill told me."

BEN WAS IN the foyer, his back to the living room and his hands on his shorts, having told himself to take the plunge—when arms came snugly around his waist. "Ben darling! How *wonderful*!"

Then Jill was in his arms, her mouth warm and greedy against his—and he was glad he had not finished stripping. She was no longer "Mother Eve"; she was wearing a priest-ess robe. Nevertheless he was happily aware that he held a double armful of live, warm, and gently squirming girl.

"Golly!" she said, breaking from the kiss "I've missed you, you old beast. Thou are God."

"Thou art God," he conceded. "Jill, you're prettier than ever."

"Yes," she agreed. "It does that. What a thrill it gave me to catch your eye at the blow-off!"

"'Blow-off'?"

"Jill means," Patricia put in, "the end of the service where she is All Mother, Mater Deum Magna. Kids, I must rush."

"Never hurry, Pattycake."

"I gotta rush so I won't have to hurry. Ben, I must put Honey Bun to bed and go down and take my class—so kiss me good-night. Please?"

Ben found himself kissing a woman wrapped in a giant snake. He tried to ignore Honey Bun and treat Patty as she deserved.

Pat then kissed Jill. "'Night, dears." She left unhurriedly.

"Ben, isn't she a lamb?"

"She is. Although she had me baffled at first."

"I grok. Patty baffles everybody—because she never has doubts; she automatically does the right thing. She's much like Mike. She's the most advanced of any of us—she ought to be high priestess. But she won't take it because her tattoos would make some duties difficult—be a distraction—and she doesn't want them taken off."

"How could you take off that much tattooing? With a flensing knife? It would kill her."

"Not at all, dear. Mike could take them off, not leave a trace, and not hurt her. But she doesn't think of them as belonging to her; she's just their custodian. Come sit down. Dawn will fetch supper—I must eat while we visit or I won't have a chance until tomorrow. Tell me what you think? Dawn tells me you saw an outsiders' service."

"Yes."

"Well?"

"Mike," Caxton said slowly, "could sell shoes to snakes."

"Ben, I grok something is bothering you."

"No," he answered. "Not anything I can put my finger on."

"I'll ask you again in a week or two. No hurry."

"I won't be here a week."

"You have columns on the spike?"

"Three. But I shouldn't stay that long."

"I think you will . . . then you'll phone in a few, probably about the Church. By then you will grok to stay much longer."

"I don't think so."

"Waiting is, until fullness. You know it's not a church?"

"Patty said something of the sort."

"Let's say it's not a religion. It *is* a church, in every legal and moral sense. But we're not trying to bring people to God; that's a contradiction, you can't say it in Martian. We're not trying to save souls, souls can't be lost. We're not trying to get people to have faith, what we offer is not faith but truth—truth they can check. Truth for here-and-now, truth as matter of fact as an ironing board and as useful as bread . . . so practical that it can make war and hunger and violence and hate as unnecessary as . . . well, as clothes in the Nest. But they have to learn Martian. That's the hitch—finding people honest enough to believe what they see, willing to work hard—it *is* hard—to learn the language it must be taught in. This truth can't be stated in English any more than Beethoven's Fifth can be." She smiled. "But Mike never hurries. He screens thousands . . . finds a few . . . and some trickle into the Nest and he trains them further. Someday Mike will have us so thoroughly trained that we can start other nests, then it can snowball. But there's no hurry. None of us is really trained. Are we, dear?"

Ben looked up at Jill's last words—was startled to find bending over to offer him a plate a woman he recognized as the other high priestess—Dawn, yes, that was right. His surprise was not reduced by her being dressed in Patricia's fashion, minus tattoos.

Dawn smiled. "Your supper, my brother Ben. Thou art God."

"Uh, thou art God. Thanks." She kissed him, got plates for herself and Jill, sat down on his right and began to eat. Ben was sorry that she did not sit where he could see her better—she had the best attributes associated with goddesses.

"No," Dawn agreed, "not yet, Jill. But waiting will fill."

"For example, Ben," Jill continued, "I took a break to eat. But Mike hasn't eaten since day before yesterday . . . and won't until he's not needed. Then he'll eat like a pig and that will carry him as long as necessary. Besides that, Dawn and I get tired. Don't we, sweet?"

"We surely do. But I'm not tired, Gillian. Let me take this service and you stay with Ben. Give me that robe."

"You're crazy in your little pointy head, my love. Ben, she's been on duty almost as long as Mike. We can take a long stretch—but we eat when we're hungry and some-times we need sleep. Speaking of robes, Dawn, this was the last in the Seventh Temple. I meant to tell Patty she'd better order a gross or two."

"She has."

"I should have known. This one seems tight." Jill wig-gled in a fashion that disturbed Ben. "Are we putting on weight?"

"A little."

"Good. We were too skinny. Ben, you noticed that Dawn and I have the same figure? Height, bust, waist, hips, weight, everything—not to mention coloration. We were almost alike when we met . . . then, with Mike's help, we matched exactly. Even our faces are more alike—but that comes from doing and thinking the same things. Stand up and let Ben look at us, dear."

Dawn put her plate aside and did so, in a pose that re-minded Ben of Jill, more than resemblance justified—then he realized it was the pose Jill had been in when she stood revealed as Mother Eve.

Jill said, with her mouth full, "See, Ben? That's me."

Dawn smiled. "A razor's edge of difference, Gillian."

"Pooh. I'm almost sorry we'll never have the same face. It's handy, Ben, for us to be alike. We must have two high priestesses; it's all two can do to keep up with Mike. And besides," she added, "Dawn can buy a dress and it fits me, too. Saves me the nuisance of shopping."

"I wasn't sure," Ben said slowly, "that you wore clothes. Except these priestess things."

Jill looked surprised. "How could we go out dancing in *these*? That's our favorite way of not getting sleep. Sit down and finish your supper; Ben has stared at us long enough. Ben, there's a man in that transition group who's a perfectly dreamy dancer and this town is loaded with night clubs. Dawn and I have kept the poor fellow up so many nights that we've had to help him stay awake in language classes. But he'll be all right; once you reach Eighth Circle you don't need much sleep. What made you think we never dressed, dear?"

"Uh—" Ben blurted out his dilemma.

Jill looked wide-eyed, barely giggled—stopped at once. "I see. Darling, I'm wearing this robe because I have to gobble and git. Had I grokked *that* was troubling you, I would have chucked it before I said hello. We're so used to dressing or not according to what we do that I forgot that it might not be polite. Sweetheart, wear those shorts—or not, exactly as suits you."

"Uh—"

"Just don't fret." Jill smiled and dimpled. "Reminds me of the time Mike tried a public beach. 'Member, Dawn?"

"I'll never forget!"

"Ben, you know how Mike is. I had to teach him every-thing. He couldn't see any point to clothes, until he grokked—to his great surprise—that we aren't invulnerable to weather. Body-modesty isn't a Martian concept, couldn't be. Mike grokked clothes as ornaments only after we started experimenting with costuming our acts.

"But while Mike always did what I told him to, whether he grokked it or not, you can't imagine how many *little* things there are to being human. We take twenty years or more to learn them; Mike had to learn almost overnight. There are still gaps. He does things not knowing that isn't how a human behaves. We all teach him—all but Patty, who is sure that anything Michael does is perfect. He's still grokking clothes. He groks they're a wrongness that keeps people apart—gets in the way of letting love cause them to grow closer. Lately he's grokked that you need a barrier—with outsiders. But for a long time Mike wore clothes only when I told him to.

"And once I failed to tell him.

"We were in Baja California; it was when we met—or remet—Dawn. Mike and I checked in at night at a beach hotel and he was so anxious to grok the ocean that he let me sleep next morning and went down by himself for his first encounter with the sea.

"Poor Mike! He got to the beach, threw off his robe, and headed for the water . . . looking like a Greek god and just as unaware of conventions—and the riot started and I came awake fast and rushed down to keep him out of jail."

Jill got a faraway look. "He needs me now. Kiss me good-night, Ben; I'll see you in the morning."

"You'll be gone all night?"

"Probably. It's a fairly big transition class." She stood up, pulled him to his feet, and went into his arms.

Presently she murmured, "Ben darling, you've been taking lessons. *Whew*!"

"Me? I've been utterly faithful to you—in my own way."

"The same way I've been to you. I wasn't complaining; I just think Dorcas has been helping you practice kissing."

"Some, maybe. Nosy."

"The class can wait while you kiss me again. I'll try to be Dorcas."

"Be yourself."

"I would, anyway. Self. Mike says that Dorcas kisses more thoroughly—'groks a kiss more'—than anyone."

"Quit chattering."

She did, then sighed. "Transition class, here I come—glowing like a lightning bug. Take care of him, Dawn."

"I will."

"And kiss him right away and see what I mean!"

"I intend to."

"Ben, be a good boy and do what Dawn tells you." She left, not hurrying—but running.

Dawn flowed up against him, put up her arms.

JUBAL COCKED AN eyebrow. "Are you going to tell me that at *that* point, you went chicken?"

"I didn't have much choice. I, uh, 'cooperated with the inevitable.'"

Jubal nodded. "You were trapped. Whereupon the best a man can do is try for a negotiated peace."

XXXII

"JUBAL," CAXTON SAID earnestly, "I wouldn't say a word about Dawn—I wouldn't tell any of this—if it weren't necessary for explaining why I'm worried about them . . . *all* of them, Duke and Mike and Dawn as well as Jill, and Mike's other victims. Mike has them fascinated. His new personality is powerful. Cocky and too much supersalesman—but very compelling. And Dawn is compelling in her own way—by morning I was lulled into thinking everything was all right. Weird, but jolly—"

BEN CAXTON AWAKENED not knowing where he was. It was dark; he was lying on something soft. Not a bed—

The night came back in a rush. The last he clearly remembered was lying on the soft floor of the Innermost Temple, talking quietly and intimately with Dawn. She had taken him there, they had immersed, shared water, grown closer—

Frantically he groped around, found nothing. *"Dawn!"*

Light swelled to dimness. "Here, Ben."

"Oh! I thought you had gone!"

"I didn't intend to wake you." She was wearing—to his sudden disappointment—her robe of office. "I must start the Sunrisers' Outer Service. Gillian isn't back. As you know, it was a big class."

Her words brought back things she had told him last night . . . things which had upset him despite her gentle explanations . . . and she had soothed him until he found himself agreeing. He still didn't grok it all—but, yes, Jill was busy with rites as high priestess—a task, or happy duty, that Dawn had offered to take for her. Ben felt that he should be sorry that Jill had refused—

But he did not feel sorry. "Dawn . . . do you *have* to leave?" He scrambled to his feet, put his arms around her.

"I must, Ben dear . . . dear Ben." She melted against him.

"Right *now*?"

"There is never," she said softly, "that much hurry." The robe no longer kept them apart. He was too bemused to wonder what had become of it.

He woke a second time, found that the "little nest" lighted when he stood up. He stretched, discovered that he felt wonderful, looked around for his shorts. He tried to recall where he had left them and had no recollection of taking them off. He had not worn them into the water. Probably beside the pool—He went out and found a bath room.

Some minutes later, shaved, showered, and refreshed, he looked into the Innermost Temple, failed to find his shorts and decided that somebody had put them in the foyer where everybody kept street wear . . . said to hell with it and grinned at himself for having made an issue out of wearing them. He needed them, here in the Nest, like a second head.

He didn't have a trace of a hangover although he had had more than several drinks with Dawn. Dawn didn't seem affected by liquor—which was probably why he had gone over his quota. Dawn . . . what a gal! She hadn't even seemed annoyed when, in a moment of emotion, he had called her Jill—she had seemed pleased.

He found no one in the big room and wondered what

time it was. Not that he gave a damn but he was hungry. He went into the kitchen to see what he could scrounge.

A man looked around. "Ben!"

"Well! Hi, Duke!"

Duke gave him a bear hug. "Gosh, it's good to see you. Thou art God. How do you like your eggs?"

"Thou art God. Are you the cook?"

"Only when I can't avoid it. Tony does most of it. We all do some. Even Mike unless Tony catches him—Mike is the world's worst cook." Duke went on breaking eggs.

Ben moved in. "You look after toast and coffee. Any Worcestershire sauce?"

"You name it, Pat's got it. Here." Duke added, "I looked in on you a while ago, but you were snoring. I've been busy or you have, ever since you got here."

"What do you do, Duke?"

"Well, I'm a deacon. I'll be a priest someday. I'm slow—not that it matters. I study Martian . . . everybody does. And I'm the fix-it boy, same as for Jubal."

"Must take a gang to maintain this place."

"Ben, you'd be surprised how little it takes. You must see Mike's unique way of dealing with a stopped-up toilet; I don't have to play plumber much. Aside from plumbing, nine-tenths of the gadgetry is in this kitchen and it's not as gadgeted as Jubal's."

"I thought you had some complicated gadgets for the temples?"

"Lighting controls, that's all. Actually—" Duke grinned. "—my most important job is no work. Fire warden."

"Huh?"

"I'm a deputy fire warden, examined and everything, and same for sanitary-and-safety inspector. We never have to let an outsider go through the joint. They can attend outer services but they never get farther unless Mike gives an up-check."

They transferred food to plates and sat down. Duke said, "You're staying, Ben?"

"I can't, Duke."

"So? I came just for a visit, too . . . went back and moped for a month before I told Jubal I was leaving. Never mind, you'll be back. Don't make any decisions before your Water-Sharing tonight."

"'Water-sharing'?"

"Didn't Dawn tell you?"

"Uh . . . I don't think so."

"I should let Mike explain. No, people will be mentioning it all day. Sharing water you grok; you're First-Called."

"'First-Called?' Dawn used that expression."

"Those who became Mike's water brothers without learning Martian. Others ordinarily do not share water and grow closer until they pass to Eighth Circle . . . by then they are beginning to think in Martian—shucks, some of them know more Martian than I do. It's not forbidden—*nothing* is forbidden—to share water with someone who isn't ready for Eighth Circle. Hell, I could pick up a babe in a bar, share water, take her to bed—and *then* bring her to the Temple. But I wouldn't. That's the point; I would never want to. Ben, I'll make a flat-footed prediction. You've been in bed with some fancy babes—"

"Uh . . . some."

"I know damn' well you have. But you will never again crawl in with one who is not your water brother."

"Hmm . . ."

"A year from now *you* tell *me*. Now Mike may decide

that someone is ready before reaching even Seventh Circle.
One couple Mike offered water when they entered Third
Circle—and now he's a priest and she's a priestess . . . Sam
and Ruth."

"Haven't met 'em."

"You will. But Mike is the only one who can be certain
that soon. Very occasionally, Dawn, or Patty, will spot
somebody . . . but never as far down as Third Circle and
they always consult Mike. Not that they have to. Anyhow,
into Eighth Circle and sharing and growing-closer starts.
Then Ninth Circle and the Nest itself—and that's the
transition service we mean when we say 'Sharing Water'
even though we share water all day long. The whole Nest
attends and the new brother becomes forever part of the
Nest. In your case you already are . . . but we've never held
the service, so tonight everything is pushed aside to welcome you. They did the same for me. Ben, it's the most
wonderful feeling in the world."

"I still don't know what it is, Duke."

"Uh . . . it's lots of things. Ever been on a real luau, the
kind the cops raid and usually ends in a divorce or two?"

"Well . . . yes."

"Brother, you've only been on Sunday School picnics!
That's one aspect. Have you ever been married?"

"No."

"You *are* married. After tonight there will never be any
doubt in your mind." Duke looked happily pensive. "Ben,
I was married before . . . and at first it was nice and then it
was steady hell. This time I like it, all the time. Shucks, I
love it! I don't mean just that it's fun to shack up with a
bunch of bouncy babes. I *love* them—all my brothers,
both sexes. Take Patty—Patty mothers us. I don't think

anybody gets over needing that. She reminds me of Jubal . . . and that old bastard had better get down here and get the word! My point is that it is not just that Patty is female. Oh, I'm not running down tail—"

"Who is running down tail?" a contralto voice interrupted.

Duke swung around. "Not me, you limber Levantine whore! Come here, babe, and kiss your brother Ben."

"Never charged for it in my life," the woman denied as she glided toward them. "Started giving it away before anybody told me." She kissed Ben carefully and thoroughly. "Thou art God, Brother."

"Thou art God. Share water."

"Never thirst. Don't mind Duke—from the way he behaves he must have been a bottle baby." She kissed Duke even more lingeringly while he patted her ample fundament. She was short, plump, brunette to swarthiness, and had a mane of heavy blue-black hair almost to her waist. "Duke, did you see a *Ladies' Home Journal* which you got up?" She took his fork and started eating his scrambled eggs. "Mmm . . . good. You didn't cook these, Duke."

"Ben did. Why would I want a *Ladies' Home Journal?*"

"Ben, stir up a couple of dozen more and I'll scramble 'em in relays. There's an article I want to show Patty, dear."

"Okay," agreed Ben.

"Don't get ideas about redecorating this dump! And leave some of that for me! You think us men can do our work on mush?"

"Tut, tut, Dukie darling. Water divided is water multiplied. Ben, Duke's complaints never mean anything—as long as he has enough women for two men and food for three, he's a perfect lamb." She shoved a forkful into Duke's mouth. "Quit making faces, brother; I'll cook you a second breakfast. Or will it be your third?"

"Not even the first, yet. You ate it. Ruth, I was telling Ben how you and Sam pole-vaulted to Ninth. He's uneasy about the Sharing-Water tonight."

She pursued the last bite on Duke's plate, moved over, and started preparations to cook. "Duke, I'll send you out something other than mush. Take your coffee and skedaddle. Ben, I was worried, too—but don't you be, dear; Michael does not make mistakes. You belong here or you wouldn't be here. You're going to stay?"

"Uh, I can't. Ready for the first installment?"

"Pour them in. You'll be back. Someday you'll stay. Duke is correct—Sam and I pole-vaulted. It was too fast for a middle-aged, prim and proper housewife."

"Middle-aged?"

"Ben, one bonus of the discipline is that as it straightens out your soul, your body straightens out, too. That's a matter in which Christian Scientists are right. Notice any medicine bottles in the bathrooms?"

"Uh, no."

"There aren't any. How many people have kissed you?"

"Several."

"As a priestess I kiss more than 'several,' but there's never so much as a sniffle in the Nest. I used to be the sort of whiny woman who is never quite well and given to 'female complaints.'" She smiled. "Now I'm more female than ever but I'm twenty pounds lighter, years younger, and have nothing to complain about—I *like* being female. As Duke flattered me, 'a Levantine whore' and unquestionably more limber—I sit in lotus position when I'm teaching, whereas it used to be all I could do just to bend over.

"But it did happen fast," Ruth went on. "Sam was a professor of Oriental languages; he started coming because it was the only way to learn Martian. Strictly professional, he wasn't interested in the church. I went along to keep an eye on him. I was jealous, even more possessive than the average.

"So we worked up to Third Circle, Sam learning rapidly and myself grimly studying because I didn't want him out of my sight. Then *boom!* the miracle happened. We began to *think* in it, a little . . . and Michael felt it and had us stay after service one night . . . and Michael and Gillian gave us water. Afterwards, I knew that I was all the things I despised in other women and I despised my husband for letting me and hated him for what he had done. All this in English, with the worst parts in Hebrew. So I wept and moaned and made myself a stinking nuisance to 3am . . . and couldn't *wait* to share and grow closer again.

"After that things were easier but not easy as we were pushed through the circles as fast as possible. Michael knew we needed help and wanted to get us into the safety of the Nest. When it came time for our Sharing-Water, I was still unable to discipline myself without help. I wanted to enter the Nest—but wasn't sure I could merge with seven other people. I was scared silly; on the way over I almost begged Sam to turn around and go home."

She looked up, unsmiling but beatific, a plump angel with a big spoon in one hand. "We walked into the Innermost Temple and a spotlight hit me and our robes were whisked away . . . and they were in the pool calling to us in Martian to come share the water of life—and I stumbled in and submerged and haven't come up since!

"Nor ever want to. Don't fret, Ben, you'll learn the language and acquire the discipline and you'll have loving help all the way. You jump in that pool tonight; I'll have my arms out to catch you. All of us will, welcoming you home. Take this to Duke and tell him I said he was a pig . . . but a charming one. And take this for yourself— oh, you can eat that much!—give me a kiss and run along; Ruthie has work to do."

Ben delivered the kiss, the message, and the plate. He found Jill, apparently asleep, on one of the couches; he sat down facing her, enjoying the sweet sight and thinking that Dawn and Jill were more alike than he had realized. Jill's tan was unmarked and just the shade of Dawn's; their proportions were identical—in rest even their features were more alike.

He looked up from a bite and saw that her eyes had opened, she was smiling. "Thou art God, darling—and that smells good."

"You look good. I didn't mean to wake you." He moved across and sat by her, put a bite into her mouth. "My own cooking, with Ruth's help."

"And good, too. You didn't wake me; I was just lazing until you came out. I haven't been asleep all night."

"Not at all?"

"Not a wink. But I feel grand. Just hungry. That's a hint."

So he fed her. She let him do so, not stirring. "Did you get any sleep?" she asked presently.

"Uh, some."

"How much sleep did Dawn get? As much as two hours?"

"Oh, more than that."

"Then she's all right. Two hours does as much as eight used to. I knew what a sweet night you were going to have—both of you—but I was worried that she might not rest."

"Well, it *was* a wonderful night," Ben admitted, "although I was, uh, surprised at the way you shoved her at me."

"Shocked, you mean. I know you, Ben. I was tempted to spend the night with you myself—I wanted to, dear! But you arrived with jealousy sticking out in lumps. I think it's gone now. Yes?"

"I think so."

"Thou art God. I had a wonderful night, too—free from worry by knowing you were in good hands. The best hands—better than mine."

"Oh, never, Jill!"

"So! I grok a few lumps still—but we'll wash them away." She sat up, touched his cheek, said soberly, "Before tonight, dear. Because, of all my beloved brothers, I would not have *your* Sharing-Water be less than perfect."

"Uh—" Ben stopped.

"Waiting is," she said, and reached toward the end of the couch. It looked to Caxton as if a pack of cigarettes jumped into her hand.

Glad to change the subject, he said, "You've picked up some sleight-of-hand, too."

Jill smiled. "Nothing much. 'I am only an egg,' to quote my teacher."

"How did you do that?"

"Why, I whistled to it in Martian. First you grok a

thing, then you grok what you want it to—*Mike*." She waved. "We're over here, dear!"

"Coming." The Man from Mars came straight to Ben, pulled him to his feet. "Let me look at you, Ben! Golly, it's good to see you!"

"It's good to see you. And to be here."

"What's this about three days? Three days indeed!"

"I'm a working man, Mike."

"We'll see. The girls are all excited, getting ready for your Welcome tonight. Might just as well shut down—they won't be worth a damn."

"Patty has rescheduled," Jill told Mike. "Dawn and Ruth and Sam are taking care of what's necessary. Patty sloughed the matinee—so you're through for the day."

"That's good news!" Mike sat down, pulled Jill's head into his lap, pulled Ben down, put an arm around him, and sighed. He was dressed as Ben had seen him in the outer meeting, smart tropical business suit. "Ben, don't take up preaching. I spend night and day rushing from one job to another, telling people why they must never hurry. I owe you, along with Jill and Jubal, more than anyone on this planet—yet this is the first time I've been able to say hello. How've you been? You're looking fit. Dawn tells me you *are* fit."

Ben found himself blushing. "I'm okay."

"That's good. Carnivores will be on the prowl tonight. I'll grok close and sustain you. You'll be fresher at the end than at the start—won't he, Little Brother?"

"Yes," agreed Jill. "Ben, Mike can lend you strength—physical strength, not just moral support. I can do it a little. Mike can really do it."

"Jill can do it a lot." Mike caressed her. "Little Brother is a tower of strength to everybody. Last night she certainly was." He smiled down at her, then sang:

You'll never find a girl like Jill.
No, not one in a billion.
Of all the tarts who ever will
The willingest is our Gillian!

"—isn't that right, Little Brother?"

"Pooh," answered Jill, obviously pleased, covering his hand and pressing it to her. "Dawn is exactly like me—and every bit as willing."

"But Dawn is downstairs interviewing the possibles out of the tip. She's busy—you ain't. That's an important difference—isn't it, Ben?"

"Could be." Caxton was finding their behavior embarrassing, even in this relaxed atmosphere—he wished that they would knock off necking or give him an excuse to leave.

Mike went on cuddling Jill while keeping an arm around Ben's waist . . . and Ben was forced to admit that Jill encouraged him. Mike said very seriously, "Ben, a night like last night—helping a group to make the big jump to Eighth Circle—gets me terribly keyed up. Let me tell you something out of the lessons for Sixth. We humans have something that my former people don't even dream of. I must tell you how precious it is . . . how especially precious *I* know it to be, because I have known what it is not to have it. The blessing of being male and female. Man and Woman created He them—the greatest treasure We-Who-Are-God ever invented. Jill?"

"Beautifully right, Mike—and Ben knows it is Truth. But make a song for Dawn, too, darling."

"Okay—"

Ardent is our lovely Dawn;
Ben grokked that in her glance—
She buys new dresses every morn,
But never shops for pants!

"Okay—"

Jill giggled. "Did you tune her in?"

"Yes, and she gave me a Bronx cheer—with a kiss behind it for Ben. Say, isn't there anybody in the kitchen? I just remembered I haven't eaten for a couple of days. Or years, maybe."

"I think Ruth is," Ben said, trying to stand up.

Mike pulled him down. "Hey, Duke! See if you can find somebody who'll fix me a stack of wheat cakes as tall as you are and a gallon of maple syrup."

"Sure," Duke answered. "I'll do it myself."

"I'm not *that* hungry! Find Tony. Or Ruth." Mike pulled Ben closer and said, "Ben, I grok you are not entirely happy?"

"Huh? Oh, I'm all right!"

Mike looked into his eyes. "I wish you knew the language, Ben. I can feel your uneasiness but can't see your thoughts."

"Mike . . ." Jill said.

The Man from Mars looked at her, then looked back at Ben and said slowly, "Jill just now told me your trouble, Ben—and it's a thing I never have been able to grok in fullness." He looked worried, and hesitated almost as long as when he was learning English. "But I grok that we can't hold your Sharing-Water tonight. Waiting is." Mike shook his head. "I'm sorry. But waiting will fill."

Jill sat up. "No, Mike! We *can't* let Ben leave without it. Not *Ben*!"

"I do not grok it, Little Brother," Mike said reluctantly. A long pause followed, silence more tense than speech. At last Mike said doubtfully to Jill, "You speak rightly?"

"You will see!" Jill got up suddenly and sat down on Ben's other side, put her arms around him. "Ben, kiss me and stop worrying."

She did not wait but kissed him. Ben did stop worrying, was lulled into a sensuous glow that left no room for misgivings. Then Mike tightened the arm he still had around Ben's waist and said softly, "We grok closer. Now, Jill?"

"Now! Right here, at once—oh. Share Water, my darlings!"

Ben turned his head—and was snatched out of euphoria by utter surprise. Somehow, the Man from Mars had rid himself of every stitch of clothing.

XXXIII

"WELL?" SAID JUBAL. "Did you accept their invitation?"

"*Huh*! I got out of there fast! Grabbed my clothes, ignored the sign, jumped into the bounce tube with my arms full."

"You *did*? I think, if I were Jill, I would be offended."

Caxton turned red. "I *had* to leave, Jubal."

"Hmmm—Then what?"

"Why, I put on my clothes—found I had forgotten my bag and didn't go back. In fact I left so fast I durned near killed myself. You know how the ordinary bounce tube—"

"I do not."

"Huh? Well, if you don't dial it to lift, you sink slowly, like cold molasses. But I didn't sink, I *fell*—six stories. When I was about to splash, something caught me. Not a safety net, some sort of field. Scared me silly, on top of everything else."

"Put not your faith in gadgets. I'll stick to stairs and, when unavoidable, elevators."

"Well, the bugs aren't out of that gadget. Duke is safety inspector but whatever Mike says is Gospel to Duke; Mike's got him hypnotized. Hell, he's got 'em all hypnotized. When the crash comes it will be worse than any faulty bounce tube. Jubal, what can we do? I'm worried sick."

Harshaw jutted out his lips. "What aspects did you find disquieting?"

"Huh? All of it."

"So? You gave me to think that you enjoyed your visit— up to the point where you behaved like a scared rabbit."

"Uh—So I did. Mike had *me* hypnotized, too." Caxton looked puzzled. "I might not have snapped out of it if it hadn't been for that odd thing at the last. Jubal, Mike was sitting by me, his arm around me—he couldn't possibly have taken his clothes off."

Jubal shrugged. "You were busy. Probably wouldn't have noticed an earthquake."

"Oh, piffle! I don't close my eyes like a school girl. How did he do it?"

"I can't see its relevancy. Or are you suggesting that Mike's nudity shocked you?"

"I was shocked, all right."

"When your own arse was bare? Come, sir!"

"No, no! Jubal, do I have to draw a diagram? I simply have no stomach for group orgies. I almost lost my breakfast." Caxton squirmed. "How would *you* feel if people started acting like monkeys in a cage in the middle of your living room?"

Jubal fitted his fingers together. "That is the point, Ben; it was not *my* living room. You go into a man's house, you accept his household rules. That's a universal rule of civilized behavior."

"You don't find such behavior shocking?"

"Ah, you raise another issue. Public displays of rut I find distasteful—but this reflects my early indoctrination. A large part of mankind do not share my taste; the orgy has a very wide history. But 'shocking'? My dear sir, I am shocked only by that which offends me ethically."

"You think *this* is just a matter of taste?"

"Nothing more. And my taste is no more sacred than the very different taste of Nero. Less sacred—Nero was a god; I am not."

"Well, I'll be damned."

"Possibly—if damnation is possible. But, Ben, this wasn't public."

"Huh?"

"You told me this group was a plural marriage—a group theogamy, to be technical. Therefore whatever took place—or was about to take place; you were mealy-mouthed—was not public but private. 'Ain't nobody here but just us gods'—so how could anyone be offended?"

"*I* was offended!"

"Your apotheosis was incomplete. You misled them. You invited it."

"Me? Jubal, I did nothing of the sort."

"Oh, rats! The time to back out was when you got there; you saw at once that their customs were not yours. But you stayed—enjoyed the favors of one goddess— behaved as a god toward her. You knew the score and they knew you knew; their error lay in accepting your hypocrisy as solid coin. No, Ben, Mike and Jill behaved with propriety; the offense lay in *your* behavior."

"Damn it, Jubal, you twist things! I did get too involved—but when I left, I had to! I was about to throw up!"

"So you claim reflex? Anyone over the emotional age of twelve would have clamped his jaws and walked to the bathroom, then returned with some acceptable excuse after things cooled down. It was not reflex. Reflex can empty the stomach; it can't choose a course for feet, recover chattels, take you through doors and cause you to jump down a hole. Panic, Ben. *Why* did you panic?"

Caxton was long in replying. He sighed and said, "I guess when you come down to it—I'm a prude."

Jubal shook his head. "A prude thinks that his own rules of propriety are natural laws. That doesn't describe you. You adjusted to many things that did not fit your code of propriety, whereas a true-blue prude would have affronted that delightful tattooed lady and stomped out. Dig deeper."

"All I know is that I am unhappy over the whole thing."

"I know you are, Ben, and I'm sorry. Let's try a hypothetical question. You mentioned a lady named Ruth.

Suppose Gillian had not been present; assume that the others were Mike and Ruth—and they offered you the same shared intimacy: Would you have been shocked?"

"Huh? Why, yes. It's a shocking situation. *I* think so, even though you say it's a matter of taste."

"How shocking? Nausea? Panic flight?"

Caxton looked sheepish. "Damn you, Jubal. All right, I would just have found an excuse to go out to the kitchen or something . . . then left as soon as possible."

"Very well, Ben. You have uncovered your trouble."

"I have?"

"What element was changed?"

Caxton looked unhappy. At last he said, "You're right, Jubal—it was because it was Jill. Because I love her."

"Close, Ben. But not dead center."

"Eh?"

"'Love' is not the emotion that caused you to flee. What is 'love,' Ben?"

"What? Oh, come off it! Everybody from Shakespeare to Freud has taken a swing at that; nobody has answered it yet. All I know is, it hurts."

Jubal shook his head. "I'll give an exact definition. 'Love' is that condition in which the happiness of another person is essential to your own."

Ben said slowly, "I'll buy that . . . because that's the way I feel about Jill."

"Good. Then you are asserting that your stomach turned and you fled in panic because of a need to make Jill happy."

"Hey, wait a minute! I didn't say—"

"Or was it some other emotion?"

"I simply said—" Caxton stopped. "Okay, I was

jealous! But, Jubal, I would have sworn I wasn't. I knew I had lost out, I had accepted it long ago—hell, I didn't like Mike the less for it. Jealousy gets you nowhere."

"Nowhere one would wish, certainly. Jealousy is a disease, love is a healthy condition. The immature mind often mistakes one for the other, or assumes that the greater the love, the greater the jealousy—in fact, they're almost incompatible; one emotion hardly leaves room for the other. Both at once can produce unbearable turmoil—and I grok that was your trouble, Ben. When your jealousy reared its head, you couldn't look it in the eye—so you fled."

"It was the *circumstances*, Jubal! This hands-around harem upsets the hell out of me. Don't misunderstand me; I would love Jill if she were a two-peso whore. Which she is *not*. By *her* lights, Jill is moral."

Jubal nodded. "I know. Gillian has an invincible innocence that makes it impossible for her to be immoral." He frowned. "Ben, I am afraid that you—and I, too—lack the angelic innocence to practice the perfect morality those people live by."

Ben looked startled. "You think that sort of thing is *moral*? I meant that Jill doesn't *know* she is doing wrong—Mike's got her hornswoggled—and Mike doesn't know it's wrong, either. He's the Man from Mars; he didn't get a fair start."

Jubal frowned. "Yes, I think what those people—the entire Nest, not just our kids—are doing is moral. I haven't examined details but—*yes*, all of it. Bacchanalia, unashamed swapping, communal living, and anarchistic code, everything."

"Jubal, you astound me. If you feel that way, why don't you join them? They want you. They'll hold a jubilee—Dawn is waiting to kiss your feet and serve you; I wasn't exaggerating."

Jubal sighed. "No. Fifty years ago—But now? Ben my brother, the capacity for such innocence is no longer in me. I have been too long wedded to my own brand of evil and hopelessness to be cleansed in their water of life and become innocent again. If I ever was."

"Mike thinks you have this 'innocence'—he doesn't call it that—in full measure now. Dawn told me, speaking ex officio."

"Then I would not disillusion him. Mike sees his own reflection—I am, by profession, a mirror."

"Jubal, you're chicken."

"Precisely, sir! But my worry is not over their morals but dangers to them from outside."

"Oh, they're in no trouble that way."

"You think so? If you dye a monkey pink and shove him into a cage of brown monkeys, they'll tear him to pieces. Those innocents are courting martyrdom."

"Aren't you being rather melodramatic, Jubal?"

Jubal glared. "If I am, sir, does that make my words less weighty? Saints have burned at stakes ere this—would you dismiss their holy anguish as 'melodrama'?"

"I didn't mean to get your back up. I simply meant that they aren't in that sort of danger—after all, this isn't the Dark Ages."

Jubal blinked. "Really? I hadn't noticed the change. Ben, this pattern has been offered to a naughty world many times—and the world has always crushed it. The Oneida Colony was much like Mike's nest—it lasted a while but out in the country, not many neighbors. Or take the early Christians—anarchy, communism, group marriage, even that kiss of brotherhood—Mike has borrowed a lot from them. Hmm . . . if he picked up that kiss of brotherhood from them, I would expect men to kiss men."

Ben looked sheepish. "I held out on you. But it's not a pansy gesture."

"Nor was it with the early Christians. D'you think I'm a fool?"

"No comment."

"Thank you. I wouldn't advise anyone to offer the kiss of brotherhood to the pastor of some boulevard church today; primitive Christianity is no more. Over and again it's been the same sad story: a plan for perfect sharing and perfect love, glorious hopes and high ideals—then perse- cution and failure." Jubal sighed again. "I've been fretting about Mike; now I'm worried about them all."

"How do you think *I* feel? Jubal, I can't accept your sweetness-and-light theory. What they are doing is *wrong*!"

"It's that last incident that sticks in your craw."

"Uh . . . not entirely."

"Mostly. Ben, the ethics of sex is a thorny problem. Each of us is forced to grope for a solution he can live with—in the face of a preposterous, unworkable, and *evil* code of so-called 'Morals.' Most of us know the code is wrong, almost everybody breaks it. But we pay Danegeld by feeling guilty and giving lip service. Willy-nilly, the code rides us, dead and stinking, an albatross around the neck.

"You, too, Ben. You fancy yourself a free soul—and break that evil code. But faced with a problem in sexual ethics new to you, you tested it against the same Judeo- Christian code . . . so automatically your stomach did flip- flops . . . and you think that proves you're right and they're wrong. *Faugh!* I'd as lief use trial by ordeal. All your stomach can reflect is prejudice trained into you before you acquired reason."

"What about *your* stomach?"

"Mine is stupid, too—but I don't let it rule my brain. I see the beauty of Mike's attempt to devise an ideal ethic and applaud his recognition that such must start by junking the present sexual code and starting fresh. Most philosophers haven't the courage for this; they swallow the basics of the present code—monogamy, family pattern, continence, body taboos, conventional restrictions on intercourse, and so forth—then fiddle with details . . . even such piffle as discussing whether the female breast is an obscene sight!

"But mostly they debate how we can be made to *obey* this code—ignoring the evidence that most tragedies they see around them are rooted in the code itself rather than in failure to abide by it.

"Now comes the Man from Mars, looks at this sacrosanct code with a fresh viewpoint—and rejects it. I don't know the details of Mike's code, but it clearly violates laws of every major nation and would outrage 'right-thinking' people of every major faith—and most agnostics and atheists, too. Yet this poor boy—"

"Jubal, he is *not* a boy, he's a man."

"Is he a 'man'? This poor ersatz Martian is saying that sex is a way to be happy. Sex *should* be a means of happiness. Ben, the worst thing about sex is that we use it to hurt each other. It ought *never* to hurt; it should bring happiness, or at least, pleasure.

"The code says, 'Thou shalt not covet thy neighbor's wife.' The result? Reluctant chastity, adultery, jealousy, bitterness, blows and sometimes murder, broken homes and twisted children—and furtive little passes degrading to woman and man. Is this Commandment ever obeyed? If a man swore on his own Bible that he refrained from coveting his neighbor's wife *because* the code forbade it, I would suspect either self-deception or subnormal sexuality. Any male virile enough to sire a child has coveted many women, whether he acts or not.

"Now comes Mike and says: 'There is no need to covet my wife . . . *love* her! There's no limit to her love, we have everything to gain—and nothing to lose but fear and guilt and hatred and jealousy.' The proposition is incredible. So far as I recall only pre-civilization Eskimos were this naive—and they were so isolated that they were almost 'Men from Mars' themselves. But we gave them our 'virtues' and now they have chastity and adultery just like the rest of us. Ben, what did they gain?"

"I wouldn't care to be an Eskimo."

"Nor I. Spoiled fish makes me bilious."

"I had in mind soap and water. I guess I'm effete."

"Me, too, Ben. I was born in a house with no more plumbing than an igloo; I prefer the present. Nevertheless Eskimos were invariably described as the happiest people on Earth. Any unhappiness they suffered was not through jealousy; they didn't have a word for it. They borrowed spouses for convenience and fun—it did not make them unhappy. So who's looney? Look at this glum world around you, then tell me: Did Mike's disciples seem happier, or unhappier, than other people?"

"I didn't talk to them all, Jubal. But—yes, they're happy. So happy they seem slap-happy. There's a catch in it somewhere."

"Maybe you were the catch."

"How?"

"It's a pity your tastes canalized so young. Even three days of what you were offered would be something to treasure when you reach my age. And you, you young idiot, let jealousy chase you away! At your age I would have gone Eskimo—why, I'm so vicariously vexed that my only consolation is the sour certainty that you will regret it. Age does not bring wisdom, Ben, but it does give perspective . . . and the saddest sight of all is to see, far behind you, temptations you've resisted. I have such regrets—but nothing to the whopper *you* will suffer!"

"Quit rubbing it in!"

"Heavens, man!—or are you a mouse?—I'm trying to goad you. Why are you moaning to an old man? When you should be heading for the Nest like a homing pigeon! Hell, if I were even *twenty* years younger, I'd join Mike's church myself."

"Lay off, Jubal. What do you really think of Mike's church?"

"You said it was just a discipline."

"Yes and no. It is supposed to be 'Truth' with a Capital 'T' as Mike got it from the Martian 'Old Ones.'"

"The 'Old Ones,' eh? To me, they're hogwash."

"Mike believes in them."

"Ben, I once knew a manufacturer who believed that he consulted the ghost of Alexander Hamilton. However— Damn it, why must *I* be the Devil's advocate?"

"What's biting you now?"

"Ben, the foulest sinner of all is the hypocrite who makes a racket of religion. But we must give the Devil his due. Mike does believe and he's teaching the truth as he sees it. As for his 'Old Ones,' I don't *know* that they don't exist; I simply find the idea hard to swallow. As for his Thou-Art-God creed, it is neither more nor less credible than any other. Come Judgment Day, if they hold it, we may find that Mumbo Jumbo the God of the Congo was Big Boss all along."

"Oh, for Heaven's sake, Jubal!"

"All names belong in the hat, Ben. Man is so built that he cannot imagine his own death. This leads to endless invention of religions. While this conviction by no means proves immortality to be a fact, questions generated by it are overwhelmingly important. The nature of life, how ego hooks into the body, the problem of ego itself and why each ego *seems* to be the center of the universe, the purpose of life, the purpose of the universe—these are paramount questions, Ben; they can never be trivial. Science hasn't solved them—and who am I to sneer at religions for *trying*, no matter how unconvincingly to me? Old Mumbo Jumbo may eat me yet; I can't rule him out because he owns no fancy cathedrals. Nor can I rule out one god-struck boy leading a sex cult in an upholstered attic; he might be the Messiah. The only religious opinion I feel sure of is this: self-awareness is *not* just a bunch of amino acids bumping together!"

"Whew: Jubal, you should have been a preacher."

"Missed it by luck. If Mike can show us a better way to run this fouled-up planet, his sex life needs no vindication. Geniuses are justifiably contemptuous of lesser opinion and are always indifferent to sexual customs of the tribe; they make their own rules. Mike *is* a genius. So he ignores Mrs. Grundy and diddles to suit himself.

"But from a theological standpoint Mike's sexual

behavior is as orthodox as Santa Claus. He preaches that all living creatures are collectively God . . . which makes Mike and his disciples the only self-aware gods on this planet . . . which rates him a union card by all the rules for godding. Those rules *always* permit gods sexual freedom limited only by their own judgment.

"You want proof? Leda and the Swan? Europa and the Bull? Osiris, Isis, and Horus? The incredible incests of the Norse gods? I won't cite eastern religions; their gods do things that a mink breeder wouldn't tolerate. But look at the relations of the Trinity-in-One of the most widely respected western religion. The only way that religion's precepts can be reconciled with the interrelations of what purports to be a monotheos is by concluding that breeding rules for deity are not the rules for mortals. But most people never think about it; they seal it off and mark it: 'Holy—Do Not Disturb.'

"One must allow Mike any dispensation granted other gods. One god alone splits into at least two parts, and breeds, not just Jehovah—they all do. A group of gods will breed like rabbits, and with as little regard for human proprieties. Once Mike entered the godding business, orgies were as predictable as sunrise—so forget the standards of Podunk and judge them by Olympian morals."

Jubal glowered. "Ben, to understand this, you must start by conceding their sincerity."

"Oh, I do! It's just that—"

"*Do* you? *You* start by assuming that they must be wrong, judging them by that very code you reject. Try logic instead. Ben, this 'growing-closer' by sexual union, this plurality-into-unity, logically has no place for monogamy. Since shared-by-all sexual congress is basic to this creed—a fact that your account makes crystal clear—why expect it to be hidden? One hides what one is ashamed of—but *they* are not ashamed, they glory in it. To duck behind closed doors would be a sop to the very code they have rejected . . . or it would shout aloud that *you* were an outsider who should never have been admitted in the first place."

"Maybe I shouldn't have been."

"Obviously you shouldn't have been. Mike clearly had misgivings. But Gillian insisted. Eh?"

"That only makes it worse!"

"How? She wanted you to be one of them 'in all fullness,' as Mike would say. She loves you—and is not jealous of you. But you are jealous of her—and, while you claim to love her, your behavior doesn't show it."

"Damn it, I *do* love her!"

"So? As may be, you clearly did not understand the Olympian honor you were being offered."

"I guess I didn't," Ben conceded glumly.

"I'm going to offer you a way out. You wondered how Mike got rid of his clothes. I'll tell you."

"How?"

"A miracle."

"Oh, for God's sake!"

"Could be. One thousand dollars says it was a miracle. Go ask Mike. Get him to show you. Then send me the money."

"Hell, Jubal, I don't want to take your money."

"You won't. Bet?"

"Jubal, *you* go see what the score is. I can't go back."

"They'll take you back with open arms and never ask why you left. One thousand on that prediction, too. Ben, you were there less than twenty-four hours. Did you give them the careful investigation that you give something smelly in public life before you blast it?"

"But—"

"Did you?"

"No, but—"

"Oh, for God's sake, Ben! You claim to *love* Jill . . . yet you won't give her the fair shake you give a crooked politician. Not a tenth the effort *she* made to help *you* when you were in trouble. Where would you be if she had made so feeble a try? Roasting in Hell, most likely. You're bitching about friendly fornication—do you know what *I'm* worried about?"

"What?"

"Christ was crucified for preaching without a police permit. Sweat over *that*, instead!"

Caxton chewed a thumb and said nothing—then stood up suddenly. "I'm on my way."

"After lunch."

"Now."

Twenty-four hours later Ben wired Jubal two thousand dollars. When, after a week, Jubal received no other message, he sent a stat care of Ben's office: *"What the hell are you doing?"* The answer was somewhat delayed:

"Studying Martian—aquafraternally yours—Ben"

PART FIVE

His Happy Destiny

XXXIV

FOSTER LOOKED UP from work in progress. "Junior!"

"Sir?"

"That youngster you wanted—he's available now. The Martians have released him."

Digby looked puzzled. "I'm sorry. There was some young creature toward whom I have a duty?"

Foster smiled angelically. Miracles were *never* necessary—in Truth the pseudo-concept "miracle" was self-contradicting. But these young fellows always had to learn it for themselves. "Never mind," he said gently. "It's a minor martyrdom and I'll guard it myself—and Junior?"

"Sir?"

"Call me 'Fos,' please—ceremony is all right in the field but we don't need it in the studio. And remind me not to call you 'Junior'—you made a very nice record on that temporary duty assignment. Which name do *you* like to be called?"

His assistant blinked. "I have another name?"

"Thousands. Do you have a preference?"

"Why, I really don't recall at this eon."

"Well . . . would you like to be called 'Digby'?"

"Uh, yes. That's a very nice name. Thanks."

"Don't thank me. You earned it." Archangel Foster turned back to his work, not forgetting the minor duty he had assumed. Briefly he considered how this cup might be taken from little Patricia—then chided himself for such unprofessional, almost human, thought. Mercy was not possible in an angel; angelic compassion left no room for it.

The Martian Old Ones had reached an elegant trial solution to their major esthetic problem and put it aside for a few filled-threes to let it generate new problems. At which time, unhurriedly and almost absentmindedly, the alien nestling which they had returned to his proper world was tapped of what he had learned of his people and dropped, after cherishing, since he was of no further interest to their purposes.

They took the data he had accumulated and, with a view to testing that trial solution, began to work toward considering an inquiry leading to an investigation of esthetic parameters involved in the possibility of the artistic necessity of destroying Earth. But much waiting would be, before fullness would grok decision.

The Daibutsu at Kamakura was again washed by a giant wave secondary to a seismic disturbance 280 kilometers off Honshu. The wave killed 13,000 people and lodged a male infant high in the Buddha image's interior, where it was found and succored by surviving monks. This infant lived ninety-seven Terran years after the disaster that wiped out his family and produced no progeny nor anything of note aside from a reputation for sustained belching. Cynthia Duchess entered a nunnery with all benefits of modern publicity and left without fanfare three days later. Ex–Secretary General Douglas suffered a stroke which impaired the use of his left hand but not his ability to conserve assets entrusted to him. Lunar Enterprises, Ltd., published a prospectus on a bond issue for the wholly-owned subsidiary Ares Chandler Corporation. The Lyle-Drive Exploratory Vessel *Mary Jane Smith* landed on Pluto. Fraser, Colorado, reported the coldest February of its recorded history.

Bishop Oxtongue, at the New Grand Avenue Temple, preached on the text (Matt. XXIV:24): "For there shall arise false Christs, and false prophets, and shall shew great signs and wonders; insomuch that, if it were possible, they shall deceive the very elect." He made clear that his dia-tribe did not refer to Mormons, Christian Scientists, Roman Catholics, nor Fosterites—especially not the last—nor to any fellow travelers whose good works counted more than inconsequential differences in creed or ritual . . . but solely to upstart heretics who were seducing faithful contributors away from the faiths of their fathers. In a sub-tropical resort city in the same nation three complainants swore on information charging public lewdness on the part of a pastor, three of his assistants, and John Doe, Mary Roe, et al., plus charges of running a disorderly house and contributing to delinquency of minors. The county attorney had no interest in prosecuting as he had on file a dozen like it—complaining witnesses always failed to appear at arraignment.

He pointed this out. Their spokesman said, "You'll have plenty of backing this time. Supreme Bishop Short is determined that this antichrist shall flourish no longer."

The prosecutor was not interested in antichrists—but there was a primary coming up. "Well, just remember I can't do much without backing."

"You'll have it."

Dr. Jubal Harshaw was not aware of this incident but knew of too many others for peace of mind. He had succumbed to that most insidious vice, the news. Thus far he had merely subscribed to a clipping service instructed for "Man from Mars," "V. M. Smith," "Church of All Worlds," and "Ben Caxton." But the monkey was on his back—twice lately he fought off an impulse to order Larry to set up the babble box.

Damn it, why couldn't those kids tape him an occasional letter?—instead of letting him worry. *"Front!"*

Anne came in but he continued to stare out at snow and an empty swimming pool. "Anne," he said, "rent us a tropical atoll and put this mausoleum up for sale."

"Yes, Boss."

"But get a lease before you hand this back to the Indians; I will not put up with hotels. How long has it been since I wrote pay copy?"

"Forty-three days."

"Let that be a lesson to you. Begin 'Death Song of a Wood's Colt.'"

The depths of winter longing are ice within my heart
The shards of broken covenants lie sharp against my soul
The wraiths of long-lost ecstasy still keep us two apart
The sullen winds of bitterness still keen from turn to pole.

The scars and twisted tendons, the stumps of struck-off
  limbs,
The aching pit of hunger and throb of unset bone,
My sanded burning eyeballs, as light within them dims,
Add nothing to the torment of lying here alone . . .

The shimmering flames of fever trace out your blessed face
My broken eardrums echo yet your voice inside my head
I do not fear the darkness that comes to me apace
I only dread the loss of you that comes when I am dead.

"There," he added briskly, "sign it 'Louisa M. Alcott' and send it to *Togetherness* magazine."

"Boss, is that your idea of 'pay copy'?"

"Huh? It will be worth something later; put it on file and my literary executor can use it to help settle death duties. That's the catch in artistic pursuits; the best work is worth most after the workman can't be paid. The literary life—*Dreck!* It consists in scratching the cat till it purrs."

"Poor Jubal! Nobody ever feels sorry for him, so he has to feel sorry for himself."

"Sarcasm yet. No wonder I don't get any work done."

"Not sarcasm, Boss. Only the wearer knows where the shoe pinches."

"My apologies. All right, here's pay copy. Title: 'One for the Road.'"

There's amnesia in a hang knot,
And comfort in the ax,
But the simple way of poison will make your nerves
relax.

There's surcease in a gunshot,
And sleep that comes from racks,
But a handy draft of poison avoids the harshest tax.

You find rest upon the hot squat,
Or gas can give you pax,

But the closest corner chemist has peace in packaged
stacks.

There's refuge in the church lot
When you tire of facing facts,
And the smoothest route is poison prescribed by
kindly quacks.

"Chorus—"

With an ugh! and a groan, and a kick of the heels,
Death comes quiet, or it comes with squeals—
But the pleasantest place to find your end
Is a cup of cheer from the hand of a friend.

"Jubal," Anne said worriedly, "is your stomach upset?"

"Always."

"That's for file, too?"

"Huh? That's for the *New Yorker*."

"They'll bounce it."

"They'll buy it. It's morbid, they'll buy it."

"And besides, there's something wrong with the scansion."

"Of course! You have to give an editor *something* to change, or he gets frustrated. After he pees in it, he likes the flavor better, so he buys it. My dear, I was avoiding honest work before you were born—don't teach Grandpa how to suck eggs. Or would you rather I nursed Abby while you turn out copy? Hey! It's Abigail's feeding time! You weren't 'Front,' Dorcas is 'Front.'"

"It won't hurt Abby to wait. Dorcas is lying down. Morning sickness."

"Nonsense. Anne, I can spot pregnancy two weeks fore a rabbit can—and you know it."

"Jubal, you let her be! She's scared she didn't catch . . . and she wants to think she did, as long as possible. Don't you know *anything* about women?"

"Mmm . . . come to think about it—no. All right, I won't heckle her. Why didn't you bring our baby angel and nurse her here?"

"I'm glad I didn't. She might have understood what you were saying—"

"So I corrupt babies, do I?"

"She's too young to see the marshmallow syrup underneath, Boss. But you don't do any work if I bring her; you just play with her."

"Can you think of a better way of enriching empty hours?"

"Jubal, I appreciate the fact that you are dotty over my daughter; I think she's pretty nice myself. But you've been spending all your time either playing with Abby . . . or moping."

"How soon do we go on relief?"

"That's not the point. If you don't crank out stories, you get spiritually constipated. It's reached the point where Dorcas and Larry and I are biting our nails—when you yell 'Front!' we jitter with relief. But it's always a false alarm."

"If there's money to meet the bills, what are you worried about?"

"What are *you* worried about, Boss?"

Jubal considered it. Should he tell her? Any doubt as to the paternity of Abigail had been settled, in his mind, in her naming; Anne had wavered between "Abigail" and

"Zenobia"—then had loaded the infant with both. Anne never mentioned the meanings of those names . . . presumably she did not know that he knew them—

Anne went on firmly, "You're not fooling anyone, Jubal. Dorcas and Larry and I all know that Mike can take care of himself. But you've been so frenetic about it—"

"'Frenetic!' *Me?*"

"—Larry set up the tank in his room and one of us has been catching the news, every broadcast. Not because *we* are worried—except about you. But when Mike gets into the news—and of course he does—we know it before those silly clippings reach you. I wish you would quit reading them."

"How do you know about any clippings? I went to a lot of trouble to see that you didn't."

"Boss," she said in a tired voice, "somebody has to dispose of the trash. Do you think Larry can't read?"

"So. That confounded oubliette hasn't worked right since Duke left. Damn it, nothing has!"

"Just send word to Mike—Duke will show up at once."

"You know I can't do that." It graveled him that what she said was almost certainly true . . . and the thought was followed by bitter suspicion. "Anne! Are you still here because Mike told you to?"

She answered promptly, "I am here because I wish to be."

"Mmm . . . I'm not sure that's responsive."

"Jubal, sometimes I wish you were small enough to spank. May I finish what I was saying?"

"You have the floor." Would *any* of them be here? Would Maryam have married Stinky and gone off to Beirut if Mike had not approved? The name "Fatima Michele" might be an acknowledgment of her adopted faith plus her husband's wish to compliment his closest friend—or it might be code as explicit as baby Abby's double name. If so, did Stinky wear his antlers unaware? Or with serene pride as Joseph was alleged to have done? Uh . . . it must be concluded that Stinky knew the minutes of his houri; water-brothership permitted no omission so important. If it was important, which as a physician and agnostic Jubal doubted. But to *them* it would be—

"You aren't listening."

"Sorry. Woolgathering."—and stop it, you nasty old man . . . reading meanings into names that mothers give their children! Next you'll be taking up numerology . . . then astrology . . . then spiritualism—until senility has progressed so far that all there is left is custodial treatment for a hulk too dim-witted to discorporate in dignity. Go to locked drawer nine in the clinic, code "Lethe"—and use two grains, although one is more than enough—

"There's no need for those clippings, because we check the news about Mike . . . and Ben has given us a water promise to let us know any private news we need at once. But, Jubal, Mike *can't* be hurt. If you would visit the Nest, as we three have, you would know this."

"I have never been invited."

"We didn't have invitations, either. Nobody has to have an invitation to his own home. You're making excuses, Jubal. Ben urged you to, and both Dawn and Duke sent word."

"Mike hasn't invited me."

"Boss, that Nest belongs to me and to you quite as much as it does to Mike. Mike is first among equals . . . as you are here. Is this Abby's home?"

"Happens," he answered, "that title vests in her . . . with lifetime tenancy for me." Jubal had changed his will, knowing that Mike's will made it unnecessary to provide for any water brother of Mike's. But not being sure of the 'water' status of this nestling—save that she was usually wet—he had made redispositions in her favor and in favor of descendants of certain others. "I hadn't intended to tell you, but there is no harm in your knowing."

"Jubal . . . you've made me cry. And you've almost made me forget what I was saying. And I must say it. Mike would never hurry you, you know that. I grok he is waiting for fullness—and I grok you are, too."

"Mmm . . . I grok you speak rightly."

"All right. I think you are especially glum today because Mike has been arrested again. But that's happened many—"

"'Arrested?' I hadn't heard about this!" He added, "Damn it, girl—"

"Jubal, Jubal! Ben hasn't called; that's all we need to know. You know how many times Mike has been arrested—in the army, as a carnie, other places—half a dozen times as a preacher. He never hurts anybody; he lets them do it. They can never convict him and he gets out as soon as he wishes."

"What is it this time?"

"Oh, the usual nonsense—public lewdness, statutory rape, conspiracy to defraud, keeping a disorderly house, contributing to the delinquency of minors, conspiracy to evade truancy laws—"

"Huh?"

"Their license to operate a parochial school was canceled; the kids didn't go back to public school. No matter, Jubal—none of it matters. The one thing they are technically guilty of can't be proved. Jubal, if you had seen the

Nest you would know that even the F.D.S. couldn't sneak a spy-eye into it. So relax. After a lot of publicity, charges will be dropped—and crowds will be bigger than ever."

"Hmm! Anne, does Mike rig these persecutions himself?"

She looked startled. "Why, I never considered the possibility, Jubal. Mike can't lie, you know."

"Does it involve lying? Suppose he planted true rumors? But ones that can't be proved in court?"

"Do you think Michael would do that?"

"I don't know. I do know that the slickest way to lie is to tell the right amount of truth—then shut up. It wouldn't be the first time that persecution has been courted for its headline value. All right, I'll forget it unless it turns out he can't handle it. Are you still 'Front'?"

"If you can refrain from chucking Abby under the chin and saying cootchy-coo and similar uncommercial noises, I'll fetch her. Otherwise I had better tell Dorcas to get up."

"Bring in Abby. I'm going to make an honest effort to make commercial noises—a brand-new plot, known as boy-meets-girl."

"Say, that's a *good* one, Boss! I wonder why nobody thought of it before? Half a sec—" She hurried out.

Jubal did restrain himself—less than one minute of uncommercial activity, just enough to invoke Abigail's heavenly smile, then Anne settled back and let the infant nurse. "Title:" he began. "'Girls Are Like Boys, Only More So.' Begin. Henry M. Haversham Fourth had been carefully reared. He believed that there were only two kinds of girls: those in his presence and those who were not. He vastly preferred the latter sort, especially when they stayed that way. Paragraph. He had not been introduced to the young lady who fell into his lap, and he did not consider a common disaster as equivalent to a formal intro—' What the hell do *you* want?"

"Boss—" said Larry.

"Get out, close the door, and—"

"*Boss!* Mike's church has burned down!"

They made a disorderly rout for Larry's room, Jubal a half length behind Larry at the turn, Anne with eleven pounds up closing rapidly. Dorcas trailed through being late out the gate; the racket wakened her.

"—midnight last night. You are viewing what was the main entrance of the cult's temple, as it appeared immediately after the explosion. This is your Neighborly Newsman for New World Networks with your midmorning roundup. Stay switched to this pitch for dirt that's alert. And now a moment for your sponsor—" The scene shimmered out and medclose shot of a lovely housewife replaced, with dolly-in.

"Damn! Larry, unplug that contraption and wheel it into the study. Anne—no, Dorcas. Phone Ben."

Anne protested, "You know the Temple never had a telephone. How can she?"

"Then have somebody chase over and—no, the Temple wouldn't have anybody—uh, call the police chief there. No, the district attorney. The last you heard Mike was in jail?"

"That's right."

"I hope he still is—and the others, too."

"So do I. Dorcas, take Abby. I'll do it."

As they returned to the study the phone was signalling, demanding hush & scramble. Jubal cursed and set the combo, intending to blast whoever it was off the frequency.

It was Ben Caxton. "Hi, Jubal."

"Ben! What the hell is the situation?"

"I see you've had the news. That's why I called. Everything is under control."

"What about the fire? Anybody hurt?"

"No damage. Mike says to tell you—"

"No *damage*? I just saw a shot of it; it looked like a total—"

"Oh, that—" Ben shrugged. "Jubal, please listen. I've got other calls to make. You aren't the only person who needs reassurance. But Mike said to call you first."

"Uh . . . very well, sir."

"Nobody hurt, nobody even scorched. Oh, a couple of million in property damage. The place was choked with experiences; Mike planned to abandon it soon. Yes, it was fireproof—but anything will burn with enough gasoline and dynamite."

"Incendiary job, huh?"

"Please, Jubal. They had arrested eight of us—all they could catch of the Ninth Circle, John Doe warrants, mostly. Mike had us bailed out in a couple of hours, except himself. He's in the hoosegow—"

"I'll be right there!"

"Take it easy. Mike says for you to come if you want to, but there is no need for it. I agree. The fire was set last night while the Temple was empty, everything canceled because of the arrests—empty, that is, except for the Nest. All of us in town, except Mike, were in the Innermost Temple, holding a Sharing-Water in his honor, when the explosion and fire were set off. So we adjourned to an emergency Nest."

"From the looks of it, you were lucky to get out."

"We were cut off, Jubal. We're all dead—"

"*What?*"

"We're all listed as dead or missing. You see, nobody left the building after that holocaust started . . . by any known exit."

"Uh . . . a 'priest's hole'?"

"Jubal, Mike has methods for such things—and I'm not going to discuss them over the phone."

"You said he was in jail?"

"So I did. He still is."

"But—"

"That's enough. If you come, don't go to the Temple. It's kaput. I'm not going to tell you where we are . . . and I'm not calling from there. If you come—and I see no point in it; there's nothing you can do—just come as you ordinarily would—we'll find you."

"But—"

"That's all. Good-by. Anne, Dorcas, Larry—and you, too, Jubal, and the baby. Share water. Thou art God." The screen went blank.

Jubal swore. "I knew it! That's what comes of mucking around with religion. Dorcas, get me a taxi. Anne—no, finish feeding your child. Larry, pack me a bag. Anne, I'll want most of the iron money and Larry can go tomorrow and replenish the supply."

"Boss," protested Larry, "we're *all* going."

"Certainly we are," Anne agreed crisply.

"Pipe down, Anne. Close your mouth, Dorcas. This is not a time when women have the vote. That city is the firing line and anything can happen. Larry, you stay here and protect two women and a baby. Forget about going to the bank; you won't need cash because none of you is to stir off the place until I'm back. Somebody is playing rough and there is enough hook-up between this house and that church that they might play rough here, too. Larry, flood lights all night, heat up the fence, don't hesitate to shoot. And don't be slow about getting everybody into the vault if necessary—put Abby's crib there at once. Now get with it—I've got to change clothes."

Thirty minutes later Jubal was alone in his suite. Larry called up, "Boss! Taxi landing."

"Be right down," he called back, then turned to look at the Fallen Caryatid. His eyes were filled with tears. He said softly, "You tried, didn't you, youngster? But that stone was always too heavy . . . too heavy for anyone."

Gently he touched a hand of the crumpled figure, turned and left.

XXXV

THE TAXI DID what Jubal expected of machinery, developed trouble and homed for maintenance. Jubal wound up in New York, farther from his goal than ever. He found that he could make better time by commercial schedule than by any available charter. He arrived hours late, having spent the time cooped up with strangers, and watching stereo.

He saw an insert of Supreme Bishop Short proclaiming a holy war against the antichrist, i.e., Mike, and he saw many shots of an utterly ruined building—he failed to see how any had escaped alive. Augustus Greaves viewed with alarm everything about it . . . but pointed out that, in every spite-fence quarrel, one neighbor supplies the incitements—and in his weasel-worded opinion, the so-called Man from Mars was at fault.

At last Jubal stood on a municipal landing flat—sweltering in winter clothes, noted that palm trees still looked like a poor grade of feather duster, regarded bleakly the sea beyond, thinking that it was a dirty unstable mass contaminated with grapefruit shells and human excrement—and wondered what to do.

A man wearing a uniform cap approached. "Taxi, sir?"

"Uh, yes." He could go to a hotel, call in the press, and give an interview that would publicize his whereabouts.

"This way, sir." The cabby led him to a battered Yellow Cab. As he put his bag in after Jubal, he said quietly, "I offer you water."

"Eh? Never thirst."

"Thou art God." The cab pilot sealed the door and got into his own compartment.

They wound up on one wing of a big beach hotel—a private four-car space, the hotel's landing flat being on another wing. The pilot set the cab to home-in alone, took Jubal's bag and escorted him in. "You couldn't have come in via the lobby," he said, "as the foyer on this floor is filled with cobras. So if you go down to the street, be sure to ask somebody. Me, or anybody—I'm Tim."

"I'm Jubal Harshaw."

"I know, Brother Jubal. In this way. Mind your step." They entered a suite of the large, extreme luxury sort, and on into a bedroom with bath; Tim said, "This is yours," put Jubal's bag down and left. On a table Jubal found water, glasses, ice cubes, and brandy—his preferred brand. He mixed himself a quick one, sipped it and sighed, took off his winter jacket.

A woman came in bearing a tray of sandwiches. Her dress Jubal took to be the uniform of a hotel chambermaid since it was unlike the shorts, halters, sarongs, and other ways to display rather than conceal that characterized this resort. But she smiled at him, said, "Drink deep and never thirst, our brother," put the tray down, went into his bath and started a tub, then checked around in bath and in bedroom. "Is there anything you need, Jubal?"

"Me? Oh, no, everything is fine. Is Ben Caxton around?"

"Yes. He said you would want to bathe and get comfortable first. If you want anything, just say so. Ask anyone. Or ask for me. I'm Patty."

"*Oh!* The Life of Archangel Foster."

She dimpled and suddenly was much younger than the thirtyish Jubal had guessed. "Yes."

"I'd like very much to see it. I'm interested in religious art."

"Now? No, I grok you want your bath. Unless you'd like help?"

Jubal recalled that his tattooed Japanese friend had made, many times, the same offer. But he simply wanted to wash away the stink and get into summer clothes. "No, thank you, Patty. But I do want to see them, at your convenience."

"Any time. There's no hurry." She left, unhurried but moving very quickly.

Jubal refrained from lounging. Shortly he was checking through what Larry had packed and grunted with annoyance to find no summer-weight slacks. He settled for sandals, shorts, and a bright shirt, which made him look like a paint-splashed emu and accented his hairy, thinning legs.

But Jubal had ceased worrying about such decades earlier; it would do, until he needed to go out on the street . . . or into court. Did the bar association here have reciprocity with Pennsylvania?

He found his way into a large living room having that impersonal quality of hotel accommodations. Several people were watching the largest stereovision tank Jubal had ever seen outside a theater. One glanced up, said, "Hi, Jubal," and came toward him.

"Hi, Ben. What's the situation? Is Mike still in jail?"

"Oh, no. He got out shortly after I talked to you."

"Is the preliminary hearing set?"

Ben smiled. "It's not that way, Jubal. Mike wasn't released, he escaped."

Jubal looked disgusted. "What a silly thing to do. Now the case will be eight times as difficult."

"Jubal, I told you not to worry. The rest of us are presumed dead—and Mike is missing. We're through with this city, it doesn't matter. We'll go elsewhere."

"They'll extradite him."

"Never fear. They won't."

"Well . . . where is he? I must talk to him."

"He's a couple of rooms down from you. But he's withdrawn in meditation. He left word to tell you to take no action. You can talk to him if you insist; Jill will call him out of it. But I don't recommend it. There's no hurry."

Jubal was damnably eager to talk to Mike—and chew him out for getting into such a mess—but disturbing Mike while in trance was worse than disturbing Jubal himself when dictating a story—the boy always came out of self-hypnosis when he had "grokked the fullness," whatever that was—or if he hadn't, then he needed to go back into it. As pointless as disturbing a hibernating bear.

"All right. But I want to see him when he wakes up."

"You will. Now relax and get the trip out of your system." Ben urged him toward the group around the tank.

Anne looked up. "Hello, Boss." She moved over. "Sit down."

Jubal joined her. "May I ask what the devil *you* are doing here?"

"The same thing you're doing—nothing. Jubal, please don't get heavy-handed. We belong here as much as you do. But you were too upset to argue with. So relax and watch what they're saying about us. The sheriff has announced that he's going to run all us whores out of town." She smiled. "I've never been run out of town before. Does a whore get ridden on a rail? Or will I have to walk?"

"I don't think there's protocol. You all came?"

"Yes, but don't fret. Larry and I made an arrangement with the McClintock boys a year ago—just in case. They know how the furnace works and where switches are and things; it's all right."

"Hmm! I'm beginning to think I'm just a boarder there."

"You expect us to run it without bothering you. But it's a shame you didn't let us all travel together. We got here hours ago—you must have had trouble."

"I did. Anne, once I get home I don't intend to set foot off the place again in my life . . . and I'm going to yank out the telephone and take a sledgehammer to the babble box."

"Yes, Boss."

"This time I mean it." He glanced at the giant babble box. "Do those commercials go on forever? Where's my goddaughter? Don't tell me you left her with McClintock's idiot sons!"

"Of course not. She's here. She even has her own nurse-maid, thank God."

"I want to see her."

"Patty will show her to you. I'm bored with her—she was a little beast all the way down. Patty dear! Jubal wants to see Abby."

The tattooed woman checked an unhurried dash through the room. "Certainly, Jubal. I'm not busy. Down this way.

"I've got the kids in my room," she explained, while Jubal strove to keep up, "so that Honey Bun can watch them."

Jubal was mildly startled to see what Patricia meant. The boa was arranged on a bed in squared-off loops that formed a nest—a twin nest, as one bight of the snake had been pulled across to bisect the square, making two crib-sized pockets, each padded with a baby blanket and each containing a baby.

The ophidian nursemaid raised her head inquiringly as they came in. Patty stroked it and said, "It's all right, dear. Father Jubal wants to see them. Pet her a little, and let her grok you, so she will know you next time."

Jubal cootchy-cooed at his favorite girl friend when she gurgled at him and kicked, then petted the snake. It was the handsomest specimen of *Boidae* he had ever seen—longer, he estimated, than any other boa constrictor in captivity, its cross bars sharply marked and brighter colors of the tail quite showy. He envied Patty her blue-ribbon pet and regretted that he would not have time in which to get friendly with it.

The snake rubbed her head against his hand like a cat. Patty picked up Abby, said, "Honey Bun, why didn't you tell me? She tells me at once if one of them gets tangled up, or needs help, since she can't do much except nudge them back if they try to crawl out. But she just can't grok that a wet baby ought to be changed—Honey Bun doesn't see anything wrong about that. And neither does Abby."

"I know. We call her 'Old Faithful.' Who's the other cutie pie?"

"That's Fatima Michele. I thought you knew."

"Are *they* here? I thought they were in Beirut!"

"Why, they did come from one of those foreign parts. Maryam told me but it wouldn't mean anything to me; I've never been anywhere. I grok all places are alike—just people. There, do you want to hold Abigail while I check Fatima?"

Jubal did and assured her that she was the most beautiful girl in the world, then assured Fatima of the same thing. He was sincere each time and the girls believed him—Jubal had said the same thing on countless occasions starting in the Harding administration, had always meant it and had always been believed.

Regretfully he left, after petting Honey Bun and telling her the same thing.

They ran into Fatima's mother. "Boss honey!" She kissed him and patted his tummy. "I see they've kept you fed."

"Some. I've been smooching with your daughter. She's an angel doll, Miriam."

"Pretty good baby, huh? We're going to sell her down to Rio."

"I thought the market was better in Yemen?"

"Stinky says not. Got to sell her to make room." She put his hand on her belly. "Feel? Stinky and I are making a boy—got no time for daughters."

"Maryam," Patricia said chidingly, "that's no way to talk."

"Sorry, Patty. I won't talk that way about your baby. Aunt Patty is a lady, and groks I'm not."

"I grok you aren't, too, you little hellion. But if Fatima is for sale, I'll give you twice your best commercial offer."

"Take it up with Aunt Patty; I'm merely allowed to see her occasionally."

"And you don't bulge, so you may want to keep her yourself. Let me see your eyes. Mmm . . . could be."

"Is. Mike grokked it most carefully and tells Stinky he's made a boy."

"How can Mike grok that? I'm not even sure you're pregnant."

"Oh, she is, Jubal," Patricia confirmed.

Miriam looked at him serenely. "Still the skeptic, Boss? Mike grokked it while we were still in Beirut, before Stinky and I were sure we had caught. So Mike phoned us. So Stinky told the university that we were taking a sabbatical. So here we are."

"Doing what?"

"Working. Harder than you made me work, Boss—my husband is a slave driver."

"Doing what?"

"They're writing a Martian dictionary," Patty told him.

"Martian to English? That must be difficult."

"Oh, no!" Miriam looked almost shocked. "That would

be impossible. A Martian dictionary in Martian. There's never been one; Martians don't need such things. My part is just clerical; I type what they do. Mike and Stinky—mostly Stinky—worked out a phonetic script for Martian, eighty-one characters. So we had an I.B.M. typer worked over, using both upper and lower case—Boss darling, I'm *ruined* as a secretary; I type touch system in Martian now. Will you love me anyhow? When you shout 'Front!' and I'm not good for anything? I can still cook . . . and I'm told I have other talents."

"I'll dictate in Martian."

"You will, when Mike and Stinky get through with you. I grok. Eh, Patty?"

"You speak rightly, my brother."

They returned to the living room, Caxton joined them and suggested finding a quieter place, led Jubal down a passage and into another living room. "You seem to have most of this floor."

"All of it," agreed Ben. "Four suites—the Secretarial, the Presidential, the Royal, and Owner's Cabin, opened into one and not accessible other than by our own landing flat . . . except through a foyer that is not very safe. You were warned about that?"

"Yes."

"We don't need much room right now . . . but we may; people are trickling in."

"Ben, how can you hide so openly? The hotel staff will give you away."

"The staff doesn't come up here. You see, Mike owns this hotel."

"So much the worse, I would think."

"Not unless our doughty police chief has Mr. Douglas

on his payroll. Mike has it through about four links of dummies—and Douglas doesn't snoop into why Mike orders a thing. Douglas doesn't hate me since Os Kilgallen took over my column, I think, but he doesn't want to surrender control. The owner of record is one of our clandestine Ninth-Circlers. So the owner takes this floor for the season and the manager doesn't ask why—he likes his job. It's a good hide-out. Till Mike groks where we will go."

"Sounds like Mike had anticipated a need."

"I'm sure he did. Two weeks ago Mike cleared out the nestlings' nest—except Maryam and her baby; Maryam is needed. Mike sent parents with children to other cities—places he means to open temples, I think—and when the time came, there were about a dozen of us to move. No sweat."

"But you barely got out with your lives. You lost all your personal possessions?"

"Oh, everything important was saved. Stuff like Stinky's language tapes and a trick typer that Maryam uses—even that horrible Madame-Tussaud of you. And Mike grabbed some clothes and cash."

Jubal objected, "You say *Mike* did this? I thought Mike was in jail then?"

"His body was in jail, curled up in withdrawal. But he was with us. You understand?"

"I don't grok."

"Rapport. He was inside Jill's head, mostly, but we were all closely together. Jubal, I can't explain it; you have to *do* it. When the explosion hit, he moved us here. Then he went back and saved the minor stuff."

Jubal frowned. Caxton said impatiently, "Teleportation, of course. What's so hard to grok, Jubal? You told me to open my eyes and know a miracle when I saw one. So I did and they were. Only they aren't miracles, any more than radio is. Do you grok radio? Or stereovision? Or electronic computers?"

"Me? No."

"Nor I. But I could if I took the time and sweat to learn the language of electronics; it's not miraculous—just complex. Teleportation is simple, once you learn the language—it's the language that is difficult."

"Ben, you can teleport things?"

"Me? They don't teach that in Kindergarten. I'm a deacon by courtesy, simply because I'm 'First Called'—but my progress is about Fourth Circle. I'm just beginning to get control of my own body. Patty is the only one who uses teleportation regularly . . . and I'm not sure she ever does it without Mike's support. Oh, Mike says she's capable of it, but Patty is curiously naive and humble for the genius she is and feels dependent on Mike. Which she needn't be. Jubal, I grok this: we don't actually need Mike. You could have been the Man from Mars. Or me. Mike is like the first man to discover fire. Fire was there all along—after he showed them how, anybody could use it . . . anybody with sense enough not to get burned with it. Follow me?"

"I grok, somewhat."

"Mike is our Prometheus—but that's all. Mike keeps emphasizing this. Thou art God, I am God, he is God—all that groks. Mike is a man like the rest of us. A superior man, admittedly—a lesser man, taught the things the Martians know, might have set himself up as a pipsqueak god. Mike is above that temptation. Prometheus . . . but that's all."

Jubal said slowly, "Prometheus paid a high price for bringing fire to mankind."

"Don't think that Mike doesn't! He pays with twenty-four hours of work every day, seven days a week, trying to teach us how to play with matches without getting burned. Jill and Patty lowered the boom on him, made him take one night a week off, long before I joined." Caxton smiled. "But you can't stop Mike. This burg is loaded with gambling joints, mostly crooked since it's against the law here. So Mike spent his night off bucking crooked games—and winning. They tried to mug him, they tried to kill him, they tried knock-out drops and muscle boys—he simply ran up a reputation as the luckiest man in town . . . which brought more people into the Temple. So they tried to keep him out—a mistake. Cold decks froze solid, wheels wouldn't spin, dice rolled nothing but box cars. At last they put up with him . . . requesting him to move on after he had won a few grand. Mike would do so, if asked politely."

Caxton added, "So that's one more power bloc against us. Not just the Fosterites and other churches—but now the syndicate and the city machine. I think that job on the Temple was done by professionals—I doubt if the Fosterite goon squads touched it."

While they talked, people came in, went out, formed groups. Jubal found in them a most unusual feeling, an unhurried relaxation that was also dynamic tension. No one seemed excited, never in a hurry . . . yet everything they did seemed purposeful, even gestures as apparently unpremeditated as encountering one another and marking it with a kiss or a greeting. It felt to Jubal as if each move had been planned by a choreographer.

The quiet and the increasing tension—or 'expectancy,' he decided; these people were not tense in any morbid fashion—reminded Jubal of something. Surgery? With a master at work, no noise, no lost motions?

Then he remembered. Many years earlier when chemically-powered rockets were used for the earliest human probing of space, he had watched a count-down in a blockhouse. He recalled the same low voices, the relaxed, very diverse but coordinated actions, the same rising exultant expectancy. They were "waiting for fullness," that was certain. But for what? Why were they so happy? Their Temple and all they had built had been destroyed . . . yet they seemed like kids on a night before Christmas.

Jubal had noted when he arrived that the nudity Ben had been disturbed by on his first visit to the nest did not seem to be the practice here, although private enough for it. He failed to notice it when it did appear; he had become so much in the unique close-family mood that being dressed or not was irrelevant.

When he did notice, it was not skin but the thickest, most beautiful cascade of black hair he had ever seen, gracing a young woman who came in, spoke to someone, threw Ben a kiss, glanced gravely at Jubal, and left. Jubal followed her with his eyes, appreciating that flowing mass of midnight plumage. Only after she left did he realize that she had not been dressed other than in that queenly glory . . . and then realized that she was not the first of his brothers in that fashion.

Ben noticed his glance. "That's Ruth," he said. "New high priestess. She and her husband have been on the other coast—to prepare a branch temple, I think. I'm glad they're back. It looks as if the whole family will be home."

"Beautiful head of hair. I wish she had tarried."

"Why didn't you call her over?"

"Eh?"

"Ruth certainly came in here to catch a glimpse of you—they must have just arrived. Haven't you noticed that we have been left pretty much alone?"

"Well . . . yes." Jubal had been braced to ward off undue intimacy—and found that he had stepped on a step that wasn't there. He had been treated hospitably, but it was more like the politeness of a cat than that of an over-friendly dog.

"They are all terribly interested in the fact that you are here and very anxious to see you . . . but they are in awe of you."

"Me?"

"Oh, I told you last summer. You're a myth, not quite real and more than life size. Mike has told them that you are the only human he knows who can 'grok in fullness' without learning Martian. Most of them suspect that you read minds as perfectly as Mike does."

"What poppycock! I hope you disabused them?"

"Who am I to destroy a myth? If you do, you wouldn't admit it. They are a bit afraid of you—you eat babies for breakfast and when you roar the ground trembles. Any of them would be delighted to have you call them over . . . but they won't force themselves on you. They know that even Mike stands at attention when you speak."

Jubal dismissed the idea with one explosive word. "Certainly," Ben agreed. "Mike has blind spots—I told you he was human. But you're the patron saint—and you're stuck with it."

"Well . . . there's somebody I know, just came in. Jill! *Jill!* Turn around, dear!"

The woman turned hesitantly. "I'm Dawn. But thank you." She came over and Jubal thought that she was going to kiss him. But she dropped to one knee, took his hand and kissed it. "Father Jubal. We welcome and drink deep of you."

Jubal snatched his hand away. "Oh, for Heaven's sake, child! Get up and sit down. Share water."

"Yes, Father Jubal."

"Huh? Call me Jubal—and spread the word that I don't appreciate being treated like a leper. I'm in the bosom of my family—I hope."

"You are . . . Jubal."

"So I expect to be called Jubal and treated as a water brother—no more, no less. The first one who treats me with respect will stay after school. Grok?"

"Yes, Jubal," she agreed. "I've told them."

"Huh?"

"Dawn means," explained Ben, "that she's told Patty, probably, and that Patty is telling everybody who can hear—with his inner ear—and they are passing the word to any who are still a bit deaf, like myself."

"Yes," agreed Dawn, "except that I told Jill—Patty has gone outside for something Michael wants. Jubal, have you been watching stereo? It's very exciting."

"Eh? No."

"You mean the jail break, Dawn?"

"Yes, Ben."

"We hadn't discussed that. Jubal, Mike didn't merely crash out and come home; he gave them miracles to chew on. He threw away every bar and door in the county jail as he left . . . did the same at the state prison near here—and disarmed all police. Partly to keep 'em busy . . . and partly because Mike purely despises locking a man up for any reason. He groks it great wrongness."

"That fits," Jubal agreed. "Mike is gentle. It would hurt him to have anybody locked up. I agree."

Ben shook his head. "Mike isn't gentle, Jubal. Killing a man wouldn't worry him. But he's the ultimate anarchist—locking a man up is a wrongness. Freedom of self—and utter personal responsibility for self. Thou art God."

"Wherein lies the conflict, sir? Killing a man may be necessary. But confining him is an offense against his integrity—and your own."

Ben looked at him. "Mike is right. You do grok in fullness—his way. I don't quite . . . I'm still learning." He added, "How are they taking it, Dawn?"

She giggled slightly. "Like stirred-up hornets. The mayor is frothing. He's demanded help from the state and from the Federation—and getting it; we've seen lots of troop carriers landing. But as they climb out, Mike is stripping them—not just weapons, even their shoes—and as soon as a carrier is empty, it goes, too."

Ben said, "I grok he'll stay withdrawn until they give up. Handling that many details he would almost have to stay on eternal time."

Dawn looked thoughtful. "I don't think so, Ben. I would have to, to handle even a tenth. But I grok Michael could do it riding a bicycle standing on his head."

"Mmm . . . I wouldn't know, I'm still making mud pies." Ben stood up. "Sometimes you miracle workers give me a slight pain, honey child. I'm going to watch the tank." He stopped to kiss her. "You entertain old Pappy Jubal; he likes little girls." Caxton left and a package of cigarettes followed him, placed itself in one of his pockets.

Jubal said, "Did you do that? Or Ben?"

"Ben. He's always forgetting his cigarettes; they chase him all over the Nest."

"Hmm . . . fair-sized mud pies he makes."

"Ben is advancing much faster than he admits. He's a very holy person."

"Umph. Dawn, you *are* the Dawn Ardent I met at Foster Tabernacle, aren't you?"

"Oh, you remember!" She looked as if he had handed her a lollipop.

"Of course. But you've changed. You seem much more beautiful."

"That's because I am," she said simply. "You mistook me for Gillian. And she is more beautiful, too."

"Where is that child? I expected to see her at once."

"She's working." Dawn paused. "But I told her and she's coming in." She paused again. "I am to take her place. If you will excuse me."

"Run along, child." She got up and left as Dr. Mahmoud sat down.

Jubal looked at him sourly. "You might have had the courtesy to let me know that you were in this country instead of letting me meet my goddaughter through the good offices of a snake."

"Oh, Jubal, you're always in a bloody hurry."

"Sir, when one is of—" Jubal was interrupted by hands placed over his eyes. A voice demanded:

"Guess who?"

"Beelzebub?"

"Try again."

"Lady Macbeth?"

"Closer. Third guess, or forfeit."

"Gillian, stop that, come around, and sit beside me."

"Yes, Father." She obeyed.

"And knock off calling me 'Father' anywhere but home. Sir, I was saying that when one is of my age, one is necessarily in a hurry about some things. Each sunrise is a precious jewel . . . for it may never be followed by its sunset."

Mahmoud smiled. "Jubal, are you under the impression that if you stop cranking, the world stops going around?"

"Most certainly, sir—from my viewpoint." Miriam joined them silently, sat down on Jubal's free side; he put an arm around her. "While I might not yearn to see your ugly face again . . . nor even the somewhat more acceptable one of my former secretary—"

Miriam whispered, "Boss, are you honing for a kick in the stomach? I'm exquisitely beautiful; I have it on highest authority."

"Quiet—new goddaughters are another category. Through your failure to drop me a postcard, I might have missed seeing Fatima Michele. In which case I would have returned to haunt you."

"In which case," Miriam pointed out, "you could look at Micky at the same time . . . rubbing strained carrots in her hair. A disgusting sight."

"I was speaking metaphorically."

"I wasn't. She's a sloppy trencherman."

"Why," asked Jill quietly, "were you speaking metaphorically, Boss?"

"Eh? 'Ghost' is a concept I feel no need for, other than as a figure of speech."

"It's more than that," insisted Jill.

"Uh, as may be. I prefer to meet baby girls in the flesh, including my own."

Dr. Mahmoud said, "But that is what I was saying, Jubal. You aren't about to die. Mike has grokked you. He says you have many years ahead."

Jubal shook his head. "I set a limit of three figures years ago."

"Which three figures, Boss?" Miriam inquired innocently. "The three Methuselah used?"

He shook her shoulders. "Don't be obscene!"

"Stinky says women should be obscene but not heard."

"Your husband speaks rightly. The day my clock first shows three figures I discorporate, whether Martian style or my own crude methods. You can't take that away from me. Going to the showers is the best part of the game."

"I grok you speak rightly, Jubal," Jill said slowly, "about its being the best part of the game. But don't count on it any time soon. Your fullness is not yet. Allie cast your horoscope just last week."

"A horoscope? Oh, my God! Who is 'Allie'? How dare she! Show her to me! Swelp me, I'll turn her into the Better Business Bureau."

"I'm afraid you can't, Jubal," Mahmoud put in, "as she is working on our dictionary. As to who she is, she's Madame Alexandra Vesant."

Jubal looked delighted. "Becky? Is *she* in this nut house, too?"

"Yes, Becky. We call her 'Allie' because we've got another

Becky. Don't scoff at her horoscopes, Jubal; she has the Sight."

"Oh, balderdash, Stinky. Astrology is nonsense and you know it."

"Oh, certainly. Even Allie knows it. And most astrologers are clumsy frauds. Nevertheless Allie practices it even more assiduously than she used to, using Martian arithmetic and Martian astronomy—much fuller than ours. It's her device for grokking. It could be a pool of water, or a crystal ball, or the entrails of a chicken. The means do not matter. Mike has advised her to go on using the symbols she is used to. The point is: she has the Sight."

"What the hell do you mean by 'the Sight,' Stinky?"

"The ability to grok more of the universe than that piece near you. Mike has it from years of Martian discipline; Allie was an untrained semi-adept. That she used as meaningless a symbol as astrology is beside the point. A rosary is meaningless, too—a Muslim rosary, I'm not criticizing our competitors." Mahmoud reached into his pocket, got out one, started fingering it. "If it helps to turn your hat around during a poker game—then it helps. It is irrelevant that the hat has no magic powers."

Jubal looked at the Islamic device and ventured a question. "You are still one of the Faithful? I thought perhaps you had joined Mike's church all the way."

Mahmoud put away the beads. "I have done both."

"Huh? Stinky, they're incompatible."

"Only on the surface. You could say that Maryam took my religion and I took hers. But, Jubal my beloved brother, I am still God's slave, submissive to His will . . . and nevertheless can say: 'Thou art God, I am God, all that groks is God.' The Prophet never asserted that he was the last of all prophets nor did he claim to have said all there was to say. Submission to God's will is not to be a robot, incapable of choice and thus of sin. Submission can include—*does* include—utter responsibility for the fashion in which I, and each of us, shape the universe. It is ours to turn into a Heavenly garden . . . or to rend and destroy." He smiled. "'With God all things are possible,' if I may borrow— except the one Impossible. God cannot escape Himself, He cannot abdicate His own total responsibility—He forever must remain submissive to His own will. Islam remains—He cannot pass the buck. It is His—mine . . . yours . . . Mike's."

Jubal heaved a sigh. "Stinky, theology always gives me the pip. Where's Becky? I've seen her only once in twentyodd years; that's too long."

"You'll see her. But she can't stop now, she's dictating. Let me explain. Up to now, I've spent part of each day in rapport with Mike—just a few moments although it feels like an eight-hour day. Then I immediately dictated all that he poured into me onto tape. From those tapes other people, trained in Martian phonetics, made longhand transcriptions. Then Maryam typed them, using a special typer—and this master copy Mike or I—Mike by choice, but his time is choked—would correct by hand.

"But now Mike groks that he is going to send Maryam and me away to finish the job—or, more correctly, he has grokked that *we* will grok such a necessity. So Mike is getting months and years of tape completed in order that I can take it away and break it into phonetics. Besides that, we have stacks of Mike's lectures—in Martian—that need to be transcribed when the dictionary is finished.

"I am forced to assume that Maryam and I will be

leaving soon, because, busy as Mike is, he's changed the method. There are eight bedrooms here equipped with tape recorders. Those who can do it—Patty, Jill, myself, Maryam, your friend Allie, some others—take turns in those rooms. Mike puts us into trance, pours language—definitions, idioms, concepts—into us for moments that feel like hours . . . then we dictate at *once* what he has poured into us, while it's fresh. But it can't be just anybody. It requires a sharp accent and the ability to join trance rapport and then spill out the results. Sam, for example, has everything but the accent—he manages, God knows how, to speak Martian with a Bronx accent. Can't use him, it would cause endless errata. That is what Allie is doing—dictating. She's in the semi-trance needed for total recall and, if you interrupt her, she'll lose what she hasn't recorded."

"I grok," Jubal agreed, "although the picture of Becky Vesey as a Martian adept shakes me a little. Still, she was one of the best mentalists in show business; she could give a cold reading that would scare a mark out of his shoes. Stinky, if you are going away for peace and quiet while you unwind this, why don't you come home? Plenty of room in the new wing."

"Perhaps we shall. Waiting is."

"Sweetheart," Miram said earnestly, "that's a solution I would love—if Mike pushes us out of the Nest."

"If we grok to leave the Nest, you mean."

"Same thing."

"You speak rightly, my dearest. But when do we eat around here? I feel a most unMartian urgency. The service was better in the Nest."

"You can't expect Patty to work on your dratted old

dictionary, see to it that everyone is comfortable, run errands for Mike, and still have food on the table the instant you get hungry, my love. Jubal, Stinky will never achieve priesthood—he's a slave to his stomach."

"Well, so am I."

"You girls might give Patty a hand," her husband added.

"That's a crude hint. You know we do all she'll let us—and Tony will hardly allow anyone in his kitchen." She stood up. "Come on Jubal, let's see what's cooking. Tony will be flattered if you visit his kitchen."

Jubal went with her, met Tony, who scowled until he saw who was with Miriam, then was beamingly proud to show off his workshop—accompanied by invective at the scoundrels who had destroyed "his" kitchen in the Nest. In the meantime a spoon, unassisted, continued to keel a pot of spaghetti sauce.

Shortly thereafter Jubal refused to sit at the head of a long table, grabbed a place elsewhere. Patty sat at one end; the head chair remained vacant . . . except for a feeling which Jubal suppressed that the Man from Mars was sitting there and that everyone but himself could see him.

Across the table was Dr. Nelson.

Jubal discovered that he would have been surprised only if Dr. Nelson had not been present. He nodded and said, "Hi, Sven."

"Hi, Doc. Share water."

"Never thirst. What are you? Staff physician?"

Nelson shook his head. "Medical student."

"So. Learning anything?"

"I've learned that medicine isn't necessary."

"If youda ast me, I coulda told yuh. Seen Van?"

"He ought to be in late tonight or early tomorrow. His ship grounded today."

"Does he always come here?" inquired Jubal.

"He's an extension student. Can't spend much time here."

"It'll be good to see him. I haven't laid eyes on him for a year." Jubal picked up a conversation with the man on his right while Nelson talked with Dorcas, on his right. Jubal noticed the same tingling expectancy at the table which he had left before, but reinforced. There was nothing he could put his finger on—a quiet family dinner in relaxed intimacy. Once, a glass of water was passed all around the table. When it reached Jubal, he took a sip and passed it to the girl on his left—round-eyed and too awed to make chit-chat with him—and said, "I offer you water."

She managed to answer, "I thank you for water, Fa—Jubal." That was all he got out of her. When the glass completed the circuit, reaching the vacant chair at the head of the table, there was a half inch of water in it. It raised itself, poured, and water disappeared; the tumbler placed itself on the cloth. Jubal decided that he had taken part in a 'Sharing-Water' of the Innermost Temple . . . probably in his honor—although it was not like the Bacchanalian revels he had thought accompanied such welcome. Was it because they were in strange surroundings? Or had he read into unexplicit reports what his own id wanted to find?

Or had they toned it down out of deference to him?

That seemed a likely theory—and it vexed him. He told himself that he was glad to be spared the need to refuse an invitation that he did not want—and would not have relished at any age, his tastes being what they were.

But just the same, damn it—"Don't anybody mention ice skating; Grandmaw is too old and frail and it wouldn't be polite. Hilda, you suggest dominoes and we'll all chime in—Grandmaw *likes* dominoes. We'll go skating some other time. Okay, kids?"

Jubal resented the idea—he would almost prefer to go skating anyhow, even at the cost of a broken hip.

He put it out of mind with the help of the man on his right. His name, Jubal learned, was Sam.

"This setback is only apparent," Sam assured him. "The egg was ready to hatch and now we'll spread out. Of course we'll go on having trouble—because no society will allow its basic concepts to be challenged with impunity. And we are challenging everything from the sanctity of property to the sanctity of marriage."

"Property, too?"

"Property the way it is today. So far Michael has merely antagonized a few crooked gamblers. But what happens when there are thousands, tens of thousands, hundreds of thousands and more, of people who can't be stopped by bank vaults and have only self-discipline to restrain them from taking anything they want? To be sure, that discipline is stronger than any legal restraint—but no banker can grok that until he himself travels the thorny road to discipline . . . and he'll no longer be a banker. What happens to the market when illuminati know which way a stock will move?"

"Do *you* know?"

Sam shook his head. "Not interested. But Saul over there—that other big Hebe, my cousin—gives it grokking, with Allie. Michael has them be cautious, no big killings and they use a dozen dummy accounts—but any of the

disciplined can make any amount of money at anything—
real estate, stocks, horse races, gambling, you name it—
when competing with the un-awakened. No, money and
property will not disappear—Michael says that both concepts are useful—but they're going to be turned upside
down and people will have to learn new rules (the hard way,
just as we have) or be hopelessly outclassed. What happens
to Lunar Enterprises when the common carrier between
here and Luna City is teleportation?"

"Should I buy? Or sell?"

"Ask Saul. He might use the present corporation, or
bankrupt it. Or it might be left untouched a century or two.
But consider *any* occupation. How can a teacher handle a
child who knows more than she does? What becomes of
physicians when people are healthy? What happens to the
cloak and suit industry when clothing isn't necessary and
women aren't so engrossed in dressing up (they'll never lose
interest entirely)—and nobody gives a damn if he's caught
with his arse bare? What shape does 'the Farm Problem' take
when weeds can be told not to grow and crops can be har-
vested without benefit of International Harvester? Just name
it; the discipline changes it beyond recognition. Take one
change that will shake both marriage—in its present form—
and property. Jubal, do you know how much is spent each
year in this country on Malthusian drugs and devices?"

"I have some idea, Sam. Almost a billion on oral con-
traceptives alone . . . more than half on worthless patent
nostrums."

"Oh, yes, you're a medical man."

"Only in passing."

"What happens to that industry—and to the shrill
threats of moralists—when a female conceives only as an

act of volition, when she is immune to disease, cares only for the approval of her own sort . . . and has her orientation so changed that she desires intercourse with a whole-heartedness that Cleopatra never dreamed of—but any male who tried to rape her would die so quickly, if she so grokked, that he wouldn't know what hit him? When women are free of guilt and fear—but invulnerable? Hell, the pharmaceutical industry will be a minor casualty—what other industries, laws, institutions, attitudes, prejudices, and nonsense must give way?"

"I don't grok its fullness," admitted Jubal. "It concerns a subject of little personal interest to me."

"One institution won't be damaged. Marriage."

"So?"

"Very much so. Instead it will be purged, strengthened, and made endurable. Endurable? Ecstatic! See that wench down there with the long black hair?"

"Yes. I was delighting in its beauty earlier."

"She knows it's beautiful and it's grown a foot and a half since we joined the church. That's my wife. Not much over a year ago we lived together like bad-tempered dogs. She was jealous . . . and I was inattentive. Bored. Hell, we were both bored and only our kids kept us together—that and her possessiveness; I knew she would never let me go without a scandal . . . and I didn't have any stomach for trying to put together a new marriage at my age, anyhow. So I grabbed a little on the side, when I could get away with it—a professor has many temptations, few safe opportunities—and Ruth was quietly bitter. Or sometimes not quiet. And then we joined up." Sam grinned happily. "And I fell in love with my wife. Number-one gal friend!"

Sam had spoken only to Jubal, his words walled by

noise. His wife was far down the table. She looked up and said clearly, "That's an exaggeration, Jubal. I'm about number six."

Her husband called out, "Stay out of my mind, beautiful!—we're talking men talk. Give Larry your undivided attention." He threw a roll at her.

She stopped it in orbit, propelled it back. "I'm giving Larry all the attention he wants . . . until later, maybe. Jubal, that brute didn't let me finish. Sixth place is wonderful! Because my name wasn't on his list till we joined the church. I hadn't rated as high as six with Sam for twenty years."

"The point," Sam said quietly, "is that we are now partners, more so than we ever were outside—and we got that way through the training, culminating in sharing and growing-closer with others who had the same training. We all wind up in partnerships inside the group—usually with spouses-of-record. Sometimes not . . . and if not, the readjustment takes place without heartache and creates a warmer, better relationship between the 'divorced' couple than ever, in bed and out. No loss and all gain. Shucks, this pairing needn't be between man and woman. Dawn and Jill for example—they work together like an acrobatic team."

"Hmm . . . I had thought of them as being Mike's wives."

"No more so than they are to any of us. Or than Mike is to the rest. Mike has been too busy to do more than make sure that he shared himself all the way around." Sam added, "If anybody is Mike's wife, it's Patty, although she keeps so busy that the relation is more spiritual than physical. Both Mike and Patty are short-changed when it comes to mauling the mattress."

Patty was farther away than Ruth. She looked up and said, "Sam dear, I don't feel short-changed."

"Huh?" Sam announced bitterly, "The only thing wrong with this church is that a man has *absolutely no privacy!*"

This brought on him a barrage from distaff brothers. He tossed it all back without lifting a hand . . . until a plateful of spaghetti caught him full in the face—thrown, Jubal noticed, by Dorcas.

For a moment Sam looked like a crash victim. Then his face was clean and even sauce that spattered on Jubal's shirt was gone. "Don't give her any more, Tony. She wasted it; let her go hungry."

"Plenty in the kitchen," Tony answered. "Sam, you look good in spaghetti. Pretty good sauce, huh?" Dorcas's plate sailed out, returned loaded.

"Very good sauce," agreed Sam. "I salvaged some that hit me in the mouth. What is it? Or shouldn't I ask?"

"Chopped policeman," Tony answered.

Nobody laughed. Jubal wondered if the joke was a joke. Then he recalled that his brothers smiled a lot but rarely laughed—and besides, policeman should be good food. But the sauce couldn't be "long pig," or it would taste like pork. This had a beef flavor.

He changed the subject. "The thing I like best about this religion—"

"'Religion'?" Sam interposed.

"Well, call it a church."

"Yes," agreed Sam. "It fills every function of a church, and its quasi-theology matches up with some real religions. I jumped in because I used to be a stalwart atheist—and now I'm a high priest and don't know what I am."

"I understood you to say you were Jewish."

"From a long line of rabbis. So I wound up atheist. Now look at me. But Saul and my wife Ruth are Jews in the religious sense—talk to Saul; you'll find it's no handicap. Ruth, once she broke past the barriers, progressed faster than I did; she was a priestess long before I became a priest. But she's the spiritual sort; she thinks with her gonads. Me, I have to do it the hard way, between my ears."

"The discipline," repeated Jubal. "That's what I like. The faith I was reared in didn't require anybody to know anything. Just confess and be saved, and there you were, safe in the arms of Jesus. A man might be too stupid to count sheep . . . yet conclusively presumed to be one of God's elect, guaranteed an eternity of bliss, because he had been 'converted.' He might not even be a Bible student and certainly didn't have to know anything else. This church doesn't accept 'conversion' as I grok it—"

"You grok correctly."

"A person must start with a willingness to learn and follow it with long, hard study. I grok that is salutary."

"More than salutary," agreed Sam. "Indispensable. The concepts can't be thought about without the language, and the discipline that results in this horn-of-plenty of benefits—from how to live without fighting to how to please your wife—all derive from conceptual logic . . . understanding who you are, why you're here, how you tick—and behaving accordingly. Happiness is functioning the way a being is organized to function . . . but the words in English are a tautology, empty. In Martian they are a complete set of working instructions. Did I mention that I had a cancer when I came here?"

"Eh? No."

"Didn't know it myself. Michael grokked it, sent me out for X-rays and so forth so that *I* would be sure. Then we got to work on it. 'Faith' healing. A 'miracle.' The clinic called it 'spontaneous remission' which I grok means 'I got well.'"

Jubal nodded. "Professional double-talk. Some cancers go away, we don't know why."

"I know why this one went away. By then I was beginning to control my body. With Mike's help I repaired the damage. Now I can do it without help. Want to feel a heart stop beating?"

"Thanks, I have observed it in Mike. My esteemed colleague, Croaker Nelson, would not be here if what you are talking about was 'faith healing.' It's voluntary control. I grok."

"Sorry. We all know that you do."

"Mmm . . . I can't call Mike a liar because he isn't. But the lad is prejudiced in my case."

Sam shook his head. "I've been talking with you all through dinner. I wanted to check it myself, despite what Mike said. You grok. I'm wondering what you could disclose if you troubled to learn the language?"

"Nothing. I'm an old man with little to contribute."

"I reserve my opinion. All the other First Called have had to tackle the language to make any real progress. Even the three you've kept with you have had powerful coaching, kept in trance during most of the few occasions we've had them with us. All but you . . . and you don't need it. Unless you want to wipe spaghetti from your face without a towel, which I grok you aren't interested in."

"Only to observe it."

Most had left the table, without formality when they wished. Ruth came over and stood by them. "Are you two going to sit here all night? Or shall we move you out with the dishes?"

"I'm henpecked. Come on, Jubal." Sam paused to kiss his wife.

They stopped in the room with the stereo tank. "Anything new?" asked Sam.

"The county attorney," someone said, "has been orating that today's disasters are our doing . . . without admitting that he doesn't know how it was done."

"Poor fellow. He's bitten a wooden leg and his teeth hurt." They found a quieter room; Sam said, "I had been saying that these troubles can be expected—and will get worse before we will control enough public opinion to be tolerated. But Mike is in no hurry. We close down the Church of All Worlds—it *is* closed. So we move and open the Congregation of the One Faith—and get kicked out again. Then we reopen elsewhere as the Temple of the Great Pyramid—that will bring flocking the fat and fatuous females, and some will end up neither fat nor foolish—and when we have the Medical Association and the local bar and newspapers and politicos snapping at our heels there—why, we open the Brotherhood of Baptism somewhere else. Each one gains a hard core of disciplined who can't be hurt. Mike started less than two years ago, uncertain himself and with only the help of three untrained priestesses. Now we've got a solid Nest . . . plus advanced pilgrims we can get in touch with later. Someday we'll be too strong to persecute."

"Well," agreed Jubal, "Jesus made quite a splash with only twelve disciples."

Sam grinned happily. "A Jew boy. Thanks for mention-
ing Him. He's the top success story of my tribe—and we
all know it, even though many of us don't talk about Him.
He was a Jew boy Who made good and I'm proud of Him.
Please note that Jesus didn't try to get it all done by
Wednesday. He set up a sound organization and let it grow.
Mike is patient, too. Patience is so much part of the disci-
pline that it isn't patience; it's automatic. Never any sweat."

"A sound attitude at any time."

"Not an attitude. The functioning of discipline. Jubal?
I grok you are tired. Would you become untired? Or
would you rather go to bed? If you don't our brothers will
keep you up all night, talking. We don't sleep much, you
know."

Jubal yawned. "I choose a long, hot soak and eight
hours sleep. I'll visit with our brothers tomorrow . . . and
other days."

"And many other days," agreed Sam.

Jubal found his room, was immediately joined by Patty,
who drew his tub, turned back his bed without touching
it, placed his setup for drinks by his bed, mixed one and
placed it on the shelf of the tub. Jubal did not hurry her
out; she had arrived displaying all her pictures. He knew
enough about the syndrome which can lead to full tattooing to be sure that if he did not ask to examine them, she
would be hurt.

Nor did he feel the fret that Ben had felt on a similar
occasion; he undressed—and discovered with wry pride
that it did not matter even though it had been years since
the last time he had allowed anyone to see him naked. It
seemed to matter not at all to Patty; she simply made sure
that the tub was just right before letting him step into it.

Then she remained and told him what each picture was and in what sequence to view them.

Jubal was properly awed and appropriately complimentary, while completely the impersonal art critic. It was, he admitted to himself, the goddamndest virtuosity with a needle he had *ever* seen—it made his Japanese friend look like a cheap carpet as compared with the finest Princess Bokhara.

"They've been changing a little," she told him. "Take the holy birth scene here—that rear wall is beginning to look curved . . . and the bed looks almost like a hospital table. I'm sure George doesn't mind. There hasn't been a needle touched to me since he went to Heaven . . . and if miraculous changes take place, I'm sure he has a finger in it."

Jubal decided that Patty was dotty but nice . . . he preferred people who were a little dotty; "the salt of the earth" bored him. Not too dotty, he amended; Patty had whisked his discarded clothes into his wardrobe without coming near them. She was probably a clear proof that one didn't have to be sane, whatever that was, to benefit by this discipline; the boy apparently could teach anyone.

He sensed when she was ready to leave and suggested it by asking her to kiss his goddaughters goodnight—he had forgotten. "I was tired, Patty."

She nodded. "And I am called for dictionary work." She leaned over and kissed him, warmly but quickly. "I'll take that one to our babies."

"And a pat for Honey Bun."

"Yes, of course. She groks you, Jubal. She knows you like snakes."

"Good. Share water, brother."

"Thou art God, Jubal." She was gone. Jubal settled back in the tub, was surprised to find that he was not tired and his bones no longer ached. Patty was a tonic . . . happiness on the hoof. He wished that he had no doubts— then admitted that he didn't want to be anything but himself, old and cranky and self-indulgent.

Finally he soaped and showered and decided to shave so that he wouldn't have to before breakfast. Presently he bolted the door, turned out the overhead light, and got into bed.

He looked around for something to read, found nothing to his annoyance, being addicted to this vice above all else. He sipped part of a drink instead and turned out the bed light.

His chat with Patty seemed to have wakened and rested him. He was still awake when Dawn came in.

He called out, "Who's there?"

"It's Dawn, Jubal."

"It can't be dawn yet; it was only—Oh."

"Yes, Jubal. Me."

"Damn it, I thought I bolted that door. Child, march straight out of—*Hey!* Get out of this bed. Git!"

"Yes, Jubal. But I want to tell you something first."

"Huh?"

"I have loved you a long time. Almost as long as Jill has."

"Why, the very—Quit talking nonsense and shake your little fanny out that door."

"I will, Jubal," she said humbly. "But please listen to something first. Something about women."

"Not now. Tell me in the morning."

"*Now*, Jubal."

He sighed. "Talk. Stay where you are."

"Jubal . . . my beloved brother. Men care very much how we women look. So we try to be beautiful and that is a goodness. I used to be a peeler, as you know. It was a goodness, to let men enjoy the beauty I was for them. It was a goodness for *me*, to know that they needed what I had to give.

"But, Jubal, women are not men. *We* care what a man *is*. It can be something as silly as: Is he wealthy? Or it can be: Will he take care of my children and be good to them? Or, sometimes, it can be: Is he good? As you are good, Jubal. But the beauty we see in you is not the beauty you see in us. You are beautiful, Jubal."

"For God's sake!"

"I think you speak rightly. Thou art God and I am God—and I need you. I offer you water. Will you let me share and grow closer?"

"Uh, look, little girl, if I understand what you are offering—"

"You grok, Jubal. To share all that we have. Ourselves. Selves."

"I thought so. My dear, you have plenty to share—but . . . myself—well, you arrived years too late. I am sincerely regretful, believe me. Thank you. Deeply. Now go away and let an old man sleep."

"You will sleep, when waiting is filled. Jubal . . . I could lend you strength. But I grok clearly that it is not necessary."

(Goddamit—it *wasn't* necessary!) "No, Dawn. Thank you, dear."

She got to her knees and bent over him. "Just one more word, then. Jill told me that if you argued, I was to cry.

Shall I get my tears all over your chest? And share water with you that way?"

"I'm going to spank Jill!"

"Yes, Jubal. I'm starting to cry." She made no sound, but in a second or two a warm, full tear splashed on his chest—was followed by another . . . and another—and still more. She sobbed almost silently.

Jubal cursed and reached for her . . . and cooperated with the inevitable.

XXXVI

JUBAL WOKE UP alert, rested, and happy, realized that he felt better before breakfast than he had in years. For a long, long time he had been getting through that black period between waking and the first cup of coffee by telling himself that tomorrow might be a little easier.

This morning he found himself whistling. He noticed it, stopped himself, forgot it and started up again.

He saw himself in the mirror, smiled wryly, then grinned. "You incorrigible old goat. They'll be sending the wagon for you any minute now." He noticed a white hair on his chest, plucked it out, didn't bother with many others just as white, went on making himself ready to face the world.

When he went outside his door Jill was there. Accidentally? He no longer trusted any 'coincidence' in this menage; it was as organized as a computer. She came straight into his arms. "Jubal—Oh, we *love* you so! Thou art God."

He returned her kiss as warmly as it was given, grokking that it would be hypocritical not to—and discovered that kissing Jill differed from kissing Dawn only in some fashion unmistakable but beyond definition.

Presently he held her away from him. "You baby Messalina . . . you framed me."

"Jubal darling . . . you were *wonderful*!"

"Uh . . . how the hell did you know I was *able*?"

She gave back a gaze of clear-eyed innocence. "Why, Jubal, I've been certain ever since Mike was asleep—in trance—he could see around him quite a distance and sometimes he would look in on you—a question to ask or something—to see if you were asleep."

"But I slept alone! Always."

"Yes, dear. That wasn't what I meant. I always had to explain things that he didn't understand."

"Hrrrmph!" He decided not to pursue it. "Just the same, you shouldn't have framed me."

"I grok you don't mean that in your heart, Jubal. We had to have you in the Nest. All the way in. We need you. Since you are shy and humble in your goodness, we did what was needful to welcome you without hurting you. And we did not hurt you, as you grok."

"What's this 'we' stuff?"

"It was a full Sharing-Water of all the Nest, as you grok—you were there. Mike woke up for it . . . and grokked with you and kept us all together."

Jubal hastily abandoned this inquiry, too. "So Mike is awake at last. That's why your eyes are shining."

"Only partly. We are always delighted when Mike isn't withdrawn, it's jolly . . . but he's never really away. Jubal, I grok that you have not grokked the fullness of our way of Sharing-Water. But waiting will fill. Nor did Mike grok it, at first—he thought it was only for quickening of eggs, as it is on Mars."

"Well . . . that's the primary purpose. Babies. Which makes it silly behavior on the part of a person, namely me, who has no wish, at my age, to cause such increase."

She shook her head. "Babies are one result . . . but not the primary purpose. Babies give meaning to the future, and that is a great goodness. But only three or four or a dozen times in a woman's life is a baby quickened in her . . . out of thousands of times she can share herself— and *that* is the primary use for what we can do so often but would need to do so seldom if it were only for reproduction. It is sharing and growing-closer, forever and always. Jubal, Mike grokked this because on Mars the two things— quickening eggs, and sharing-closer—are entirely separate . . . and he grokked, too, that *our* way is best. What a *happy* thing it is not to have been hatched a Martian . . . to be human   and a woman!"

He looked at her closely. "Child, are you pregnant?"

"Yes, Jubal. I grokked that waiting had ended and I was free to be. Most of the Nest have not needed to wait—but Dawn and I have been busy. But when we grokked this cusp coming, I grokked there would be waiting after cusp—and you can see that there will be. Mike will not rebuild the Temple overnight—so this high priestess will be unhurried in building a baby. Waiting always fills."

From this high-flown mishmash Jubal abstracted the central fact . . . or Jill's belief concerning such a possibility. Well, no doubt she had had plenty of opportunity. He resolved to keep an eye on the matter and bring her home for it. Mike's superman methods were all very well, but it wouldn't hurt to have modern equipment at hand, too. Losing Jill to eclampsia or some other mishap he would not let happen, even if he had to get tough with the kids.

He wondered about another such possibility, decided not to mention it. "Where's Dawn? And where's Mike? The place seems awfully quiet." No one else was in sight and he heard no voices . . . and yet that odd feeling of happy expectancy was even stronger. He would have expected a release from tension after the ceremony he had apparently joined in himself—unbeknownst—but the air was more charged than ever. It suddenly reminded him of how he had felt, as a very small boy, when waiting for his first circus parade . . . and someone had called out: "There come the elephants!"

Jubal felt as if, were he just a little taller, he could see the elephants, past the excited crowd. But there was no crowd.

"Dawn told me to give you a kiss for her; she'll be busy for the next three hours, about. And Mike is busy, too— he went back into withdrawal."

"Oh."

"Don't sound so disappointed; he'll be free soon. He's making a special effort so that he will be free on your account . . . and to let us all be free. Duke spent all night scouring the city for the highspeed recorders we use for the dictionary and now we've got everybody who can possibly do it being jammed full of Martian phonic symbols and then Mike will be through and can visit. Dawn has just started dictating; I finished one session, ducked out to say good-morning . . . and am about to go back and get poured full of my last part of the chore, so I'll be gone a little longer than Dawn will be. And here's Dawn's kiss— the first one was just from me." She put her arms around his neck and put her mouth greedily to his—at last said, "My goodness! Why did we wait so long? 'Bye for a little!"

Jubal found a few in the dining room. Duke looked up, smiled and waved, went back to hearty eating. He did not look as if he had been up all night—nor had he; he had been up two nights.

Becky Vesey looked around when Duke waved and said happily, "Hi, you old goat!"—grabbed his ear, pulled him down, and whispered: "I've known it all along—but why weren't you around to console me when the Professor died?" She added aloud, "Sit down and we'll get some food into you while you tell me what devilment you've been plotting lately."

"Just a moment, Becky." Jubal went around the table. "Hi, Skipper. Good trip?"

"No trouble. It's become a milk run. I don't believe you've met Mrs. van Tromp. My dear, the founder of this feat, the one and only Jubal Harshaw—two of him would be too many."

The Captain's wife was a tall, plain woman with the calm eyes of one who has watched from the Widow's Walk. She stood up, kissed Jubal. "Thou art God."

"Uh, thou art God." He might as well relax to the ritual—hell, if he said it often enough, he might lose the rest of his buttons and believe it . . . and it did have a friendly ring with the arms of the Skipper's vrouw firmly around him. He decided that she could teach even Jill something about kissing. She—how was it Anne described it?—she gave it her whole attention; she wasn't going anywhere.

"I suppose, Van," he said, "that I shouldn't be surprised to find you here."

"Well," answered the spaceman, "a man who commutes to Mars ought to be able to palaver with the natives, don't you think?"

"Just for powwow, huh?"

"There are other aspects." Van Tromp reached for a piece of toast; the toast cooperated. "Good food, good company."

"Um, yes."

"Jubal," Madame Vesant called out, "soup's on!"

Jubal returned to his place, found eggs-on-horseback, orange juice, and other choice items. Becky patted his thigh. "A fine prayer meeting, me bucko."

"Woman, back to your horoscopes!"

"Which reminds me, dearie, I want to know the exact instant of your birth."

"Uh, I was born on three successive days. They had to handle me in sections."

Becky made a rude answer. "I'll find out."

"The courthouse burned down when I was three. You can't."

"There are ways. Want to bet?"

"You keep heckling me and you'll find you're not too big to spank. How've you been, girl?"

"What do you think? How do I look?"

"Healthy. A bit spread in the butt. You've touched up your hair."

"I have not. I quit using henna months ago. Get with it, pal, and we'll get rid of that white fringe you've got. Replace it with a lawn."

"Becky, I refuse to grow younger. I came by my decrepitude the hard way and I propose to enjoy it. Quit prattling and let a man eat."

"Yes, sir. You old goat."

Jubal was just leaving as the Man from Mars came in. "*Father!* Oh, Jubal!" Mike hugged and kissed him.

Jubal gently unwound him. "Be your age, son. Sit down and enjoy your breakfast. I'll sit with you."

"I didn't come here for breakfast, I came looking for you. We'll find a place and talk."

"All right."

They went to an unoccupied living room, Mike pulling Jubal by the hand like an excited small boy welcoming his favorite grandparent. Mike picked a big chair for Jubal and sprawled on a couch near him. They were on the side of the wing having the private landing flat; high French windows opened to it. Jubal got up to shift his chair so that he would not be facing the light; he was mildly annoyed to find that the chair shifted itself—remote control over objects was a labor-saver and probably a money-saver (certainly on laundry!—his spaghetti-splashed shirt had been so fresh that he had put it on again), and obviously to be preferred to the blind balkiness of mechanical gadgets. Nevertheless Jubal was not used to telecontrol done without wires or waves; it startled him the way horseless carriages had disturbed decent, respectable horses about the time Jubal was born.

Duke came in and served brandy. Mike said, "Thanks, Cannibal. Are you the new butler?"

"Somebody has to do it, Monster. You've got every brain in the place slaving away over a hot microphone."

"Well, they'll be through in a couple of hours and you can revert to your usual lecherous sloth. The job is done, Cannibal. Pau. Thirty. Ended."

"The whole damn Martian language in one lump?

Monster, I had better check you for burned-out capacitors."

"Oh, no! Only the primer knowledge that I have—had, I mean; my brain's an empty sack. Highbrows like Stinky will be going to Mars for a century to fill in what I never learned. But I did turn out a job—six weeks of subjective time since five this morning or whenever it was we adjourned the sharing—and now the stalwart steady types can finish it while I loaf." Mike stretched and yawned. "Feels good. Finishing a job always feels good."

"You'll be slaving away at something else before the day is out. Boss, this Martian monster can't take it or leave it alone. This is the first time he has relaxed in over two months. He ought to sign up with 'Workers Anonymous.' Or you ought to visit us more often. You're a good influence."

"God forbid that I should ever be."

"Get out of here, Cannibal, and quit telling lies."

"Lies, hell. You turned me into a compulsive truth-teller . . . and it's a handicap in the joints where I hang out." Duke left.

Mike lifted his glass. "Share water, Father."

"Drink deep, son."

"Thou art God."

"Mike, I'll put up with that from the others. But don't *you* come godding at me. I knew you when you were 'only an egg.'"

"Okay, Jubal."

"That's better. When did you start drinking in the morning? Do that at your age and you'll ruin your stomach. You'll never live to be a happy old soak, like me."

Mike looked at his glass. "I drink when it's a sharing. It

doesn't have any effect on me, nor on most of us, unless we want it to. Once I let it have its effect until I passed out. It's an odd sensation. Not a goodness, I grok. Just a way to discorporate for a while without discorporating. I can get a similar effect, only much better and with no damage to repair afterwards, by withdrawing."

"Economical."

"Uh huh, our liquor bill isn't anything. Matter of fact, running that whole Temple hasn't cost what it costs you to keep up our home. Except for initial investment and replacing some props, coffee and cakes was all—we made our own fun. We needed so little that I used to wonder what to do with the money that came in."

"Then why did you take collections?"

"Huh? Oh, you have to charge 'em, Jubal. The marks won't pay attention if it's free."

"I knew that, I wondered if you did."

"Oh, yes, I grok marks, Jubal. At first I did preach free. Didn't work. We humans have to make considerable progress before we can accept a free gift, and value it. I never let them have anything free until Sixth Circle. By then they can accept . . . and accepting is much harder than giving."

"Hmm . . . son, maybe you should write a book on human psychology."

"I have. But it's in Martian. Stinky has the tapes." Mike took a slow sybaritic sip. "We do use some liquor. A few of us—Saul, myself, Sven, some others—like it. I've learned to let it have just a little effect, then hold it, and gain a euphoric growing-closer much like trance without having to withdraw." He sipped again. "That's what I'm doing this morning—letting myself get the mildest glow and be happy with you."

Jubal studied him closely. "Son, you've got something on your mind."

"Yes."

"Do you want to talk it out?"

"Yes. Father, it's always a great goodness to be with you, even if nothing is troubling me. But you are the only human I can talk to and know that you will grok and not be overwhelmed. Jill . . . Jill always groks—but if it hurts me, it hurts her still more. Dawn the same. Patty . . . well, Patty can always take my hurt away, but she does it by keeping it herself. They are too easily hurt for me to share in full with them anything I can't grok and cherish before I share it." Mike looked very thoughtful. "Confession is needful. Catholics know that—they have a corps of strong men to take it. Fosterites have group confession and pass it around and thin it out. I need to introduce confession in the early purging—oh, we have it, but spontaneously, after the pilgrim no longer needs it. We need strong men for that—'sin' is rarely concerned with a real wrongness but sin is what the sinner groks as sin—and when you grok with him, it can hurt. I know."

Mike went on earnestly, "Goodness is not enough, goodness is never enough. That was one of my first mistakes, because among Martians goodness and wisdom are identical. But not with us. Take Jill. Her goodness was perfect when I met her. Nevertheless she was all mixed up inside—and I almost destroyed her, and myself too—for I was just as mixed up—before we got squared away. Her endless patience (not common on this planet) was all that saved us . . . while I was learning to be human and she was learning what I knew.

"But goodness alone is *never* enough. A hard, cold

wisdom is required for goodness to accomplish good. Goodness without wisdom always accomplishes evil." Mike added most soberly, "And that's why I *need* you, Father, as well as loving you. I need your wisdom and your strength . . . for I must confess to you."

Jubal squirmed. "Oh, for Pete's sake, Mike, don't make a production out of it. Just tell me what's eating you. We'll find a way out."

"Yes, Father."

But Mike did not go on. Finally Jubal said, "Do you feel busted up by the destruction of your Temple? I wouldn't blame you. But you aren't broke, you can build again."

"Oh, no, that doesn't matter at all!"

"Eh?"

"That temple was a diary with its pages filled. Time for a new one, rather than write over filled pages. Fire can't destroy the experiences   and from a standpoint of practical politics, being chased out in so spectacular a fashion will help, in the long run. Churches thrive on martyrdom and persecution; it's their best advertising. In fact, Jubal, the last couple of days have been an enjoyable break in a busy routine. No harm done." His expression changed. "Father . . . lately I learned that I was a spy."

"What do you mean, son?"

"For the Old Ones. They sent me here to spy on our people."

Jubal thought about it. Finally he said, "Mike, I know you are brilliant. You possess powers that I don't have and have never seen before. But a man can be a genius and still have delusions."

"I know. Let me explain and you decide whether or not

I'm crazy. You know how the surveillance satellites used by the Security Forces operate."

"No."

"I don't mean details that would interest Duke; I mean the general scheme. They orbit around the globe, picking up data and storing it. At a particular point, the Sky-Eye is keyed and it pours out all that it has seen. That is what they did with me. You know that we of the nest use what is called telepathy."

"I've been forced to believe it."

"We do. But this conversation is private—and besides, no one would attempt to read you; I'm not sure we could. Even last night the link was through Dawn's mind, not yours."

"Well, that is some comfort."

"I am 'only an egg' in this art; the Old Ones are masters. They linked with me but left me on my own, ignored me—then triggered me, and all I had seen and heard and done and felt and grokked poured out and into their records. I don't mean that they wiped my mind of it; they simply played the tape, so to speak, made a copy. But the triggering I could feel—and it was over before I could stop it. Then they cut off the linkage; I couldn't even protest."

"Well . . . it seems to me that they used you shabbily—"

"Not by their standards. Nor would I have objected—I would have been happy to volunteer—had I known it before I left Mars. But they didn't want me to know; they wanted me to grok without interference."

"I was going to add," Jubal said, "that if you are free of this damnable invasion of your privacy now, then what harm has been done? It seems to me that you could have had a Martian at your elbow all these past two and a half years, with no harm other than attracting stares."

Mike looked very sober. "Jubal, listen to a story. Listen all the way through." Mike told him of the destruction of the missing Fifth Planet of Sol, whose ruins are asteroids. "Well, Jubal?"

"It reminds me of the myths about the Flood."

"No, Jubal. The Flood you aren't sure about. Are you sure about the destruction of Pompeii and Herculaneum?"

"Oh, yes. Those are established facts."

"Jubal, the destruction of the Fifth Planet by the Old Ones is as certain as that eruption of Vesuvius—and is recorded in much greater detail. No myth. Fact."

"Uh, stipulate it. Do I understand that you fear that the Old Ones of Mars will give this planet the same treatment? Will you forgive me if I say that is hard for me to swallow?"

"Why, Jubal, it wouldn't take the Old Ones to do it. It merely takes knowledge of physics, how matter is put together—and the same control you have seen me use time and again. Simply necessary first to grok what you want to manipulate. I can do it, right now. Say a piece near the core of Earth about a hundred miles in diameter— much bigger than necessary but we want to make this fast and painless, if only to please Jill. Feel out its size and place, grok carefully how it is put together—" His face lost all expression and his eyeballs started to turn up.

"Hey!" broke in Harshaw. "Stop it! I don't know whether you can or not but I don't want you to try!"

* * *

THE FACE OF the Man from Mars became normal. "Why, I would never *do* it. For me, it would be a wrongness—I am human."

"But not for them?"

"Oh, no. The Old Ones might grok it as beauty. I don't know. Oh, I have the discipline to do it . . . but not the volition. Jill could do it—that is, she could contemplate the exact method. But she could never *will* to do it; she is human, too; this is her planet. The essence of the discipline is, first, self-awareness, and then, self control. By the time a human is able to destroy this planet by this method—instead of by clumsy things like cobalt bombs—it is not possible, I grok fully, for him to entertain the volition. He would discorporate. And that would end any threat; our Old Ones don't hang around the way they do on Mars."

"Mmmm . . . son, as long as we are checking you for bats in your belfry, clear up something else. You've always spoken of these 'Old Ones' as casually as I speak of the neighbor's dog—but I find ghosts hard to swallow. What does an 'Old One' look like?"

"Why, just like any other Martian."

"Then how do you know it's not just an adult Martian? Does he walk through walls, or such?"

"Any Martian can do that. I did, yesterday."

"Uh . . . shimmers? Or anything?"

"No. You see, hear, feel them—everything. It's like an image in a stereo tank, only perfect and put right into your mind. But—Look, Jubal, the whole thing would be a silly question on Mars, but I realize it isn't, here. If you were present at the discorporation—death—of a friend, then helped eat his body . . . and *then* you saw his ghost, talked with it, touched it, anything—would you then believe in ghosts?"

"Well, either that, or I had slipped my leash."

"All right. Here it could be hallucination . . . if I grok correctly that we don't hang around when we discorporate. But in the case of Mars, there is either an entire planet all run by mass hallucination—or the straightforward explanation is correct . . . the one I was taught and all my experience led me to believe. Because on Mars 'ghosts' are the most powerful and the most numerous part of the population. The ones still alive, the corporate ones, are hewers of wood and drawers of water, servants to the Old Ones."

Jubal nodded. "Okay. I'll never boggle at slicing with Occam's Razor. While it runs contrary to my experience, mine is limited to this planet—provincial. All right, son, you're scared they might destroy us?"

Mike shook his head. "Not especially. I think—this is not a grokking but a guess—that they might do one of two things; either destroy us . . . or attempt to conquer us culturally, make us over into their own image."

"But you're not fretted about us being blown up? That's a pretty detached viewpoint."

"No. Oh, they might decide to. You see, by their standards, we are diseased and crippled—the things we do to each other, the way we fail to understand each other, our almost complete failure to grok with one another, our wars and diseases and famines and cruelties—these will be insanity to them. I *know*. So I think they will decide on a mercy killing. But that's a guess, I'm not an Old One. But, Jubal, if they decide to, it will be—" Mike thought a long time. "—a minimum of five hundred years, more likely five thousand, before anything would be done."

"That's a long time for a jury to be out."

"Jubal, the greatest difference between the two races is that Martians never hurry—and humans always do. They would much rather think about it an extra century or half dozen, to be sure that they grok all the fullness."

"In that case, son, don't worry about it. If, in another five hundred or a thousand years, the human race can't handle its neighbors, you and I can't help it. However, I suspect that they will be able to."

"So I grok, but not in fullness. I said I wasn't worried about *that*. The other possibility troubled me more, that they might move in and try to make us over. Jubal, they *can't*. An attempt to make us behave like Martians would kill us as certainly but not painlessly. It would be a great wrongness."

Jubal took time to answer. "But, son, isn't that what *you* have been trying to do?"

Mike looked unhappy. "It was what I started out to do. It is *not* what I am trying to do now. Father, I know that you were disappointed in me when I started this."

"Your business, son."

"Yes. Self. I must grok each cusp myself alone. And so must you . . . and so must each self. Thou art God."

"I don't accept the nomination."

"You can't refuse it. Thou art God and I am God and all that groks is God, and I am all that I have ever been or seen or felt or experienced. I am all that I grok. Father, I saw the horrible shape this planet is in and I grokked, though not in fullness, that I could change it. What I had to teach couldn't be taught in schools; I was forced to smuggle it in as a religion—which it is not—and con the marks into tasting it by appealing to their curiosity. In part it worked as I knew it would; the discipline was just as available to others as it was to me, who was raised in a Martian nest. Our brothers get along together—you've seen, you've shared—live in peace and happiness with no bitterness, no jealousy.

"That alone was a triumph. Male-femaleness is the greatest gift we have—romantic physical love may be unique to this planet. If it is, the universe is a poorer place than it could be . . . and I grok dimly that we-who-are-God will save this precious invention and spread it. The joining of bodies with merging of souls in shared ecstasy, giving, receiving, delighting in each other—well, there's nothing on Mars to touch it, and it's the source, I grok in fullness, of all that makes this planet so rich and wonderful. And, Jubal, until a person, man or woman, has enjoyed this treasure bathed in the mutual bliss of minds linked as closely as bodies, that person is still as virginal and alone as if he had never copulated. But I grok that you have; your very reluctance to risk a lesser thing proves it . . . and, anyhow, I know it directly. You grok. You always have. Without needing the language of grokking. Dawn told us that you were as deep into her mind as you were into her body."

"Unh . . . the lady exaggerates."

"It is impossible for Dawn to speak other than rightly about this. And—forgive me—we were there. In her mind but not in yours . . . and you were there with us, sharing."

Jubal refrained from saying that the only times he had ever felt that he could read minds was precisely in that situation . . . and then not thoughts, but emotions. He simply regretted without bitterness that he was not half a century younger—in which case Dawn would have had that "Miss" taken off her name and he would have boldly risked another marriage, despite his scars. Also that he would not trade the preceding night for all the years that might be left him. In essence, Mike was right. "Go on, sir."

"That's what sexual union should be. But that's what I slowly grokked it rarely was. Instead it was indifference and acts mechanically performed and rape and seduction as a game no better than roulette but less honest and prostitution and celibacy by choice and by no choice and fear and guilt and hatred and violence and children brought up to think that sex was 'bad' and 'shameful' and 'animal' and something to be hidden and always distrusted. This lovely perfect thing, male-femaleness, turned upside down and inside out and made horrible.

"And every one of those wrong things is a corollary of 'jealousy.' Jubal, I couldn't believe it. I still don't grok 'jealousy' in fullness, it seems insanity to me. When I first learned what this ecstasy was, my first thought was that I wanted to share it, share it at once with all my water brothers—directly with those female, indirectly by inviting more sharing with those male. The notion of trying to keep this never-failing fountain to myself would have horrified me, had I thought of it. But I was incapable of thinking it. And in perfect corollary I had no slightest wish to attempt this miracle with anyone I did not already cherish and trust—Jubal, I am physically unable even to attempt love with a female who has not shared water with me. And this runs all through the Nest. Psychic impotence—unless spirits blend as flesh blends."

Jubal was thinking mournfully that it was a fine system—for angels—when a sky car landed on the private flat diagonally in front of him. He turned his head to see and, as its skids touched, it vanished.

"Trouble?" he asked.

"No," Mike denied. "They are beginning to suspect that we are here—that I am, rather; they think the rest are dead. The Innermost Temple, I mean. The other circles aren't being bothered . . ." He grinned. "We could get a good price for these rooms; the city is filling up with Bishop Short's shock troops."

"Isn't it about time to get the family elsewhere?"

"Jubal, don't worry. That car never had a chance to report, even by radio. I'm guarding us. It's no trouble, now that Jill is over her misconceptions about 'wrongness' in discorporating persons who have wrongness in them. I used to have to use complicated expedients to protect us. But now Jill knows that I do it only as fullness is grokked." The Man from Mars grinned boyishly. "Last night she helped me with a hatchet job . . . nor was it her first time."

"What sort of a job?"

"Oh, just a follow-up on the jail break. Some few I couldn't release; they were vicious. So I got rid of them before I got rid of bars and doors. But I have been slowly grokking this whole city for months . . . and quite a few of the worst were not in jail. I have been waiting, making a list, making sure of fullness in each case. So, now that we are leaving this city—they don't live here any more. They were discorporated and sent back to the foot of the line to try again. Incidentally, that was the grokking that changed Jill's attitude from squeamishness to hearty approval: when she finally grokked in fullness that it is *impossible* to kill a man—that all we were doing was much like a referee removing a player for 'unnecessary roughness.'"

"Aren't you afraid of playing God, lad?"

Mike grinned with unashamed cheerfulness. "I *am* God. Thou art God . . . and any jerk I remove is God, too. Jubal, it is said that God notes each sparrow that falls. And so He does. But the closest it can be said in English is that God cannot avoid noting the sparrow because the Sparrow *is* God. And when a cat stalks a sparrow both of them are God, carrying out God's thoughts."

Another sky car started to land and vanished; Jubal did not comment. "How many did you toss out of the game last night?"

"Oh, about four hundred and fifty—I didn't count. This is a largish city. But for a while it is going to be an unusually decent one. No cure, of course—there is no cure, short of the discipline." Mike looked unhappy. "And that is what I must ask you about, Father. I'm afraid I have misled our brothers."

"How, Mike?"

"They're too optimistic. They see how well it works for us, they know how happy they are, how strong and healthy and aware—how deeply they love each other. And now they think they grok that it is just a matter of time until the whole human race will reach the same beatitude. Oh, not tomorrow—some of them grok that two thousand years is but a moment for such a mission. But eventually.

"And I thought so, Jubal, at first. I led them to think so.

"But, Jubal, I had missed a key point:

"Humans are not Martians.

"I made this mistake again and again—corrected myself . . . and still made it. What works for Martians does not necessarily work for humans. Oh, the conceptual logic which can be stated only in Martian *does* work for both races. The logic is invariant . . . but the data are different. So the results are different.

"I couldn't see why, when people were hungry, some of them didn't volunteer to be butchered so that the rest could eat . . . on Mars this is obvious—and an honor. I couldn't understand why babies were so prized. On Mars our two little girls in there would be dumped outdoors, to live or die—and nine out of ten nymphs die their first season. My logic was right but I misread the data: here babies do not compete but adults do; on Mars adults never compete, they've been weeded out as babies. But one way or another, competing and weeding takes place . . . or a race goes downhill.

"But whether or not I was wrong in trying to take the competition out at both ends, I have lately begun to grok that the human race won't let me, no matter what."

Duke stuck his head into the room. "Mike? Have you been watching outside? There is a crowd gathering around the hotel."

"I know," agreed Mike. "Tell the others that waiting has not filled." He went on to Jubal, "'Thou art God.' It's not a message of cheer and hope, Jubal. It's a defiance—and an unafraid unabashed assumption of personal responsibility." He looked sad. "But I rarely put it over. A very few, just these few here with us, our brothers, understood me and accepted the bitter along with the sweet, stood up and drank it—grokked it. The others, hundreds and thousands of others, either insisted on treating it as a prize without a contest—a 'conversion'—or ignored it. No matter what I said they insisted on thinking of God as something outside themselves. Something that yearns to take every indolent moron to His breast and comfort him. The notion that the effort has to be *their own* . . . and that the trouble they are in is all their own doing . . . is one that they can't or won't entertain."

The Man from Mars shook his head. "My failures so greatly out-number my successes that I wonder if full grokking will show that I am on the wrong track—that *this* race *must* be split up, hating each other, fighting, constantly unhappy and at war even with their own individual selves . . . simply to have that weeding out that every race must have. Tell me, Father? You must tell me."

"Mike, what in hell led you to believe that I was infallible?"

"Perhaps you are not. But every time I have needed to know something, you have always been able to tell me—and fullness always showed that you spoke rightly."

"Damn it, I refuse this apotheosis! But I do see one thing, son. You have always urged everyone else never to hurry—'waiting will fill,' you say."

"That is right."

"Now you are violating your own rule. You have waited only a little—a very short time by Martian standards—and you want to throw in the towel. You've proved that your system works for a small group—and I'm glad to confirm it; I've never seen such happy, healthy, cheerful people. That ought to be enough for the short time you've put in. Come back when you have a thousand times this number, all working and happy and unjealous, and we'll talk it over again. Fair enough?"

"You speak rightly, Father."

"I ain't through. You've been fretting that since you

failed to hook ninety-nine out of a hundred, the race couldn't get along without its present evils, had to have them for weeding out. But damn it, lad, you've been *doing* the weeding—or rather, the failures have been doing it by not listening to you. Had you planned to eliminate money and property?"

"Oh, no! Inside the Nest we don't need it, but—"

"Nor does any healthy family. But outside you need it in dealing with other people. Sam tells me that our brothers, instead of getting unworldly, are slicker with money than ever. Right?"

"Oh, yes. Money making is a simple trick once you grok."

"You've just added a new beatitude: 'Blessed is the rich in spirit, for he shall make dough.' How do our people stack up in other fields? Better or worse than average?"

"Oh, better, of course. You see, Jubal, it's *not* a faith; the discipline is simply a method of efficient functioning in anything."

"You've answered yourself, son. If all you say is true— and I'm not judging; I'm asking, you're answering—then competition, far from being eliminated, is rougher than ever. If one tenth of one percent of the population is capable of getting the news, then all you have to do is *show* them—and in a matter of some generations the stupid ones will die out and those with your discipline will inherit the Earth. Whenever that is—in a thousand years or ten thousand—will be soon enough to worry about some new hurdle to make them jump higher. But don't get fainthearted because only a handful have turned into angels overnight. I never expected *any* to manage it. I thought you were making a damn fool of yourself by pretending to be a preacher."

Mike sighed and smiled. "I was beginning to be afraid I was—worrying that I had let my brothers down."

"I still wish you had called it 'Cosmic Halitosis' or some such. But the name doesn't matter. If you've got the truth you can demonstrate it. Talking doesn't prove it. *Show* people."

Mike did not answer. His eyelids drooped, he held perfectly still, his face was without expression. Jubal stirred restlessly, afraid that he had said too much, crowded the lad into a need to withdraw.

Then Mike's eyes opened, he grinned merrily. "You've got me all squared away, Father. I'm ready to show them now—I grok the fullness." The Man from Mars stood up. "Waiting is ended."

XXXVII

JUBAL AND THE Man from Mars strolled into the room with the big stereo tank. The entire Nest was gathered, watching it. It showed a dense and turbulent crowd, somewhat restrained by policemen. Mike glanced at it and looked serenely happy. "They come. Now is the fullness." The sense of ecstatic expectancy Jubal had felt growing ever since his arrival swelled greatly, but no one moved.

"It's a mighty big tip, sweetheart," Jill agreed.

"And ready to turn," added Patty.

"I'd better dress for it," Mike commented. "Have I got any clothes around this dump? Patty?"

"Right away, Michael."

Jubal said, "Son, that mob looks ugly to me. Are you sure this is time to tackle them?"

"Oh, sure," said Mike. "They've come to see me . . . so now I go down to meet them." He paused while some clothing got out of the way of his face; he was being dressed at break-neck speed with the unnecessary help of several women—each garment seemed to know where to go and how to drape itself. "This job has obligations as well as privileges—the star has to show up for the show . . . grok me? The marks expect it."

Duke said, "Mike knows what he's doing, Boss."

"Well . . . I don't trust mobs."

"That crowd is mostly curiosity seekers, they always are. Oh, there are some Fosterites and some others with grudges—but Mike can handle any crowd. You'll see. Right, Mike?"

"Keerect, Cannibal. Pull in a tip, then give 'em a show. Where's my hat? Can't walk in the noonday sun without a hat." An expensive Panama with a sporty colored band glided out and settled itself on his head; he cocked it jauntily. "There! Do I look all right?" He was dressed in his usual outer-services mufti, a smartly tailored, sharply creased, white business suit, shoes to match, snowy shirt, and luxurious dazzling scarf.

Ben said, "All you lack is a briefcase."

"You grok I need one? Patty, do we have one?"

Jill stepped up to him. "Ben was kidding, dear. You look just perfect." She straightened his tie and kissed him—and Jubal felt kissed. "Go talk to them."

"Yup. Time to turn the tip. Anne? Duke?"

"Ready, Mike." Anne was wearing her Fair Witness

cloak, wrapping her in dignity; Duke was just the opposite, being sloppily dressed, with a lighted cigarette dangling from his face, an old hat on the back of his head with a card marked "PRESS" stuck in its band, and himself hung about with cameras and kit.

They headed for the door to the foyer common to the four penthouse suites. Only Jubal followed; all the others, thirty and more, stayed around the stereo tank. Mike paused at the door. There was a hall table there, with a pitcher of water and glasses, a dish of fruit and a fruit knife. "Better not come any farther," he advised Jubal, "or Patty would have to escort you back through her pets."

Mike poured himself a glass of water, drank part of it. "Preaching is thirsty work." He handed the glass to Anne, then took the fruit knife and sliced off a chunk of apple.

It seemed to Jubal that Mike sliced off one of his fingers . . . but his attention was distracted as Duke passed the glass to him. Mike's hand was not bleeding and Jubal had grown somewhat accustomed to legerdemain. He accepted the glass and took a sip, finding that his own throat was very dry.

Mike gripped his arm and smiled. "Quit fretting. This will take only a few minutes. See you later, Father." They went out through the guardian cobras and the door closed. Jubal went back to the room where the others were, still carrying the glass. Someone took it from him; he did not notice, as he was watching images in the big tank.

The mob seemed denser, surging about and held back by police armed only with night sticks. There were a few shouts but mostly just the unlocalized muttering of the crowd.

Someone said, "Where are they now, Patty?"

"They've dropped down the tube. Michael is a little ahead, Duke stopped to catch Anne. They're entering the lobby. Michael has been spotted, pictures are being taken."

The scene in the tank resolved into enormous head and shoulders of a brightly cheerful newscaster: "This is NWNW New World Networks' mobile newshound on the spot while it's hot—your newscaster, Happy Holliday. We have just learned that the fake messiah, sometimes known as the Man from Mars, has crawled out of his hide-out in a hotel room here in beautiful St. Petersburg the City that Has Everything to Make You Sing. Apparently Smith is about to surrender to the authorities. He crashed out of jail yesterday, using high explosives smuggled in to him by his fanatic followers. But the tight cordon placed around this city seems to have been too much for him. We don't know yet—I repeat, we don't know yet—so stay with the chap who covers the map—and now a word from your lo cal sponsor who has given you this keyhole peep at the latest leap—"

"Thank you, Happy Holliday and all you good people watching via NWNW! What Price Paradise? Amazingly Low! Come out and see for yourself at Elysian Fields, just opened as home-sites for a restricted clientele. Land re claimed from the warm waters of the glorious Gulf and every lot guaranteed at least eighteen inches above mean high water and only a small down payment on a Happy— oh, oh, later, friends—phone Gulf nine-two eight two eight!"

"And thank *you*, Jick Morris and the developers of Ely sian Fields! I think we've got something, folks! Yes, sir, I think we do—"

("They're coming out the front entrance," Patty said quietly. "The crowd hasn't spotted Michael yet.")

"Maybe not yet . . . but soon. You are now looking at the main entrance of the magnificent Sans Souci Hotel, Gem of the Gulf, whose management is in no way responsible for this hunted fugitive and who have cooperated with the authorities throughout according to a statement just issued by Police Chief Davis. And while we're waiting to see what will happen, a few highlights in the strange career of this half-human monster raised on Mars—"

The live scene was replaced by quick cuts of stock shots: The *Envoy* blasting off years earlier, the *Champion* floating upwards silently and effortlessly under Lyle Drive, Martians on Mars, the triumphant return of the *Champion*, a quick of the first faked interview with the "Man from Mars"— "What do you think of the girls here on Earth?" . . . "*Gee!*"— a quicker shot of the conference in the Executive Palace and the much-publicized awarding of a doctorate in philosophy, all with rapid-fire commentary.

"See anything, Patty?"

"Michael is at the top of the steps, the crowd is at least a hundred yards away, being kept off the hotel grounds. Duke has grabbed some pix and Mike is waiting to let him change lenses. No hurry."

Happy Holliday went on, as the tank shifted to the crowd, semi-close and panning: "You understand, friends, that this wonderful community is in a unique condition today. Something strange has been going on and these people are in no mood to trifle. Their laws have been flouted, their security forces treated with contempt, they are angry, righteously so. The fanatic followers of this alleged antichrist have stopped at nothing to create turmoil in a futile effort to let their leader escape the closing net of justice. Anything can happen—anything!"

The announcer's voice climbed: "Yes, he's coming out now—he's walking toward the people!" The scene cut to reverse; Mike was walking directly toward the camera. Anne and Duke were behind and dropping farther behind. "This is it! This is it! This is the blow-off!"

Mike continued to walk unhurriedly toward the crowd until he loomed up in the stereo tank in life size, as if he were in the room with his water brothers. He stopped on the grass verge in front of the hotel, a few feet from the crowd. "You called me?"

He was answered with a growl.

The sky held scattered clouds; at that instant the sun came out from behind one and a shaft of light hit him.

His clothes vanished. He stood before them, a golden youth, clothed only in beauty—beauty that made Jubal's heart ache, thinking that Michelangelo in his ancient years would have climbed down from his high scaffolding to record it for generations unborn. Mike said gently, "Look at me. I am a son of man."

The scene cut for a ten-second plug, a line of can-can dancers singing:

Come *on,* la*dios,* do *your* duds!
In *the* smoo*thest,* yumm*iest* suds!
Lo*ver* Soap *is* kind *to* hands—
But *be* sure *you* save *the* bands!

The tank filled with foamy suds amid girlish laughter and the scene cut back to the newscast:

"God damn you!" A half brick caught Mike in the ribs.

He turned his face toward his assailant. "But you yourself are God. You can damn only yourself . . . and you can never escape yourself."

"Blasphemer!" A rock caught him over his left eye and blood welled forth.

Mike said calmly, "In fighting me, you fight yourself . . . for Thou art God . . . and I am God . . . and all that groks is God—there is no other."

More rocks hit him, he began to bleed in several places. "Hear the Truth. You need not hate, you need not fight, you need not fear. I offer you the water of life—" Suddenly his hand held a tumbler of water, sparkling in sunlight. "—and you may share it whenever you so will . . . and walk in peace and love and happiness together."

A rock caught the glass and shattered it. Another struck him in the mouth.

Through bruised and bleeding lips he smiled at them, looking straight into the camera with an expression of yearning tenderness on his face. Some trick of sunlight and stereo formed a golden halo back of his head. "Oh my brothers, I love you so! Drink deep. Share and grow closer without end. Thou art God."

Jubal whispered it back to him. The scene made a five-second cut: *"Cahuenga Cave!* The night club with *real* Los Angeles smog, imported fresh every day. Six exotic dancers."

"Lynch him! Give the bastard a nigger necktie!" A heavy gauge shotgun blasted at close range and Mike's right arm was struck off at the elbow and fell. It floated gently down, then came to rest on the cool grasses, its hand curved open in invitation.

"Give him the other barrel, Shortie—and aim closer!"

The crowd laughed and applauded. A brick smashed Mike's nose and more rocks gave him a crown of blood.

"The Truth is simple but the Way of Man is hard. First you must learn to control your *self*. The rest follows. Blessed is he who knows himself and commands himself, for the world is his and love and happiness and peace walk with him wherever he goes." Another shotgun blast was followed by two more shots. One short, a forty-five slug, hit Mike over the heart, shattering the sixth rib near the sternum and making a large wound; the buckshot and the other slug sheared through his left tibia five inches below the patella and left the fibula sticking out at an angle, broken and white against the yellow and red of the wound.

Mike staggered slightly and laughed, went on talking, his words clear and unhurried. "Thou art God. Know that and the Way is opened."

"God damn it—let's *stop* this taking the Name of the Lord in vain!"—"Come on, men! Let's finish him!" The mob surged forward, led by one bold with a club; they were on him with rocks and fists, and then with feet as he went down. He went on talking while they kicked his ribs in and smashed his golden body, broke his bones and tore an ear loose. At last someone called out, "Back away so we can get the gasoline on him!"

The mob opened up a little at that warning and the camera zoomed to pick up his face and shoulders. The Man from Mars smiled at his brothers, said once more, softly and clearly, "I love you." An incautious grasshopper came whirring to a landing on the grass a few inches from his face; Mike turned his head, looked at it as it stared back at him. "Thou art God," he said happily and discorporated.

XXXVIII

FLAME AND BILLOWING smoke came up and filled the tank. "Golly!" Patty said reverently. "That's the best blow-off ever used."

"Yes," agreed Becky judicially, "the Professor himself never dreamed up a better one."

Van Tromp said very quietly, apparently to himself: "In style. Smart and with style—the lad finished in style."

Jubal looked around at his brothers. Was he the *only* one who felt anything? Jill and Dawn were seated each with an arm around the other—but they did that whenever they were together; neither seemed disturbed. Even Dorcas was dry-eyed and calm.

The inferno in the tank cut to smiling Happy Holliday who said, "And now, folks, a few moments for our friends at Elysian Fields who so graciously gave up their—" Patty cut him off.

"Anne and Duke are on their way back up," she said. "I'll let them through the foyer and then we'll have lunch." She started to leave.

Jubal stopped her. "Patty? Did you *know* what Mike was going to do?"

She seemed puzzled. "Huh? Why, of course not, Jubal. It was necessary to wait for fullness. None of us knew." She turned and left.

"Jubal—" Jill was looking at him. "Jubal our beloved father . . . please stop and grok the fullness. Mike is not dead. How can he be dead when no one can be killed? Nor can he ever be away from us who have already grokked him. Thou art God."

"'Thou art God,'" he repeated dully.

"That's better. Come sit with Dawn and me—in the middle."

"No. No, just let me be." He went blindly to his own room, let himself in and bolted the door after him, leaned heavily with both hands gripping the foot of the bed. *My son, oh my son! Would that I had died for thee!* He had had so much to live for . . . and an old fool that he respected too much had to shoot off his yap and goad him into a needless, useless martyrdom. If Mike had given them something *big*—like stereo, or bingo—but he gave them the Truth. Or a piece of the Truth. And who is interested in Truth? He laughed through his sobs.

After a while he shut them off, both heart-broken sobs and bitter laugh, and pawed through his traveling bag. He had what he wanted with him; he had kept a supply in his toilet kit ever since Joe Douglas's stroke had reminded him that all flesh is grass.

Now his own stroke had come and he couldn't take it. He prescribed three tablets to make it fast and certain, washed them down with water, and lay quickly on the bed. Shortly the pain went away.

From a great distance the voice reached him. "Jubal—"

"'M resting. Don't bother me."

"Jubal! *Please*, Father!"

"Uh . . . yes, Mike? What is it?"

"Wake up! Fullness is not yet. Here, let me help you."

Jubal sighed. "Okay, Mike." He let himself be helped and led into the bath, let his head be held while he threw up, accepted a glass of water and rinsed out his mouth.

"Okay now?"

"Okay, son. Thanks."

"Then I've got some things to attend to. I love you, Father. Thou art God."

"I love you, Mike. Thou art God." Jubal puttered around a while longer, making himself presentable, changing clothes, taking one short brandy to kill the slightly bitter taste still in his stomach, then went out to join the others.

Patty was alone in the room with the babble tank and it was switched off. She looked up. "Some lunch now, Jubal?"

"Yes, thanks."

She came up to him. "That's good. I'm afraid most of them simply ate and scooted. But each of them left a kiss for you. And here it is, all in one package." She managed to deliver in full all the love placed in her proxy cemented together with her own; Jubal found that it left him feeling strong, with her serene acceptance shared, no bitterness left.

"Come out into the kitchen," she said. "Tony's gone so most of the rest are there—not that his growls ever really chased anybody out." She stopped and tried to stare down the back of her neck. "Isn't that final scene changing a little? Sort of smoky, maybe?"

Jubal solemnly agreed that he thought it was. He couldn't see any change . . . but he was not going to argue with Patty's idiosyncrasy. She nodded. "I expected it. I can see around me all right—except myself. I still need a double mirror to see my back clearly. Mike says my Sight will include that presently. No matter."

In the kitchen perhaps a dozen were lounging at a table and elsewhere; Duke was at the range, stirring a small sauce pan. "Hi, Boss. I ordered a twenty-place bus. That's the biggest that can land on our little landing flat . . . and we'll need one almost that big, what with the diaper set and Patty's pets. Okay?"

"Certainly. Are they all coming home?" If they ran out of bedrooms, the girls could make up dosses that would do in the living room and here and there—and this crowd would probably double up anyhow. Come to think of it, he might not be allowed to sleep solo himself . . . he made up his mind not to fight it. It was friendly to have a warm body on the other side of the bed, even if your intentions weren't active. By God, he had forgotten how friendly it was! Growing-closer—

"Not everybody. Tim will pilot us, then turn in the bus and go to Texas for a while. The Skipper and Beatrix and Sven we're going to drop off in New Jersey."

Sam looked up from the table. "Ruth and I have got to get back to our kids. And Saul is coming with us."

"Can't you stop by home for a day or two first?"

"Well, maybe. I'll talk it over with Ruth."

"Boss," put in Duke, "how soon can we fill the swimming pool?"

"Well, we never filled it earlier than April before—but with the new heaters I suppose we could fill it anytime." Jubal added, "But we'll still have some nasty weather—snow still on the ground yesterday."

"Boss, lemme clue you. This gang can walk through snow hip deep on a tall giraffe and not notice it—and will, to swim. Besides that, there are cheaper ways of keeping that water from freezing than with those big oil heaters."

"Jubal!"

"Yes, Ruth?"

"We'll stop for a day or maybe more. The kids don't

miss me—and I'm not aching to take over being motherly without Patty to discipline them anyhow. Jubal, you've never really seen me until you've seen me with my hair floating around me in the water—looking like Mrs. DoAsYouWouldBeDoneBy."

"It's a date. Say, where is the Squarehead and the Dutchman? Beatrix has never been home—they can't be in such a hurry."

"I'll tell 'em, Boss."

"Patty, can your snakes stand a clean, warm basement for a while? Until we can do better? I don't mean Honey Bun, she's people. But I don't think the cobras should have the run of the house."

"Of course, Jubal."

"Mmm—" Jubal looked around. "Dawn, can you take short-hand?"

"She doesn't need it," put in Anne, "any more than I do."

"I should have known. Use a typewriter?"

"I will learn, if you wish it," Dawn answered.

"Consider yourself hired—until there's a vacancy for a high priestess somewhere. Jill, have we forgotten anybody?"

"No, Boss. Except that all those who left feel free to camp on you anytime, too. And they will."

"I assumed that. Nest number two, when and as needed." He went over to the range, glanced into the pan Duke was stirring. It held a small amount of broth. "Hmm . . . Mike?"

"Yup." Duke dipped out a little in the spoon, tasted it. "Needs a little salt."

"Yes, Mike always did need a little seasoning." Jubal took the spoon and tasted the broth. Duke was correct;

the flavor was sweet and could have used salt. "But let's grok him as he is. Who's left to share?"

"Just you. Tony left me here with strict instructions to stir by hand, add water as needed, and wait for you. Not to let it scorch."

"Then grab a couple of cups. We'll share it and grok together."

"Right, Boss." Two cups came sailing down and rested by the sauce pan. "This is a joke on Mike—he always swore that he would outlive me and serve me up for Thanksgiving. Or maybe the joke's on me—because we had a bet on it and now I can't collect."

"You won only by default. Split it evenly."

Duke did so. Jubal raised his cup. "Share!"

"Grow ever closer."

Slowly they drank the broth, stretching it out, savoring it, praising and cherishing and grokking their donor. Jubal found, to his surprise, that although he was overflowing with emotion, it was a calm happiness that did not bring tears. What a quaint and gawky puppy his son had been when first he saw him . . . so eager to please, so naive in his little mistakes—and what a proud power he had become without ever losing his angelic innocence. I grok you at last, son—and would not change a line!

Patty had his lunch waiting for him; he sat down and dug in, hungry and feeling that it had been days since breakfast. Sam was saying, "I was telling Saul that I grok no need to make any change in plans. We go on as before. If you've got the right merchandise, the business grows, even though the founder has passed on."

"I wasn't disagreeing," Saul objected. "You and Ruth will found another temple—and we'll found others. But we'll have to take time now to accumulate capital. This isn't a street corner revival, nor yet something to set up in a vacant shop; it requires staging and equipment. That means money—not to mention such things as paying for a year or two on Mars for Stinky and Maryam . . . and that's just as essential."

"All *right* already! Who's arguing? We wait for fullness . . . and go ahead."

Jubal said suddenly, "Money's no problem."

"How's that, Jubal?"

"As a lawyer I shouldn't tell this . . . but as a water brother I do what I grok. Just a moment—Anne."

"Yes, Boss."

"Buy that spot. The one where they stoned Mike. Better get about a hundred-foot radius around it."

"Boss, the spot itself is public parkway. A hundred-foot radius will cut off some public road and a piece of the hotel grounds."

"Don't argue."

"I wasn't arguing. I was giving you facts."

"Sorry. They'll sell. They'll reroute that route. Hell, if their arms are twisted properly, they'll donate the land— twisting done through Joe Douglas, I think. And have Douglas claim from the morgue whatever was left when those ghouls got through with him and we'll bury him on that spot—say a year from now . . . with the whole city mourning and the cops that didn't protect him today standing at attention." What to put over him? The Fallen Caryatid? No, Mike had been strong enough for his stone. The Little Mermaid would be better—but it wouldn't be understood. Maybe one of Mike himself, just as he was when he said, "Look at me. I am a Son of Man." If Duke didn't catch a shot of it, New World did—and maybe there was a brother, or would be a brother, with the spark of Rodin in him to do it right and not fancy it up.

"We'll bury him there," Jubal went on, "unprotected, and let the worms and the gentle rain grok him. I grok Mike will like that. Anne, I want to talk to Joe Douglas as soon as we get home."

"Yes, Boss. We grok with you."

"Now about that other." He told them about Mike's will. "So you see, each one of you is at least a millionaire— just how much more than that I haven't estimated lately . . . but much more, even after taxes. No strings on it at all . . . but I grok that you will spend as needed for temples and similar stuff. But there's nothing to stop you from buying yachts if you wish. Oh, yes! Joe Douglas stays on as manager for any who care to let the capital ride, same pay as before . . . but I grok Joe won't last long, whereupon management devolves on Ben Caxton. Ben?"

Caxton shrugged. "It can be in my name. I grok I'll hire me a real businessman, name of Saul."

"That wraps it then. Some waiting time but nobody will dare really fight this will; Mike rigged it. You'll see. How soon can we get out of here? Is the tab settled?"

"Jubal," Ben said gently, "we *own* this hotel."

Not long thereafter they were in the air, with no trouble from police—the town had quieted down as fast as it had flared up. Jubal sat forward with Stinky Mahmoud and relaxed—discovered that he was not tired, not unhappy, not even fretting to get back to his sanctuary. They discussed Mahmoud's plans to go to Mars to learn the language more deeply . . . after, Jubal was pleased to learn, completing the diction, which Mahmoud estimated at a year for his own part in checking the phonetic spellings.

Jubal said grumpily, "I suppose I shall be forced to learn the pesky stuff myself, just to understand the chatter around me."

"As you grok, brother."

"Well, damn it, I won't put up with assigned lessons and regular school hours! I'll work as suits me, just as I always have."

Mahmoud was silent a moment. "Jubal, we used classes and schedules at the Temple because we were handling groups. But some got special attention."

"That's what I'm going to need."

"Anne, for example, is much, much farther along than she ever let you know. With her total-recall memory, she learned Martian in nothing flat, hooked in rapport with Mike."

"Well, I don't have that sort of memory—and Mike's not available."

"No, but Anne is. And, stubborn as you are, nevertheless Dawn can place you in rapport with Anne—if you'll let her. And you won't need Dawn for the second lesson; Anne will then be able to handle it all. You'll be thinking in Martian inside of days, by the calendar—much longer by subjective time, but who cares?" Mahmoud leered at him. "You'll enjoy the warming-up exercises."

Jubal bristled. "You're a low, evil, lecherous Arab—and besides that you stole one of my best secretaries."

"For which I am forever in your debt. But you haven't lost her entirely; she'll give you lessons, too. She'll insist on it."

"Go 'way and find another seat. I want to think."

Somewhat later Jubal shouted, *"Front!"*

Dorcas came forward and sat down beside him, steno gear ready.

He glanced at her before he started to work. "Child, you look even happier than usual. Glowing."

Dorcas said dreamily, "I've decided to name him 'Dennis,'"

Jubal nodded. "Appropriate. Very appropriate." Appropriate meaning even if she were mixed up about the paternity, he thought to himself. "Do you feel like working?"

"Oh, yes! I feel grand."

"Begin. Stereoplay. Rough draft. Working title: 'A Martian Named Smith.' Opener: zoom in on Mars, using stock or bonestelled shots, unbroken sequence, then dissolving to miniature matched set of actual landing place of *Envoy.* Space ship in middle distance. Animated Martians, typical, with stock as available or rephotographed. Cut to close: Interior space ship. Female patient stretched on ―"

XXXIX

THE VERDICT TO be passed on the third planet around Sol was never in doubt. The Old Ones of the fourth planet were not omniscient and in their way were as provincial as humans. Grokking by their own local values, even with the aid of vastly superior logic, they were certain in time to perceive an incurable "wrongness" in the busy, restless, quarrelsome beings of the third planet, a wrongness which would require weeding, once it had been grokked and cherished and hated.

But, by the time they would slowly get around to it, it would be highly improbable approaching impossible that the Old Ones would be able to destroy this weirdly complex race. The hazard was so slight that those concerned with the third planet did not waste a split eon on it.

Certainly Foster did not. "Digby!"

His assistant looked up. "Yes, Foster."

"I'll be gone a few eons on a special assignment. Want you to meet your new supervisor." Foster turned and said, "Mike, this is Archangel Digby, your assistant. He knows where every thing is around the studio and you'll find him a very steady straw boss for anything you conceive."

"Oh, we'll get along," Archangel Michael assured him, and said to Digby, "Haven't we met before?"

Digby answered, "Not that I remember. Of course, out of so many when-wheres—" He shrugged.

"No matter. Thou art God."

"Thou art God," Digby responded.

Foster said, "Skip the formalities, please. I've left you a load of work and you don't have all eternity to fiddle with it. Certainly 'Thou art God'—but who isn't?"

He left, and Mike pushed back his halo and got to work. He could see a lot of changes he wanted to make—